A MIND OF WINTER

a novel by

Shira Nayman

Acknowledgements

Warm thanks to Johnny Temple at Akashic, game-changer and visionary; also to Johanna Ingalls and the rest of Akashic's team. I'm grateful as well to Erin Cox for finding this book its home. My deep gratitude and love go to my family: Lucas, Juliana and Louis, my mother Doreen, my late father Jack, sisters Michèle and Ilana, and brother Marc.

This project has been assisted by the Australian government through the Australia Council for the Arts, its arts funding and advisory body.

Published by Akashic Books
©2012 by Shira Nayman

ISBN-13: 978-1-61775-103-5
Library of Congress Control Number: 2011960948

Akashic Books
PO Box 1456
New York, NY 10009
info@akashicbooks.com
www.akashicbooks.com

To Michèle Nayman and Andrea Masters
who helped me find this book

"The Snow Man," by Wallace Stevens

One must have a mind of winter
To regard the frost and the boughs
Of the pine-trees crusted with snow;

And have been cold a long time
To regard the junipers shagged with ice,
The spruces rough in the distant glitter

Of the January sun; and not to think
Of any misery in the sound of the wind,
In the sound of a few leaves,

Which is the sound of the land
Full of the same wind
That is blowing in the same bare place

For the listener, who listens in the snow,
And, nothing himself, beholds
Nothing that is not there and the nothing that is.

PROLOGUE

Oscar

The North Shore of Long Island. Late Summer, 1951.

I do not fail to see the irony in it—being taken, once again, for someone else. Of course, the circumstances this time could not be more different.

Anyone who has traveled much knows the curiosity of catching sight on a foreign street of someone you're certain you know, or knew long ago. It's not a vague similarity of features that seizes your attention but something specific: the exact angle of the protruding teeth, the way the lips pull back with the smile to reveal too much gum; or the elongation of a forehead, the hairline too even. Of all people, you wonder, what could your schoolteacher from decades ago, with his inimitable gait, be doing here? Though you know that by now the teacher, who was old then, must surely be dead. You conclude there must be a finite number of physicalities, of shapes of jaws and brows, of ways a limp can set in or a mouthful of teeth can crowd. You don't however imagine this to be true, too, of you—that your form is a composite of human parts that, meted out to an unknown individual somewhere else, have achieved a similar effect: that in a distant country you will never visit, a person you once knew will think that a stranger he sights on the street is you.

Or, as in my present troubling case, that the specifics of my own features would evoke so precisely, so insistently—in the eyes not of one person, if my visitor is to believed, but of several—the exact image of someone else. And for this to have happened not once in my life, fluke enough, but twice? In two far-flung countries, involving a likeness to two different people—and me, leading two wholly disconnected lives?

I could not begin to defend myself against the present accusation. I would not presume even to try. My visitor has not been unfriendly: on the contrary. He maintains a posture of respect, bows when he greets me and again when he leaves. He is careful to phrase things in the interrogative, and makes liberal use of the words *alleged* and *supposed* and *perhaps*. He keeps impulse and enthusiasm at bay, prides himself on reaching conclusions through careful compilation of fact. A thoughtful and diligent young man; I bear him no malice.

His office appears to be sparing no expense in the investigation.

He, too, is an immigrant. I cannot help noting how comfortable he seems; he carries himself as if he belongs.

Though I have not angled for such declarations, he has on several occasions assured me that no legal action will proceed unless they are absolutely certain—*Beyond*, as he put it, breaking into American idiom, *the shadow of a doubt*. I am impressed by the sense of security I have in being an American citizen.

Never once has he asked if the accusations are true. This makes me feel oddly safe—as if he were not a representative of the prosecutor but, rather, my lawyer. This is unfortunate. For one thing, it contributes to a sense of myself as a criminal. It is also likely to put me off guard.

It was clear from the moment I opened the door that evening, three weeks ago, to find Wallace standing there with the stranger, that something sinister was afoot. For Wallace to disturb me at that late hour—11:48 p.m., I checked my wristwatch when I heard the tap on the door—was unprecedented. And then, there was the grimness I sensed beneath Wallace's professional reserve, as if he could see some danger barreling toward me but was powerless to stop it.

When the young man, with his fastidious good looks and elegant attire, addressed me in German, I knew that Wallace's fear had not been misplaced. These people know what they are doing: the ambush, the trump card played first, before their subject is even aware that a high-stakes game is under way. Instinctively, I knew I didn't stand a chance; one cannot undo the reflexive indication of comprehension that surely shows in the face upon hearing one's mother tongue. Pretending I did not speak German would have been pointless; I had sense enough to realize that.

Sitting behind my desk, looking across at the tapestry of the fox hunt which I'd bought from my antique dealer in London a few months before setting sail for New York, the sound of the German issuing from my own lips seemed like a violation. It was a Tuesday night, so there were virtually no houseguests about, except for Marilyn, who had only lately accepted my invitation to move in for the rest of the summer, and Barnaby, at the tail end of his recuperation. I was aware, however, of the danger—that someone might hear us, that someone might hear us speaking German. When I could no longer tolerate the strain, I switched to English, attempting as much nonchalance as the situation would allow. Thankfully, my visitor followed suit, without a remark.

Since then, it has become, for me, a bit of a game. My visitor begins each meeting by addressing me in German; I wait until an apt moment presents itself and then slip into English. I have perhaps invested this aspect of our meetings with too much significance, as if I am in danger only while speaking German, regaining a return to safety the moment the world is again cast in the language of my adopted country, the only language I have spoken—until my visitor first appeared three long weeks before today—since alighting on American soil almost six years ago.

The fact is, there may never again be, for me, safe ground of any kind. This realization infuses everything; it is as if someone has placed before me a screen of acrid smoke, sickening my senses and tainting the world I have so carefully pieced together. When I walk, now, in the gardens, the flowers appear remote, closed to me, as if I had done them, too, some wrong. The halls of my beloved house seem either painfully empty or painfully crowded: when I am alone, they echo with isolation; on weekends, when the guests abound, I feel encroached upon. Even the woods, where I have always found peace, seem alive with disruption—the birdcalls too shrill, the leaf cover too dense, the occasional scuttlings underfoot now alive with threat. I feel ridiculous, and yet find myself creeping about in a state of diffuse fear, afraid that I will be bitten or stung, or else set upon by some official or artist I invited months ago from the vantage of my prior sportive, socializing self.

I have no intention, however, of canceling any of the planned festivities. It would likely draw attention, even suspicion. The only moments of equanimity I can still count on are my late-night visits to the basement studio where Marilyn is working on the catalog for her exhibition. I know it is a refuge for her too—from the goings-on of the house, from the strains of her marriage, and the affair I suspect she has embarked upon with Barnaby. As she works, I simply sit, and either read or think.

Marilyn reminded me of Christine from the moment we met—on the second-floor landing, I recall. Though opposite in coloring (Marilyn, dark; Christine, fair), there was something uncannily similar about their eyes: a distinctive quality of both vibrancy and distress, a vitality shot through with unease. Perhaps it was this likeness that made me feel immediately at home with Marilyn. I am not a person who readily makes attachments.

In any event, I find myself seeking Marilyn's company more and more. Her simultaneous presence and distance is calming; she is both absorbed in her work and also aware of my troubled state, concerned while showing a deep respect for my privacy. Bless her.

And yet, being with Marilyn also makes me more keenly aware of the span of years during which I have willed Christine from my consciousness. I have come to realize, through Marilyn, that despite my efforts to devote myself single-mindedly to my new life—which is to say, life without Christine—

Christine has in fact been there all along, stored, with care, in the attic of my soul.

It was with Christine that I crossed from purgatory and rejoined the living. I do not know why she chose to flee; perhaps I never will. This no longer torments me as it once did. I soothe myself with thoughts of Christine's new life across the farthest ocean, in China: a culture that could not be more different from that of her native England. Surely she found the peace she was seeking—the peace that for some reason she was not able to find with me. I see her dressed in crisp cotton, engrossed in a book while sipping oolong tea in a stately, colonial club, relieved of the Shanghai heat by a giant wooden fan circling overhead. Her face, smoothed of its disquiet, now gives full play to her unusual beauty.

I dwell for long moments on such images: not to punish myself, but only that I might touch Christine protectively in my mind's eye, that I might whisper on her image a blessing. A paltry blessing, to be sure, given its source, one that begs forgiveness at the same time as it bestows whatever sorry sparks of hope I have left in this heavy chest. It is all I have to give.

Did I have to lose her, so that she might find herself and flourish? Is this to be the case, too, with Marilyn?

We could not be more different from one another— Christine, Marilyn, and I. And yet, I see us as three comparable figures, up against the same squall. Only this too: I may be battling alongside them, but I am also the eye of the storm, the terrible, still center. Not merely one of the hurricane's combatants, but somehow also its source, and therefore, as it happens, a void, which is to say, nothing at all.

That first meeting with the visitor seemed interminable, though it was probably no more than an hour. For the first half of it we were speaking at cross-purposes, a dark version of an Oscar Wilde comedy. All the time he was talking about "the accusation," I simply assumed that I had been found out, that the visitor had come to discuss the paintings. Why would I not? Harboring such a secret—one that cuts to the quick of your being—can turn the world to a parliament of watchful eyes, and fill every unexpected situation with the threat of discovery.

When I finally realized my mistake, that this meeting had nothing to do with the selling of the paintings—that my visitor in fact appeared to have no inkling of that sorry excursion of mine into more than murky waters—I felt a rush of relief. This lasted the merest flash of a second, followed, as it had to be, by the understanding that what I stand accused of makes child's play of those particular dealings of mine.

I stand accused of murder. A crime of war. A crime, to be precise, against Humanity.

PART I

Christine

CHAPTER ONE

There were times, back home, when the beauty of things willfully withdrew. The grounds of the school where I taught would become suddenly aloof, the old stone paths confusing, the great leafy trees as distant as the hundred or more years they held aloft. Sitting on a bench in the sun, a chill would settle on my skin beneath the layers of my clothes. *England*, I remember thinking, looking out from my rooms at the slow gray drizzle that would hang for days in the air like a pinched complaint. *It is England against which nature is closing herself off.*

It was different here, the rain never drizzled; it released in ardent torrents from a thick sea-green sky. And the heat, always the heat.

Yes, it is true that the civil unrest was beginning to bleed into Shanghai—betrayals and shifting allegiances, warlords posturing threat, late-night clashes on the street that readily erupted into violence. Still, it seemed unthinkable that Mao's thugs would prevail. I kept to the Foreign Quarter, which remained fairly free of disturbance. Compared with the nightly bombings I'd endured in London, along with the sense of constant danger from a fierce and unitary enemy, the situation in Shanghai seemed of a different order: scattered and avoidable. Besides, I had other things on my mind.

How could I describe the mornings? Before the first pipe, when along with my tea I savored the soft gnawing that felt akin to hunger but was really a condition of the spirit.

I sat in my room awaiting Barnaby—opened the window, breathed in the odor of stagnant pools and decaying timber.

I crossed my arms on the sill and looked out onto the street. Here, in place of ancient trees, were saplings as spindly and spotted with sores as the children who hopped about in the alleys, and I thought I saw in them the same urchin cheer.

It had been dry all morning, long enough for a handful of misshapen birds to gather on the broken ledge of the building next door. Without warning, water splashed in bucketfuls from the sky; in a commotion of screeching and awkward flapping, the birds rose as one and disappeared over the roof. Glancing back down at the street, I sighted Barnaby rounding the corner, his collar raised—pointlessly, force of habit, I guessed—against the soaking rain. Before crossing the street, he paused; there was no traffic, save for a passengerless rickshaw being pulled slowly along, and two men on bicycles, crisscrossing the roadway to avoid potholes that had already turned to glossy black pools. Even through the downpour I could see that Barnaby, hands shoved into his pockets, the water splashing up around him, was frowning. This surprised me; I did not think of Barnaby as a man who was easily perturbed.

I knew what would ensue when Barnaby finally climbed the three flights to my room, knew the sequence as well as if I had just witnessed it played by actors on a stage. He would peel off his wet clothes, put on the silk bathrobe I kept for him behind the door of the water closet, and emerge looking fresh, his wet hair combed away from his face. He would look at me with amused eyes and spin me around the room to the beating sound of the rain, then sashay more slowly until we were no longer dancing but just swaying to and fro. (He was still there outside, looking down, now, at the ground.) By then, the discomfort would be spreading through my body, gripping my stomach, clutching my head. At the thought, my lips soured. Finally, he would reach for the pouch he had managed to keep dry and with steady hands, prepare the opium pipe that would pass between us. I would be aware of how briefly

Barnaby would inhale, and the indulgence, by comparison, with which he would press me to linger when the pipe was in my hands.

Then I might glance out the window, only the sky would look suddenly vast, and Barnaby might lean down and kiss me, the acrid-smoke taste on his lips subtle and full as opening roses. His hands on my hips would tighten, and I would shut my eyes. My own lips would taste of ash, dusty and sweet, my own breath the breath of the pipe. The street outside would narrow to a straggly thin line, the casual charcoal stroke of an artist. In between kisses, we would now pass a cigarette, still swaying together, Barnaby's hands moving slowly on my hips. The room would turn blue and then black with night though the hour would elongate, seem not to pass.

Still Barnaby stood there, out in the rain, the frown no longer visible. Finally, he crossed the street and disappeared into the doorway below, the entrance to the narrow green building where for more than a year I have had my lodgings.

When Barnaby opened the door, he moved through the room, stripped off his wet clothes, and changed into the blue robe. As we glided together, he bunched the material of my skirt in his hands, raising the hem halfway up my thighs. I glimpsed myself each time we passed the dressing glass that stood in the corner—the red flash of my skirt, my thigh a white blur; how curiously distant I felt from my reflection. From time to time, Barnaby spoke into my ear; the rich sound of his voice gave me pleasure, though I paid no attention to what he was saying.

The gnawing heightened unpleasantly; I held Barnaby with an urgency that made him also tighten his grasp on me. He rode my dress higher in his hands and reached under the lace of my camisole, pressing both hands so tightly around my waist that his fingers almost touched. He seemed to be waiting until the last possible moment before producing the pouch.

"Darling, why don't we set up the pipe—" I said.

Barnaby's hands glided upward under the front of my camisole. We slid to the floor. Barnaby's robe fell open. With one hand, he unbuttoned my blouse, pausing over each one, the other hand still on my breast.

I attempted a small laugh. "The pipe," I repeated softly.

Barnaby pulled away, looked at me appraisingly, then smiled. "Of course, my sweet, I'd forgotten your greed."

He crossed to where his wet clothes were hanging on the coat rack and from an inner pocket, removed a small oilskin bag. Back beside me, he unfastened the pouch with what seemed like excruciating slowness—untying the leather thong, curling its ends into a loose knot.

"Where is the pipe?" Barnaby asked. I darted to the desk by the window and retrieved my small, cloisonné pipe. Outside, the sky held its cloud banks of sludge.

When I handed the pipe to Barnaby he placed his hand on the back of my neck and drew my face down to his. He pressed his lips over mine, and I had a peculiar sensation of collision, as if I were slamming up against steel. My efforts to mask my panic must have been successful for when we drew apart Barnaby still had a slow, dreamy face.

"I don't know which appetite to satisfy first," he said.

"The devil's choice," I said, forcing a smile. Waiting does this, I thought, looking at Barnaby through the pulsing red blurs at the corners of my eyes.

"It's so wonderful, before we smoke," he murmured.

Everything ached; where he nuzzled my breast it burned.

Time at a standstill. Gazing at Barnaby: frozen, distracted. For a moment I forgot him, I was thinking of somebody else. I was thinking of Robert. I'd heard he'd changed his name— how odd, that he would take on the name of his sad refugee friend from the Internment Center, *Oskar*, anglicizing it to Oscar. Of course, I can only think of him as Robert. Robert holding me, touching me, taking my spirit between his soothing palms. I closed my eyes. I might almost float there, I thought; I might almost float home.

"Here, Christine—" I opened my eyes. Not Robert, not home, but Barnaby, naked beneath his open robe, carefully handing me the pipe.

From the moment I set eyes on Archibald in the ship's shabby dining room—which the crew, to their credit, had tried to spruce up with paper streamers and a few crystal pieces that had survived the war—I knew that Archibald and I would be friends. I drew a chair up to the crowded table, where Archibald was holding court among a group of fellow passengers, and soon found myself in the kind of lighthearted spirits I had not known since my university days.

Archibald was wily and clever, though never really serious, even when his talk turned lofty. This I knew from the inflamed joviality in his small, strangely pink eyes, and from the quizzical expression that never entirely abandoned his features. He was a strange fellow, at odds with himself, in a way that was stamped into his physical being. In contrast to the rest of his form—the thickened features of his face, whiskers like two gray scrubbing brushes at the sides of his jowls, the solid limbs arrayed awkwardly around his massive protruding center—Archibald's hands were unaccountably beautiful. He must have known this for he kept them creamed and manicured and, on occasion, when mulling something over, would spread his fingers before him and regard them admiringly.

The mood on board was festive. Less than one short year since V-J Day, I found myself among people who, like myself, were eager to leave the drabness of wartime England behind. Archibald was the exception. He had only good things to say about his Beloved Motherland, as he called it. For reasons still unclear to me, Archibald had spent the war years in China. He had waited some months before booking his passage home.

But, for all the expense and effort and anticipation of the journey, he had stayed in England a scant few weeks. "No point hanging about," he said to me with a wink. "Just wanted to lay eyes on the Dear Lady, make sure she was still intact."

The social life established on board continued uninterrupted once we were ashore. My first months in Shanghai were all parties and gay conversation. Archibald knew everybody—everybody who counted as far as expatriate society went. I soon discovered that my new friend had a deeper nature. We were sitting in the bar of the hotel where Archibald made his home, when he turned the conversation to his own early life.

"I've always known I had a calling," he'd said. "Since I was a little boy. I wouldn't have known what to name it but it was there, an irascible creature hanging around my neck wherever I went, wriggling and whining and giving me nasty little nips. Heavens, the days I spent wandering around Knightsbridge in a state. One thing frightened me: that the path, my *North Star*, when it finally revealed itself, would be unworthy—and please excuse the self-indulgence—of my largesse of spirit, of all the effort and duress."

A tear bulged from the corner of Archibald's eye. His self-pity seemed absurd, yet I could feel the prickle of tears myself—was aware of how I, too, as a child, had a similar desperate intimation of my own destiny.

"My severe trepidations were, alas, in the end, borne out," he continued. "But by then, it was too late to alter my course." Archibald fixed me with a disturbing stare, his pinkish eyes suddenly hard. "I say, how about an excursion? You must have heard about Han Shu's café, on the Great Western Road. I've been meaning to take you there for some time. I have a feeling you and Han Shu will get along."

I immediately liked the smokey, dim bar, with its cushioned chairs, polished wood beams, and well-attired clientele. Unlike other expatriate nightspots, Han Shu's café—more of a nightclub, really—had held its own throughout the war. Rumor had it that after the Japanese occupiers had brutalized Han Shu's friend, a Dutchman and fellow club owner, for refusing to comply with their extortionist demands, Han Shu had done what was necessary to secure his own safety and prosperity.

When Han Shu appeared, well into the evening, he turned out to be surprisingly tall, and of an unusual build: muscular and pudgy, both. His hair was a slick black cap, oiled and parted, razor sharp down the middle, and he emanated a potent scent—part floral, part musk. A single detail marred his otherwise meticulous grooming: when Han Shu smiled, which he did unself-consciously and often, his glossy lips revealed a stunted forest of richly stained teeth.

"A dear shipboard friend," Archibald said, by way of introduction, nodding to me. Han Shu eyed me approvingly. "Meet Han Shu, a long-standing connoisseur of things British. And an important person in these parts."

"A privilege, to meet such a beautiful woman. I am indeed most honored."

Han Shu took my hand in dough-soft fingers and gave a low bow. I had not before encountered such a large Chinese man. As he lingered, half bent over, I studied the girth of his back and noticed him taking me in. There it was again, that almost palpable sense of thrill rising from a man, directed at me, which had long ago ceased to interest me. I wondered absently why physical beauty should occasion such worship.

Archibald looked first at me and then at Han Shu, and I fancied I saw in his face a paternalistic glow. His next words seemed addressed to himself.

"Yes. I'd like you to meet your spiritual guide."

The rains scrubbed the city clean. Even the mosquitoes festering in the pools that gathered along the streets seemed like emissaries of goodwill.

I had not expected to find Barnaby in Han Shu's smoking

room—in the same building as the café but secreted from the bar at the end of a long corridor. So it was a surprise to see his square-jawed face appear above the rice-paper screen of the booth where I was sitting among a small group of customers. I stiffened and drew slightly away from my new acquaintance, a middle-aged specimen with mustard-colored hair and startled eyes.

"Why Barnaby, what a pleasant surprise! Meet Stephen—Stephen Stonehill," I said awkwardly. Stonehill, smiling excitedly, seemed at a loss for words. "You will join us for a drink," I added, aware of the anxiety in my voice. "We're all going out for a drive later, in Stonehill's car."

I smoothed the ripple of hair above my ear. Barnaby's eyes followed the movement; their warmth felt like a caress.

"I have a quick errand to run," I said quickly. "Why don't you two get acquainted."

I rose, lifting the hem of my dress, which I noticed was slightly frayed.

The corridor was almost completely dark; narrow glass shingles near the ceiling let in a greasy red glow. At the end of the hallway, by the front door, I recognized my contact, a thin Chinese man whose face was a plane of hard angles. Our business took barely a minute. Nodding curtly, the man left through the front door. He'd granted my request for an extension on the loan, but there was still the matter of finding fresh funds. I stood for a moment, alone, twisting my handkerchief in my hands, wondering how my savings, which had seemed so robust—surely enough to sustain me here for two years, possibly three—could have dwindled so rapidly. Archibald, I thought. He would help me figure out how to dig my way out of the mess I was in. I would visit him later at his hotel. Starting back down the corridor, I almost collided with Barnaby and hastily resumed my cheerful air.

"You will come with us, won't you?" I said. "Stonehill's a bit simple, but he's awfully nice."

"You're in trouble, aren't you," Barnaby said.

"Don't be a silly boy," I replied brightly, linking my arm in his. "We're going to have a wonderful evening. We'll go to the American Bar and dance. I'll take turns, though I can assure you that every moment I'm dancing with Red, I'll be thinking of you."

After a languid day spent with Barnaby, I readied myself for my nightly sortie to Han Shu's café.

"Let's give it a miss tonight," Barnaby said. "I'm rather bored with the place."

"You're not going to give me reason to call you a stick-in-the-mud. You, of all people."

Barnaby eyed me with uncharacteristic seriousness. "What do you see in a buffoon like Stonehill, anyway?"

I smiled. "Barnaby Harrington. I do believe you're just the teensiest bit jealous."

He smiled back. "Haven't you heard? Life is painful, hard, and short."

"Darling, that's not how the saying goes," I said.

"Well, I've got the short part right, and that's my point. Life—time—it's precious. Spend it with me. Don't throw yourself away."

He regretted his words immediately, I could see that; something in the air between us altered, like a sudden plunge in barometric pressure.

"There's something else," he said, unable to mask the darkness in his face.

"Yes?"

"You should stay away from Han Shu's. It's not good for you."

I lit a cigarette, inhaled deeply, turned to face him.

"Barnaby, dear. You stick to your pleasures, I'll stick to mine."

～

Archibald was at his usual table in the hotel bar, his giant belly like a lost, friendly sea creature perched in his lap. Barnaby slung his panama onto the hat rack and sat opposite his friend in a cushioned chair.

"Out late again last night, I presume?" Archibald's small eyes glistened beneath bushy brows. "Official business? Or intrigues of another kind? Nothing that a thick bristle from the dog that bit you won't fix."

Barnaby tapped down a cigarette on the side table. "Decidedly *unofficial*. And a decidedly fiendish dog."

Barnaby enjoyed his little tête-à-têtes with Archibald.

"The usual suspects?" Archibald inquired.

"And a new chum of Christine's."

Archibald nodded glumly. "Christine was here earlier. We both know she's a woman of broad gifts. As it happens, though, I'm a mite worried about her. She seems to be having trouble—how can I put it?—staying afloat. I'm afraid there's some disappointment on the horizon."

Barnaby drew on his cigarette.

Archibald craned his neck in search of the waiter. "Damn it," he said good-naturedly. "Never there when you need them."

"What do you mean—about Christine?" Barnaby asked.

"I've noticed a change in her. Not sure I can put my finger on it. I do believe the Romantics were right when it came to the charms of women. Innocence and grace. Call me old-fashioned, but it's all in the manner. Unadorned coyness, that's the measure of a woman's regard for her own worth."

Archibald stroked his belly with tender concentration.

Barnaby knew the man's penchant for drama, and sensed that this was all a springboard for the real story he wished to tell. At last a waiter arrived with their drinks. Barnaby took a few slow sips.

"Which brings me to something I've been meaning to chew over with you, Barnaby—of a personal nature. If I may be permitted to prevail on your generous attention."

Barnaby raised his drink in a toast, and Archibald continued.

"Imagine, if you will, a country under siege. Wartime. Shanghai cowers under the yoke of occupation. And there you are, as worried as the next fellow about your weekly ration of noodles, hoping you might have a few shavings of pork.

"You spend the morning on your toilette, making the best of the wafer of shaving soap left at the bottom of the dish. You rub only three drops of oil into your whiskers. You notice the dirt gathering in the head of your walking cane, in the creases of the lion's mane. You didn't ask for this war and you're none too happy about it.

"You head down to the water, breathing in the smell of the quay. It smells human: sweaty, unclean. It smells like a brothel. This makes you hungry. Dirty children crowd around; the pier is rotting, you can almost hear the termites gnashing their teeth. The children have sores on their faces and feet. Some of the girls have babies tied to their backs with rags. They slip their filthy little hands into your pockets. You pat their heads and wonder if you should worry about lice jumping onto your fingers.

"The junks are bobbing up and down. You step onto the deck of the fifth junk from the end of the pier, balancing yourself with your cane. There are boys and girls inside the junk too, you know that. They're older, old enough to know about life. Their mothers sit on crates, arguing about something.

"Now, Barnaby, here's the question. Are you responsible for what happens next? Are you a person making a choice, or simply a cork in the current of history, caught in the timeless web of human misery? Oh dear, I'm mixing my metaphors. Let me put it another way. Are you, in the end, no more than an instrument of the human urge to destroy?"

Barnaby was aware of a creeping discomfort. He squinted

through the smoke at his friend, whose face was the picture of affability.

"I've always thought that destruction was a form of creation," Archibald went on. "Take a fire. I don't mean a bonfire or a small kitchen blaze. I'm talking a real forest fire, an out-of-control devouring beast of a fire. Splendid, I say. Nature's sylph. Alive. Even if what it's alive with is its own end."

He laughed roundly then leaned forward, earnest, his voice falling to a whisper. "Have you ever seen a house burn, my boy? All the way to the ground?"

Archibald finished his drink in a swift gulp, then glanced impatiently around the room. Sighting the waiter at the bar, he held up his empty glass, his face almost vibrating with anticipation. "And a little something to nibble, if you wouldn't mind!"

He turned back to Barnaby. "Now, where was I? Oh yes, the junk. I know you're a fellow after adventure; heaven knows the stories I've heard you tell about Africa. Now here's an admission. Never have had a bit of ebony. But I'm awfully fond of the smooth jade you can collect out here—quite a bargain too—and the tigereye. Up north, if you look hard enough, a nice long sliver of hematite. They're taller in the northern villages, you probably know that. Thinner too. Still tender, though, if you catch them at the right age. But a nice smooth onyx for my collection—did I say onyx? I meant ebony. Never mind, it's all the same."

The idea of Archibald being sinister struck Barnaby as absurd. Then why the feeling of alarm? Barnaby let out a quick laugh to mask what he was feeling, then tried to relax into the soothing languor afforded by the drink: was this his second, or already his third?

The waiter set down a plate, and Archibald greedily eyed its contents: a dozen or more small pastry shells, each containing a shrimp smothered in creamy sauce. Delicately, he picked one up between forefinger and thumb and popped it into his small red mouth, which was set like a shiny bright egg in the nest of his whiskers.

⤫

Outside, the skies were clear; a brief respite from the rains. As I waited for Barnaby—how many months had it been, these trysts with Barnaby?—I felt the familiar stirrings of disaffection. When Barnaby rounded the corner, and I saw the eager set of his face, my spirits dampened further.

As I opened the door, I could feel his ardor spilling into the room, sucking up the oxygen. I tried to return his smile, gripped by a desire to flee. Not Barnaby—I'd thought things would be different with him. The wine did nothing to quell the panic, so I reached for the bourbon, trying to distract myself from the fact that we had no opium to smoke.

"Darling, what is it?" Barnaby asked with genuine concern. Then, playfully: "You look like you've seen a ghost."

I attempted to smooth the trouble from my face, puzzling over the tricks that feelings could play—little inner sprites that frolicked and squealed, then disappeared on a whim. I watched as Barnaby unpacked his satchel. He'd brought delicious morsels, as always, and whistled quietly as he set them out. Then, in a burst of cheer, he swept me into his arms and twirled me around. Around, around, the feel of his strength enfolding me, the room a sudden discombobulation.

"Barnaby," I whispered, distress in my voice. "Put me down."

He laughed. "Christine, you *are* wonderful." His voice trembled with happiness.

He continued to spin me around; the room sped up. I threw back my head, fixed my eyes on the blur of the light, a sorry earthly comet, plummeting nowhere. No use, I thought, aware for a moment of a great, crashing sadness.

It was there, always: the fallen sun. I have loved once, only once, and unwisely, to say the least.

I thought of the thunderbolt, the way it had hit me, that first day, when Robert—before I knew anything about him, before I even knew his name—walked into my classroom along with the scraggly contingent of his fellow Internment Center residents. *He* was not scraggly—a misfit, rather, of dignified elegance, as if a case of mistaken identity had landed him someplace he did not belong. It was his carriage, and the intelligence and clarity that poured from his eyes. I knew in that moment that Robert and I would be lovers. I also knew something else, though I could not have known where it would lead, what this fact would come to mean (about him, about me): that Robert and I were two of a kind.

Barnaby was still twirling me. I wanted desperately for him to put me down.

"Christine," Barnaby breathed.

It was already too late. No sadness now: only numbness, stillness, drought.

He came to a sudden halt; still holding me, he brought his lips close to mine.

"I love you, Christine. Did you know?"

"Barnaby. Put me down. Please."

He gently set me down on the couch. I caught my breath, then reached for a cigarette.

"Let's not fuss with the food," I said, attempting nonchalance. "We can go out to the noodle house."

Barnaby glanced at the items he'd lain out on the table: a handful of green beans, some sticks of dried beef, a bamboo box containing cold steamed rice, and two small, perfectly ripe mangoes.

"But it's so much nicer here, just the two of us."

I drew deeply on my cigarette. I was aware of the awful familiar restlessness in my feet, my legs, my arms: it took some effort to stop myself from fleeing the room.

"Barnaby, you know I'm not much of a homebody."

He seemed finally to register that something was wrong; he approached the couch, knelt beside me.

"Darling," he said, reaching down to stroke my hair. I carefully removed his hand, peered into his eyes, certain, suddenly, of what I must do.

"Maybe we just need a little air," I said.

"But it's muggy as hell out there."

"That's not what I mean."

"Then what, Christine. What do you mean?"

"Breathing room. Perhaps we've been spending too much time together."

"You can't mean that."

I said nothing. I gazed over at the mirror, stared at the tassels of the peacock-blue scarf; stirred by the overhead fan, they flared up like the hair of a running child.

"Why are you doing this?" Barnaby asked. "I don't see the reason in it."

His words seemed distant, as if his voice were echoing in my memory, rather than here, with me, in the room. When I turned to him, I was momentarily surprised to find that he was still there.

"It's not about reason, Barnaby."

"Then what?"

I looked at him—Barnaby flustered. Not the Barnaby I knew. And, bridling a little at my own callousness, not the Barnaby I wanted.

"Well," I said, calm now, measuring my words, "if you must know, I'm not fond of being told that I'm wonderful."

Barnaby looked like a child who'd been slapped. I ground out my cigarette in the alabaster ashtray on the side table, steeling myself.

"I'm also not fond of those three little words that other women seem so intent on extracting."

Crossing to the window, I drew aside the curtain. Outside, the heat was almost visible: liquid ripples shimmying around the hard edges of the world. When I turned back to Barnaby, I glimpsed on his face a contorted look of helpless rage. It was his turn to quickly rearrange his features.

"Christine," he said quietly, "I only wanted to—"

"Yes?" Even I was surprised by the hardness in my voice. I tried it again. "Yes, Barnaby?"

He looked at me for a long moment, his brown eyes flat as mud: gone, the twinkle I had found so amusing; gone, the warmth, the expectation of imminent delight.

"I am sorry," I said, managing some softness.

"I wonder why I don't believe you," Barnaby said, composed now, reaching for his hat.

"That I'm sorry? But darling, I am."

"That's not what I mean." He surveyed the room. "I guess I just don't quite believe any of it. What you want. What you think you want. The way you're living. The parties, your friends. All this *fun*."

He waited by the door holding his hat, studying the brim. "Be careful, Christine," he said sadly, brushing the crown of my head with his lips.

Afterward, I stared for a long time at the closed door, studied the faded patches, the random pattern in the paintwork of peelings and blisters. Then, collecting my purse and stole, I stepped into my best evening shoes and headed out into the wet heat of the night.

At the party, there was a small orchestra with that perfect combination of tightness and abandon. Someone spun me around the room. A newcomer. He gripped my waist in a tender, possessive way. It had been a boisterous evening; I'd left drained tumblers and wine glasses on tables and sills. Overhead, enormous fans ground away at the thick heat. Now and then I looked up to see the slope of the man's face. Charles, yes, that was his name. Young, very young, with a hovering eagerness about him; his eyes darted about with expectation and surprise.

As the evening wore on, the music changed, as it always did: fewer swing numbers, entire sets, now, of ballads. Of course, he pulled me closer, his hand caressed my waist. The wine was good, the whiskey exceptional, but the liquor could not stay the whirring ache that began somewhere deep within and fanned out to every inch of my flesh. I glanced up at him, at Charles, and tried to look happy, but something was wrong. This man seemed so innocent, so taken with me, so alive to my every movement. I could almost feel the tingling in his fingertips as they moved stealthily upward along my middle back, sliding discreetly; through the chiffon of my dress, they brushed the side of my breast. My practiced eye had plucked him immediately from the crowd: the expensive cut of his suit, the heavy gold of his watch chain, the Italian leather shoes. He had succumbed so readily, and yet now my heart was not in it.

"How old are you?" I asked. The man's brow momentarily creased.

"Fancy asking such a thing," he protested, trying to sound unperturbed.

Something at the base of my skull tightened and for one ghastly moment I saw myself as a giant bird of prey, swooping down with extended talons. I smiled, trying to make it a winning smile, but could tell, by the twittering of the man's eyelashes, that I had distressed him. It was late; the band slowed still further to a deliberate languor. I gently pulled away.

"I'm sorry," I muttered, abandoning the smile.

It was no use, I thought, making my way through the crowd. For a moment, in the midst of the dance floor, listening to the saxophone moaning in rhythm to the swaying hips of the dancers, I wondered if I might chance upon Barnaby, almost hoped I would run into him, right into his arms. I lowered my eyes and hurried toward the door. Barnaby had long since lost interest in such gatherings. Besides, there'd be no reason he'd come looking for me; I'd made my feelings about him all too clear. I knew that Charles was probably standing bewildered among the other dancers watching my retreating figure. But I didn't care. Not even the promise of smoke—and I knew from experience that Charles would have been un-stinting in that regard—made me want to go back. His gleam-ing face above mine had become abhorrent; I needed to get some air.

But outside, the air was thicker and coarser than it had been on the dance floor. I hurried along the thoroughfare, which glowed in black blurry ovals where the streetlights hung from loopy metal necks. My lungs labored against the viscous air; more than anything, I wanted the freeing thrust of momentum.

A creaky rumble up ahead and then, over a hump in the road, a trolley car ambled into view. I waved it to a stop, then climbed onto the worn running board and rested there a moment, rummaging in my purse for a coin. Once my breath steadied, I glanced around the car. My fellow passengers sat in silence, staring disturbingly into the middle distance. To a person, they were dressed in simple canvas garb. Their eyes were like hard brown eggs, opaque and somehow fragile, their skin leathery, prematurely aged by the sun.

After some minutes, the trolley car turned off the main road and headed away from the harbor. At first, it was a relief to be seated in the car, to see the world moving steadily by. But as the minutes passed, the bland silence began to feel op-pressive. I looked at the woman across from me, whose brow, despite the deep lines, was expressionless. Won't somebody say something? I thought. Anything but this dreadful silence. The woman opposite me grimaced, revealing several rotted tooth stumps in her lower jaw. I jumped to my feet and pressed myself to the door, trying to pry it open with my fingers.

"Let me off!" I called out in Shanghainese dialect to the

driver. My finger jammed in the door, which clamped onto the nail bed; I felt a burning pain and the ooze of blood. The tram was now moving at a pace. I applied all my strength to the rubber grip and finally inched it open, just wide enough to wedge in my foot. I tugged and kicked at the doors and, as they sprang open, flung myself through, tumbling onto the road. The door snapped shut, catching a corner of my hem, which tore off in a long coil.

Shakily, I stood. I had no idea where I was. Instinct, I thought, I'll do this by instinct. I ducked into a side street and headed east. It must have been very late, as there was no sign of life; the only sound that reached my ears, besides the clicking of my heels on the road and the labored draw of my own breath, was the lone warble of a cock, hours ahead of schedule. The air was tainted with the pungent odor of overripe fruit. I imagined papaya and mango, scattered on the ground with skins split, their yellow and orange flesh crawling with plump red-eyed flies.

The streets were a narrow chaos, curving odd-shaped bends running haphazardly into one another. I thought again of the young man at the party—what was his name, Christopher? Carl? The fluttering of his eyelashes, the timid sweetness I saw in the upward arc of his combed eyebrow: those had been my undoing.

But the blooming in my belly was ugly now and fierce. Food, I thought, wondering how long it had been since I had eaten. For the second time that night I thought about Barnaby, recalled a sumptuous meal he had produced in the meager kitchenette of my room. Barnaby had watched approvingly as I pried the meat from the tiny bones of the pigeon, as I scooped up another spoonful of the rice flour he had turned to a delicately spiced soufflé. I could not remember when food had tasted so good. I wondered where Barnaby was, what he was doing, what adventure he was embarked upon to add to his ever-mounting stockpile.

A retch rose in my throat. Something was happening to the air: it was sinking, lowering itself to the ground. No, not the air—the sky. Above the decaying tenements and shacks, a faint glowing rectangle of red seemed to be trying to press through the blackness.

Chan wanted the rent. This time, he was adamant. I knew he would throw me out—change the lock, perhaps, cast my belongings onto the street or, more likely, sell them.

It was easy to get lost in these streets. Now, small group-ings of men stood about; heads turned, the slinging of surly glances. I snapped to alertness: guns in plain sight, the shabby blue uniforms of the Nationalists. Not a woman in sight. These men were looking to do harm. I turned the cor-ner before hastening my step. I saw with some relief that this street was deserted, and the next. I came to a halt, looked around at the disheveled buildings eyeing me emptily with grime-smeared panes. I'm done with it, I thought, I've had enough of that place. I looked down at my ivory dress. I had to admit it was a little worse for wear, not just because of the torn hem; the filth in the air had arranged itself in damp patches on the bodice and skirt. I wondered where I would go.

When, some weeks earlier, Han Shu had vaguely offered me "some manner of employ," I laughed breezily and patted his pork chop of a hand.

"Han Shu, darling," I said, "I'm far more comfortable having the flow of cash go from me to you. Besides, I'm not certain I have any talents that would prove lucrative in your trade, whereas we all know the quality of the goods you have to offer me."

I had peered over his shoulder into the foyer of the café, trying to determine whether the party just entering from the street included anyone I knew. Despite the casual way in which I dismissed Han Shu's offer, I had been keenly aware that, besides my lipstick, key, and the vial of pills I kept for an emergency, there was but a single coin rattling around in my purse.

"I suspect you may change your mind," Han Shu had said in a respectful tone, which seemed at odds with the sinister shadow crossing his face. "You are welcome at any time to take up my offer."

"Han Shu, I won't have you turning serious on me," I answered in an attempt at lightheartedness. Han Shu bowed, but when he righted himself, there was an angry glaze in his eyes.

I had, after all, known someone in the group who had entered—a high-spirited Dane who was delightfully free with his billfold. After I led him to the large back chamber, he took it upon himself to foot the expenses I incurred in the space of that long and amusing evening.

The next day, I returned to Han Shu's alone. I sat at the bar and ordered a drink. My mind flew to the back room; I could almost taste the oily blue smoke in my nostrils. The bartender freshened my drink once, twice. At the third refill, my earlier pleasant feeling of anticipation turned to familiar restlessness.

"I think I'll slip into the back and see if my friends are waiting for me there," I said.

The bartender glanced up and down the bar. "Look, Christine. Han Shu told me I could fill your glass a few times, but your credit's no good in the back room. Not anymore."

"Don't be a donkey," I snapped. "I'm expecting a wire any day now. I've been through this with him before."

But the man only shook his head, rested his hand over mine on the bar. "Don't go back there, Christine. It will only cause a scene."

"You're being ridiculous," I said, pulling away my hand. "We're the best of friends, Han Shu and I. There would never be a scene between us." I emptied my glass, collected my stole and white satin purse.

It took a little while for my eyes to adjust to the smoky depths of the back room. I stood in the doorway blinking, then scanned the dim space: a few solitary figures seated or sprawled on divans in a state of intoxication, but no one I knew well enough to join. I made my way to a red upholstered chair and sat down, watching the boys with their trays silently crisscrossing the room, pausing now and then to adjust a footstool, fill somebody's pipe, deposit a glass of steaming tea. None of the boys stopped to attend to me. Finally, jumping out of my skin, I called a little too loudly to one as he passed, but he averted his eyes and moved by. I called out to a second boy; again, the averted gaze. When, some minutes later, the first boy passed by again, I took hold of his arm.

"I'd like a pipe," I said steadily.

"I'm sorry, miss," he whispered in Chinese, "the master has issued orders."

"And what kind of orders, may I ask?" My voice rose, which sent a flicker of alarm into the boy's face. "I'd like to see the master," I said loudly. Several stupefied faces turned calmly in my direction.

It was only then that I noticed Han Shu's bulky frame looming in the arch that opened onto the passageway. He said something curt to the boy that I didn't quite catch.

"May I help you, madam?" Han Shu asked, reverting to English.

"You're just in time to clear up a misunderstanding," I said with relief.

"And what kind of misunderstanding, madam, might that be?" Han Shu's voice was brusque, though I was heartened by his odd repeated use of the word *madam*.

"Well, sir," I said, going along with the game, "I was simply ordering some refreshment, and—"

"I'm afraid if you want refreshments," he cut in, "you'll have to visit some other establishment," and he turned and disappeared.

I jumped up and followed Han Shu into the hallway, calling after him: "You know I'm good for it, I've always been good for it."

He stopped short; I found myself staring at his back.

"I'm not playing with you, Christine, and no, I do not assume you are, as you put it, good for it. If you have no friends here this evening who can pick up your tab, I'm afraid I will have to ask you to leave."

Han Shu proceeded toward his office.

"Wait." I grabbed hold of his thick arm.

He spun around and gripped my shoulder. "I don't think you want to play with me," he said hoarsely.

Still gripping me, Han Shu pushed me down the corridor, pulled a key ring from his pocket with his free hand, and unlocked the door. Few people set foot in Han Shu's private rooms; I had not visited them before. I had trouble taking in the unusual appointments, so startled was I by Han Shu's unexpected behavior. He flung me roughly onto a gold chaise lounge, then walked behind an elaborately carved desk. Using another key to open a drawer, he pulled out a large leather-bound ledger. He opened the book and carefully leafed through the pages.

"Yes, here it is," he said, marking a spot on the page with his forefinger. "Your account now stands at 178 pounds sterling, adjusting for my modest conversion fee. Now." He looked up. "You are clearly not liquid as you were when you arrived. You therefore no longer represent a sound business proposition. I did not have to make very extensive inquiries to ascertain that you have no steady source of income, that you were living on the savings of a—let me see." He peered down again at the book. "Of a school teacher, which I imagine, given your current rather desperate manner, have dwindled down to nothing."

Han Shu closed the book and replaced it in the drawer, which he then relocked.

"I regret that you have forced my hand," he said, moving back around the desk, the rage gone from his face, replaced by dispassionate calculation. "I had taken you for someone who would play by the rules," he continued, drawing a fountain pen from his pocket and tapping it slowly against the palm of his hand. "But I suppose I can't be right about all of the people all of the time."

He paused, seemed lost for a moment in thought.

"I gave you a chance to redeem yourself. Why do you think I offered you employment?"

I listened to the soft *tap tap* of the pen against the padded surface of his hand. The conversation did not seem entirely real to me and, though I heard every word Han Shu said, I had trouble piecing it together. I did, however, understand the seriousness of his tone.

"Han Shu," I said quietly, "I've always considered you a friend."

"The people I call my friends do not try to cheat me." He squatted on his heavy haunches and brought his face close to mine. Grasping my chin firmly in his thick fingers, he spoke right into my face: "You are not my friend, Christine. You are a business investment gone bad. Is that clear?"

I squirmed my head to escape Han Shu's unpleasant breath, but he tightened his grip, pressing painfully into the soft underside of my gullet.

"Now, what are you going to do? You're a clever woman."

The room tightened; Han Shu peered into my eyes, his fingers pushing under my chin, his breath rancid in my face.

"I only want one pipe," I whispered. "Just one pipe."

"Do I really need to tell you?" he cooed. "This is no longer about what I can give you. There's no mystery here. Both of us know what it is I have to give you. The question, now, is what can *you* give *me*?"

He paced before his desk.

"Well?"

My eyes filled with tears. I fidgeted with the chain on my purse. "I don't know what to say, Han Shu. I simply—"

"Then get out. I don't wish to see your—your—" His eyes skipped around the room, in search of something. "Your simpering face, yes, that's it. I don't want to look at your simpering face."

He reached for the thick gold cord hanging by the window and pulled it. A stocky man with pockmarked skin entered from what I'd thought was a bookcase but now showed itself to be a hidden doorway.

"Madam would like to leave," Han Shu said. "Kindly show her out."

The man picked me up by the arm and shunted me across the room. He handled me roughly all the way down the hallway and through the foyer. When we reached the front door, he opened it and pushed me. I stumbled out onto the street.

Now, hurrying through the damp roads, I found myself replaying this scene from some weeks ago in my mind. I was no longer baffled, nor even particularly angry. In place of the fury I'd felt since that evening whenever Han Shu came to mind, was now a fluttery hope.

Dawn, finally, was beginning to break; I could see its pallid ripple spreading on the horizon. My feet were aching in my high heels; I slipped off my shoes and continued barefoot, walking awkwardly in the middle of the uneven road.

An elderly woman, tiny and alert as a sparrow, poked her head through a paneless window.

"The harbor?" I queried hopefully.

The woman nodded vigorously and jabbed the air with a small crooked finger. I headed in the direction she indicated. It was not long before I was back on evenly paved road. When, finally, I rounded the corner and caught a glimpse of the murky bay—the dull gleam of the water, the ramshackle silhouettes of the junks—I cried out in relief.

With renewed energy I hastened along the roadway. For the first time in a very long while, I found myself thinking beyond the moment, beyond what was to happen that day or that evening, beyond who might call on me or who I was hoping to run into. The pain in my belly receded to a dull throb as I thought about what I would say when I got to Han Shu's— about how I was going to change things, to turn the clock back to an earlier, happier self. I kept my eyes on the horizon. The sky, the whole sky, was gently aglow with the new day.

The front of the building was still in darkness when I arrived. Knowing Han Shu was an early riser I lifted the handle of the iron knocker and struck three firm raps. The door was opened almost immediately by a servant boy.

"He'll see me," I said breathlessly, "I know he will. Tell Han Shu it's Christine."

The boy dipped his head apologetically and closed the door, leaving me standing out in the street. I slipped my shoes back on, then waited. After some minutes, the boy reappeared and gestured for me to enter. He led me down the hallway and ushered me into Han Shu's office. I felt unusually alert and in command of myself as I entered the room. Han Shu was seated behind his desk, fully dressed, down to the silk handkerchief peeking from the breast pocket of his jacket, a benign expression on his face.

"Why, Christine," he said pleasantly, remaining seated. "I thought I might see you back here again."

I did not fail to notice how brazenly he eyed me—up and down, lingering first on my breasts, then at my hips, and taking in, to be sure, the stains on my dress, the jagged edge of my hem. This only made me square my shoulders; when I spoke, my voice was steady.

"Hello," I said, sitting in the leather chair on the other side of the desk. "I'd like to know the precise nature of your proposal. Regarding the job."

"Let me get you a drink," Han Shu replied, taking a shot

glass from a shelf above his desk and filling it from a crystal decanter. He handed it to me.

"This establishment, as you know, is a respectable business. And, while my aim is to cater fully to my clients' needs and desires, where business is concerned, I pride myself on running a tight ship." He paused, giving me time, I supposed, to recall my own brush with his strict business practices.

"It may, therefore, come as a surprise that I keep an establishment of a different order on the other side of the city, one that does not provide much of a return. Given the nature of the enterprise, I cannot provide the accoutrements I am happily able to proffer here." He swept his arm in an arc to indicate the plush office. The smugness on his face seemed less to do with the opulence of the room than with his appreciation of his own use of the English language.

"The place I am speaking of is serviceable and clean, as I hope you will see. But we operate on a bare-bones budget. You will appreciate, therefore, that I will not be able to pay you a princely wage. And, if you will permit me to remind you, there is the matter of your debt.

"The position comes with a room. Your other needs will be taken care of. Including, of course, your predilection for the pipe. At Manor House, I will ask you to, ah, nurse those needs in private.

"One of your duties will be to serve as a chaperone, what I believe in England you might call a House Mother. Your other duties will capitalize on your professional expertise. May I freshen your drink?"

I nodded. Han Shu rose, pulled down a tumbler this time, and filled it almost to the brim.

"Let me come straight to the point. I run a home for girls without parents, or without parents who can adequately provide for them. Alley children, street children, call them what you will. I look for girls who show the potential to rise above their origins, and cultivate them to become young ladies. No

point taking in a girl who will show a poor return on the effort I put into her."

My head was swimming pleasantly. An old exhilarating
anticipation tickled my limbs. Behind Han Shu, the dull yellow glow in the window filled the room with a filmy light.
Another glow, sickly and wan, straining to break through
cloud, stirred in my memory: a lifetime away, in a room by the
Port of Southampton. How many hours had I sat there, in my
freshly ironed traveling dress, my suitcase by the door, waiting for my pocket watch to indicate it was time to head down
to the quay where I would board the steamer that would take
me away?

For days, the grief had been like a beast, threatening to
tear me apart. I had raged against it—against Robert, for shattering the only real dream I'd ever had. I had cried until I could
not shed one more tear, I had pounded so hard on the bed of
the hotel to which I'd fled that I damaged the springs. Finally,
in the middle of one of those black nights, I had walked like
a sleepwalker to the dressing table and looked hard into the
tarnished mirror at my swollen, almost unrecognizable face,
and called an end to it. In that moment, my dreams seemed
worthy only of scorn. What had I been thinking?

And then I'd clung onto the date of departure as onto a
buoy, clung to the thought of that boat pulling away from
the shore, obliterating everything—Robert, our life together,
England, the self I had been and the self I now was—so that
I might begin anew. I remembered looking out at the dull sky
and thinking, *No room there for heaven*. But where I was going, it
was different: the hot bright fulcrum—

"You would instruct the girls as befits the refinement of
young ladies." Han Shu's voice was tinged with excitement.
"First and foremost, the English language. Through literature.
I think that's the best way, don't you? It was how I received
my instruction, as I presume is obvious."

For a long moment, I was silent. Han Shu, the proprietor

of an orphanage? Looking at him—his polished attire, vanity inscribed in every gesture—it did not add up. Could it really be? That, tucked away in that great barrel of a chest, was a tender heart with room enough for a houseful of misbegotten waifs?

"I never thought I'd find myself teaching again," I said, almost to myself.

"Perhaps a little refreshment would help you think the matter over." Han Shu reached for the gold braided cord and gave it a quick tug. The panel of books swung open to reveal the same burly fellow who at last meeting had thrown me out. This time, he was carrying a tray laid with paraphernalia. He lit the lamp and then carefully prepared the little nugget of opium, dexterously passing it back and forth over the flame using two long, silver needles. When it was sticky and soft, he placed it over the hole in the cloisonné pipe and handed it to me.

I glanced slowly around the room, taking in the silk wall hangings and warm colors of the rugs. Inhaling my first deep breath of smoke, I relaxed. I smiled at the stony countenance of the man who hovered above me. Suddenly the earlier incident with him seemed no more than a harmless vaudeville sketch.

"Well then," Han Shu ventured, "do we have a deal?"

I peered through the smoke at my new employer, puzzling over why I had, in the first place, troubled to say no. What harm could there be, after all, in teaching Han Shu's young ladies? I inhaled again, a long slow draw of what seemed to be life itself. I could feel the muscles of my face soften; I knew from the look in Han Shu's eyes that a glimpse of what people called my radiance must be evident. I relaxed into it, the way I'd learned, long ago, to do.

"I've always thought you an interesting woman," Han Shu said quietly, his voice transformed.

"You will make it worth my while," I murmured, losing

myself now in the trouble-free sinking, in the openness that unclenched my fingers, massaged the balls of my burning feet, blossomed peculiarly within as a simultaneous seizing and abdication of will.

"Yes," Han Shu breathed, "I believe it will be a pleasing partnership for us both."

"Then it's settled. When do I start?"

CHAPTER TWO

I called out directions to the rickshaw man, glancing at the map Han Shu had drawn: spindly meandering lines, mostly unnamed streets that twisted inland. Wearing my most sedate dress—a floral cotton with a crocheted collar—and cream, low-heeled pumps, my satchel of papers balanced on my lap, I could almost imagine I was a young school teacher again, newly trained, eager about my profession.

It was a bright morning. Instead of the oozing heat were unusual splashes of sunlight, which gave the streets, even the dirty alleyways, a freshly painted feel. I enjoyed the long ride. Han Shu had treated me to several days of pampering: hot tea and sweet buns for breakfast, mounds of white rice and thinly sliced chicken for dinner; the peace and quiet of his guest room, with its feathered mattress and quilt; and the discreet though ready replenishment of the pipe. My strength returned in full force and now, being spirited through the quirky and unfamiliar streets, I relaxed into the bamboo seat, took note of the unusual flora: papery blue flowers that sprang out here and there on the vines, waxy conical pods that hung orange and creaturelike from stunted crooked branches.

The map had been drawn carefully, and I had no trouble directing the rickshaw man. Finally, I came to the place marked by an X, and told the man to stop. When I saw the narrow wooden structure, sandwiched between two smaller, more ramshackle tenements, I had to restrain myself from laughing. Manor House indeed!

I stepped down from the rickshaw, taking care to avoid a muddy patch in the unpaved road. Standing by the front door,

I was struck by a distinctive, unreasonable feeling that I had seen this house before—that I had known the sloping red tiles of the roof and the slanted wooden beams, visible beneath the rusted tin guttering, all my life. The clay-brick walls were damaged in places, showing uneven layers of muted color: sandy yellow, reddish charcoal, muddy brown. Studying the patterns of erosion and distress, I wondered what lives had passed within these walls.

A girl, who looked to be about fourteen, opened the door and appraised me warily. She showed me into the foyer. When I asked to see Han Shu, she disappeared through a green swinging door. Inside, the house exuded the same humble dignity as the exterior. The entrance hall was neatly swept, and though the ceiling and walls needed paint, they were brushed clean of loose peelings and adorned with several simple wall hangings. A vase of fresh flowers, the same blue papery blooms I had seen on the vines, sat on a wooden sideboard, which also held a silk-bound visitors' book.

After several minutes, Han Shu appeared. He enfolded my hand up to the wrist in his soft padded palms.

"Welcome," he said warmly, caressing my hand. "Welcome to your new home."

He showed me into a long narrow room, sparsely appointed but clean, where the girl who had greeted me at the door stood meekly by a long trestle table.

"Toung-Yang, please assemble the girls," Han Shu said. "I would like to introduce you all to your new *school mistress*." He enunciated the words as if he were saying *Her Majesty the Queen*.

The girl soon returned, followed by eight or nine others of varying ages and heights. They were all dressed in a similar and decidedly odd fashion: garments that fit perfectly and yet seemed incongruous, on the wrong scale. Then I realized what it was. The girls were wearing women's evening gowns of a dated European style that had been altered to suit the contours of a young girl's shape.

* * *

That first meeting with my new wards was tense. The girls remained silent and would not look me directly in the eye.

Their reticence, however, soon lifted. Within days, the girls were talking happily in the school room, using the street slang I quickly learned to decipher, and showing me their few, but prized childish treasures.

My days fell into a pleasant routine. I would rise early, help prepare breakfast, and eat with my charges; then, while the girls cleared the dishes, I set up the schoolroom for the day's lessons. Mercifully, my lesson plans came back to me, though I had to strip things back to basics. The small cache of books I'd brought with me from England sufficed for teaching basic courses in English; as their language improved, I would be able to use the novels in my collection to teach literature along with a little history.

Classes ended at two o'clock, when my pupils retired for a siesta. I spent the afternoons and evenings alone in my room—reading, correcting homework, preparing the next day's lessons. When my work was done, I would lose myself slowly in the smoke of the pipe. It felt like an oddly pure existence.

Sometimes I would find myself casting a thought back to the street where my lodgings had been. Then, I would see the lone scrawny tree in the middle of the block and imagine creaking up the wooden stairs to my room. Invariably, I would think of Barnaby and wonder how he was getting along. I missed Barnaby—I could not deny this—yet I had no real desire to see him.

Behind everything was Robert. Behind and within the life I was living here. An uncanny, parallel world. I kept the postcard Robert had sent me in the cardboard box by my bed; on occasion, I would take it out and look at it. It was from this postcard that I'd realized he now called himself *Oscar Harcourt*, joining the first name of his friend from the Internment Center with the surname of his wealthy British mentor, Earnest Frederick Harcourt, creating an unlikely hybrid. But then, what was there in a name? The postmark read, *Long Island, New York*; the address he gave was that of his solicitor. Long Island—oddly evocative. Islands were places of respite, of escape; how much better, then, an island that was long, a place one could long to be, a place one could belong.

I saw Robert's face, felt his touch; I would close my eyes and feel his warmth, find myself back in my London boarding house—those long hours, hazy with pleasure—find myself gazing once more into eyes that were searching and keen. No man had ever looked at me that way; I'd found it settling.

Robert hadn't wanted anything from me, not the way other men had: only that I allow myself to be seen. Instead of the little ploys that go on between people, between lovers, there was, between us, only nakedness and light. With Robert, the ancient agitation that had accompanied me from my earliest memory simply dissolved. In its place, at least for a time, had been a gentle shared pleasure: unhurried, undemanding, undeclared.

"I'd like to know how it was," Robert had said, his usually guarded eyes now piercing. "Your English childhood, before everything happened to the world. I can't help thinking of Wordsworth—his daffodils, the sparkling lake he talks about in "The Prelude." I've read him only in German translation, so I'm sure the version in my mind is heavily accented, and therefore inaccurate."

"I grew up in Manchester. Not the most romantic of English cities, I'm afraid. I doubt Wordsworth would ever have been moved to write poetry about it."

Robert had taken my hand and stroked it. "I'd like to hear. Really."

I found myself telling Robert about a little girl in a white cotton dress with an eyelet collar. Of a mother who doted on her husband and only child, who'd made a haven of their cottage: lavender and geraniums in the window box, hand-stitched quilts on the beds. A childhood spent running with friends in the cobbled alley at the back of their houses, playing games on the grassy patch in front of the schoolhouse. Picnics in the surrounding countryside, threading daisy chains while my mother unpacked the lunch and my father napped on a blanket in the shade of a tree. And hunting for treasures: shiny pieces of quartz and flint, tiny bright ladybirds, and fragments of speckled eggshell.

I watched Robert's face as I talked; saw in the softening of his features that each brushstroke I painted fulfilled the hopes of the portrait he had unwittingly commissioned—this picture of haven and innocence, of a child coming to full flower, untainted, free, within the benevolent bosom of her family.

At some point, I realized that this is what had made a refuge of our lovemaking: Robert's utter belief in my goodness, in the idea of an eyelet-collared dress, lovingly ironed. It was there in my soul, this other self that could have been, should have been, that was every child's birthright and shining hope. That inner spark that would one day become the North Star that Archibald was so fond of talking about, and without which the heavens would only smolder, empty and black.

Robert had given me this. And, for a time, it had held: my innocence, his longing, the belief in the construct we each clung to and shared.

Except there had been no picnics, no simple quartz and eggshell treasures, no father I had known, and certainly no white eyelet dress. Perhaps it was the knowledge of my own deceit that aroused in me the gnawing suspicion about Robert. If we were two of a kind, would *he* not also have lied to *me*?

The logic was inexorable. What secrets, like mine, did Robert have to hide?

I did not consciously decide to spy on Robert. I simply found myself, one afternoon, arriving an hour early at his club, where we were to meet. I slipped into the elegant building across the street and waited in the vestibule, peering through the glass panels of the door out onto the street. A car pulled up to the curb and Robert emerged, wearing a navy overcoat with wide lapels. A fellow member, leaving the club, engaged him in conversation and I could see the seriousness of Robert's expression; he was nodding, his intelligent face taut with concern. The other man I saw in profile, the even small features arranged in impenetrable aristocratic politeness, though the hands, clenched together before him, betrayed agitation. There was something odd about them—as if the two men were engaged in some sort of charade. Had I imagined it, or did the other man cast a furtive glance in my direction? Once again, I wondered if Robert were up to something, guarding a secret beyond that of his origins.

There must have been clues, clues I chose to close my eyes to. How could there not have been?

I was struck by how much alike the two men looked: both slimly built and moderately tall, both with neat, fair hair. And oddly similar, too, in their bearing, the way each seemed to lean forward while remaining erect. Would a stranger walking by have seen it?

They shook hands, and then the man consulted his pocket watch and disappeared through the glass and brass door. Robert remained there some minutes before drawing a pair of gloves from his pocket and carefully pulling them on, his face transformed: private and mild and closed. Then he walked toward the street corner and disappeared to the right.

I pushed against the heavy doors; for a moment, it seemed as if the thick panes held my fate in their glassy palms. When they closed behind me, I had the unnerving feeling of being swallowed into a looking glass, of crossing to the other side. The cold leapt up at my face.

At the corner I turned right: there he was, Robert, up ahead. I became aware of something unusual about the condition of my own feet: a buoyancy that seemed to belong to the pavement, as if it were guiding me toward a destination. I was aware, too, of an irrational urge, every now and then, to turn and look behind me, as if I were the one being followed.

Robert kept a good pace. I worked hard to maintain the right distance, adapting my own stride to his while keeping a certain number of steps behind. When Robert made a turn, I worried that by the time I also turned, he'd no longer be in sight. Then something about his manner seemed to change— as if he'd decided suddenly that he were looking for something, something specific, which he knew he would find. I could feel my nerve slipping; I wanted to turn back, go home to my comfortable lodgings. But then Robert broke into a run, gained the corner, and made another turn. We were on a dark street; the height and closeness of the buildings muted the dim light coming from the sky. The pavement was uneven, slabs of old slate unbalanced by a hundred years of swollen tree roots. Up ahead, Robert was moving effortlessly, unhampered by the cracks and depressions and jutting slate edges underfoot. And then he came to an abrupt halt.

I pulled up against the façade of a town house. Robert, dwarfed by a church, was looking up at the steeple, which I could see presided over a massive jagged hole in the roof; one of many bombed-out buildings throughout the city, awaiting repair. I could almost feel the dissolving of his tension; this was the place he'd been looking for. He climbed the steps, holding the thick stone rail. The huge medieval door swung open; a black velvet shadow swept across the steps, soft and unsavory as a bat's wing. I waited several minutes then followed.

Inside the vault of the church, the smell of stone: limey and cold. Gray light, a thickness of sky pouring through the belly of the space, the ragged edges of the hole etched onto the mosaic floor. A feeling of being underwater: a fluid, slow-moving haze. Robert was nowhere to be seen. I slid into a pew at the back.

The silence was ruptured by a gentle, precise murmur, which echoed strangely in the disrupted space. The words became clearer, louder: no longer a whisper but boldly spoken. Latin, a prayer of some kind. I rested my head on the pew before me, breathed in the scent of frankincense and old candles baked into the wood.

And then I saw Robert, kneeling in the front row, directly beneath the open sky. Beside him lay mounds of rubble not yet cleared away: large asymmetrical stones, chunks of ancient beam. He was bowed over, and though his voice rang out clearly, his shoulders heaved with grief.

I don't know when I first admitted to myself what I must have known from the start; walking along the corridor, perhaps, seeing, through a crack in the door, three of the younger girls sitting in front of the dressing table, leaning close into the mirror, chatting together while carefully applying color to their faces. I saw again the glossy lips, skillful gray lines encircling the eyes, the shading of those broad smooth cheekbones—and the flush of excitement, the guarded knowledge in the back of the eyes.

It is true I had heard things that first night, sitting in my room with the door ajar: the hushed voices of the girls as they made their way downstairs, conspiratorial and childlike. The sounds of people coming and going; I couldn't be sure—there was quite a distance between my tiny room at the back and the main entrance. But my interest had soon waned. Closing the door, I picked up my pipe, along with a book, then lost the house, the girls, and their goings-on as I sank into that marshy green place and watched the words dance on the page before they exploded with images.

"Do sit down," Han Shu said, gesturing toward a large white couch. "Well, now. How are the classes coming along?"

Compared with his rooms at the café, the office Han Shu

kept at Manor House was a simple affair, dominated by a plain ashwood desk and an overstuffed couch where I now sat. In one corner, two wicker armchairs were placed opposite each other, separated by a small wicker and glass table.

"We have to make up for lost time but I think we're making progress," he continued, giving me a probing look. "I believe you're ready to assume another duty I've had in mind for you from the start. Something that requires judgment—and ingenuity. Quite naturally, the time comes for each of the girls to go out and make her way in the world. I feel it is incumbent on me to keep the house full. Besides, there is always room for a little—how might one put it—expansion.

"In the past, the girls have come to us in one of two ways. Family members, usually the mother or father—poor people, it goes without saying—hear about Manor House and bring the girl. I must then make a decision. Will she fit in? Is she equipped with the necessary talents to make use of what we have to offer? It is not an easy process. The parent gets upset if I send the girl away—and even when I take her in, the parent can get ideas. We've had some unpleasant encounters, to say the least. I prefer, therefore, to take in orphans, or children who've been abandoned. The streets are full of them, as you know."

Han Shu leaned forward conspiratorially.

"And now, with all the refugees from the provinces, swarming into Shanghai. I've seen mothers leaving children by the side of the road—just walking away. Perhaps they imagine that some kindly stranger will be able to feed their children better than they have any hope of doing.

"That's where we come in. Me—and now, you."

Han Shu gave a rare grin that showed his stained teeth to full advantage.

"We are those kindly strangers. Even so, we have to be careful not to make a mistake. Once a girl is here, there is no sending her back." Han Shu clapped his hands. "This is where your experience can help. I don't expect any of the girls are quite ready to leave at the moment, but we could accommodate two, maybe three new additions. One at a time, over the course, say, of a month. The right girls, mind you; I cannot impress on you enough how important that is."

I nodded dumbly. I had seen the street children often enough, with their scabby pox and dirt-caked skin. The idea of taking one in seemed a worthy task: cleaning her up, giving her a home.

"Tonight might be a good time to begin," he said as I rose. "It's better to work at night, I'm sure you'll agree."

I had skipped dinner again. As the evening wore on, I became aware of that insectlike crawling in my belly. A drink, I thought, might settle my stomach.

The back of the house was in darkness. I passed through the hallway and down the stairs, feeling my way along the walls. In the kitchen, I filled my cup from the pitcher of cold tea and took a rice biscuit from the tin in the cupboard. I trained my ears on the darkness but, aside from a faint creaking and a low mechanical hum, heard nothing.

I left by way of the door leading to the front of the house. As I approached the main stairway, I heard voices: dim, at first, they grew louder with each step. And then the sound of the green door swinging. I ducked into the schoolroom.

What was that? A man's voice? Followed by the calm, steady reply of a girl speaking broken but confident English. The stairs creaked. I pushed the door gently with one finger and peered through the crack. I glimpsed only the girl's back, so it was hard to tell who it was. Behind her was the man, portly, of medium height, a Westerner with a full head of wavy light-brown hair. He said something inaudible; the girl laughed. His hand darted out as the two of them mounted the stairs, and patted—no, grasped—the girl's small behind. Then he laughed as well: a deep-throated male rumble. He had lowered his hand immediately, but I fancied I saw it still, a ghostly white imprint on the back of the girl's emerald taffeta dress.

I let the door close and retreated to the kitchen. Better return the way I came, I thought, letting the image of the white hand on shiny green fabric slip from my mind like the thinning of blue smoke into air. Something Archibald used to say wafted to mind: there's knowing and there's *knowing*. Then this, too, went the way of smoke as I climbed the back stairs, my mind a singular dart of concentration aimed solely at my cloisonné pipe.

I'm on a mission of mercy, I thought, as I stepped into the muggy gloaming.

Though the existence at Han Shu's was simple, I knew that to a child accustomed to scavenging for food and spending nights under leaky eaves, Han Shu's provision of clothing, hot meals, and a bed would seem nothing short of bountiful.

I had no idea where I was going, yet I felt more sure than I had felt in a long time. I looked up, almost expecting to see a burning North Star, but all I saw was pregnant cloud dragging the sky earthward. I could not have explained it, but as I turned the corner and headed toward what the foreigners of the bar and café crowd called the Rat Quarter, I had the feeling that I was homeward bound, that I was going back, finally, to where I belonged.

To a Westerner newly landed, this was all just poverty—a uniformity of filth and want and disrepair. But I had been in Shanghai for long enough to register the changing nuances of the districts I passed through: thin poles strung with tatty clothes appearing here and there from a window frame in one area but wholly absent further on—a sign of owning more than one set of clothes and of some measure of hygiene. The occasional squawk of a hen, or hiss of a fat meaty snake, the sounds of women with humor enough to laugh, the mingled scents of pickled cabbage and steaming rice, of glazed duck sizzling in grease or the charred salt smell of fish baking among hot coals: the emblems, hereabouts, of relative plenty. And then, stepping across an invisible divide, such smells were extinguished, replaced by the stench of a hundred stagnant puddles festering with mosquitoes, of unwashed bodies and open rivulets of human sewerage. The animal life here did not hiss or squawk but was beady-eyed and mute, making itself known in wretched gnawings and scuttlings. The occasional sickening odor of singed fur and putrid cooked flesh were evidence that these vermin were being put to use as food.

Several times, I passed children who stopped what they were doing to watch as the white woman in the floral dress passed by. It was my light hair they looked at most; I could see their dark eyes fly there and settle. I took the children in with a quick sweep of my eyes: the ankles like twigs poking up from the ground, the firm straight posture, the item or two of clothing that each of them wore, the dark matted hair and alert gaze. Once, the look of a child almost made me stop: the intelligent stillness of the face, the soft, thoughtful set of the mouth. When I realized it was a boy, I kept on, with a twinge of regret.

It was instinct that told me, suddenly, to come to a halt and listen. Cocking my head, I located the sound of the scrambling and turned, finding myself in a closed-off alley. In the far corner, a sheet of corrugated tin with jagged holes was propped up by brick fragments and sticks. Beneath this, a group of children played. A few yards away, several older ones combed through a mound of garbage, calling to each other in street slang. They noticed me collectively, as if linked by invisible antennae: stopped as one in their movements and fixed me with intense and calculating stares. I could feel what had been a bolt of vigilance melt into simple curiosity. I took two steps forward. From beneath the tin roofing, and from atop the hill of peelings and rotting fish heads, the children's eyes followed me.

Slowly, I approached the corner and peered under the roofing. I did not even register the look of two of the children there, could not have said whether they were female or male, so blinded was I by the third, a girl. Her eyes were somber and yet crinkled at the edges with humor; unexpectedly, she smiled. The grime on her face made her teeth seem especially white. I reached out my hand and the girl raised herself on her haunches as a cat might, regarding me with chocolate eyes.

"Come," I said softly, using the slang I had learned from Han Shu's girls, and she stepped over the packed-down dirt that was the floor of the dwelling and offered me her greasy warm hand. As we walked the length of the alley, the girl stole a look at me, then again, every few minutes, as we climbed over the sty and made our way back along the narrow, winding street. It was only when we rounded the corner more than an hour later, onto the street where Manor House stood, that I realized the girl, whom I had already named Ma Ling ("No name," the girl had insisted when I asked. "My name is no name."), had uttered no word of farewell to her playmates, had not so much as given a backward glance in the direction of the world she now left.

Han Shu was wearing a white silk smoking jacket; his black hair was slicked back, showing the broad flattened shape of his skull and emitting the familiar floral and musky scent. Gingerly, he approached the girl. Ma Ling eyed him steadily. A sliver in her dirt-caked cheek marked the site of a dimple.

"Well, well, and who do we have here?" he said. "Why, Christine. I do believe we have ourselves a beauty." He switched to street slang: "Your name, child, what is it?"

"No name," the girl replied as before, with the same determined set of her jaw.

"I've called her Ma Ling," I said.

"Ma Ling. Yes, that's fine." Han Shu took her hand and led her to the couch. "I'd like the two of us to have a little talk."

Ma Ling walked with Han Shu and sat beside him on the white couch. He told her about the house, about the other girls, about the three meals a day, the bed of her own, and the lessons from me. The child listened attentively, for all the world as if she regularly sat through such briefings. Han Shu patted her shoulder and helped her to her feet.

"Now," he said. "You go along with Christine. She'll clean you up and show you to your room, and tomorrow you'll have a pretty new dress."

Ma Ling did have a pretty new dress the next morning. It was draped over the foot of her bed when she awoke: a blue satin gown reaching almost to the ground, with lace at the sleeves and throat. After heating several cauldrons of water and then washing the girl gently with a washcloth, I had stayed up most of the night refashioning the dress I had chosen from the walnut chest Han Shu kept in the attic.

While the other girls slept, I helped Ma Ling into the dress and showed her how to brush her hair, which still smelled of the lye I'd used to remove the lice. Fully dressed, Ma Ling stood before me with that same matter-of-fact air she had displayed the previous night, and it was clear that Han Shu had been right; she was a natural beauty. Ma Ling could not have been more than fourteen, and looked both older and younger than her years: still childlike in stature, but with an uncannily poised and mature bearing.

In all the time I had been at Manor House, Han Shu had never joined us for breakfast. So when, as I was bringing the steaming rice to the table, I heard the clatter of a rickshaw from the street, followed by the click of heels in the hall, I realized he must be even more pleased about the new resident than he had let on.

As the girls filed in, each curtsied to Han Shu before taking her seat. Having observed the others, Ma Ling plucked up the sides of her skirt and executed a competent dip. Han Shu let out a delighted laugh. He motioned for Ma Ling to come toward him. I saw shyness in her face as she moved into his outstretched arm.

"I see you've already met the daughters of the house. They will teach you about the life here. We have happy times and many comforts, as you can see." Han Shu swept his arm toward the table to indicate the rice and puffy white buns.

"Here, we will equip you for life. Discipline, whole-hearted application to all of your tasks. The art of being a young lady." He passed his gaze down the length of the table. "Girls, I'd like you to welcome Ma Ling to Manor House."

The girls chimed their welcome in unison. Ma Ling took her seat to the right of Han Shu and the meal began.

After breakfast, Han Shu lingered to enjoy a cigarette.

As I stood to take my leave, he said through the smoke: "Christine, come to my room this evening for a nightcap. I'd like to thank you for your marvelous work. Ma Ling is a find; I have a feeling she's going to bring honor and good fortune to this house."

All that day, I was aware of the spark of pride in my chest and of a growing anticipation as the evening approached. At dinner, I had no appetite, just picked with my chopsticks at the food in my bowl. The meal over, I retired to the bathing room where I took a long time over my toilette. Refreshed, every pore tingling, I returned to my room where I dabbed perfumed oil behind my ears and on my wrists. The three dresses I'd retrieved from my lodgings—which, along with a few smaller items were the only things my landlord had not sold—were beginning to look shabby. I chose the pink. Standing before the small mirror by my cot, I held up a lavender handkerchief I had bargained down to almost nothing at the market the previous week, then twisted it into a flower and pinned it to the neck of my dress. I examined myself for a moment in the glass, aware of my thinness, but pleased with the effect of the knotted handkerchief.

I hesitated outside Han Shu's door, then reached up and knocked twice.

"Come in," he said.

The room seemed changed, patterned by wavering shadows flung out onto the ceiling and walls by a row of candles along the windowsill. I sat across from Han Shu in the wicker armchair. A decanter of whiskey stood on the table between us, and two crystal goblets from which flashed a splinter of light. Han Shu, in his ivory smoking jacket, filled first my glass and then his own.

"You have had a real impact on Manor House," he said, lifting his glass and motioning for me to do the same. "I'd like especially to toast your effort of last evening. Two or three more finds like that would usher in a whole new era here."

Han Shu tapped his glass against mine, took a long sip, then slid something across the table.

"For your efforts," he said.

I saw it was a blue velvet pouch of considerable size and could easily guess what it contained. I dropped the pouch into my purse.

"I don't want to jump the gun," Han Shu continued, "but I did want to mention one other thing. Some time ago when we were, how might I put it, on somewhat different terms, I made plain to you the financial realities of Manor House—that the establishment is not exactly a money-making venture. However, the fact is, with the two of us working hand-in-hand, we could turn it around. I believe we could make this organization quite profitable. If you are able to maintain the level of your contribution, we might begin to think about some sort of limited partnership. I leave the opportunity in your hands."

I tried to attend to Han Shu's words but my mind was on the pouch I had just slipped into my purse—on the square weight of it, the soft human give of the fabric as it briefly made contact with my hand.

Han Shu took a cigar from the wooden box on his desk, struck a match, and frowned thoughtfully as he waited for the flame to set it alight.

"Let's see how things progress," he said. "I can be harsh, I know that, but I believe in acknowledging work well done."

A flake of ash drifted to the waist of his smoking jacket; carefully, he flicked it away.

"I know!" his face brightened. "You appreciate photography, I am sure, a cultured woman like yourself. How would you like to sample my slide collection? We'll kill two birds with one stone!" He jumped from his chair. "Entertainment—and at the same time the history of Manor House!"

Han Shu disappeared behind a red curtain at the back of the room and returned carrying a black leather case. He placed it on his desk and unsnapped the clasp. Inside was a cumbersome goggle-like viewing device and hundreds of slides arranged in velveteen slots.

"Let's see, where shall we begin." He held a slide above one of the candles and examined it briefly. "This was taken before the war, just after I established Manor House."

Han Shu placed the slide along with another he took from an adjoining slot into the viewer and handed me the device. I held it to my eyes and found myself suddenly surrounded by the greenery of a large estate; in the foreground stood an assemblage of British officers in uniform, several men in helmets and riding clothes, and a younger, slimmer Han Shu in a white morning suit, all holding still for an instant to allow the photograph to be taken. It looked as though the men would at any moment resume ambling across the lawn. The effect was so vivid, so real, it was if I had stepped into another place, another time.

"Three-dimensional slides," Han Shu said. "You must have seen them before—in England?"

I handed back the device.

"And here is Manor House, in the early days," Han Shu said, changing the slides.

This time, when I raised the viewer, I beheld Han Shu standing behind a group of girls, one more solemn than the next. Their faces and hair looked clean, but instead of the miniature gowns the girls at Manor House now wore, they were wearing street rags.

"After a time, they become like one's own children," Han Shu sighed. "As you'll see, we had not yet found a solution to the problem of their garments, but then, war was in the air."

They were standing in front of the house, which was in greater disrepair than its current state. The window casements were cracked, and several panes were missing. The tin sheeting of the roof was rusted and showed several black patches where it had eroded through. But what struck me most about the picture was Han Shu's expression: an almost kindly, sincere regard, directed unblinklingly into the lens. I wondered who the person on the other side of the camera had been.

Several more slides of Han Shu in front of the house followed, taken across a span of years. The girls changed from picture to picture: new faces appeared while others vanished, and their attire became less tatty. The house, too, showed improvement: the missing panes replaced, the window casements repaired; and in the last pair of slides Han Shu offered for my consideration, I noted the new roof. As the sequence progressed, Han Shu's mien also altered by shades, though in his case the changes were more subtle and of reverse order: not the signs of gradual repair, but a fugitive undoing. The uncharacteristic kindly visage of the first Manor House photograph turned gradually to a sheen of dissimulation. And by the eighth or ninth slide, Han Shu's face had evolved into the one I knew.

"But here I am chatting away," Han Shu said, with his usual mixed tone of calculation and conviviality. "You're probably ready for some refreshment."

I put down the viewer.

"Allow me." He reached for the device and exchanged it for a delicate porcelain pipe. I waited while he prepared the pellet, watched as he passed it back and forth over the flame until it became sticky and soft and then placed it over the hole in the pipe. I closed my eyes and drew in the smoke. Han Shu walked to where an open glass cabinet stood against the wall and surveyed the rows of crystal on the shelves. Selecting a small cocktail glass, he filled it with cherry brandy, then returned to his seat.

"Your health," he said, raising the glass to me.

I smiled at him through the smoke.

He drained his glass in one toss, then rose to refill it. The second shot he drank while standing, directing an intent gaze toward me. This time, he did not sit down but simply stood there, holding his empty glass and continuing to stare at me as if trying to decide something. Then his face took on a queasy pallor, but for his cheeks, which turned a mottled pink.

"I know this was not part of our initial arrangement," he stammered. "Might I suggest—"

This was something new, I thought: Han Shu, uncertain. He crossed the room tentatively, and when he placed his hand on my bosom, his touch was tender. I closed my eyes, allowed the tender feeling to seep through me. I found myself drifting back, back to my London lodgings. Even in the seismic drift, I knew the association to be absurd: two people more different from each other surely did not exist on the entire planet. Robert, Han Shu. And yet, there was something about the way Han Shu was touching me that recalled how I'd felt with Robert—something about the way he entered me while still leaving me free to travel to my own private place. Spiraling into the confusion—losing myself as children do in dreams, as perhaps the dying do in their approach to the blinding, all-healing light—I held one flickering, changeling thought: *It's a terrible thing to be known, it's a glorious thing to be known.*

A beautiful odd sound reached my ears through the cottony fog: a filigreed tinkle as angels might make.

✳ ✳ ✳

We were lying together on the floor when I opened my eyes to the astonishing fact of Han Shu quietly sleeping in my arms, the girth of him suddenly not *Power* or *Force* as it had been, but an amorous plumpness, soft to the touch.

His eyes snapped open. He sprang up, looked at me with bafflement, then averted his eyes, the look on his face turning opaque.

"Christine, forgive me. I don't know what came over me."

I rose, smoothed my dress, attempted to rearrange the lavender handkerchief into the decorative knot.

"It's just that I, well, ah—" Han Shu muttered, batting a hand at his mouth as if to coax out the right words. He clutched my hand. "A beautiful woman like you. And me, a man—"

I smiled. Looking at Han Shu, I felt oddly happy, as though I had reclaimed some piece of myself that had gone missing.

"Really, Han Shu. It's all right."

He stood stiffly opposite me, a terse smile on his lips. I retrieved my purse from the floor, where I noticed the shards of porcelain scattered under the chair. The pipe, I thought. That had been the tinkling sound.

"Well, good evening, my dear," Han Shu said formally, as he escorted me across the room. "Until—the next time. And thank you again for your fine . . ." but he closed the door before he had finished, allowing the sentence to dangle.

I stood there, staring at the door, aware of the rise of something in my chest, a surge of—what? Aliveness? Was that it? I glimpsed a new world—some undiscovered continent I'd known existed all along. The place I sensed was dark, unencumbered by civilization or law, a place that had long called out to me, perhaps all my life, in the fluid thin voices of Sirens—and I having strapped myself, one way or another, to the mast on the deck of the slow-moving unstoppable ship.

Finally, this evening, I had wrenched myself free.

"There are souls which need altering, if they are to come into their own," Archibald announced as Barnaby sat down. "So often, I find, people don't know what it is they want."

Archibald's tiny eyes twinkled. "Actually, I introduced them. *Meet your spiritual guide*, I said. They both looked a bit perplexed, Han Shu and Christine, as if neither knew which of them I meant."

The waiter set down a plate of half shells.

"Did I ever tell you about my theory of the North Star?" Archibald continued. "Well, I do believe the one will turn out to be the North Star of the other. I do love symmetry, don't you?"

Archibald's new passion was oysters; it was miraculous that Harry, the restaurant owner, managed to keep up with Archibald's culinary whims.

"You see, Han Shu and I are masters of the hovering life within, to borrow a phrase. Christine is also a visionary of a sort; she and Han Shu are destined to play a key role in each other's lives. Every imagination is only a fragment in need of its complement. Artists understand this. Until the artist has found his North Star—the transcendent counterpart that is to be his guide—he despairs, flounders in search of *that something* which has gone lost.

"I know all too well what it is like. Oh—the heavenly hurrahs when you stumble upon it! It only seems like chance, my boy. Believe me, it is anything but. After all, that's the only thing we have: *imagination*. Besides oysters!"

Archibald picked up a shell and gently sucked the flesh from it. "I must ask you, while we are on the subject of finding one's spiritual complement: how go things with Christine?"

Barnaby hesitated. He was not in the habit of confiding in Archibald. And yet, he found himself feeling a level of desperation he'd not felt in years—perhaps ever.

"I think I've lost her. I thought it was only temporary—that she would come to her senses, realize, after a month or so, what we really have together. I thought I'd just back off, let her taste her old life without me in it, and she'd know it wasn't a satisfying life. Some breathing room, she said. So I let her be. I waited. One week. Then another." Barnaby pulled out a white handkerchief and drew it across his brow.

"Dear boy, I am sorry." Archibald looked genuinely pained.

"She's disappeared. Clear disappeared." Barnaby could hear the crack in his own voice. The look in Archibald's face came as a shock: the depth of his sympathy and concern. "I went to her lodgings. She's gone. That vile landlord of hers told me he sold her belongings weeks ago."

Archibald nodded somberly. "Destiny involves Darkness, there's no getting around it. She is going where she needs to go, and there's not a damn thing you or I can do about it. We're neither of us a Virgil, I'm afraid. Which isn't to say she won't find one, further down the line."

He leaned across to Barnaby and whispered into his face: "There is always another side to consider. Let us not forget Coleridge. Where would English poetry be without 'Kubla Khan'? And without the exquisite poppy—well, there simply wouldn't have been any 'Kubla Khan' at all."

Archibald slid another oyster into his mouth and chewed thoughtfully. "There's a brilliance to Christine," he added. "You must have sensed it. She feels the pulse of the universe."

"I only know I have to find her," Barnaby said.

Archibald squinted meaningfully through the smoke of his cigar. "Destiny has to be thought through, Barnaby. It doesn't descend like some ghostly visitation. I met a young man at the club, on my short trip home to London. Charming chap, frightfully good looking, half his luck. Made a killing on the stock market. Toward the end of the war, he devised an ingenious scheme. Something to do with mapping troop movements in the major theaters of war, deducing military tactics.

He'd pour over newspapers while the ticker tape spewed from his machine. He was a refugee. Imagine. Arrived in England with nothing but the shirt on his back. A stowaway—that was the rumor. Sociable fellow, but get him on the subject of his background and he was tight as a clam. You'd never have suspected from the look of him, from the way he spoke, that he was anything but an Englishman. Thoroughbred.

"That fellow—can't think of his name now. There'll be no thickets for him, come middle life. More like this—at the helm of a yacht on the Riviera. He'll fill his chest with fresh, salty air, thinking, *The past was the past; this is now.* He decided upon his scheme and then saw it to its inevitable conclusion. Quite a project, really. To take that grimy war machine—how many thousands mown down at Normandy? Derelict buildings, bombed and deserted and crawling with rats—and make it grind out cold hard cash."

Archibald paused. "Come to think of it, Barnaby, where did you spend the war? I've heard so many of your stories but I can't say I've ever heard you talk about your army days. You did have army days, how could you not? A strapping chap like yourself."

Barnaby sipped his drink but said nothing. It was just like Archibald to find the raw spot and put his finger on it. Did he sense Barnaby's shame? At not having seen action, stuck, as he'd been throughout the war, on home soil, an officer in charge of supplies and requisitions shipped to the real fighting men at the front.

"Let's come back to that later; you must remind me." Archibald chuckled. "Hats off to him. A refugee translating the war into the trappings of a good English life. A town house in London, a country estate, a full staff to manage it all. In the end, that's the task: take what we're given and turn it into a reflection of our own True Self."

Archibald stared distractedly forward. "I was still a young man, about your age, when I fashioned my own compass, for better or worse." He cupped his elongated fingers as though now holding that very compass in his hand. "I pointed it straight ahead of me, and lo and behold! It guided me here, straight to the seething heart of the matter!"

Barnaby set down his drink. He was beginning to find Archibald exasperating. "Archibald, I must ask you. As a friend. Do you have any idea where Christine is? Or how I could go about tracking her down?"

Archibald shook his head sadly. "Christine has seized her destiny, my boy, whatever you or I might think of her journey."

"Then you *do* know where she is?"

"Barnaby, I do not believe you've heard a single word I've said. It's not for us to interfere. I'm afraid I can't be budged on that point. I am a man of principle, and that happens to be one of the principles I prize most."

⌇

Ma Ling settled in immediately. I had a small calendar, printed on handmade paper, that Han Shu gave me; I marked with a star the day I found Ma Ling. One month to that day, I placed another star. And upon rising one morning, I realized with surprise that it was already time to mark a third. How quickly two months had passed. I descended for our usual late breakfast; looking from girl to girl, I saw it again, the stamp of a kind of knowledge not entirely at home with such youth, and for the first time, I told myself explicitly what it was they knew.

That night, after my customary long evening of solitude, I felt restless. With no more secrets to keep from myself, I left my small room, taking care to remain unnoticed, which was not difficult given the layout of the house, the two sections, front and back, being almost completely self-contained. I avoided the main passageway connecting the halves and roamed the halls at the back section, making several passes up and down the long, rickety staircase.

The next night, I did the same. And the next. It became a habit and, as the days passed, I found myself drawn to the place I had previously avoided, the main passageway connecting the two halves of the house, one of the few sections of flooring that Han Shu had at some point replaced, so that, unlike the creaky boards elsewhere, these lengths were solid and quiet. There was something reassuring about the small enclosed place. Slow pacing eased my mind.

When I first heard the odd three-part rhythm on the stairs, I didn't know what to make of it: a heavy tread with a syncopated thud, and now and then a pause, silent and laden. A man with a wooden leg? I wondered. A war veteran? After a week, I realized he was a regular visitor; on my nightly sorties to the enclosed passageway, I found myself listening for him expectantly.

Sometimes, after a long bout with the pipe, snippets of my time with Robert came back to me with unalloyed sweetness. I would emerge from such moments refreshed, then settle in for the evening with my books, floating, still, in the magical freedom bestowed by the smoke: to live and relive and unlive as one pleased.

And while I did not feel I had turned back the clock as I had hoped, I did, on occasion, have the feeling that I had at least stopped the movement of time, as though I'd found a way to keep the present from sliding forward, from leaving its trail of slime in the shadowy, airless plane of memory.

I thought, too, of my mother. For years, I had shuttered her from my mind; now, she wafted back as if from the beyond, a strangely comforting, ghostlike presence. As a young child, I had thought my mother a princess. I'd had no trouble seeing our cramped quarters as a Renaissance Court, at least in the evenings. There had been gentlemen callers, mostly well-dressed, often jovial, always with beautiful manners and the kind of grateful, heightened, even worshipful attentiveness that I imagined was reserved for royalty.

One evening, a beau had tried to draw me in. I had been excited, and was hurt when my mother snapped, "Leave the girl be. Leave her out of it." She steered me back to my room, placing one of my beloved books in my hands, and whispered sweetly: "Read, love, read your book," the perfume lifting from her soft, full form. The sounds coming from our small parlor—and later, across the length of our apartment, from my mother's room—were baffling and enticing both.

The gentlemen were always gone by the time I awoke, and my mother would be transformed—hair in pins and rags, bustling about the small kitchen, tending to eggs sizzling in lard, the loose housedress only emphasizing her lovely shape.

I understood that there were two realities in my world. The colorless humdrum of the days metamorphosed late each evening to a climate of expanding spirits, of paste jewels and shimmering silk, of jangling color and sound. Laughter and texture and warm bared skin and fondness and stroking and mouthfuls of sweets—chocolates, caramels, boiled peppermints—slipped to me by my mother's callers.

By day, I applied myself to school work at the grim schoolhouse a mile's walk away. Back at home in the afternoons, I sat at the streaked window of my tiny room—no larger than a closet but mine, all mine—reading by the dull northern light. It provided a sure escape from the dreary streets below, this wandering through fanciful written worlds, as I waited for what I thought of as our true life: the Royal Night Court that my mother had created. I came to think of my life as neatly spliced down the middle: Day Words, Night Music.

And when the men started coming into my tiny, private space—occasions when the gentlemen lavished on my mother too many glasses of the amber stuff, so that she would end up draped across the green brocade couch, which in the candlelight showed only its deep sheen, not the worn patches visible in the flat light of day—when they came to me on those nights, I felt drawn into the magic: Cinderella flung into the whirl of the ball.

My mother could not have known that this beau or that might have brought a particularly fine bottle or two for the sole purpose of silencing her own stern injunction, *Leave the girl be*, or that the men passed this information among themselves.

They were kind to me for the most part. Not one of them ever hurt me, not really. They smiled tenderly, the way I imagined a father might smile at a daughter. They held me, stroked my hands and hair. Sometimes they even read aloud to me. I loved this most of all. They fondled and cooed. And when they turned earnest, I watched with interest the change that would come upon their features. I felt a strange power in the way my own small self could bring about the extraordinary concentration I witnessed: the way the entire world, for them, seemed to fall away. *I'm bringing about the end of the world*, I would think, staring at the disappeared gaze before my own, at the contortion of the brow, the tight grimace of the mouth. (Had this been before or after my fourteenth birthday? It hardly mattered; it simply was as it was.)

Not one ever retreated without bestowing a treasure: a porcelain doll with blue glass for eyes and eyelashes made of human hair; a hand-painted tea set covered in roses; and, when I started asking for them, books. Soon, the books were stacked high along the wall of my little room, all the way to the ceiling.

The men loved me; this, I could feel. Sometimes, the word was even uttered—or my name whispered, breathed into my ear. Tears, on occasion: tears from manly eyes—of gratitude and affection. And as my own body swelled, and I developed the full, high breasts, which brought pleasures of my own, my mother's men became more ardent, more appreciative, more grateful. They brought more expensive bottles of spirits for my mother and seemed hardly able to contain their excitement as they waited for the drink to take effect. And then, in my closet room, it was *Darling* or *Precious* or *Chérie*. And soon I learned to sip the warm fire myself and learned, from the men, to give myself to the exotic waves that came from my own fiery center, and the days no longer wore their drab colors, as all of it, all of my own life, my own being, became focused on the musical flames of the night.

Throughout, the world of my books continued to exert their pull. Eventually, they drew me to teacher's college, out and away from my mother and the electric goings-on.

But I never let go of the night.

Ma Ling picked up English so quickly and effortlessly it was as if she imbibed it from air. I secretly imagined that this was because she wanted to be able to communicate better with me. Another star in my calendar marked the third month, and then the fourth. I was soon assigning Ma Ling more advanced exercises, which she worked on in the back of the classroom while I instructed the other girls. It was hard to believe that, only a few short months earlier, Ma Ling had been a lice-ridden alley child who spoke street slang and had never set eyes on a book. The early missionaries, I thought, would have admired my success in civilizing this grubby young savage.

The first crate arrived with a certain amount of ceremony. Parcels seldom made their way to these backstreets, and certainly never parcels of such grand dimensions. The wooden box created interest, with its smooth-planed boards, light coat of varnish, and gray-blue lettering, *84 Charing Cross Road*, stenciled on the side: the famous bookstore in London popular here among expatriates, who placed their orders by wire and could count on delivery within a month. The package was for Ma Ling, who took calm delivery of it in the breakfast room to the *oohs* and *ahs* of the other girls. Ma Ling pried it open with a tool I unearthed in the kitchen. Inside, sealed in an inner lining of oilskin, were stacks of leather-bound books with gold embossed covers and spines. I fingered the volumes as respectfully as the girls did, enjoying the smell of new paper and fresh leather. Whoever put together the package—it had to be Ma Ling's special gentleman friend—had thoughtfully assembled the classic English literary works of the nineteenth century. The girls examined the books one by one then passed them back to Ma Ling. Of course, it would be some time before she would be able to read them herself. Perhaps it was an awareness of this, I mused, that touched the girl's face with awe as I packed the books back into the crate, as if I were handling the reassuringly sturdy blocks of the future itself.

The following week Han Shu made another of his rare morning appearances at the house.

"Ma Ling will be moving to the third floor where she will have her own room," he announced, once we were all seated. Ma Ling sat demurely, her breakfast untouched, her face glowing gently with pride.

Two other packages arrived for Ma Ling in quick succession: another crate from Charing Cross Road, and a few days later, a shiny black trunk with brass fittings, which Ma Ling and her friends immediately ferried up to her new room. The trunk was a mystery, until Ma Ling descended after the afternoon rest period in a beautifully cut jade suit, the long pointed collar of a cream blouse showing stylishly at the throat, and on her feet, black patent pumps with the look of Italy about them. Most impressive of all were the sheer silk stockings. The seam at the back was expertly placed, as if Ma Ling had been wearing silk stockings all her life. The following day, she appeared in another equally stylish outfit, and the day after that, a third.

With the arrival of these worldly goods, I felt a distance spring up between Ma Ling and me. Of course, the gifts had to have an origin—there was clearly, somewhere, a sender—but I found myself focusing on the things themselves, on the books and the beautiful clothing, secretly blaming these items for the change. It was the politeness in Ma Ling's eyes that most mortified me, where before there had been the eagerness of discovery, gratitude, and an occasional flicker of admiration. Now, Ma Ling spent long hours alone with her books, taking what I had to offer with what seemed like a dismissive air.

Two light raps roused me from my stupor. I opened the door. It was Ma Ling, dressed in a crisp sky-blue dress.

"I was wondering if you'd like to go for a walk," she said. I gazed distractedly around the room. My eyes fell on the pink scarf draped across the foot of the cot and trailing along the floor. I shook the dust from it and retrieved the small white purse from the cardboard box by my bed, which served as a nightstand.

It was only when we were outside and exposed to the eyes on the street that I became aware of how shabby I must look beside my ward. Countless washings had failed to dislodge the faint rust-colored splotches on my own dress, which I realized had never looked as fine as the cotton of Ma Ling's skirt, even on the day it was bought.

It was a dank evening. We found a noodle shop and chose a table by the sweat-coated window. I noticed with some alarm how out of place Ma Ling seemed here, with her balletic posture and smooth, carefully brushed hair; delicately, she raised the tea bowl to her lips. The din of voices ricocheting around the room muted to a dull background buzz.

"How many years were you a teacher?" Ma Ling asked. "I mean, in England?"

"A long time. Too long," I replied, a little surprised by the question.

"Is it so different there, teaching pupils?"

"From here? Well, yes, of course. To begin with, the climate is very different, and that changes everything—even the kinds of lessons we teach and the way we go about teaching them."

I pictured myself holding my satchel as I approached Shropshire Hall, saw again the redbrick path leading from the iron gates, with their grillwork scrolls and veined black leaves and feathers at the top pointing deadly as arrows. I recalled assembly in the great hall, prayers, then history and literature all day long, beginning with the third form on the ground floor and working my way up the eighteenth-century staircase to the top floor, from where the upper sixth classroom commanded a view of gently sloping hills and lofty-headed trees.

Ma Ling was watching me expectantly. I scrambled for words that had long since rolled away into some forgotten cobwebbed corner.

"There's something you start understanding when you teach," I said. I swallowed a mouthful of tea, aware of the taste of rust on my tongue. "When you teach, you remember how it was to sit at a pupil's desk and think that there is an order to it all: truth, packed away in some huge trunk, alphabetized and complete, and all you have to do is turn the pages in the right order. I remember, when I first began to teach, walking into the classroom full of hope. How could one not? There they were, my students, sitting in their little halos of light, ready to learn."

Ma Ling was looking at me with a curiously uncomprehending eye; what I was saying could hardly hold meaning for her, but I found I couldn't stop.

"I used to have them recite important phrases. They loved that, heaven knows why. Toward the end of the war, one of my former students, a girl named Jennifer, came back to visit me. She had married soon after leaving school and her husband had been shipped off to fight. She had come to tell me her news: that her husband was being sent home—wounded, but only lightly."

Ma Ling was sitting stone still in the bamboo chair.

"She told me that the day after she got the news, she

awoke with words going around in her head. Sentences I had given her, years earlier, to memorize. And then she began to recite: *The Renaissance was a period of time in history when there was a new spirit of enquiry, of interest in learning, of desire to develop new ideas and take part in new activities.* When she'd memorized those words in my classroom, she'd had only an inkling of what they meant. But when it came flashing back in her mind only a few days earlier, she said she finally understood what they meant."

I had no idea why I was telling all this to Ma Ling. Looking at the girl, I felt muddled and sad. A glance at the watch around my neck informed me that it was almost time for the daily supply to be delivered by one of the girls to my room.

"The funny thing was," I continued, "I never truly understood the implications of those words myself until Jennifer relayed to me that experience of hers. Knowledge is mysterious; that's one of the things I learned as a teacher. You can think you know something and even pass it along, without really knowing it at all."

Now, Ma Ling looked entirely baffled.

"Oh dear, I'm afraid I'm not answering your question," I said, trying to remember what the question had been.

"Why did you stop teaching there? At the school in England?"

I tried to untangle my thoughts. "I was supposed to say certain things to my students. It became harder and harder, until finally I could no longer say them."

A lost experience loomed up from the past: Awards Day, the last formal day of the school year. I was standing at the lectern, preparing to deliver my speech.

"About two years into the war, the headmistress asked me to address the student body. The remarks I prepared were what was expected—praising the contributions women had made to the war effort. Like everybody else, the girls had seen the newsreels: former housewives in head scarves, assembling guns and shells in munitions factories; nurses wearing the starched uniforms of the Red Cross; and everywhere—on buses, in parlors, at the movies—women and girls knitting socks. Our own girls were no exception. You could hear the *click click* of needles at assembly every morning.

"But that morning at the podium, looking at the first page of my address, I just couldn't read what I'd written. Instead, I talked to the girls about what kind of new world they could help to make. I spoke about being independent, about developing ideas and ways of living that were new—no longer under the thumb of men: it was men, after all, who had waged this war, and every other war I knew of."

I was no longer talking to Ma Ling, though the girl sat attentively, attempting, it seemed, to take it all in.

"After a few minutes of this, the headmistress approached the podium and whispered that she thought I should step down. I knew then that my teaching career in England was over."

I stared hard at Ma Ling. For an instant, I felt as if she had become a creature from another world: an ancient queen, or some other reincarnated spirit. But the moment passed and there, again, was Ma Ling, restored to her earthly self. What I had just told her was a lie: the same lie I'd been telling myself for years. Yes, those events had happened, but they had not been the real reason for my departure from the school.

A fresh furrow appeared between Ma Ling's brows. "It must be different there, now that the war is over," she said.

I was taken aback. "You want to be a schoolteacher, Ma Ling? Is that it?"

She blushed and bent her head. "We all have plans. For when we leave Manor House," she said quietly, into her empty tea bowl. Was there a trace of sarcasm, I wondered, in the slightly exaggerated way she'd said *Manor House*? When she looked up, her eyes had turned to flint.

I became newly aware of the healthy fullness of the girl's

arms and cheeks. I glanced down at my own arms on the table and was so startled I almost upset the bowl I held in my hands. How had my limbs become these sticks, covered in downy dry skin the color of parchment? Ma Ling's gaze passed from my face to my torso; I followed it, noting my own sunken chest and the billowy look of my once close-fitting dress.

Ma Ling nudged her tea bowl toward the middle of the table, pushing back her chair. "We should be going."

We walked back in silence. I knew that something had changed between us, that whatever it is that snaps sometimes between people had snapped.

The beginnings of dusk floated through the air. We wound back by way of the market, where the farmers and merchants were well advanced in the dismantling of their stalls. A man barked orders to an elderly woman; she reached above her head to unhook the glazed orange ducks, elegant as swans, strung by their necks on a wooden pole. Beside them, a boy stood by a basket of wilted radish tops, calling out the end-of-day price in a shrill child's voice.

That night, lying awake in my cot, naked against the thick wet heat, Ma Ling's flinty eyes came back to me: nubs of condemnation punched from the darkness. Where had I seen that expression before? I remembered another time, sitting beside Ma Ling as she brushed her hair before the cracked glass; seeing the calm of her features reflected in the mirror as she struggled to say—or not say—what she meant, I had felt my own happiness peel away. *My patron*, Ma Ling had said. To hear her refer to him that way, to see the coyness in her face—and pride! It was then that it came to me, watching the steady brushstrokes that turned Ma Ling's hair to burnished metal: that innocence is not something you're born to, it's something you must construct with the scraps life throws you. A painstaking labor, grain by grain, brick by tiny brick.

How much of sin could be effaced in this way? What of me? And what of Robert?

Here I was, witness to Ma Ling's own fastidious labor—
Ma Ling, sitting at her makeshift dressing table, brushing her
hair in careful, relentless rhythm.

Another rhythm. Of course! Ma Ling's patron was the
man of the three-part rhythm on the stairs. I imagined her
sitting on the four-poster bed beneath maroon drapings,
propped against a mountain of silk pillows and struggling to
read aloud from Wordsworth, Jane Austen, George Elliot. Lying beside her, I pictured a man just the other side of youth,
handsome and trim, wearing a fine linen shirt and smoking
a cigarette. The man's cane leaned against the bed and, although the injury I fancied he had sustained in the war was
not immediately apparent, the aura of the hero hung about
him. An incongruous image—not a hundred feet from my own
meager room: the two of them luxuriating among pillows re-
citing the words of the English poets.

From that time on, when I descended at night to the passageway joining the front of the house to the back, I waited in
the airless oblong space with a sense of dread until I heard the
sound of croup on the stairs. When it finally came (and some
nights this was not until dawn), I slowly made my way back
upstairs to my room, which had also changed—no longer a
place of respite but a chamber of tense confinement.

Just as initially the house had welcomed me, its spare tidy
rooms offering a new chance of order and peace, now it
seemed to be shutting me out. Wherever I went in its rickety
confines, I began to feel as if I were intruding, as if my presence were an affront. Even the schoolroom began to feel like a
no-man's-land, cordoned off, a site of potential danger. I kept
my duties to a minimum: preparing and conducting my lessons, avoiding going anywhere I was not absolutely required
to be. Dining I kept to the barest necessity, on some days appearing only for breakfast, when I would pocket one or two of
the white buns that would serve later for my supper.

And then my late-night wanderings ceased. During those interminable black hours, I now committed myself to the immobile punishment of my room. It bit into me, this loneliness. How distant this room was from my cozy, neat suite at the country school I'd taught in—a hemisphere, a lifetime away: the study, with its chintz-covered couch and antique writing table, and beyond double doors, the sleeping quarters, a pleasing room with gauzy white curtains that fluttered by day, and at night were still before a heavy tar cloth that blocked the light of my reading lamp from the whirring steel enemy prowling the skies.

There my life had buzzed with purpose, even more so when the girls had begun arriving from war-ravaged London to stay in those relatively safe parts.

Penelope arrived with the first trainload. I noticed immediately the fraught, dreamy look in her face that signaled a girl with a passion for books. In the classroom, Penelope attended to my words with a mixture of distraction and fervor. One evening in the common room, two weeks after her arrival, she asked nervously if she might show me some verses she'd written. I suggested she visit my rooms during the evening study period.

In my sitting room, Penelope seemed different: older, more confident. When she finished reading aloud the verses she'd brought—which held the promise of a true poet—the girl seemed curiously indifferent to my response. Why the anxious request in the common room, I wondered, if she had no interest in her teacher's thoughts? The cool, almost arrogant look on her face as she left came back to me, as if Penelope had set me some kind of challenge that I'd failed. And yet, behind those cool eyes, there had been the shadow of coy pleasure.

Penelope showed up at my rooms the following Thursday evening and again, the week after that. Without either of us discussing it, this meeting became a routine.

It was some weeks before I realized just how much I looked forward to those visits, odd as they were. Penelope would arrive, wary and reserved. The moment she began reading, the haughtiness would settle over her. And yet, as the weeks passed, she also seemed more open to my comments, scribbling in the margins of her notebook as I gave my response.

"I've heard you'll be staying over the summer," I said at the end of the spring term. Most of the girls were to be billeted to families in the surrounding villages; only a few were to remain at the school, along with a skeleton staff.

Penelope's face flashed with irritation; she reached for her notebook and began to read. Everything fell away: the school, my work, the other mistresses and girls. The poem at an end, Penelope looked at me with deep eyes—and there, a smile on her lips, happy and shy. The smile seemed an omen; I felt released from a stricture I'd not until that moment known I was constrained by, and reached for her hand. The girl remained motionless, then turned her head slowly toward me as a startled animal might, an opaque muffled look in her eyes.

"Penelope," I said softly. I found myself drawing toward that beautiful, clouded, enigmatic face. But the girl's lips suddenly twisted; she snatched her hand away. A rustle of papers, a flurry of movement, the click of schoolgirl heels: a blurred expression of disgust. Then the sound of a door opening and closing. Bewildered, I looked around the room. All was as it had been: I was alone.

A few short weeks and the summer was upon us. All but the five girls boarding for the summer were dispatched to their billets, and the school seemed suddenly large and gracious, alive with the promise of some delightful invitation.

It was one of those rare days that in any given year the English can count on one hand, when the sun is strong and hot. At breakfast, the girls were in high spirits; I suggested an outing to the lake. The cook packed us a picnic of potted meat, carrots, chalky ration-flour buns, and for dessert, squares of hard dark chocolate. The walk in the heat was marvelous, and I found myself feeling content, humming a melody under my breath as I watched the girls chatting happily up ahead. Even the icy remove Penelope had adopted since our last private meeting failed to unsettle me.

At the lake, I spread a faded checked tablecloth on the grass and readied lunch while the girls splashed in the water. The heat showed no sign of letting up. How lovely it would be, I thought, gazing out at the shiny white limbs of the girls, to be in a climate where one was always surrounded by syrupy heat, where bright rays layered the world into dappled textures of glow and shade. The girls emerged from the water, shaking droplets from their hair and skin as they ran up the bank. Penelope wrapped herself in her towel, the others preferring to dry themselves in the sun.

After lunch, the girls slipped on their tunics, put on socks and shoes, gathered up their belongings. On the long walk back, they sang rounds. Once we reached the school grounds, they dropped their satchels and raced to the bathhouse to rinse off. I climbed the driveway at my own slower pace, deposited the picnic basket at the kitchen door, and then doubled back to the bathhouse. By the time I got there, the girls were stripped down, standing above the long metal trough, their backs to the door where I stood, lathering themselves with bars of rough yellow soap. It was cool within the barn-like structure, and I imagined their shoulders and arms to be covered with goose bumps. One girl reached down to the faucet, cupped a handful of water, and, giggling, splashed the face of the girl beside her. Soon all five were spraying each other, gasping with fun. I stood silently behind them, watching the fluid and unself-conscious grace of their movements.

When one girl twisted around in her play, she caught sight of me at the half-open door and turned fully to face me. Immediately, the others turned too. I found myself confronted by five naked, shivering, suddenly quiet girls, their hair dripping onto their shoulders. Unthinkingly, I sought out Penelope and again, unthinkingly, lowered my eyes and found my gaze fixed on the girl's well-developed bosom. The girls seemed to be waiting for me to say something, to explain my presence.

I cleared my throat and began, awkwardly, "When you're ready, girls . . ." There was a pause, an endless ringing, and then I retrieved my will, forced my gaze back up to the level of the girls' faces in time to see a look of dark despisement in Penelope's eyes.

"When you're ready, cook has tea for you in the common room." I turned and walked from the outhouse, aware of the stony silence that continued to fill the vast draughty room behind me.

When I got back to my room, I drafted a letter of resignation. There would be no reconciliation. I knew that Penelope would not again appear at my door on Thursday or any other afternoon. It was three weeks to the day that I had made my disastrous speech to the assembled school, not truly the reason for my departure, as I had presented it to Ma Ling, though an important moment in the souring. It was only after the trip to the lake, after that deathly still moment in the doorway of the outhouse, that I knew my long years of devotion to the students at the school had come to an end.

I did not leave, however, with a sense of despair, nor did I feel anything but gratitude toward Penelope. She had shown me that my heart was not barren; it was with Penelope that I had experienced the first real stirrings of love.

CHAPTER THREE

I counted the minutes to my next pipe. Seventy-three. I concentrated on the small face of the clock I wore on a chain around my neck, watching the second hand make its way round and round the dial. *Round and round the merry-go-round*, I said softy to myself. *Round and round we go*.

A knock sounded at the door. I looked up. The door opened a crack, and one wide polished shoe slunk sluglike into view.

Han Shu's voice was a blast of molasses: "My dear, allow me an audience." His ample body followed. "I've brought you your pipe." He strode toward me, swinging the pipe before him as if it were some kind of divining rod he was using to determine my mood. When he reached the cot he leaned down, close enough so that his breath blew damply into my face.

"Don't worry," he said thickly. "You will get your four o'clock pipe as well. Consider this a gift."

I took the pipe and waited for Han Shu to prepare the pellet over the small lamp and then, when it was oozy and puffy, place it over the hole in the stem of the pipe. Slowly, I inhaled.

"Word has spread apparently about Ma Ling," he said, giving an odd little flourish of his hand. "We are on the cusp of a new era. An era of powerful reputation. We might, in fact, start a little specialization. *Private girls*, so to speak. There are certainly more than a few exclusive men like Mr.—like Ma Ling's gentleman—who prefer the use of a girl who is, well, limited to them."

Han Shu seemed for a moment to be chewing some pleasing morsel in his mouth. "I imagine they might like to train them too, to their own predilections." He paused. "Let me come to the point. I must ask you, Christine, to return to that most important of all duties which you have, if you don't mind me remarking, let slip."

I inhaled again and watched as the burned little lump of opium shriveled to almost nothing.

"It's imperative. I'd never thought it possible—people here left and right, selling up and leaving in droves. Even Victor Sassoon! I've heard he has plans to remove to some island in the Caribbean. They're driving away my friends, my comrades—my clientele! Han Shu's Bar is threatened . . . after surviving so much . . ." He placed his hand over his heart, his brow tensed, his dark eyes wide and glistening.

"Manor House is our only future, I see that now. Christine, I must exhort you. We need more girls. I cannot make this more plain. And soon. It's every bit as much your future as mine, my dear. Would you permit me to remind you of that?"

Han Shu was stroking my hand; his expression of pleading was not one I'd seen before in his face.

"Stick to the street children, of course," he continued. "A mother catching wind of her daughter's success might suddenly develop an inconvenient bout of maternal devotion." He pulled back his lips in what I had learned was supposed to be jocularity, but which gave the impression of a donkey preparing to bray.

"Consider it your contribution to our joint endeavor. I mean it, Christine. With your talents and my business sense—but let's not get ahead of ourselves. I'd recommend an evening stroll, my dear. Tonight. Inland, where you had such luck finding Ma Ling. The pickings might be quite . . ." Han Shu paused, a man preparing to draw his trump card. "Salubrious. Yes! Salubrious!" He turned and left the room.

❧

"You will tell me if I'm chewing your ear off, won't you?" Archibald began as Barnaby planted himself in his usual chair.

"Strange words to pass your lips," said Barnaby.

"I know I'm a bit of a scoundrel, but I'm terribly troubled all the same, right at this moment."

Barnaby glanced at his watch. He had tried to take Archibald's advice—to put Christine out of his mind, to wait until she resurfaced, until she was ready to seek him out. It had been much harder than he could have imagined; the strain of it was wearing him down.

"I wouldn't want to keep you," Archibald was saying uncertainly.

"I'm not meeting the others until ten," Barnaby replied, trying to be gracious, though seeing the inflamed look on Archibald's face made him wish he could leave. He ordered a drink and sat back in his chair.

These meetings with Archibald had been a welcome distraction for Barnaby, but he was beginning to tire of his friend's sordid eccentricities. Perhaps, he found himself thinking, it was time to return home, to reclaim his life on American soil.

"Here's the point," Archibald said. "A question, really, that I would put to you. Have you ever smelled a mixture of hot-buttered crumpets and honeysuckle? Picture it, Barnaby, a room in a comfortable boarding house overlooking the hills of the Lake District. Honeysuckle spills from the window boxes, the air coming in at the window is fresh as apples. A maid in a bonnet—no more than a child, really—brings tea and crumpets to your room on a tray. Your senses are reeling, her red cheeks glow. A knob of butter shines on her finger; she's mortified! Her eyelashes flutter, poor dear, you think she might burst into tears. You want to take her into your arms and comfort her. That buttery odor makes your mouth water, the honeysuckle sends you into a swoon; those

plump arms, that tender look of remorse on the child's face—
all make you feel you have clumsily stumbled upon heaven.
I'm sorry, sir, it was an accident, she whispers. *Come here, my sweet,*
you say, and you know by the throaty sound of your voice
and the look on the child's face that you have scared her half
to death. So you slip your finger into the middle of the soft
crumpet, like Tom Thumb poking about for his plum, and you
pull up a lovely warm gobbit of butter and lick it right off. To
show the girl that her buttery finger has not upset you in the
least. You laugh and hope she will too but there's terror in
her face. She's staring at you as if you're the big bad wolf—it
makes you sad. You see, more than anything, at that moment
you want her company. All those tantalizing fragrances! You
spoon some blackberry jam onto the crumpet; you must take
a bite, you want to detain her, you try to do both at the same
time. An embarrassment of riches: a mouthful of crumpet, the
warm sweet jam and melted butter fresh from the farm, and
a frightened little beauty by your side, plump as a suckling.

"*And how old are you, my precious?* you say, trying to sound
kind. *Thirteen and a half, sir,* she replies. You are surprised; she
looks younger. *Well, not to worry,* you say, meaning to put her
mind at rest about the buttery finger. *Come over here, let me pat
your arm.* She takes a few frightened steps toward you and you
pat her plump shoulder. How your fingers ache to caress her!
How you long to breathe in the child's odor from her hair and
skin.

"But here's the problem; you know it as well as the sound
of your own name. This is England! There's a funny look in
her face now, piteous, confused, and you realize it is because
there are tears streaming from your eyes. *My sweet,* you say, no
longer the big bad wolf, just a pitiful fat old man."

Archibald wiped away a tear. "You spend a good minute
or two trying to refrain but you cannot stop yourself, and you
let your hand slip to her rump, and you stroke her there a few
times, firmly enough to get a sense of her dear shape. The fear

is back in her face, and that makes it all the more delicious, and you let your hand linger. Your fingers are aching, how dearly you'd love to . . . But no. *England*, you say to yourself, *Almighty England*, and you go back to patting the child's arm.

"*Thank you, my dear*, you say innocently enough, *for the tea*, and she takes that to mean she may go, which she does, and you are left alone with your grief."

Barnaby pushed his drink away. He was used to Archibald's waywardness—he had depended on it, in fact, for amusement—and had come over time to admire his friend, in some peculiar, roundabout way. But, for the first time, he found himself feeling frankly disgusted by him. Could it be, he wondered, that all this was *not* bravado, the tawdry musings of a man staring down old age? Could it be that Archibald was, in fact, truly a pedophile?

Archibald swatted his face with his handkerchief, then drained his glass. He began his customary scan of the room, his internal radar set to spot anyone in the post of barman or waiter.

"That, my old fellow, is why I came to the East. Heaven and beyond! Of course, it's almost impossible to find a plump one here. But I cherish a secret little hope, and mark my words— ah, waiter!" Archibald winked. "Damn the glassful. We'll take the bottle, my man. From beneath the counter. Harry's special port." And then, to Barnaby: "Marvelous, don't you think? Don't have a clue where he gets it. But drink up! Never did see you such a nursemaid with a drink as you are tonight, dear fellow."

Watching Archibald stare impatiently in the direction of the bar, Barnaby remembered the real reason for his visit; he was certain that Archibald knew Christine's whereabouts.

A moment later, the waiter hurried toward them, carrying a bottle wrapped in a starched white napkin, above which a cracked label was visible. He filled Archibald's glass then set the bottle on the table. Archibald flicked a note from his billfold and handed it to the waiter, who bowed rapidly several times and mumbled something self-deprecatory in broken English.

"Now, where was I? Oh yes, my little secret. You see, I have found just the girl. I'm trying to fatten her up. Pâté de foie gras, bowls of hot chocolate, that sort of thing—Harry furnishes it all, isn't he marvelous? It's all devilishly hard to get hold of here, as you can imagine, but Harry's quite the resourceful genius."

Archibald, his face red from emotion and from the very good port, leaned over to refill Barnaby's glass. Barnaby flattened his hand across the rim and shook his head. He could not bring himself to ask about Christine; he felt desperate to get away from Archibald, and he also felt certain that the man would not in fact yield up Christine. With a sudden pang of desperation, he fancied that she had been swallowed up by this place, had disappeared into some great churning gut from which she would never be released. That she was, perhaps, lost to him forever.

"Saving yourself?" Archibald asked sorrowfully.

"Just trying to slow down the train," Barnaby said, standing, unable even to attempt a gracious departure. "I'm afraid I really must be going."

Archibald shook his head. "I suppose you think I am a scoundrel, after all," he said, setting the bottle down on the table.

⟿

I lay perfectly still on my cot in the silence, blinking my eyes in an attempt to relieve the stale itch. I threw the thin cover to the ground but it made little difference. I could feel the perspiration at my temples, at the back of my neck, on the inside of my elbows, behind my knees. And then, a recollection, oozing in upon the bland stupor, so vivid that, for a moment, I wondered if I hadn't chanced upon a mysterious form of time travel.

There I was again in my rooms at the school, tidying up, putting things away. I could see the tailored green lawns; could feel in the air the orderliness of an orderly people confronting the chaos of war. In my recollection, there was something odd about the set of my face: a stiffness of the muscles, a tightness in my jaw that was both familiar and foreign—a lost habit from the past.

That night, in my rooms at the school, I had glanced at my watch—half-past eleven—and, on a whim, decided to make a quick circuit of the flower garden, which the gardeners had managed to bring to full bloom, despite the constrictions of war. In the hallway, I breathed in the familiar oiled wood smell. Thinking about the sterling roses and the sprays of baby's breath, wondering whether their fragrance would be different in the dead of night, a noise made me stop. I turned in the direction of the sound. Backtracking the way I had come, I passed the empty rooms of those teachers who were away for the summer. Empty rooms, I thought, an open invitation for rodents. The sound grew louder, a soft padding. Perhaps a squirrel, having entered though an open window and unable to find his way out?

I reached the cul-de-sac at the end of the corridor, outside the headmistress's rooms; not squirrels, but muffled footsteps, stockinged feet upon rug-covered floors. And a light chiffon voice as one might hear rising from a dance floor. Seized by giddiness, I leaned against the door; the old wood felt solid, I breathed in its mulled scent. Slowly, I turned the handle. The sitting room, where the headmistress received her callers, was lit by a single lamp on the reading table by the window. The dim bulb cast a yellowy light onto the glass, turning the pane slickly dark, blotting the outside world to incomprehensible shadows. The headmistress had left the blackout curtains undrawn! On tiptoe, in a confused flurry,

I crossed the room and pulled the tarred cloth shut. A heavy silence emanated from the inner chamber, the sound of someone holding their breath. I walked as if in a trance, the air turned to water, slowing my movements and heightening the feel of my skin. The internal skip of anticipation—of something exciting and proscribed. There, within reach, the second doorknob, this one of cut glass. The door swung inward. Uncertain light, the stuttering hesitations of a single candle, and suddenly, directly before me, the headmistress sitting up in bed, clasping the cover inadequately to her breast, squinting at me with angry eyes.

"How dare you." Beside the headmistress, Penelope's enigmatic face with its curious expression of contempt. I turned my eyes slowly back to the headmistress. Though she still clasped the sheet, it had slipped and, as she repeated the accusatory mantra, her pendulous breasts, in an oddly suitable gesture of negation, swung gently back and forth across her torso.

I tried to shriek, but the words stuck in my throat. *Oh, Penelope! Don't you see? Don't you see that I love you?* I ran from the room, across the office, into the hallway, and clattered down the back stairway. Out into the cool air, blindly across the gravel driveway, into the dark. The lawn opened up beneath me; I kicked off my shoes and ran barefoot. My mind clouded over, my legs and arms turned to wax. I clamped my eyes shut and slowed to a halt.

The green hooded smell of beech trees, the crinkly cool feel of grass underfoot.

But then, suddenly, another world, somewhere else, both close by and distant, the here and now of four narrow walls, a ceiling, and a small square cut in one side that passed for a window. No bars, though it might as well have had them, and no moonlight.

What was that? A rapping at the door?

Like everything else, I thought: *My dreams are playing tricks on me.* The door opened and a slim figure slipped into the room.

"Some food, miss," a voice said. Something set down on the table: a bowl of rice. It was one of the girls. Beside the bowl, she set down the glass box.

"Thank you," I managed, attempting to lift my head from the pillow. I glimpsed yellow; the girl was wearing a yellow dress. "Wait," I croaked, but it was too late. The girl had disappeared. The rice cooled on the table, the turquoise box glinted slyly.

I'd been wearing the yellow chiffon, that night with Robert: our last evening together. It is still there, I imagine—that dress, shut up inside my cedar trunk, which Mrs. Lassiter, my landlady, had agree to store in her attic. Still there, smelling of mothballs and disuse.

Robert had touched my arm, drawn his forefinger along my shoulder and down to my wrist.

All doubt, all the suspiciousness that had been dogging me about him—his past, his goings-on—all my concerns and fears: vanished in the beam of his gaze, which was fiery and soft, both. He moved to speak.

"Christine." His voice was steady, though I heard in it something urgent.

I imagined I saw, in his face, the words he was about to speak. I reached out my finger and touched it to his lips. Not to silence him, no. But in order that I might declare myself first.

"Go and dress," I said, aware of a sudden flicker of anxiety in Robert's face. "We'll have time later to talk."

London, cheerless and cold. But I was more alive that night than I'd ever been; the air pulsed with readiness. I remember thinking that the whole odd arc of my life had led to this moment. Absurd imaginings, to think that Robert, dear, brilliant Robert, with his longings and stoic reserve and his secret history of suffering, could possibly be involved in dubious dealings of any kind. No, I reasoned, all of that was nothing more than my own faulty self, intent on painting others black, like me.

It sounds childish, but at that moment, I pictured Robert's soul as a dewdrop, delicate and true.

Yes, I thought. I would write it down. I would find my own way to turn words that had once filled me with dread—words of love that had in the past been for me a kind of betrayal—to sweetness and truth.

A quick tender kiss: Robert's soft, full lips, pressed against mine.

"Later, then," he whispered, spots of pink growing in his cheeks.

Why do I still hold onto that instant? Why do I still close my eyes and recall the imprint of his lips, the sigh of his breath as he drew away? All of my own longing and loss, coiled into that brief moment?

But then it springs back at me every time, forked tongue out, venomous tooth at the ready. Along with the hatred that has grown familiar as a vicious pet—hatred toward Robert, for taking it all away.

My Manor House cell, sparse and ungiving. I rolled from my cot, thudded to the floor. I crawled to the table, reached up with one hand, fumbling at its edge. I touched it with the tip of my forefinger, tapped at the side of it; the smooth box nudged forward, then toppled and crashed to the floor.

Damn it, damn it to hell, I half sobbed. Up on all fours, I batted at the floor beneath the table. The box was there, not shattered, though the lid had rolled off somewhere. Under the table, still on elbows and knees, I licked at the floor. The tarry crumblings clung bitterly to my parched tongue; the dust made it difficult to swallow. Enough of the resinous shavings remained in the box, though; I could see that, even in the faint light seeping through the window. With a sudden revival of bodily strength, I rose to my feet, pressed the shavings into a tiny, firm pellet, and set about preparing the pipe.

I breathed on my fingers to steady them, dragged a wooden match across the table, and held it to the paktong lamp. *Breathe*, I instructed myself. The hovering flame flirted with the wick until it made contact. My fingers trembled as I handled the needles, maneuvering the tiny lump over the flame until it succumbed, trembled, still, as I placed the swelling pellet over the hole in the stem. Finally, I felt the thin angel stream that made my veins ache with pleasure.

Then, something in that narrow exposed beam of the world filled me with fright. My own fingers: shaky, pale, like fated scraps of sea life left to shrivel on the shore. *I have also disappeared*, I thought bitterly. I watched as the wick in the oil lamp burned down. Watched as the sputtering flame extinguished in the oil. *A tiny drowning*, I thought. Numbly, I dipped my finger in the oil, aware of the searing heat, though from a distance. It didn't feel bad so I left my finger there. After a time, I removed it, staring absently at the red burn in the flesh. I rubbed the shiny, raw spot with my thumb.

A racket at the end of the hall. At first, it sounded like barking, as if a street mongrel, too mangy to be seized for food, had made its way in through a window and was yelping in some closed-off room. As I made my way down the hallway, the yelping turned into Han Shu's voice. He rarely lost his temper but when he did, he lost his English accent along with it; now, he sounded like a market hawker defending his pride. The shouting voice came in bursts, punctuated by the sound of another voice—an indecipherable rumble. I paused by the door.

"The future," Han Shu was saying. "I have to think of the future! I have many girls to feed."

The other voice, a man's, said something I could not make out, though I could hear he was calm, in control.

"Is this how you think?" Han Shu again. I heard pacing, a thud—the sound of a fist coming down hard on a table. "This is not a *cabbage* you are talking about, my dear friend. We are talking about—" Another thud, and then the sound of breaking glass. "We are talking about my prize treasure!"

Again, the low mumble.

"If that is your final offer, you may as well leave. And I'll ask you not to frequent my house anymore."

There was a creak and the thud of a cane. And then the low voice—audible now, and so very familiar. "I can assure you, Han Shu, if this is your decision, Ma Ling will no longer work for you."

"She does what she is told!" Han Shu shrieked. "She is *my* girl, do you hear?"

From inside the room, footsteps approached the door, accented by a wooden tap: *thud thud tap, thud thud tap.* The door flew open, I jumped out of the way.

"Why Christine, my dear. What a surprise," Archibald said. Behind him was Han Shu, his face contorted.

"Bartering over her as if she were a goat," I replied, my voice a squeak.

"The Orient, my dear," Archibald winked. "We are in the Orient."

"I won't have you bartering over Ma Ling." I felt my own voice squeezing tight; I feared I would lose the capacity to speak altogether.

"I would ask you to stay out of this discussion," Han Shu said, his throat gurgling strangely in what I imagined was a vain attempt to retrieve his British inflection.

"She is not a goat," I repeated.

"That, I know," Han Shu said. "But may I remind you of the fee you were paid to bring her in?"

Ignoring this, I turned back to Archibald. "You want to buy her for good, don't you? That's what this is all about. You want to take her away . . ."

Archibald hung his head, seemed to weigh something in his mind. He turned to Han Shu. "I think we should continue our business another time. Feelings are running hot. Think about my offer, Han Shu. All I'm asking is that you think about it." Archibald waved his arm before him, and I stepped away from the door.

For a long moment, Archibald examined me with his small pink eyes. "I wondered where you had disappeared to, Christine," he said. "I hope you're taking care of yourself." He patted my arm, then labored toward the stairs.

"What I do with my girls is really not your business, Christine, dear," Han Shu said. "I trust you are aware of that."

I sat on my cot staring out at the wet summer sky. I let Han Shu's words slip over me.

"I don't understand what's happened to you," he said with growing agitation. "You may very well have scotched the deal." He was pacing; the warped floorboards whined. "Archibald's a wealthy man. He's used to paying for what he wants. The bargaining is just a game with him; he doesn't take it seriously."

I could feel Han Shu's eyes on my back.

"It's all in the timing. I suppose I can't expect you to understand that. Your presence, at the worst possible moment, just as . . ."

Outside, a sticky blood substance leaked from the setting sun onto the corroding, ramshackle roofs.

"Christine, what's happened to you?" There was real distress now in Han Shu's voice. "The girls tell me you are making little sense in your lessons. And have you given up entirely on finding a new girl?"

He approached my cot and took gentle hold of my shoulder.

"I meant it, Christine," he said carefully. "When I talked of a partnership. It's not too late. We can salvage things still. But I need your help." Han Shu took my hand.

Familiar territory, I thought. A laugh curdled bitterly in my throat. Back where I belong.

"But do not despair. I have a secret little hope, my dear. Call me a fool, but I picture us—together. You and me. At the country club. You in your prettiest frock, and me, well, dressed for polo." He paused. "Who knows, perhaps we'll even . . ."

I could hardly make sense of what Han Shu was saying. What had the country club to do with—*this*? This life? This Manor House?

"Even what, Han Shu?"

"Go back. To England. Settle there, where we belong."

I stared into his face, took note of his odd dreamy expression, my mind drifting away, the tiny buzzing pockets in my lungs suddenly silent, and my flesh, where Han Shu now stroked my shoulder, strangely unfeeling, as if I were made of nothing but rags.

⟿

Barnaby dismissed the rickshaw when the rain started, and ran the last half-mile at a sprint, less to escape the rain than to set the blood flowing. He paused under the canopy, slipped off his jacket, and shook the water from it. A frail, thin man in an elaborate red and gold costume bowed as he opened the door.

A reception of some sort was underway in the main ballroom; the sound of a brass band spilled into the foyer. Three women in evening gowns passed by on their way to the ladies' lounge. Dressed in tight-fitting skirts, they moved with mincing steps. Barnaby recognized the wife of a fellow consul worker; he nodded, she waved back a hand tipped with shiny red nails.

Barnaby made his way down a long corridor until he came to a black door. He rapped gently, twice. The door was opened by a very old man with a cleanly shaven pate, and a stoop so pronounced he was almost doubled over. He peered up at Barnaby, his friendly features compressed into a smile.

"Hello, Li," Barnaby said. The thick smell of incense filled the room and, for a moment, he felt light-headed. He followed Li across the room, then sat opposite him in a hard-backed chair.

"I'm looking for Christine," Barnaby said.

Li nodded again, a grave look replacing his smile. "She's gone, Barnaby." He paused. "Maybe Archibald knows where she is."

"Where has Archibald been keeping these days?" Barnaby asked.

Li clicked his tongue. "Not good times for Archibald. These days Archibald is not happy."

"Do you know where I might find him?"

Li shook his head. "He's a private man. He doesn't like everybody in his business."

"We're old friends, Archibald and I. There's not much about him I don't already know."

Li was silent a moment. He seemed to be thinking something over. "Sometimes, he visits the junks," he said finally.

Barnaby nodded. "Thanks." He reached across and patted Li's narrow shoulder before taking his leave.

The man in the red and gold flagged down a rickshaw and Barnaby climbed aboard. They skirted along Bubbling Well Road for a good mile, made the jog onto Nanking Road, and then took a sharp turn into a small unnamed street that wound toward the harbor. There was a pause in the rain and, for ten or fifteen minutes, the rickshaw man picked up speed. Then the rain came down again in sheets, spiking up from the pavement in hot, angry bursts. Through half-open doorways, Barnaby glimpsed distant figures: an old woman sprawled on a cot in the light of a candle; a group of men huddled around a table; a toddler at its mother's breast.

The alleys became narrower and more difficult to negotiate. The rickshaw bounced roughly over stones and threatened to stall in places where the roadway had become soft patches of mud. Barnaby called out for the man to stop. He paid, dismounted, and continued on foot. The harbor, black and unsettled by the rains, sprang into view. He made his way to the curve where the junks were lined up by a section of wharf in a dismal state of disrepair.

Surveying the oddly shaped vessels, which bobbed before him in syncopated rhythms, Barnaby felt a vague feeling of dread. It had been some time since Archibald told him about his harbor visits, but with no other clue to go on, Barnaby counted to the fifth boat from the end of the pier. It was the largest of the junks and the most curious, seeming both hulking and fragile at the same time. A tent-shaped construction of corrugated metal, like the misshapen beak of a giant bird, had been affixed to the stern, and at the other end was an open deck, scattered with wooden barrels and crates. The junk's middle consisted of several small chambers made up of old planks. As he got closer, Barnaby could see places where metal sheets had been soldered to join the little rooms together. He stepped onto the deck and through an uneven doorway hung with an old bedsheet.

Inside, he had to bow his head to keep from banging against the ceiling. The space was filled with the sound of voices, but it was a moment before he could make out the two women sitting on crates in the corner. A kerosene lamp, spewing black fumes, blinked ineffectually on the floor. Barnaby was about to speak when one of the women, without interrupting her conversation, motioned toward another crude doorway, also hung with a faded sheet, and Barnaby stooped still lower to pass through this. He found himself in another chamber, with two more women, and again fumes from a kerosene lamp. Passing through the third doorway, he was relieved to discover a larger room, which accommodated his full height—and no sputtering lamp. What light there was here was moonlight, which entered through slits punched out at the top of one metal-sheeted wall.

Feeling a tug on the hem of his jacket, Barnaby looked down to see a little girl with a toothy smile.

"Hey, mister," she said easily in English, pointing across the room to where a group of children crouched against the wall, engaged in some kind of game. She was wearing a garment that was clearly too large for her, holding the skirt with one hand to keep it from dragging on the floor. The deep scoop of the neckline revealed her thin and undeveloped chest.

"Choose, mister, any one yours."

He heard the sound of tiny claws scratching against wood, and from where the children were playing, the *clack clack* of tiles being flipped.

"We clean girls," she said, lifting the hem of her dress to show a pair of spindly legs and a smooth white groin. Barnaby gently lowered the fabric and hunkered down on his haunches.

"Archibald," he said quietly to the girl. "I'm looking for Archibald."

The girl nodded, eyes bright with a child's desire to please, and pointed a grubby finger in the direction of yet another doorway, this one hung with a piece of rough cloth. Barnaby patted her hand.

Beyond the rough curtain, the room was in almost complete darkness, but for a single taper burned down to a stump, which sat waist-high in a hollow in the wall. In the middle of the floor was a mammoth dark shape, moving and thumping against the boards and emitting a horrible low bark. It was a man. From the floor, the white sphere of a face turned toward Barnaby.

"Why Barnaby, is that you?" he heard Archibald's voice say. "Well, fancy . . . I'm sorry to be, ah, indisposed right at the moment."

Another pause. Beneath Archibald's bulk, the owner of the face: a small girl, pressed flat against the floorboards. Barnaby's eyes had adjusted to the dark and now he could see that she, too, was wearing one of the oversized dresses, carefully unbuttoned and splayed around her like a butterfly's torn cocoon.

Barnaby felt paralyzed, but before he could decide what to do next, he heard Archibald say something to the girl in a soothing voice. There was a commotion of clattering as Archibald rose, with the help of his cane, to his feet. Barnaby looked away.

"I've come back to my little dears," Archibald said, fastening his pants as he approached Barnaby. "Ah, but then, you don't know how I've neglected them of late."

"I'm looking for Christine," Barnaby responded tersely. "Li seems to think you know where she is."

"Christine," Archibald said sadly. "Now there's another story. And, strangely enough, not altogether unrelated to the terrible misfortune that has befallen me." Archibald came closer. He took Barnaby's arm and peered at him morbidly. "It's all gone. Everything I've worked for, for so long. Collapsed. Destroyed. Burned to the ground."

"Christine, where is she?" Barnaby asked harshly.

"Now, now, we've been over this before."

"*Where*, Archibald."

"No need to get short. Are not manners the touchstone of civilization?" He took a white silk handkerchief from his pocket and wiped his fingers carefully, one at a time. "Now where were we? Oh yes, you were asking about Christine." He frowned. "As it happens, I've only just seen her. And not, I'm afraid, under very favorable circumstances. It's all linked up, her misfortune and my own. Dear boy, never have I suffered so great a disappointment. My scheme was well underway, with only the final details to be put into place. But Han Shu has pulled the rug out from under my feet. He may speak the King's English but I'll be damned if he knows a thing about being a gentleman!"

Archibald reddened and a few fat tears made their way down his cheeks.

"Christine," Barnaby said coldly. "What about Christine?"

"I was getting to that, Barnaby. Honestly, if we weren't such dear friends, I'd suspect you had no heart at all. Christine." Archibald let out a deep, deflating sigh. "Who knew she'd turn out to be nothing more than your poor little swallow who should long since have flown to Egypt? You do know the story of the Little Prince—the statue, who relied on the swallow to be his eyes, to fly forth and harvest real experience for him. He kept her so long from her instinctual migration that the bitter winter killed her. It was the Nile the little bird longed for; nothing festers there, not by those waters. Brings to mind Palestine, *the holy hush of ancient sacrifice, the porch of spirits lingering, the grave of Jesus where he lay . . .*"

Archibald perched for a moment on tiptoe, the wide globe of his belly tipping down, and peered through one of the slits that looked out onto the black waters of the harbor.

"I suppose she did head northward after all. Though not to any limpid destination. Perhaps I must take some portion of the blame. But then, is one man ever really responsible for another's destiny?"

Barnaby tapped his foot impatiently.

"Yes, yes, dear fellow," Archibald sighed. "I've not forgotten you. You want to know about Christine. Well, she has been in Han Shu's employ. Schoolmistress, I believe. At his other establishment. You do know about Manor House, don't you? The very same place I met my princess. Who was to have been Lady of my Oxfordshire estate . . ."

Archibald wiped at his eyes with a fresh white handkerchief. "The passage to England booked—first class. The inaugural visit: Ma Ling's exposure to the height of English society. *He* wants to take it all away, Barnaby, right when I have it in the palm of my hand."

He reached outstretched fingers toward Barnaby, his face a pitiful mask. "I have seized my North Star," he whispered, tears sliding down and settling in his whiskers. "I can feel its tender little points up against my skin," and he closed his fist on the air as if it were something, rather than nothing.

"I will get her back," he went on. "Han Shu has not seen the last of me, I can assure you of that."

When Barnaby spoke again, the coldness was gone from his voice: "Tell me how to get there. I'm really worried about her."

"And right you are to be worried . . ." The pinkness faded from Archibald's cheeks, and a vaguely sinister gleam appeared in his eyes. "Dear boy, you don't know, do you?"

"Know what?"

"About Christine."

"What on earth are you talking about?"

"She's not like us, Barnaby. She doesn't traffic in love. At least, not love for other people." Archibald came close, whispered hotly into Barnaby's face: "Christine's not a woman of human passions. She wants to go to the Sirens. But I've told you all that already."

Archibald squinted in the way he had that made his eyes disappear. "She's willing to sacrifice her life for it. Isn't that *simply marvelous*? I mean, from a philosophical point of view. It's a splendid gift to the more fearful among us. The amateurs— that includes you and me, I'm afraid, Barnaby—those of us without the courage, let's face it, without the force of character, the true spirit of adventure to really follow Truth to its ultimate source or endpoint. You realize, of course, that they're one and the same? Origin, destination: endings, beginnings. A great coiling serpent eating its own tail, swallowing itself up as it spits itself out.

"True, she was partly to blame for my misfortune." Archibald's eyes popped back to full size; they glistened, uncannily, far away and close up at the same time. "But I have to say, I admire the hell out of her."

Barnaby had to restrain himself from grabbing the fat man and wringing his neck. "Archibald, *please*."

Archibald seemed suddenly to realize something. His face became tender. "But *you* didn't know how it would turn out. I'm sorry, Barnaby, truly I am. I thought—foolishly, I now see—that you were up for it. I didn't factor in that you might actually get snagged."

He crept back a few steps, then peered at Barnaby through the murky, airless space. "I'll let you in on the truth. Perhaps it will make it easier for you."

Barnaby felt a rise of panic.

"She's Eve," Archibald hissed. "Pure and simple. She set out to eat of the Tree of Knowledge, and eat she did. A big robust bite of Human Truth."

After a moment's silence, he mumbled, as if to himself: "I'd just as soon overlook the position that puts me in."

Barnaby could hear Archibald's shallow, wheezing breath.

"It wasn't Eve's fault. The English language got all tangled in itself, fashioning the word *Evil* from Eve's name. It is, in the end, the innocent who must be flung from the garden. It takes rigorous calculation to avoid that fate, to figure out a way to remain ensconced. And that—calculation—is precisely the measure of what the innocent lack."

In the thick, dank space of the junk, Barnaby was finding it hard to breathe.

"The address, Archibald. Tell me how to get there."

Archibald backed away further, tiny careful steps on his small, well-shod feet.

"I'm sorry, Barnaby. I see now that this is out of the question. Far be it for me to interfere, to upset the planets in their orbs. It is as it is, each journey is fated."

Archibald's voice faded, the footsteps suddenly a rapid retreat. The misshapen space offered up one final rancid whisper: "Written in the stars. Your journey too, my friend. It might as well have all happened already."

"She's gone. Ma Ling. Her books, her clothes. Gone."

Han Shu had not bothered to knock. I tried to shake the muddy half-sleep away. My watch told me it was five o'clock in the morning.

"Christine—have you forgotten our plans? My hope for Manor House? For our future?"

Han Shu was wearing a newly laundered tuxedo with a starched white shirt and he smelled, as always, of floral-musk cologne.

"We have to find her." His voice was strangely sweet, the way one talks to a child to whom one is promising a treat. He leaned down to the bed and took my chin in his hand.

"You were right, when you said that Ma Ling is not a goat. But let's be frank. Like a goat, she is worth something. To me and to others. To you too, if you consider where your livelihood comes from. I'll find someone else to take her over, I can promise you that. There will be others willing to pay even more than that scoundrel has been paying."

Han Shu patted my cheek. "Let us salvage my dreams— dare I say, *our* dreams? Let us do it together. You found Ma Ling—you can find her again. She trusts you. I have complete faith that you can bring her back."

I pulled myself up from my cot. I looked at Han Shu. Through the mud in my brain I could see it, something I'd not seen before in his face. Wistfulness.

I nodded. "Yes, Han Shu. I'm sorry, I—"

He took me into his arms. I allowed myself to be held, aware of the useless, fleshless feel of my limbs.

At this hour, the bay was a conspiracy of silence. Old boats rocked on the water, oozing decay into the depths. Ma Ling had never spoken to me of any family, but for a handful of ever-less-valuable paper currency, one of the girls had told me where I might find a relative of Ma Ling's, a distant cousin. I walked around the bay, surveying the lean-tos across from the water—haphazard structures of old board and corrugated tin. Even from that distance, I could see where heat and rain had caused the paint to hang in ragged strips.

I ducked into an alley, rehearsing in my mind the landmarks the girl had described to help me find my way: a blue shack, wire chicken coops, a rickshaw chained to a fence. The drizzle turned to rain. My throat burned for want of smoke.

The further I went inland, away from the lights of the bay, the darker it became. Wire chicken coops, I said to myself. Six of them tied together with twine, beside a blue shack. My eyes scanned from side to side. The sound of chirps, I thought: that would be a signal. But no, at this hour, the chickens were probably asleep.

A man appeared in my path. "Chicken coops," I said in Chinese. "I'm looking for six chicken coops."

The man laughed, drew twice on the stub of a foul-smelling cigarette and tossed the butt onto the street. "I'll find you some chicken coops," he said, taking me by the arm.

He walked briskly; I stumbled on the hem of my dress. A gentle rain fell.

One alleyway led into another. I started to think we were going in circles; everything had begun to look the same.

"A blue house," I mumbled.

Again, the man laughed. I was feeling dizzy, and paused to regain my balance. The man waited at my side.

"Smoke. Do you have any smoke?" I asked.

"Sure," the man said in English. "Chicken coops and smoke. I have them both."

I put out my hand, hoping he would set a pipe in it, but the man just tapped my palm lightly in the rhythm of a waltz, *one two three, one two three.*

"We're almost there," he said, pulling me back into motion by the arm.

We must have been moving even further inland, for it got

darker and darker until I could no longer see more than six feet in front of me. As I walked, my sodden dress flapped against my thighs.

"We're here," the man finally said. I had already forgotten about the chicken coops, so it didn't much matter that there wasn't a coil of wire in sight. I stood shivering at the man's side, my hair dripping onto my shoulders.

After the blackness of the wet night, the candlelight inside hurt my eyes. I stumbled alongside the man through a hallway, listening to the simultaneous creaking of the floorboards underfoot and the wet slapping of our shoes. Through a doorway, an old woman shrieked something to the man, who shouted something back in a hoarse, disgruntled voice. We climbed a narrow staircase with no railing. One thought only pierced the dense static of my mind. Light, I thought. Yellow afternoon light splashing through green leaves onto a polished floor, static to the eye but slowly moving, like the fugitive and determined motion of a planet. The thick, heavy warmth of the sun through a pane of glass. And music floating in from another room.

"A pipe," I said almost desperately. This man was as good as any, I thought. He would give me a pipe. "Do you have a pipe?"

I looked at his eyes, at the water streaming from his hair, at the pixielike triangle of his jaw. He was not a cruel man, I could see that. He shook his head.

"No pipe," he said apologetically, leading me to a cot in a corner of the room. "I'm sorry, I have no pipe."

I lowered myself onto the cot. It was made of wood and had no mattress or padding of any kind, covered only by a worn sheet. The man fumbled in a box by the bed, then withdrew a roughly rolled cigarette like the one he had been smoking earlier. He placed it between my lips.

The sound of male voices and clacking tiles suddenly filled the room, followed by a wedge of wavering candlelight that angled onto the ceiling. One voice rose above the rest: a flat voice. But I could not quite hear what it was saying.

I knew it was no good. I would never find Ma Ling. Perhaps I could find another child to bring back to Han Shu who would take the girl's place.

The flat voice grew louder. I watched the shadow of a man move in the candlelight along the wall. When it came to a stop immediately beside me, I turned my head and found myself looking into a face with pasty white skin and deep pockmarks. The owner of the flat voice. He repeated whatever it was he had said before. I heard a door slam. The room lurched, I lurched, the hard palette beneath me lurched. And in all the motion, a memory of Ma Ling, seated before her art deco dressing table (it had arrived not long after the first crate of books), pulling a comb through her dark hair. I sit on the bed, watching the fluid movement of the girl's arms. Ma Ling wears a pure linen dress that reaches to mid-calf and is bordered at hem and throat with Irish lace.

"Does he treat you well, your gentleman friend?" I ask. Ma Ling meets my gaze in the mirror and smiles.

"I am lucky," she says simply. "And I have you to thank for everything."

Ma Ling seems as if she is about to say something, but only continues to look in the mirror, her eyes now focused back on her own reflection, silently combing her hair.

"What does he want? Your gentleman friend. What does he want from you?"

"We speak English, we read out loud. I read to him, he reads to me."

"And love?" I ask. "What about love?"

Ma Ling's jaw tightens. I try to catch her eyes again in the glass, but she fixes her gaze on herself.

He's still there, the man, lurching with the room. He says something to me in that same indecipherable dialect. From the tone of his voice, I can tell that he is saying something nice. With the passing seconds, his voice becomes more cheerful. It reminds me of someone calling out at a picnic—"More wine. Would you like some more wine?" I see the banks of the River Cam. Young men in white suits and straw hats, rowing a boat. A woman strolling by the water, book in hand. Another sitting on a blanket spread on the grass, earnestly making a point; a male companion pours something frothy into her glass. A cloud rolls overhead, rolling somewhere very fast.

The man with the pockmarked skin is on top of me now and he grunts. I know this is happening, I can feel him inside me, but it is distant, as if I am remembering the moment rather than living it. He seems to be taking a very long time. His face is clenched with a look of great effort. A child's face floats above me. I am surprised to see that the child is not Chinese, but a blond boy with ruddy cheeks. He is crunching an apple. The child waves something over my head. It looks like a fishing rod. He wears a serious expression. Lying in the fog of putrid-smelling smoke, I wonder what the boy is doing here, and feel a wave of shame. I try to say something to him, but find I am unable to move my jaw. He seems to be studying my face; he is crisscrossing my face with his steady blue eyes.

"Do come with us," the child says. "I'll do the worms. I promise to do the worms."

The room spins giddily. Then, for an instant, my mind clears. The fog is gone, and in its place, a crystal light.

I know I won't find another girl to replace Ma Ling. I haven't the heart.

"The chicken coops," I say.

The boy has disappeared, and the man does not seem to have heard me. His grunting escalates for a short time and then abruptly ceases. A weight is lifted from my body, and I draw in a lungful of stale, smoky air.

"My friend," the man is saying, in English now. A horrible smile breaks his face into two slabs of scaly rock. "He wants too," and he points first to my crotch, then to a man towering above the cot, a man with the indigo tunic and short baggy trousers of General Piao's raggedy army. "For Englishwoman, my friend give pipe."

The recent arrival is clutching something. I reach up, snatch the thing, and find in my trembling fingers an oilskin pouch. I open the drawstring and pull out a pipe and a second, smaller pouch. I fumble at the tiny oily strings of the second pouch but they are tightly knotted and will not give.

"Damn it," I say, feeling hot tears in my eyes.

Both men are grinning now. The new arrival is stroking himself through his baggy trousers. Neither makes a move to help me with the pouch but watch, as if my struggle amuses them. I prop myself up against the wall, concentrate on the strings, and slowly manage to loosen the knot. The pouch open, I carefully remove a small piece of opium.

"The lamp. Where is the lamp?" I ask desperately.

Again, the men laugh. "Lamp. Yes, lamp."

One of them produces a box of some kind, crudely made, and filled with something that gives off a rank odor. With one hand still on his groin, the man pulls a match from somewhere and draws it across the wall. He teases me for a moment, holding it just out of reach, and then, laughing, sets the flame to the stuff in the box and throws the spent stick to the ground. A small flame leaps from the box, giving off an odious stink. Shoving it before me, I realize he intends me to heat the opium over the burning stuff. I have nothing to use as an instrument, so I just hold it over, feel the flame bite my fingers as the opium loosens to slime. I paste it over the hole in the stem of the pipe and with all of my strength, suck in the smoke.

An awful sound brews in his throat as he mounts me. I suck again at the pipe, only vaguely aware of his coarse movements.

The feel of the yellow chiffon as I leapt from Robert's divan, the swish a frothy sound that matched the heightened girlish joy I felt. Yes, I would find a note card or leaf of stationery—

it didn't matter what. If I could not bring myself to say those words, I would simply write them down.

I had thought myself barred from such pure happiness.

We each have our birthright—mine was the legacy of the cramped Manchester flat: paste stones, watered-down cologne, counterfeit declarations of love, and me, succumbing to the fool's gold, a child desperate to please.

Later, the crash from grace, my eyes opened onto the truth. And then, the stark knowledge—that above all else, my birthright was this: a denial of the possibility of ever really loving.

Until that moment.

Me, in yellow chiffon, my bare shoulders prickly with cold and thrill both; me, rummaging in the tiny drawers and slots at the back of Robert's rolltop desk, which typically he took care to lock, but which he had, in the fluster of his own desire to make some kind of declaration, left open. Rummaging for the note card or sheet of engraved stationery on which I'd write words I never thought would be possible to utter in truth. My heart sang with it, I'd taken flight—unaccountably, at last—on a love that Robert shared. I was more certain of it than anything I'd ever known.

Letters and documents, their seals broken, all kinds of papers and neatly arranged bills, snug in their slots and little wooden drawers. He *must* have some writing paper somewhere, I thought. In this last drawer, surely he must. But no, only stamps and sealing wax.

This slot? Something jammed in here, at the back. Too tight to properly reach.

Some premonitory sentiment. I pulled back my hand, cradled it with the other, as if it were hurt. The girlish excitement at the idea of finding the paper I was looking for suddenly froze to something else.

Do we know when the perilous moment is upon us? When the great hand is readying to slap us forward, into the maw?

The search for paper forgotten, I worked my two fingers into the space, tugged and jostled and poked until I was able to draw out the desperate contents wedged deeply within.

The man has finished with me. He rolls off the cot, reclaims the candle from where he set it down on the floor, and disappears.

"Mama," I croak aloud. To nobody. To everybody. "Are you proud of your girl? *Have I made you proud?*"

Aware of the smoke—and then, of a sickening realization that spreads like the rays of a black sun. It was for this that I had ached and yearned. Not for Ma Ling, not for anything human, but for this.

"Robert," I whisper, my voice brittle. "Don't you see? *We were made for each other.*"

Not sleep, but a blank dissociation from light and sound; a ghastly taste of the grave. A faint slapping noise penetrated the airtight seal. A sensation of something impossibly heavy, a slab of marble ten feet thick sliding open and, in the crack, that soft slapping sound: fervent little waves lapping at the shore. I opened my eyes. The room was dark and filled with a stench of fish oil and human grime. The sound, coming from the corner, growing louder. I raised my body tentatively, swung my feet onto the floor, and squinted through the darkness. My eyes adjusted quickly, revealing the outlines of a human form rocking unevenly back and forth. An old woman with stringy gray hair, her crinkled face and opaque, bleary eyes arranged into an expression of idiotic glee. Her toothless jaws gummed noisily; this was the sound that had roused me. As I drew nearer, the old woman clapped her hands merrily; a channel of drool formed at the corner of her working mouth and made its way down her stubbly chin. I stumbled toward the door.

Outside, the air was even more putrid than it had been inside. The streets were coated with an oily film—muck from the port deposited by the pummeling rains. My cracked shoes made the going treacherous. I slipped and slid and, though I did not fall, each step threatened a tumble. I thought about the pipe that had miraculously appeared at some point in the middle of the night. But sharp needles were already whirring in my skull and I cursed the inferior offering. Around me, the air thickened the way it did before a renewed onslaught of rain. I quickened my pace, moving now on the balls of my feet, which lessened the feeling that I was about to topple, and it hit me: I had lost an entire day. It had been night when I drifted off in the stranger's putrid room and night again now. Not the same night, surely: too much had happened. *No matter*, I thought. *The days may as well shrivel up and disappear.*

A faint breeze, tinged with salt, reached my nostrils. Had the flutter of air come from inland, it would have been tainted with the smell of goat dung and human waste. I turned in the direction from which it blew, hoping this would lead me back to the sea. *My North Star*, I thought bitterly, *this scrap of salty air.* Although I knew it was hopeless, the idea of finding Ma Ling beat in my mind like a trapped moth until it felt like it would knock a hole in my skull. I turned into a side alley and, for a moment, everything went black. Then, the impression of a heavy, tarred cloth being pulled back, and of light slowly entering some vast humid room. I found myself curled on the ground. As I picked myself up, a puffy sensation of pain swelled in my left knee. Limping along the alley, I felt a burst of determination.

I'm going to find Ma Ling.

The alley turned to a street and back to an alley again, and then ended abruptly at a crumbly brick wall. I sensed rather than heard human motion, and picked my way slowly over the uneven stones. Sure enough, a man, moving up against a wall. His back was toward me—a broad back, and the man too tall to be Chinese. Faint moonlight drizzled through the flat, water-heavy sky, making the smooth material of his shirt dully gleam. Silently, I tiptoed toward him until I was right beside him. It was only then that I saw the little face pressed sideways against the wall. What struck me most was the look of forbearance in the child's face. At that instant, the girl slowly moved her eyes, and I found myself peering into two steady, blank pools. Without thinking, I leapt upon the man and, possessed suddenly of uncommon strength, tore him away and flung him to the ground. The child stayed pressed against the wall, still holding the rags of her dress around her waist in delicate dirty fingers, regarding me with a calm unblinking gaze. A flicker of fear crossed the girl's face. Something had scared her. And then I realized that I was uttering a peculiar, sustained scream.

I turned around. The man, having righted himself, withdrew into the shadows; I could just make out that he was fastening his pants. I lunged at him, and found myself again sliding into muddy blackness with nothing to catch me, and nothing to grip. Next thing I knew, I was running—sure-footed, now, despite the broken heel of my shoe and my swelling knee. But I was not moving as fast as I might have been and, in a flash, realized why. There was a small hand in my own, someone beside me, trying to keep up but slowed by a child's stride and the slipperiness of bare feet on wet stone. I moved my grasp to her wrist and continued in a half-run, half-stumble, the girl flying weightlessly alongside me.

I continued to stumble and the nausea hit. My nose and eyes streamed; the little hand was limp in my own. I stopped, and turned to look at her. In place of the blank eyes, I saw flat terror. My own eyes were flooding, my chest heaved with sobs. For a moment, I faced the girl. I let go of her hand. She looked at me, bewildered.

"Go," I said harshly, using the street-slang word and shoving the child who stumbled, almost fell, then raced away, a gray streak of energy in the dark.

✳ ✳ ✳

Somebody is banging on the door. My hand flicks jerkily before my face, shooing away mosquitoes and flies that do not exist. The door bursts open. My eyes are dry but I manage to crack them open. A dim figure stands in the door frame: Han Shu, his round face distant and otherworldly as a moon.

"Just wait until you see who I've brought you!" he booms. I watch Han Shu's large frame thrusting toward me in a series of strange little jerks. He is moving that way, I realize, because there is somebody with him, someone he is prodding before him. I raise my head, squint my eyes in an attempt to focus my gaze.

"Ma Ling," I manage to croak, and I reach a bony arm in the girl's direction.

"Yes," Han Shu gaily declares. "You see? I've found her! I've brought her back! Can't say it was easy, all the sleuth work and scouting about. And the little rascal did put up some resistance. But no matter, now that we have her back *home!*"

At this Han Shu, in a spasm of joy, reaches down and clasps Ma Ling to his chest, raising her so that her legs dangle in the air. He sets the girl down again and turns her by the shoulders to face me.

"Well?" he says breathlessly. "What do you say?"

I look hollowly at my employer.

"Christine, don't you see? Our plans! It's all still possible! . . . Don't worry," he continues, apparently to Ma Ling. "She's a little under the weather, your teacher. Has been for some time. But she'll come around."

I crane toward Ma Ling, my neck aches from the effort. I take in the way the girl has draped her scarf over her shoulder—was that the olive and yellow Hermès?—in an only partially successful effort to hide a large tear in her dress.

What have you done? I want to shriek at Han Shu, but in my daze, say nothing. Ma Ling, too, remains silent. Han Shu fondles the girl's hand lovingly, then plucks at the torn silk flap of her bodice with thumb and forefinger.

"We'll fix this, my pet. You know Christine's skill with a needle. We'll have you all fixed up again in no time."

My eyelids droop. I again try to speak, there is something I want to say, but the tongue in my mouth is no longer my own, it belongs to some foreign and mechanical realm. I fumble at my side for the pipe, my hand a blunt bulbous object not wholly within my control.

"Your afternoon refreshments, my dear, that's what you want," Han Shu says.

He pulls from his pocket an enamel box, then picks up the pipe I'd been groping for. Using a tiny gold spoon, he scoops out a brown pellet.

How did you get her back? I want to say, but the effort is too great. And besides, I think dimly, the thought floating away from me at the very instant it appears, that isn't the point, the blur of Ma Ling's fierce eyes make that clear.

Someone is holding the pipe to my lips. I feel the small close heat of the sticky, swollen lump, perched above the hole on the stem of the pipe. If there is a point to it all, I sense it is somewhere in the room: somewhere between the cracked boards of the floor and the peeling paint of the ceiling; in the spaces beneath the metal frame of my cot, perhaps, which squeaks pleasantly as I lean forward to allow Han Shu to slide the slim tip of the pipe's stem into my mouth—or off in a dusty corner, fleshy and inquisitive as a mouse. I suck in the smoke, close my eyes tightly, and lower my head back down to the cot.

How desperately I had wanted to see Ma Ling again; how I had longed to encounter her, if only for one last, brief moment. Something stirs briefly within: that beautiful oval face, those clear dark eyes narrowed with loathing. I can feel my mind glazing over. I hear Archibald's voice, as though he were there in the room. "What do the English know about opium. Ha! Visions of wicked Chinamen, exotic Eastern scenes run amok! No subtlety. No imagination. A child's playroom equipped by a dull-witted adult. To strip the great treasure of Egyptian Thebes of imagination—its very essence! A crime, I tell you, a punishable crime, by my lights."

A violent clapping threatens to splice my eardrums, a thousand or more hands drawn together in a cacophony of cheer. I crack open my eyes. It is only Han Shu clapping his hands, smiling at Ma Ling who is standing, listless, beside him.

"How charming," I hear him declare. "Our family, reunited at last!"

There is no reason to leave my room. Everything I need, everything I want, is here.

When did Han Shu change his tactic? Arrange it so that every morning one of the girls would tap on the door, enter quietly, and leave a small bulging cloth bag. No more tiny turquoise box with its limited cache. It is a marvel. No more waiting, no minutes to count on the ornate face of the clock around my neck. No infuriating ticking. From time to time, the door opens; another girl appears holding a bowl of soup or a mound of rice, a glass of sweet red syrup or a goblet of wine.

A cloisonné bracelet rattles on my wrist. I straighten my arm by the bed, and the bracelet clatters to the floor. I watch it spin to rest. *Living is a horizontal fall.* Who said that? Someone Archibald was fond of quoting.

"To hell with him." I say it aloud, and I wonder who I mean. Archibald? Or Han Shu, who is giving me what I want, serving it up in great dollops? *I live in an igloo of cold black bricks,* I think. Or Robert. Is that who I mean?

Yes, I found it there, wedged in the back of Robert's roll-top desk that should have been locked but wasn't. I never gave Robert a chance to explain. *What if—*? What if—there were some explanation, other than the one I'd presumed?

I look down at my thin hands, notice, on the back of one, an unseemly scab.

I remember Ma Ling up in her room; recall the look in her eyes, last night, of loathing.

I didn't wait for Robert to come back; I remember only a frenzy. No thought, just blind animal action.

I knew only that I had found unmistakable evidence, that my suspicions about Robert had been confirmed—and worse.

I had stuffed the offending scrap back into the slot, not grasping that it was to be my ruin too. I grabbed my shawl and bag and fled—down the stairs, through the grand foyer, and out the front door into the cold evening. I walked, then ran, in my flimsy evening slippers; ran until I could hardly breathe.

I have drifted off; now, I open my eyes.

At first it is hard to tell, but then I am sure. The smoke has changed color—and odor. It is gritty and hard, it smells of wet tar. My eyes burn as it drifts upward. I stare into it, hoping for some vision.

Mold from a bowl in the corner of the room taints the air with its intimate animal scent.

No visions, no. How long has it been? How long since the smoke has offered up more than numbness?

I see Ma Ling's face again. Not filled with loathing, but—beseeching.

I sit up, brush at my face, wipe my eyes. I cross to the window. It is very dark outside, the kind of blackness that is the true heart of the night: three, maybe four in the morning. My head breaks open into clarity. Why had it not occurred to me before?

Things are not always what they seem. My words echo hollowly around me. Carefully I dress. Sandals in hand, I leave my little room, tiptoe to the third floor, and open the door. Ma Ling, still in her dress, lies curled on the bed. I touch her shoulder.

"Ma Ling," I whisper. She starts awake. The hopeful new eyes of awakening. And then, in her face, a fireworks of feeling: hatred, longing, despair, a child's wish to be held. I put a finger to her lips, batting with my other hand at the thick blue spiderwebs that swing before my eyes. I try to stifle the hollow cough that plagues me now. I reach for Ma Ling's hand, as I had reached for her hand in the thicket of another moonless night, and again she unfolds her limbs and rises. I scoop up her shoes, and together, Ma Ling and I, hand in hand, make our way down the stairs and out through the front door.

It might have been miles, it might have been the merest crossing of a street; all I recall is steady movement through heavy night air, and Ma Ling's soft hand in my own. The darkness thins in the light of a sliver moon; puddles and dubious tricklings glisten amber and white.

I feel an awful pain in my gut; my brain is a torturing buzz of want. But I do not feel that deadly longing for the smoke; the fierceness, now, is a different sort of love.

We remain silent until I come to a halt, miles distant, in front of the neat, well-cared-for building where Barnaby has his lodgings.

"We're going home," I say. "Barnaby will help us. We're going home, Ma Ling. To England."

PART II

Marilyn

The North Shore of Long Island. Summer, 1951.

CHAPTER FOUR

The year I spent in London during the war, I never made it to the Continent. One time, the Red Cross truck which was to take me from Ostende to Paris was blown up in a skirmish—news I received by telegram at my hotel in Dover where I was readying to sail. On the eve of another scheduled departure, my travel papers were destroyed in an air raid while I sat in the bomb shelter in my nightdress, sipping tea. So, I ended up documenting what was there, in London. But the closer I got to London's version of the war, the further away from the war I felt.

Now and then, I would stumble upon someone injured in a bombing. You might think being brought face-to-face with such suffering would heighten the reality of it all, but actually, on those occasions, I felt even more at a remove. One early morning, I crept from the bomb shelter minutes after an attack, before the all-clear siren had sounded, only to find, four blocks from my own unscathed lodgings, a man crawling through the ruins of his house. He was moving very slowly, seemed to be looking for something with intense and unbroken concentration. I picked my way over the rubble, got close enough to hear what he was mumbling—something about ice, how he needed a bag of ice. Then I saw the raw stump where his right hand should have been, and realized that what he was groping for with the fingers of one hand was the missing other, which must have flown off in the explosion. I knelt, yanked off my scarf, set about bandaging the man's exposed wrist. Dawn was just beginning to break, a thin glow through the billows of smoke that hung above the trees.

The rescue squad arrived minutes after I did and packed the man up in a stretcher, ignoring his pleas that they continue the search for the piece of himself he had lost. By that time I was standing behind my camera, some way off in the middle of the road; an emergency worker, a boy not older than four-teen, turned from the wounded man to look at me, brushing soot from his eyes, then swept his arm in an arc to indicate the mess which used to be the man's house, a wooden skel-eton squatting among piles of broken brick. I trained my lens on the house across the street, a neatly painted Victorian with grill-iron railings on the porch. On the window ledge of the ground floor, ivy trailed from a row of clay pots; amidst the foliage, a fat cat blinked sleepily into the first tepid light of day. At the moment I clicked the shutter, the cat's eyes sud-denly snapped alert: yellow, contemptuous.

In the course of that year, I watched German missiles flat-ten the city. It struck me as curious that, despite the wreckage, carefully searched out each day and documented by armies of middle-aged men with resigned faces, London did not seem all that altered. At what point, I remember wondering, is a city so changed that it no longer resembles itself? Roaming the streets, camera in hand, I recalled the case, pondered by philosophers, of the construction worker—Phineas Gage, from Vermont, who sometime in the late 1800s miraculously survived when an explosion propelled a steel rod through his head, gouging out part of his brain. His intelligence was not much affected, though in place of the calm, considerate man he had been was a surly new Phineas, given to hurling abuse. How different from London, skewered by countless projectiles, but without any indication of temperamental change. I decided it was a matter of the soul (though this would hardly have satisfied the philosophers), that the metal pole had somehow barreled through Phineas's soul—whereas mercifully the soul of England's capital was the one target the enemy had been unable to locate, remaining, through it all, intact: hovering as great dust clouds above the rubble, sighing when walls, centuries old, buckled and fell, glinting in the geysers of black water that shot into the air when a barrage of V-2 issues, off-target, pummeled the nighttime Thames. If anything, the city seemed to become more and more itself, as if the raids were chiseling away the superfluous, the way time sharpens a face with its own character through a process of withering and collapse.

When I was asked to put together an exhibition—World War II through the eyes of American women photographers—I took on the project, without really thinking it through. There were only a few of us, so the logistics were not difficult. Once I began reviewing the work of the others—all had documented the war throughout Europe—I cringed, knowing I should have found a way to get to the Continent. I have never shaken the unbalancing twinge that it was cowardice that kept me from going, not so much a fear for my own physical safety but something deeper, more alarming.

I was somehow not surprised when each of the women photographers expressed, in her own way, the desire to have little to do with the project, beyond furnishing their boxes of contact sheets. They wanted to put the war behind them. I envied that they had earned the right to do so.

If I could, would I go back and reverse that unthinking gesture? My running back upstairs that day, as we were loading up the car for the trip to Ellis Park, to retrieve the portfolio which contained, along with my own contact sheets, those of the other women to be featured in the exhibition, over one hundred large sheets of negatives, fifty shots to a page? Had we been going to visit Simon's parents in Maine, or my friend Rachel in Cape May, or anyone else for that matter, in any of the forty-eight states of this well-meaning geography, it wouldn't have much mattered. To any other weekend destination, I could have brought these women's entire oeuvres, some of it so awful that even I have to avert my eyes, and it would not have made one whit of difference.

But we were not driving to Maine or New Jersey or Rhode Island or Vermont. We were driving to Ellis Park, to Oscar's painstakingly crafted haven, where fairy lights stitched the contours of the mansion into the black sky, where nature and cultivation existed in equipoise, where the calibration, exquisitely unnoticed, of festivity and pleasure kept all else at bay. Into this I brought my black leather portfolio. I may as well have stamped through the polished rooms wielding a hammer and knife, smashing Chinese vases, slicing the portraits and still lifes that adorned the walls, pitching to the floor crystal glasses and decanters that stood at the ready in alcoves, on sideboards and end tables. And yet, I cannot be certain it was I who heaved memory onto the bland lawns of Ellis Park.

Two of our more well-known friends had attended a weekend gathering at the imposing Ellis Park mansion on the slightly wild north shore of Long Island, which was presided over by a refined and elusive Englishman, and had brought back news of the dinners and dances and drawing-room conversations. So when, after a gallery opening of mine that garnered its share of complimentary press, I received a letter from the almost legendary Oscar, praising my work and inviting Simon and me to Ellis Park, I talked Simon into it, curious to see what that world was like.

"I admire your work," Oscar had said when we were introduced that first day in the hallway, outside the library. He was wearing an immaculately tailored blue suit with a close-fitting jacket, the corner of a white silk handkerchief protruding carefully from the breast pocket slit. "I've been following your career. Your photographs of the new industrial frontier in *Life* magazine were a tour de force." He spoke in an upper-class British accent that was all of a piece with the house and the uniformed maids and the butler who greeted us at the door. The extreme youthfulness of Oscar's face was at odds with the gravity of his bearing—with the worldliness and accomplishment that seemed to infuse his being.

"Are those yours?" I asked, nodding toward the three photographs hanging on the wall behind him.

"Yes," he said with a quick backward glance. "Amateur dabbling."

The pictures were of a river, different angles of the same stretch taken an hour or two apart: early morning, mid-morning, late morning. "England," I ventured. "In the north?"

Oscar smiled. "Ah," he said, "and a sleuth besides."

Through the window I could see great splashes of sunlight; it seemed to be dripping off the trees.

"Why don't we take a walk before lunch?" he proposed. "I'll show you the formal gardens and we can peek at the beach."

Simon was off somewhere wandering the hallways with a mutual friend we'd encountered upon arriving, so Oscar and I headed off across the wide sweep of lawn, past clay tennis courts, where a man methodically passed a wide broom back and forth along the width of the red surface. A stone path skirted the croquet course, which was set beside an orchard of old fruit trees. Everywhere, the bright liquid sunlight, like pure draughts of cheer.

We walked awhile in comfortable silence. The pathway ended at an opening in a large rectangle of tailored hedge. I stepped into the enclosure to find row upon row of flowering plants. Some I recognized: petunia, nasturtium, nicotiana. There were also exotic varieties I'd never seen—a long-stemmed specimen with fleshy orange heads; a miniature bush with beige spotted buds.

"I do find flowers restful," Oscar said, drawing a deep breath of the sweet air. "Don't you?" He looked at me with a soft, querying smile.

I closed my eyes, savoring the complex medley of scents. Thyme, in among the nectar, and also something roundly pungent—cilantro, perhaps. Standing there, the warmth on my face, I felt an unexpected ripple of anxiety. As beautiful as it was, there was something unsettling about the place, something that was not quite right.

I snapped open my eyes to find Oscar's calm, unaltered gaze.

"Yes," I replied to his question about the flowers. "How could one not?" He must have sensed my sudden disquiet; he looked more deeply into my eyes, then nodded, almost imperceptibly. It was one of those gestures which assumes some mutual, exclusive understanding.

"Come," he said, taking my arm. We walked the length of the formal gardens, then cut through a smaller break in the hedge. We came to another wide lawn, this one sloping down to the sea where, beside a little jetty, an assemblage of rowboats bobbed gently on the Sound.

Further along the beach I could see the rise of chalky rock juttings. We walked down to the water. The sand trickling into my sandals was silky and untroubling.

Oscar shielded his eyes with one hand. "We all came from the sea," he said, looking out over the rumpled tide at the ocean's green skin.

I never brought my photographic equipment to Ellis Park, so when Oscar asked me to take a few pictures one Saturday, I set off in search of a camera. I knew somebody would have one; it was a well-heeled faddish crowd, and photography was much in fashion. Within an hour, I had obtained a Leica.

By the time I returned to the front of the house, where I stood back on the grassy shoulder of the driveway, Oscar was organizing a little crowd on the wide, semicircular steps. A woman with red hair caught in a ponytail was waving a champagne flute and calling out to him in a deep-throated voice; tiny amber droplets flew from her glass. Oscar turned and sighted me.

"There she is," he said, then jabbed a finger back in the direction of the people talking and laughing on the steps, shrugging in mock helplessness. "I've done what I can, Marilyn. Now, you're on your own."

I raised the camera, winding the strap around my wrist. Through the viewfinder the group looked rowdy and expensively dressed. Oscar stood beside me as I shot five, six frames, adjusting the angle slightly with each one. I paused to reassess the light.

I had not yet met the convalescent, though I knew, when I lifted the camera again to my eye, that the craggy face that had suddenly appeared beside the ponytailed woman must be his. I clicked, noticing how definitively his presence changed the composition. He said something to his neighbor, which must have amused her, for she threw back her head and laughed, allowing me to capture the sweep of her neck. He looked intently at the camera. I snapped the watchful face, twice, three times, four times. I focused on the square line of his jaw, which wavered, curiously, in the tiny glass box at my eye; snapped the way the jocularity rose around him, swirling in a way I imagined would show up on the film. I had the impression I was watching the place on the disturbed surface of a lake where a tossed stone has disappeared.

The convalescent's name was Barnaby, and I was formally introduced to him later that day.

Before the cocktail hour, a hush fell on the house, when people retired to their rooms to freshen up for dinner. I liked to wander the halls, then: a chance for a moment's peace among Oscar's beautiful objects—Dutch porcelain, small copper sculptures from India, elaborately carved boxes, set here and there upon the sideboards and end tables placed at intervals along the walls. I decided to stop by Oscar's study.

"Marilyn, how nice," Oscar said, opening the door. Barnaby was sitting in a leather armchair beneath a massive tapestry of a fox hunt painted in muted earth tones, but for the unseemly red of the hunters' jackets. Barnaby reached for the cane leaning up against the chair and rose for a moment, giving a crooked half-smile which caused a deep vertical dimple to appear in his right cheek.

I sat across from Barnaby in a matching leather armchair. Oscar poured a drink from the crystal decanter on his desk and brought it over to me.

"Poetic justice," Oscar said, gesturing with the drink he held to Barnaby's cane. "You see, Barnaby has a genius for survival. Our friend here works for the American Consulate. He may traffic in good will on the side, but danger's his real game. He specializes in getting into scrapes, then wriggling his way out.

"I always know something's wrong when the postcards stop coming. This last time, I tracked him down myself— hopped on a flight to Rhodesia and, through great effort, I might point out, found him in a village several hours from Salisbury. Sprawled on a mat in a mud hut. Talk about colonization: parasites, malaria, heaven knows what else."

Oscar returned to his desk and chose a pipe from the dozen or more hanging in a rack on the wall.

"Chief Ngube wouldn't be too happy to hear you refer to the tribal meeting house as a mud hut," Barnaby said. "I had a good deal of time to study the bark shields decorating the ceiling. Simple art does not mean art that's not profound."

Oscar pressed tobacco into the bowl of his pipe. "I arranged a six-month leave for him from the Consulate, then dragged him back here. A recuperation sentence, I told him. To be served at Ellis Park. No time off for good behavior. Though with Barnaby, there'd be little risk of that."

Oscar paused.

"Hello," he said, looking expectantly at his friend. "Barnaby speechless. Let me savor the moment."

"Just waiting for the *poetic justice* punch line," Barnaby replied.

Oscar struck a match, held it to the bowl of his pipe, looked across at me as he gently puffed.

"I stuffed him full of medicine and got him back in one piece. He slept for two days and woke up a new man—fever gone, appetite restored. But the first day he ventured from his room—as it happens, everybody was assembled in the foyer for drinks—I looked up and saw him hesitating at the top of the stairs. Next thing I knew, he'd toppled, and was bucking all the way down. Quite the hullaballoo—people below gasping and calling out. By the time I got to him, his ankle was blowing up like a balloon."

"Sprain," Barnaby said sheepishly, pointing to his foot, which appeared no longer to be bandaged.

"Tendons, ligaments, muscles. He managed to get everything involved," Oscar added.

"Are you quite finished, Oscar?"

"If my meaning is plain."

"Plain as a mud hut, wouldn't you say, Marilyn?" Barnaby inquired mildly, looking at me full on for the first time. His eyes had a curious hovering about them, caught somehow between stillness and action.

"The poetic justice," I said slowly. "Let's see. Barnaby survived Africa only to injure himself in the wild interiors of Ellis Park."

Oscar looked from Barnaby to me and back again. I glimpsed something in his face—some realization that glimmered for an instant behind the closed shutters of his reserve.

It was a gregarious crowd; the endless talk could be wearying. The first Saturday evening of the season, Oscar brought in a brass band. While it was setting up in the ballroom, I excused myself from a discussion about the influence of Mississippi Blues on the Big Band, and made my way along the hallway past the brightly lit front rooms to the rear foyer where a Steinway stood in the shadows. I flicked on the lamp, opened the glass doors of the music case, and selected a volume of Ancient Keyboard Music I myself happened to own.

It was my second summer as a regular weekend guest, and already I had forgotten what life without Ellis Park was like. Yet, I did not exactly feel as if I belonged. Oscar had accrued an odd collection of people: a motley group which came and went, most of them leaving only the shallow imprint of caricature—the judge given to furtively adjusting his eyeglasses; the overweight matron who would labor across the lawn, jewels crusted to her fingers and throat.

Simon and I were allotted the yellow suite in the west wing, and also invited to the occasional midweek dinner reserved for Oscar's closest friends. These gatherings invariably included a dignitary of some kind, a foreigner of distinction, a modestly celebrated artist or journalist. I suppose Simon and I slotted into the artist category—he, a writer; me, a photographer. Though despite the glittering guest list, Oscar himself was not at all pretentious. His elegance seemed to spring from the same uncalculated place as his sculpted features, some serene department of nature that dispensed dignity and grace.

I'd lost track of how many times I had repeated the piece on the piano; it was rolling from my fingers of its own accord. I'd forgotten the party, and the band, which by this time must have been swinging mightily on the other side of the house. I was aware only of my solitude, of the lilting melody that had nothing and everything to do with me. No longer looking at the music, I watched my fingers in a trance, stalled in the limpid timelessness of the melody.

I looked up. My eyes followed the balcony encircling the foyer midway up the wall. A rustle, and then I fancied I saw a pale round moon withdraw into the dark. No, not a moon: a face. *Tap, tap, tap*, fading away from the balcony toward the servant stairway at the back of the house. Barnaby, of course, it must have been Barnaby, there, on the balcony, in the dark, watching. For how long?

* * *

We retired to the green parlor after dinner, where the butler had poured out glasses of Oscar's crimson port. As the small talk dwindled, we sank more deeply into the leather couches and paisley wingback chairs and I sensed, in the room, that ambiguous moment in which the comfort of familiar faces and pleasurable habit thickens to tedium. Barnaby had a sixth sense about such awkwardnesses and a canny talent for dispelling them.

That was when Barnaby came up with the idea of the storytelling salon. "Next he'll have us playing charades," I said. But Barnaby's enthusiasm won us over.

"One rule," he announced. "Each story must contain an element of truth."

I looked over to Simon and saw him frown.

"I'm happy to get the ball rolling," Barnaby continued. "Only, I like my audience well-oiled."

He fetched the decanter from the sideboard. Barnaby was no longer using the cane; a slight limp was the only remaining sign of his tumble down the staircase. He did a slow circuit of the room, filling each glass.

Simon rose and excused himself, pausing to kiss my cheek. "I'll see you back in the room, darling," he whispered, an odd expression in his face: vaguely disapproving, but also puzzled.

Barnaby dusted off one of his Africa exploits. As I listened to him tell his story about hunting with Charlie, a swashbuckler who had once bagged an elusive white panther, it became clear to me that Barnaby was somehow making himself up. Seeing himself as a jazz-age adventurer on safari, perhaps, as he stole through the Kenyan brush, rifle in hand, a silver whiskey flask sloshing on his hip. And yet the Barnaby I pictured scouting low in the wilds was not a thumb-worn figure, not diminished for having been constructed, but the reverse: realer than real. Barnaby had a way of enlarging a situation, a sort of Midas touch of ownership and prowess. As the story progressed, I found myself shedding my critical distance, and had anybody asked me what Hemingway himself might have thought, I would have answered in a flash that both Charlie and Barnaby were the kinds of men Hemingway had always longed to be.

The story had a terrible end, as I knew it would: Charlie found mauled almost beyond recognition, having given himself over to a lioness in some mysterious compact with the animal kingdom. His final words hovering in the air, Barnaby rose for another pass with the decanter of port.

By the time I got back to our suite, Simon was already asleep. Barnaby's story was still swirling in my head. Slipping off my shoes, I crossed into the sitting room adjoining the bedroom, opened the curtains, and sat in the easy chair by the window. The trees outside were strung with lights; their tiny bulbs picked out circlets of new green from the heavy black foliage.

I wasn't particularly interested in the dance Oscar set up for the next evening. Simon, however, was in a romantic mood; I danced a few slow numbers with him, but my heart wasn't in it. I looked for a moment into his face—the stillness of his chiseled features, those eyes that melted me sometimes, at other times stopped me cold with their icy detachment. Simon wore his good looks lightly. He was not unaware of his physical charisma (he had been mistaken, on more than one occasion, for a matinee idol to whom he did, in fact, bear a strong resemblance). He simply had little interest in what others thought of him, a self-sufficiency that could spark resentment, even ire—and in my case left me, at times, feeling shamed and alone.

I started to speak. "Simon, why don't we . . ." But then, aghast at the pleading tone in my voice, muttered an excuse: "The wine, it's gone to my head." I stepped out onto the porch and breathed in the warm salt air. I made my way down the wooden steps and along the loose-stone path that led to the water.

The private beach stretched for half a mile. I walked the length of it, accompanied by three gulls the size of small geese which rose every now and then to glide above the Sound, looking straight ahead, as if waiting for something important to be borne to them on the breeze. The ocean was quiet, except where it licked the sand near my feet. I found myself thinking again, as I had on and off all day, about Charlie's white panther, its velvety coat and spellbound eyes. What had they been saying to each other, I wondered, this man, the beast, soul to soul, the moment before the shot?

The beach side of the house was in darkness when I returned. Behind me, wavelets fingered the shore. I headed for the kitchen, where a maid was busy at a frothy sink, and poured myself a glass of milk. On my way back, I noticed light under the door of Oscar's study. I knocked, then entered, but instead of Oscar, found Barnaby sitting in a halo of light, reading. He put the book down on the side table.

"Hello." He smiled. "A nightcap?"

I pointed to my glass of milk and shook my head. I leaned against the doorjamb; looking down at him sitting in the green chair, the tapestry of the fox hunt rising behind him, I had the feeling that for all his travels, Barnaby most truly belonged here, in Oscar's wood-paneled room.

"I've been thinking about Charlie," I said. "How high was the truth quotient of that story?"

"If you're asking me whether it happened, the answer is yes."

"Did you have any idea he was going to do what he did in the end? Was there ever a hint?"

Barnaby slowly rotated his glass. "There was one incident, now that I think about it. I was awoken one night by the cold. The fire had gone out, and when I saw Charlie's empty sleeping bag, I went to look for him. I found him by the water hole in a kind of daze. No rifle, just standing there, staring into the water. He looked at me as if he didn't know who I was. The whole way back to camp, he didn't say a word.

"Next morning, he was back to his old self. Whistled as he shaved and wolfed down his breakfast. As usual, it was *Ready boys?* before any of us had finished eating. No mention of the previous night."

Barnaby stared for a moment at the blackened window, then turned back to me.

"As for the truth quotient: that's not for me to judge. Besides, isn't that the business you're in? The photographer, going about the world with a camera—teasing the truth out of things?"

Barnaby rose and walked toward me, a seriousness in his face I'd not seen before. He leaned against the opposite side of the doorjamb.

"I've been wondering," I said. "Am I just imagining it, or do you sometimes follow me?"

Back at our apartment on Riverside Drive the following Thursday, as we were sitting up in bed reading, I had an idea for a story of my own. Not really an idea—more like a glimpse in the dark into an intriguing, unfamiliar room full of somebody else's belongings. I barely had time to register it and it was gone, leaving behind a wild, jumpy feeling in my chest.

"Simon, won't you join us in the green room for the story-telling tomorrow night?" I found myself asking.

Simon looked up from his book. "You know I don't have a taste for that kind of thing." He seemed a little put out by my question.

In the morning, we loaded up the Studebaker outside our apartment building. And then, the ritual leave-taking: traveling a little ways north in order to cross the city above the park, and then east to take in the wide main boulevard of Harlem, open as an honest face, its jazz clubs slumbering in the daylight like unsung notes on a stave. As we headed south, I leaned back in my seat and watched the chameleon performance of the city as it sped by, dressing and undressing itself of decorum and civility: the slouching tenements of upper Park Avenue straightening to stately apartment buildings, with doormen in navy jackets and gold-braid epaulets, who guarded their marble entrances with vaguely bewildered pride. Then, the sparkling storefronts, with their whimsical displays and piles of summer fruit. I felt myself uncoiling, returning from the chill landscape of my work where I bounced along eerily unhampered by gravity, my camera, snug in my hands, fixing me not to space but to time in tiny, stolen snippets. When we finally crossed the Queensboro Bridge, I looked back to see Manhattan transformed yet again: now the trapped beast it always seemed from any distance great enough to view it whole.

By the time we pulled into the circular driveway in front of the house, I felt alive with excitement. I glanced over at Simon. His face was tight.

"Why don't you take a walk?" I suggested.

He gave a strained smile. "Good idea."

I got everything up to our suite in two trips, then returned to park the car. Back in the room I freshened up. I sat on the chintz-covered couch and smoked two cigarettes, one after the other, looking out at the handful of guests milling about on the lawn. I changed into a light evening suit and headed down to join them.

Outside, I walked across the lawn to the croquet course where the little group was scattered among the hoops, Barnaby somehow at the center of things, leaning on his croquet stick. Beside him was the red-haired woman again, wearing freshly applied lipstick, her hand cradling the crown of her head where the ponytail sprouted, attempting to protect i suspected, from the sudden breeze that was tickling up s] and setting wide trouser legs aflap.

"Marilyn," Barnaby smiled, tipping the rim of his straw hat. The woman's face darkened to a frown she tried to hide behind a toothy grin.

"It's all the rest of us against Barnaby," she said. "Don't let the limp fool you—he's leaving us in the dust."

"Croquet's not my strong suit, I'm afraid," I said. "I always end up hitting someone's foot."

Barnaby handed his croquet stick to the woman. "Tell you what, Hilary. I'm appointing you my proxy." Barnaby took my elbow, turned me in the direction of the beach. "Do me proud," he called back to the woman, who was trying, without success, to disguise an out-and-out scowl.

"You could be kinder," I said when we were out of earshot. "The woman is clearly smitten."

"Hilary? Oh, she'll be all right," Barnaby replied absently. I was aware of the firmness of his hand on my elbow, of the way it made me feel: as if I were at the mercy of an unpredictable force of nature.

"The Consulate must be missing you," I said.

"The consul general's a friend of Oscar's. They're in cahoots, you know."

"Oh yes. Your enforced recuperation."

"Incarceration, I call it."

We entered the formal gardens. There was not a soul about. Only the gushing presence of the wild assortment of blooms, and a volley of twittering, muffled by distance, coming from the direction of the woods. Barnaby led me to a bench and we sat down.

"Do you feel at a loose end?" I asked.

"Not exactly. I'm working on a couple of ideas. Diplomatic travel writing, you might call it, about the postings I've had. Actually, the hardest thing about being here," he broke off, reached forward, and cupped his hand around an open-throated tiger lily, "is being surrounded by all this, well, beauty." He looked up to the clear and vibrantly blue sky.

"I'm afraid I'm accustomed to a little more reality than Oscar provides. But it would be wickedly ungrateful of me to complain."

"I imagine there are worse places to be incarcerated," I said.

"Do you?" Barnaby leaned back, though the bench had no back, as if he had made a cushiony support of the fresh sunny air. "And what kind of prisons are you familiar with?" The half-smile, the deep vertical dimple, the intimate conspiratorial voice.

"Actually, prisons are not my forte."

"No, the pictures of yours I've seen don't have a lot of walls. You seem to prefer the outdoors."

We both hesitated. The far-off twittering of birds seemed to grow louder, as if the woods were stealthily advancing.

"Non-fortes," he said. With his right hand, he counted out two fingers on his left. "Croquet. Prisons. I see I'll be learning about you in the negative."

Those brown eyes: I felt I might reach into them and pull out something marvelous and undiscovered.

At dinner Barnaby leaned over and whispered in my ear, "We'll be hearing from you this evening, I trust." The pounding in my chest started up. I patted his arm.

"Perhaps," I said, attempting nonchalance. "If Oscar's brandy inspires me sufficiently."

Barnaby gave a knowing smile and resumed his banter with the woman seated on his other side who was poking at her salad and looking at him in that hopeful, insecure way I'd seen women look at him before.

After dinner, we made our way upstairs to the green room. Simon, in conversation with a scholarly looking man from the Treasury Department, remained in the dining room. Climbing the stairs alongside Barnaby, I could feel the weight of his gaze.

We were the first to enter. Barnaby crossed the room to check the decanters, which had been readied on the sideboard. I sat in an overstuffed chair. Everything seemed vaguely altered; it was as if each piece of furniture had been moved two or three inches in one or another direction. The hunter-green of the walls appeared more precise, and the two paintings opposite me—a woman reading a letter, and a stiff family portrait of English aristocrats bearing no resemblance to Oscar—seemed suddenly both very still and very animated, as if the figures were holding their breath and waiting to spring to life.

The others came drifting into the room. From where Barnaby stood in the corner I could hear the sound of ice cubes clinking, one at a time, into empty glasses. I recalled the flash that had come to me the previous evening—only in the remembering it was different, larger and smaller at the same time. I could see the whole story before me in one frozen scene, the characters and setting in miniature: propped up on a bed the size of a matchbox, a minuscule girl with honey-blond braids that fell across her shoulders and onto her developing bosom, which rose nakedly above a tightly laced bodice. The picture had the feel of memory—not my own, but somebody else's, as if I had divined the source of some stranger's secret obsession. I looked around, a little bewildered. There was Barnaby, moving about with the tray of fresh drinks and an exaggerated, waiterly air. The room had filled. Barnaby set the last drink from his tray onto the coffee table in front of me and returned to the sideboard to retrieve the one he had poured for himself. Everybody turned expectantly to where he stood by the window.

"To this evening's raconteur," he said, raising his drink in my direction.

"It was discovered in the vault of a cathedral," I began, though I scarcely knew where the words were coming from. "A leather-bound notebook, rotting at the spine and filled with the writing of a feminine hand. *The Twelfth Day of the Month of May, 1601 Years After the Birth of Our Lord Jesus* was written across the top of the first page."

I found myself describing the story of a young girl, born in a servant's shack built against the inside of a monastery wall, who grew up scrabbling with other children around the straw-roofed settlement, gazing in awe at the priests when they passed by on their way out into the parish.

Every now and then I glanced across at Barnaby, who was leaning back in a leather chair, chin resting on interlaced fingers. I wondered if he had contrived this storytelling business solely to afford the chance of watching me frankly, and in the open.

"The Canon knew the girl from church," I continued. "He had not failed to notice how lovely she was. The mother, he knew, had eight other children at home; he knew, too, that her husband, an ironsmith, had recently lost the use of one hand." A hush fell over the room. The only sound, apart from my voice, was the tinkle every now and then of ice cubes in a glass.

"*I'll see to her education*, the Canon said one Sunday, taking the girl by the hand. The woman fell to her knees and covered his feet with kisses.

"The Canon believed the world sullied women, and that if he shut the girl away, she would, under his tutelage, flower. He placed her in a spacious cellar and brought in a staff to care for her: two servant girls—children themselves—along with a tutor and a cook."

I realized, as I spoke, that this strange story had all been there in that heightened glimpse, the week before, as I lay reading in bed with Simon.

"For five years, the Canon came every week to visit the girl. She noted some of their exchanges in her diary. *It's a curse to see things too clearly*, the girl had said one day, to take one example. *No vision is ever a curse*, the Canon had replied.

"But on her thirteenth birthday, the pattern changed. Late that afternoon, the staff suddenly vanished (they would reappear later in the evening). The Canon swept in, bulky beneath the heavy velvet he wore, and took the girl onto his lap.

"*The flower is formed,* he muttered. Then, in a whisper, to himself: *The sweet nectar at the core.*"

I could feel the expectancy in the room; I could see it in the faces around me. Only Barnaby seemed not to be listening, lost in some faraway private domain, an elsewhere that in some intimate way included me.

"It struck the girl as odd that with all the care her master had taken with her wardrobe he should tear so at her clothes. He repeated these same actions on the next visit, and the next.

"The girl quickly grasped that this was the new order of things. Sometimes, the Canon instructed that the clothes he tore be mended, and then the servant girls would sit stitching into the night. On other occasions, he would simply press the ruined fabric to his nose and inhale."

Barnaby took his hands from his chin. Why the look of puzzlement, as if he'd been presented with a difficult theorem it was somehow his business to solve?

The story went down well, judging from the general liveliness that replaced the crowd's prior drowsiness. Afterward, the room emptied with the usual uninhibited performance of bonhomie—too-ardent back slaps and goodnight kisses, the more sober supporting the less. Until there were just the two of us, Barnaby and me, alone.

"Misfiled," I lied, when Barnaby asked me about the tale. "In the Agriculture section at the New York Public Library. I was looking for something on the history of corn and there it was. A facsimile edition of the original diary which was published in 1821, two hundred years after it was written."

It was an unseasonably cold night and earlier Barnaby had

made a fire. Now, three burning coals—all that remained of it—eyed us redly from the grate.

"There's the matter of the truth quotient," he said quietly.

"Diaries always tell some kind of truth, don't you think?" I rejoindered.

"The question is, what is the truth of it for you?"

I took a cigarette from the polished wooden case on the table. Barnaby did not rise to light it but sat peering at me, head cocked, the vertical shadow in his cheek.

"That's changing the rules of the game," I said, striking a match. Looking at Barnaby, I was suddenly blindsided by an intuition that my marriage to Simon depended, in some crucial way, on the abiding love of this man.

"I imagine you keep a diary," he said. "A journal. Some account of your life."

Oscar furnished Galois, and now the tarry smoke hung in the air between us.

"As a matter of fact, I do."

"And how does the truth quotient figure in that?"

I flicked ash into the bronze ashtray, shook my head. "Barnaby, your parlor game and my personal life are two quite different matters."

The smoke thinned; through the dissolving, gauzy swatches, I could see that the shadow in Barnaby's cheek had disappeared, leaving not a trace of the rogue about him.

"Are they?"

Typically, when I came into the yellow suite, I would find Simon at the desk. Sometimes he would be staring out the window; then, he would turn to look at me, offering a faint smile. At other times, he seemed not to notice my presence, keeping his head lowered as his pen moved across the page. I would walk quietly into the bedroom, sit by the window in the chintz chair, and read, glancing occasionally out at the scene below me—a gardener raking the lawn, a handful of flush-cheeked guests returning from a walk, servants covering a trellis table with white linen and then lining up glasses and setting out little dishes that would later hold olives and nuts and tiny sweet gherkins.

This time, when I opened the door, Simon put down his pen and looked up. He rose and crossed to where I stood in the middle of the gold rug with its border of bright green leaves. He raised his hand and with one finger stroked the side of my neck. For an instant, I looked into eyes that were certain of what they saw and yet claimed to know nothing. In the slow time of the slowest waltz we edged toward the bedroom. The sheets were crumpled into clusters of unruly shells; we lowered ourselves onto the bed and they rustled beneath us.

Later, we lay there together sipping brandy, the curtains raised, lights out. Modest starlight gave a shady cast to the room.

"The University of Montreal has a visiting writer's fellowship," Simon said. "The person they had lined up for the summer program canceled. They've invited me to come in his place."

"Would you like to go?" In the dim light, the brandy shone black like tar.

"They want me for the month of August." He turned, looked at me calmly, openly, a little sadly. I put my snifter on the nightstand and lit a cigarette, aware that my heart was pounding.

"You'd be happy there," I said. "A chance to exercise your French and write in outdoor cafés. You could pretend it was Paris."

Simon took my chin in his hand, turned my head toward him. "Would you visit?" he asked.

"Darling, of course."

I rested my cigarette in the ashtray. We kissed. Simon closed his eyes. I looked at his lids, picturing his gaze, longing for the force of it, relieved to be free of it, aching all over for him, unsure what part of my pounding heart was panic and what part the slithering thrill of freedom.

All week long, back in Manhattan, my mind flew forward to the weekend. When Friday morning came, I found myself dawdling—packing and repacking my small valise, flitting about to tidy this and that.

I smoked the whole way there, the window unrolled, the summer air rushing in and tousling my hair. Thelonius Monk crackled on the radio, leaving me feeling slightly off-kilter; Simon relaxed, enjoying the music. Though we were driving at quite a speed, time felt irritatingly sticky and slow.

Eventually, we pulled into the driveway. My mouth felt dry. Simon smiled one of his infrequent, happy smiles and patted my hand.

"Run along, squirrel," he said sweetly. "I know you're eager to see your friends."

I stepped slowly from the car feeling puzzled, then walked around to Simon's side and kissed him through the open window.

"See you at dinner, darling," I said.

Dinner seemed to go on for hours.

Why not, I thought, taking another sip of Oscar's port, which sometimes, as on that night, when the sky outside was inky and blank, glowed so deep it was almost purple. Why not honor Barnaby's rule: really tell them some of the truth as I see it?

And then, there we were, Barnaby and I in the lead, heading up the stairs to the green room, me in the grip of an edgy desire—to show them something. Not just to tell a story, but to really make them see. Images from a troubling photographic assignment in the South clamored inside my skull, pressing for release. I sat in my usual place, waited for Barnaby to do the honors with the drinks. I could feel the grimness in my face, was uncomfortably aware of the locked bone hinge of my jaw. I surveyed the room; these people I only half knew with their cool linen jackets and sleek silk dresses, smooth brows and eyes glazed by not enough to think about and too much good wine. I wanted to take them away from all this; I wanted to take them *there*.

I had in mind a picture I had shot which appeared in a book I collaborated on years ago with a writer friend—of a sharecropper family in its shack. I had never here, in America, seen such poverty. It had seeped into the woman's face; the children, too, were all of a piece with it, the way opulence becomes similarly stamped into the physical being of the wealthy. At the epicenter of the scene was the woman; in her arms, a bowlegged boy, too old to be held, and beside her, a girl of about thirteen, who wore a threadbare dress that seemed pasted on with filth. In all their eyes, the same strained bleakness.

"In a small town in Alabama, long before the war, a sharecropper's daughter was raped," I began. As I described the woman's circumstances, I recalled following her into a small room misshapen as the poor woman's face: relived the feel of the camera before my face, the woman stone still, bearing the boy, regarding me without accusation as I focused and shot. *She's turned to salt*, I remember thinking, focusing on her pale blue eyes, which I knew would show up slug-brown in the prints.

I told the comfortable little group about how word of the rape had traveled and how the first order of business for the town was to nail a suspect. This they went about with a certain glee; it didn't much matter who it was, so long as the color of his skin was black. As I talked, I recalled how easily the pictures had slid from my eyes, how alive I'd felt with the disconcerting harmony of the compositions.

I glanced over to Barnaby; he was looking at me uncertainly. I wondered what he was thinking.

There was murmuring in the room; the guests were restless. I knew I was losing their attention, but I didn't care. This account was not for them. I wanted to show Barnaby what I'd seen. To let him know that I saw Oscar's playground as just a pleasantry, a diversion. But I realize now, too, that it was also a test. It's easy to sit back and watch. I wanted to know if Barnaby was also willing really to *see*.

Barnaby eyed me oddly, as if caught between avoidance and approach. It was the first time I'd seen him look uncomfortable, and it intrigued me. And then, I could see that he'd made some kind of decision: not to listen to what I was saying, not to hear the story, after all.

"The townsfolk were going to have a lynching. No matter that one of the sharecropper's cousins as much as owned up to the rape, with little more than a slap on the wrist as punishment. They found a young black man and the sheriff booked him, though he conveniently forgot to lock the door of the prison hut. You can imagine the man's fate."

My fellow weekenders were clearly disgruntled. A few polite and unconvincing remarks were made about the importance of my work in the South, but within very short order, the group dispelled, off to other distractions. Barnaby and I took leave of the green room along with the last of them. He offered me his arm; gingerly, I took it.

Outside, I drew my shawl around my shoulders. We strolled to the edge of the patio and Barnaby leaned against the old silver birch. Its dangly pods released a handful of delicate gray-green seed flakes down on our heads.

"I'm not sure how much longer I can stand this," Barnaby said, looking at me with smiling eyes.

"I could spare you any more accounts of the South," I responded.

"I'm not talking about your stories."

Barnaby put his hand on my waist and drew me toward him. The sureness of his reach stilled everything, snatched away my confusion. He had, of course, failed my test; there was no question about it. But in that moment, it no longer mattered; the very notion of a test seemed childish and absurd. I smiled back, allowed myself to be brought close. There *was* something marvelous in those eyes, behind the easy charm. And then, this recognition: that I liked what Barnaby had turned me into.

From the back foyer, I watched as the others headed across the lawn toward the jetty, some holding bathing suits, others with long-stemmed flutes or a bottle of champagne. When they disappeared over the hump, I sat down at the piano and turned to a Chopin prelude. I floated with the music, forgot the tepid crowd and their bland remarks. The pressure, deceptively gentle, of the descent into the musical depths.

Flashes of London: actual moments bubbling forth then flattening again to nothing. The terrible charred taste after a bombing, of inhaled ash. The feel of my camera—bewildered faces in the viewfinder, as if awaiting nothing but the snap of the shutter. The awful performance of the street, with its random guttings and deletions. And later, a house—or what was once a house—before which stood a boy, who could not have been more than seven or eight. He wore a green jacket: a drab olive-gray green, a color now burned into my memory. Everywhere, as far as the eye could see, visual compositions of gripping interest and complexity.

The sudden sense, once again, of eyes. No tapping, the cane gone, now, for some weeks. I turned my head and there he was, emerging from the shadows.

"Please, don't stop playing," he said. I turned my eyes back to the music. Barnaby's soft footfall behind me, the feel of his approach. And then the warmth of his hand, moving my hair away from the back of my neck, the warmth of his hand in my hair. I faltered at the keys.

"I enjoy listening to you play," he said, his voice a whisper.

I lifted my hands, let them fall into my lap. "Are you always there? Watching? Listening?"

Barnaby said nothing, leaned down until his lips were close to my ear. I turned to face him; found, in the shadowy light thrown down by the wall sconces, that the hovering in his face was gone. Only stillness now, and a kind of pulsing certainty. Motionless, his hand there in my hair. The sound of his calm breath. As if he were breathing me in, taking in the whole of me through his olfactory sense.

I was the one finally who drew toward him. I placed my lips on his, though I had no sense of choosing to do so.

When Barnaby drew back from the kiss, his eyes were probing. "You look different," he murmured, making warm, slow circles on the back of my neck.

"People look different when you've kissed them," I replied.

Later, sitting at the dressing table, I heard the floorboards creaking in the next room as they bore the weight of Simon crossing to the bedroom. His compact frame appeared in the doorway, reflected in the mirror. I could see him watching me as I smoothed face cream into my forehead. I was thinking of the kiss—of me kissing Barnaby, of Barnaby kissing me. In the mirror, I saw my hand frozen on my forehead, as if stuck there with glue.

"You're looking lovely tonight," Simon said.

I put down the little porcelain jar and, in the mirror, our eyes met. Simon was smiling an open, direct, unfamiliar smile. There it was, the kind of openness I so often longed for from him. The merest glimpse of it; I shuddered that it should be now, *now*—not an hour after the kiss at the piano, the only moment of infidelity in seven ecstatic, disorienting, painful years of marriage to a man I continued to love with a fearful intensity that thrilled and unbalanced me. I waited, tightening the lid onto the jar, watching the stealth return to the balanced contours of Simon's face. I reached for a tissue to wipe off my hand. Simon disappeared from the mirror and I listened as he walked back into the sitting room, puzzling over the image that had come to mind of a long dark passageway, a door cracking open, a knife of yellow light.

When Simon told me he wanted to remain in Manhattan the next weekend—that despite his efforts he found Ellis Park too much of a distraction from his work—I felt relieved; it seemed somehow right that I should go there alone.

I enjoyed the drive up; I cruised along slowly, leaving the radio off. After arriving, I took a long bath, then lay down, intending a five-minute nap. I awoke to find I had missed dinner. I dressed and made my way to the green room. I knew when I saw Barnaby sitting there alone, leafing through a copy of *Life* magazine, that he was not expecting anyone else to appear, and that he had been waiting for me.

Up until that moment, everything that had passed between us was connected with an Ellis Park event: a party or dinner, breakfast on the terrace, an amble in the woods or croquet, the storytelling evenings. Now, looking at Barnaby, I had the sense that Ellis Park and everybody who comprised it—the guests and servants, the stable hands, the endless stream of delivery men—had been a kind of scaffolding upon which we had, without realizing it, constructed something that could now exist on its own. The metal frame and planks could be removed; the structure behind it was complete.

"The troops have deserted," Barnaby said, closing the magazine and placing it on the coffee table.

"So I see." I stood in the doorway. We looked at each other.

"Marvelous pictures," he said.

"You like factories?" I asked.

"I worked in one once. Long time ago. Buttons."

I laughed.

"You wouldn't think it, but they're actually rather complicated."

"Of course. They could be large or small, have two holes or four."

Barnaby rose and moved toward me. It was as if we both understood that this room had served its purpose, that we no longer needed it and were free to leave. He reached over and touched the top button of my blouse with the tip of his forefinger.

"There's more to it than that," he said, letting his finger drift up to my cheek. A long pause. Then: "I missed you at dinner."

"I took a nap. I guess driving up by myself made me sleepy."

"By yourself?"

"Simon decided to stay in the city."

"I see," Barnaby said, reaching across me to the wall and flicking off the lights.

He took my arm and we headed downstairs, along the hallway, and into the morning room, where French doors opened onto the patio.

I had no idea where we were going, though once we stepped into the mild air it was clear, from the decisiveness of his step, that Barnaby had a destination in mind. I held onto his arm and we glided across the lawn. We cut through the vegetable garden and took a path that ended at a shed, beyond which stretched an uninviting wilderness. Barnaby unbolted the rusty door, struck a match, and led me around bits of machinery to a door at the back. This he unlocked with a key he took from his trouser pocket, and we emerged onto a tiny path, which cut through the thick brush and had to be taken single file.

Barnaby led the way, reaching behind with his arm to steer me along. Around us, the ringing silence and clinging green scent of leaves. And a sense of uncanny precision—as if even this woolly terrain, in all its disorder, were part of some larger scheme, left wild as a contrast to the carpetlike lawns and the driveway with its trained canopy of leaves: calculated, somehow, down to the squawking of magpies, the menacing slow circling of hawks, the scramblings of rabbits and squirrels away from their slithering fork-tongued foes.

We walked for some time in silence. And then: something glinting above a thicket in the beam of the new moon. We wove through the dense arbor and there it was, a glass structure the size of a large room with a pagoda-shaped roof. Barnaby pulled a second key from his pocket.

"I didn't even know this place existed," I whispered.

"Oscar keeps it a secret," Barnaby replied, turning the key in the door.

The storm, the one they called Eleanor, took us all by surprise. It plucked the pier from its pylons and dashed it against the rocks, littering the cove with giant splinters. Early July, during one of our midweek visits to Ellis Park, Simon and I had the house virtually to ourselves. On weekends, Oscar had begun to spend more and more time alone in his study, though he still attended to his hostly duties. During the week, he more or less handed the running of the place over to Wallace, emerging from his rooms only briefly in the late evening to share a nightcap. Then, he would smile his wry smile, but he was unable to disguise the gauntness of his cheeks, the black patches beneath his eyes.

It was already dark when we set out, but the lights along the pier and outlining the curve of shoreline across the Sound sufficiently illuminated our way. The first half hour, we walked in silence. The rain began slowly, light sporadic pellets that glanced our clothing and hair. It's a strange form of company, walking with somebody side by side, and yet sunk airtight in your own mind. For a while I scrounged for something entertaining or amusing to say, but the sight of Simon's distant, closed face withered my thoughts before they could take hold.

The storm quickly turned muscular, fisting up handfuls of sand, the rain stinging with cold. A scene worthy of a Romantic poet, I thought: morbid and ecstatic. I wondered about the opening in the sheer sandstone face, through which we usually made our way back up the incline toward the house; it had as good as disappeared.

For a brief instant the sky cleared, and behind Simon I saw the giant rise and curl of a wave. In the riot of the storm it was silent, flattening back to the sea with portentous ease. Simon quickened his pace; my arm fell away from his and he gained several yards on me. Beyond him, I spied a moving form, someone stumbling into the storm. I closed the gap between us and grabbed onto Simon's arm.

"Look!" I shouted, pointing at the unsteady figure just discernible in the wavery wet thickness of the storm. Simon seized my arm, quickening his pace to a run. I glanced up in time to see the slow swivel backward of the man's face. I registered an oddly mild gaze, eyes somehow unfazed by life's troubles, before the man realized he had company here, on the stormy beach. He seemed to know me, though I'd never seen him before. He pulled his jacket more tightly about him and broke into a run.

"Hey!" Simon called out. "Come back here!" We set off in pursuit, my arm beginning to ache where Simon had tightened his grip. We continued that way for some minutes; I could feel my legs weakening. I suddenly had no curiosity about the man up ahead; I was aware only of the desire to stop moving. I wrenched my arm free of Simon and stood, watching the man disappear into what must have been an opening in the sandstone wall—our *sortie*, at last, as well. Simon turned an impatient face toward me.

"Well? Do you want to lose him?" he shouted.

"What if we do?" I shouted back.

Simon shrugged and pushed on ahead. I stood, watching his back, appreciating the grace of his movements, aware of a stark and sorrowful aloneness.

There was nothing dramatic about the evening, a week or so after the storm on the beach, when I stumbled upon Oscar's darkroom. After dinner, back in the yellow suite, Simon and I had a fight, if one can use that word to describe what went on between us when things went wrong.

Trivial, that was the word Simon had used. Everything here, at Ellis Park. Not that he minded superficiality—after all, we'd both found it amusing, this anthropological mission into the heart of decadent frivolity. But he was accusing me of having become tainted with it, of having become too involved, of having become trivial myself.

I wasn't sure what, exactly, had set off Simon's opprobrium. I'd been in a particularly buoyant mood that evening, and had come into the yellow suite exuberant. I'd seen it in Simon's face the moment I entered—that barbed closedness. I foolishly thought I could cheer him out of it—in any case, I chatted happily about the evening's festivities, pretending I hadn't noticed his mood. I poured myself a drink from the decanter on the lowboy.

"Honestly," Simon said, "aren't you sick of all this?"

"It's really quite harmless. And fun. It gets me away from—"

"From what?" he interrupted, his voice almost sneering, snuffing out my high spirits, which were replaced by a panicky surge of grief.

"I was going to say from my work."

"Oh, your *work*," he responded, the same unpleasant tone in his voice.

Even after all these years, I did not understand the odd weather between Simon and me, the way the warmth would flow and then seize to ice. The way my own being would oscillate as a result—now expansive and hotly alive, now curtailed to a shivering, blank-eyed anomie. What I least understood were Simon's dissatisfactions; when the weather turned sour, he saw me as all failings and faults. Try as I might to correct these, to find my way back into Simon's graces, so that his clear, world-seeing eyes might smile again my way, I would end up feeling powerless, in the position of simply having to wait out the downturn.

But here, now, was something new. Not just the shades of unkindness and disregard I had come to dread when these moods settled over Simon. I wondered if he knew—if Simon knew about Barnaby and me. But this did not seem like the pain or anger of a jealous lover. In that moment, it was as if Simon disdained everything about me—including my life's work. As if I were some sort of deluded amateur, with nothing interesting to say or show, full of posturing and pretension and no different from the fops and frauds he saw peopling Ellis Park.

"Yes, my work," I repeated slowly, setting my drink down and turning to face him.

There it was, in his face: Simon, my husband, was looking at me with contempt.

"I'm sorry," I muttered, aware that we were caught in an awful band of misery that led nowhere but back on itself. The yellow walls were pressing in on me; I made my way to the door.

The moment I was outside, my head began to clear. I walked quickly across the stones of the courtyard and out onto the lawn. Above me, the filmy light of invisible stars seeped through a thick bank of cloud. I walked to the bottom of the long driveway and stood for a while examining the fantastic ironwork gates Oscar had shipped from Spain; adorned with netherworld characters and ferocious animallike plant life, they separated Ellis Park from the world. Not yet ready to return to our suite, I followed the driveway around behind the house and climbed the four brick steps to the back entrance. Inside, I proceeded down the dimly lit hallway.

All around me, the sleeping house: and, from some damp space in the bowels of the building, the rumbling of the boiler. Beyond the double doors at the end of the main corridor lay the servants' quarters. I pushed through the doors and tiptoed past these rooms.

I recalled something that Oscar had mentioned on one of my earliest visits: that he kept a photographic studio in the basement—a darkroom, he had called it. "Silly of me," he had remarked. "To suppose my hobby would amount to much. Actually, I've never used it." At the time I didn't give it another thought, content for Ellis Park to be the haven from work Oscar intended it to be. Once, my work had offered me refuge, but in recent years, it had begun to weigh me down; those grim fragments of the world, patched together by my camera, often felt heavy and uncomfortable as a lead apron. On my weekends here, I was happy to escape from darkrooms: sometimes makeshift affairs in motel bathrooms, but principally the maid's room in our apartment on Riverside Drive, where I had blackened the window with tar paper and corked the walls to block out sound.

But now, tired and unsettled by the encounter with Simon, I found the idea of the privacy of Oscar's darkroom, if I could find it, soothing. I took the stairs down slowly, aware of the plush feel of the runner against my bare feet. I brushed my hand along the moldings, set midway up the walls; the horizontal spine gave me the feeling of being guided, as if the wall itself were gently leading the way.

Midway along the hallway, I tried the handle of a door. Locked. The door beside it: also locked. At the very end, a door yielded; I took one step into the space, sensing, in the blackness, its vastness. I felt on the wall by the door for a switch and, when I found it, flipped it on. Soft light, thrown out by a lamp on a metal countertop, revealed a large, clean space: three stainless steel sinks stood beside long metal shelves that were stacked neatly with bottles and jars.

I made a slow circuit of the room. In the far corner, a heavy black curtain reached from ceiling to floor. The fabric gave off the same burnt-wood odor I remembered from the yards of blackout cloth I had cut and sewn and fixed to my windows in London. I drew it aside to discover a cubicle designed for developing photographs: two sinks with shiny metal pans, and thick wires overhead holding clusters of padded wooden pegs. I turned back to the main part of the studio. There was a bank of switches on the wall beside me; I flicked them all up at once. A low hum, and then a fluorescent blast. The force of it imparted a disconcerting sense of agency to the space, as if the room itself had widened a set of mindless chill eyes and taken two giant steps toward me.

But there was something missing. I ran my hand across the smooth metal countertop. Beneath it was a large drawer, equipped with a lock and key. I opened a cabinet, and surveyed the containers and bottles. I lifted a jar and shook it; inside, the liquid gently swished. A ghostlike realm of plenty, I thought. Then it clicked: no seeping acid odor, that was the problem.

I recalled a time, long ago, when I had coaxed a medical student friend to let me accompany him to the dissection room, where he would arrive before classes to clock up extra study time. I was not put off by the acrid-sweet formaldehyde in the laboratory; it was not so different from the silver chloride and bromide washes I used in my work. He'd pulled instruments from his bag and set to work on an elderly man. I leaned over my friend's shoulder and focused my lens on the blank mask with its rawhide lips and rickety teeth. How apt, I remember thinking, that this world, too, like that other silently peopled universe I inhabited, with its own vivid forms of lifelessness, should give off similarly corrosive fumes.

Not in Oscar's darkroom, though: nothing to burn tears

to the eyes. Only the mustiness of windows kept closed for too long, the empty stillness of an unused room. So different from the green room which, I now realized, I had not set foot in since the last of our storytelling evenings. Always the signs, there, of life: an empty tumbler stained at the rim, reading glasses forgotten on a lowboy beneath a series of botanical prints, a vase of carnations with one headless stem, which made you think of the bloom affixed, somewhere in the house, on the lapel of a guest.

My mind drifted back to those strange evenings in that room, to the story I told about my work in the South. I saw again the woman and child in the wretched room, both of them imbued with the frightful aliveness of Pompeians, preserved in the midst of some vibrantly quotidian act. Each detail was uncannily precise: a fly on the lacerated mattress, its tiny shadow bulging slightly on a coil of stuffing; on the table, a small shank of lamb, the fuzzy dark edges suggesting it has turned.

Describing this scene in the green room that night, I had been aware of the intimate, glassy space of the viewfinder, and of the way the room beyond the camera had looked both larger and smaller than it actually was, clearer in its details and yet reassuringly remote.

I felt overtaken by a hankering for that time—how many years ago was that?—when the photographs offered themselves to me, the world responsive and yielding both, like a lover.

And then, there he was, the little boy standing before the ruins of his house—beyond my camera, and yet for a brief moment also trapped in the glass of the viewfinder—silent, head bowed, his foot toying with a piece of rubble.

"He managed to get to the cellar," the rescue worker had whispered, pausing in his work. "It saved his life."

My camera was raised; I'd been readying for the shot. It was an exquisite composition, I could see that. The skies had obliged with curiously subtle pyrotechnics: ashy gray streaked with bright metallic shades I'd never before seen, ancient and otherworldly. But for his barely moving foot, the boy was utterly still. I wondered about the charred block his foot found so irresistible, whether it was a burnt toy, or a remnant from some piece of furniture as familiar to him, as inevitable and indestructible, as the hand of his mother, or his father's voice: the base of a nightstand, perhaps, the top of a bedpost, or a piece from the wing of a piano he'd spent countless hours practicing. Or maybe it was nothing he recognized at all, a piece of detritus as meaningless as a spent coal in a grate.

It was not the kind of shot one comes upon often; I could feel the rising thrill of a real find.

Now, I had one last look around the studio, then turned off the lights and took my leave. Back along the corridor, up one flight, and through the servants' quarters. I moved quickly through the main section of the house. It felt good to be back among these familiar rooms. I gained the stairway and took the stairs two at a time.

Entering our suite, I kicked off my shoes and headed across the room, glancing at Simon, who was not asleep as I expected but at the desk, reading. I walked through the French doors and fumbled at the lamp switch. Opening the armoire, I pulled aside the clothing, removed my portfolio, and withdrew its contents. I went through the contact sheets, one by one, each a barrage of images; it felt like being yelled at insistently by a riled crowd.

"Marilyn?" I could hear Simon calling from the next room. "Marilyn, is everything all right?"

I nodded, yes, everything was all right, as if expecting that Simon could see my silent reply through Oscar's solid, wallpapered walls.

I hastily gathered up the contact sheets and stuffed them back into the leather case. Without bothering to put on my shoes, I slipped back through the bedroom, avoiding Simon for the third time that evening.

"I'll be back soon," I mumbled. I could feel his eyes following me as I walked toward the door.

Back downstairs, the route to the studio was already charged and familiar, inevitable and compelling as a memory.

I stashed the proof sheets in the empty drawer, the one that locked, then hid the key in the developing cubicle and again took leave of the studio. Morning was upon the house; the servants would soon be up.

Deep into the writing of his book, Simon became increasingly distant, and less interested than ever in Ellis Park. This suited me. In the past three weeks, Simon had come up only once—the night, as it happened, that I discovered the darkroom—and then, his presence had felt like an intrusion. In Simon's absence, I was able to sneak out late at night to the glass house without fear of discovery.

Barnaby and I were, of course, discreet, though at first I anguished that some guest or other might figure out what was going on and let something slip that would find its way back to Simon. As time passed, however, I realized that whatever I might think of Oscar's medley of acquaintances and guests, there was a compact about the place as sturdy as the redbrick itself. That there was a mutual granting of impunity from the rules of our everyday lives, as if we were masked participants at a Renaissance ball: that no one would be likely to stand in the way of this wayward freedom—the freedom to remake oneself, to be, within the confines of Ellis Park, whomsoever one wanted to be.

That first evening, after the little glass structure had magically appeared before us in the woods, Barnaby had retrieved a number of Japanese screens from where they were stacked against one wall and arranged them around the room to afford us privacy. From a box made of knotty Moroccan root wood, he'd withdrawn a handful of candles, which he set on the floor in little glass holders at intervals around the octagonal-shaped structure. Once lit, the candles threw a wavery light out into the night.

"Won't somebody see us?" I whispered.

"Nobody comes into the woods at night. Besides, there are the screens."

"But the light . . ."

"I told you, it's a secret," Barnaby whispered back. "We're the only ones, besides Oscar, who know it's here."

I scarcely knew what I was getting into with Barnaby, but strangely I didn't seem to care, an attitude that was aided by the development in myself of a perplexing new habit of memory. From the early-morning hour, in which Barnaby and I took a sometimes calm, sometimes frantic leave of each other, until the next time we met again by the shed at the end of the vegetable garden, it was as if Barnaby, or, I should say, the Barnaby of our trysts, simply ceased to exist. When I saw him during the day—at meal times, on outings, in the library or the ground-floor sitting room—I had no vivid sense of the long slow hours in the glass house, the moonlight pouring in and washing us both a luminous white. It was not that I forgot: more a matter of being overtaken by the busy, innocuous day life of Ellis Park in which no purpose seemed possible beyond the current round of drinks, the next meal, the plan for a ride into town. Everything else took on a two-dimensional quality, so if I happened to think of the glass house, what came to mind was the image of two stick figures walking stiffly among papier-mâché trees, entering a box made of plastic squares, and lying down together, wooden and inert. I knew there was something absurd about the schism that had rent the day, for me, from the night, but I couldn't help treating it with a certain respect.

There were other schisms too.

On the third of my late-night vigils in the darkroom, where I was working on putting together my exhibition and writing the essay that would go into the catalog, I was startled by the sound of the door handle turning. Instinctively, I gathered up the proof sheets spread across the bench and covered them with my arms. Looking over my shoulder, I saw the surprised face of Oscar.

"Why, Marilyn," he said. He was holding something in his hand, what looked like a leather-bound notebook. "I see you've discovered my darkroom. I'm glad someone is making use of it." He approached the counter. "What are you up to?"

I looked down at the bench. Beneath the crisscross made by my arms, I could see the angular stubble-covered head of a girl and, below that, the corner of another picture: striped pajama-ends dangling six or seven inches above the ground and the twig-thin ankles of a man. I slid a sheet of paper over the top.

"Oh," I said lightly. "Preparing something for an exhibition. And you? What brings you down here?"

Oscar glanced at what I could now see was a portfolio of some kind. When he looked back at me, there was sorrow in his eyes, though he tried to mask this with an unconvincing smile.

"Actually, I had in mind a little project," he said casually, his tone as unconvincing as his smile. He opened the cover of the portfolio and gingerly pulled out two photographs, medium-sized sepia prints. Each had several creases running both horizontally and vertically, suggesting they had been folded into small squares. He smoothed them down on the countertop. Portraits, flamboyantly signed in the lower right-hand corner in white ink.

The larger of the two showed a formally posed family: a woman with pale eyes and light hair and a gracious smile—Oscar's mother, I supposed, her face a female version of his own. Beside her, a gray-haired man with a slender nose, his expression an unexpected mix of roguishness and duty. On each side of the couple was a child; both had the woman's pale eyes, and while the boy, the young Oscar, had his mother's light hair, the girl's curls were dark. The second picture was a close-up of the woman. Here she was less guarded, her lips slightly parted, something almost too direct about her gaze.

"I want to restore these," Oscar said.

"I'm just the woman for the job."

Oscar shook his head. "I'd like to do them myself."

When Oscar came to the studio again the next evening, he brought a newspaper, folded into a narrow column to fit into his jacket pocket. I could see a fragment of headline: something important, the letters larger and bolder than usual.

"I've brought you some tea," he said, setting a silver thermos down on the countertop. He sat on the metal chair beside me and pulled out his newspaper. I turned back to my photographs.

He seemed to read every page completely through from top to bottom, judging by the long lapse between each rustling turn. Some time must have passed, for when I next looked up I saw that Oscar had finished reading his paper and had lain it on the floor by his feet.

"How is it coming along? Your work on the exhibition," he asked.

I took off my glasses and rubbed my eyes, which smarted from the long hours of close work. "I'm focusing on the catalog now."

Oscar's eyes were ringed with weariness. He pointed to the thermos. "You look like you need it," he said. "It's probably still warm."

I nodded. Oscar rose and poured tea into a clean beaker he removed from the cabinet. I peered down at the shiny surfaces of my prints. Without my eyeglasses, the shapes swam around, bearing little relation to one another. The composition of one—a photo taken by a colleague—caught my eye, seemed, for a moment, beautiful. But for their striped garb, I could almost have believed the people in the series before me, crowded together in a large barnlike structure, had gathered for some social event—a party, perhaps, or a country dance. I was tempted to say, *A dance, Oscar, they're photographs of a dance.* I said nothing, replaced my glasses on the bridge of my nose, and picked up my beaker of tea.

Oscar lifted his own beaker and raised it toward mine. "To your exhibition," he said.

There was nothing for it but to raise my beaker and smile back.

CHAPTER FIVE

Such sashays of weather: stretches of scorching heat; dank moody spells that set the air above the Sound to festering; sudden brief downpours that freshened the lawns. On one rainy night, Barnaby slipped me a note at dinner. *The Blue Suite? After midnight . . . The rain.*

Back in the yellow suite, I took a quick shower, aware of how completely these rooms, in Simon's continued absence from Ellis Park, had come to seem my own. Then, instead of making my way down to the basement darkroom, I wound through the corridors of the west wing, glimpsing the dripping trees outside each time I passed a window. No one was about: it felt as if we were the only two souls in the house—Barnaby, waiting in his suite, and me, on my way to meet him.

When he saw me at the door, Barnaby lifted me and carried me into his sitting room, where he placed me gently in the blue velvet chair by the window so that my legs draped over the arm. Beginning at the hem, he slowly opened several of the buttons that ran the length of my green silk dress. He knelt beside me on the floor, slipped his hand through the opening, and caressed my knee.

I knew, then, that despite his conquistador persona, our affair had nothing to do with conquest. It was a more abstract, less personal matter, though nonetheless deeply felt. Barnaby knew something I had glimpsed only from afar—something sinister, though it was a knowledge he hid; he had been somewhere and did not want others to know. This was not without a certain irony—after all, Barnaby was Ellis Park's storyteller. But then, perhaps all his talk about tramping through the Himalayas, about steamy Chinese villages and the erotic dances of Tibet, were partly a way of distracting from journeys of another kind.

"Why do you think everybody stopped coming to your storytelling salon?" I asked.

"You mean *our* salon. You were, after all, the star raconteur."

"It was me, wasn't it."

Barnaby's hand, gently stroking, moved up my thigh. "You may have misjudged our fellow revelers."

"But they couldn't get enough of Africa," I said. "Of hearing about Charlie and his terrible fate, for example."

"Darling, that's precisely what I mean."

Looking into Barnaby's face, I felt a spear of fear unsettling the languid pleasure spreading through me. "But wasn't that the point of it? I know we were playing around with them—shameful, really. But why were they so put off?"

Barnaby's hand was still on my thigh. He paused. "Far-off Africa is one thing," he said. "Playing the hero, the dangers of Mother Nature. But poverty and a lynching, right here in our own backyard. That's another matter entirely."

What he said made sense, of course, though it also made me feel disgruntled. What was Oscar up to? Why had he created this place, this odd community of shallow people?

Barnaby turned his attention back to my thigh.

But Ellis Park was also *this*. Though I was ashamed to admit it, I knew that I was smitten—with Oscar, with Barnaby, with the house and its goings-on, with whatever grand, mysterious scheme of Oscar's lay behind it all.

Barnaby slowly blinked, his eyes hooded; I could see he was swimming in his own pleasure, swimming, disconcertingly, not with me, but *away*.

"You have a lot to learn about this crowd," he said. "Though don't fret, darling. I hate to see you fret." He brought his lips down to my thigh, trailed his moving hand, upward, with his mouth.

* * *

Things with Simon had oddly improved since he'd stopped coming to Ellis Park—and since, I realized with some confusion, I had begun my weekend trysts with Barnaby. This was another of those schisms: my weekday life with Simon an alternate reality to the Ellis Park weekends with Barnaby. There was something peculiarly centering about it for me, as if this divided self were an expression of my true nature—and as if some pneumatic balance had been achieved in channeling to Barnaby some of my too-abundant feelings for Simon. I imagine there was some relief in this also for Simon, though we never discussed it, and to this day I do not know whether he was aware of the affair or not.

I do know that our lives together in Manhattan, Simon's and mine, became dominated by our lovemaking. Our affection had never been casual but always heated and erotic; now, it seemed that even the most glancing touch fired intensity and we'd find ourselves returning to bed again and again, no matter the time of day.

A few days before Simon's departure for Montreal, we abandoned our respective work and spent all our time together, alternating long bouts of raw pleasure in the bedroom with strolls through Central Park and lunches where we talked about our projects, worrying through ideas we were struggling to come to terms with or express.

During the last of those lunches, sitting across from Simon at the diner we frequented, I was aware of a moment of joyous completion; looking into his eyes, eyes that really looked back, that looked deeply into me, I could scarcely contain the goblins of hope leaping about within—that this man, that his love, was mine. The feeling had barely declared itself when it slithered away, leaving behind a bleak little admonition: *Never yours, not this man, not Simon; he'll never give himself, not really, to you.* And quick on the heels of this, sitting in that spare little welcoming place, with its orange booths and beige tile floor and waiters we'd known for years, the old ache spilled forth: the knowledge of Simon's grand passion, the love he'd memorialized in his first novel (for all the world to see). The woman who had shut him out, only fueling the heat of his longing and love, the woman for whom Simon had felt the same kind of bottomless hankering I felt for him.

"Simon," I said, trying to hide my misery, the same as I'd tried moments earlier to hide the tideswell of blinding adoration, "it's your last weekend. Perhaps you'd like to come to Ellis Park."

What was I saying? Doing? Did I want Simon to discover what was going on with Barnaby? Did I want to upset the strange balance I'd achieved?

I peered across at Simon; something about the clarity of his gaze made me want to weep. In that moment, my affair with Barnaby seemed like some terrible mistake someone else had made: what business had such sordid goings-on here, in the crystalline space of my marriage?

I did, in fact, start to weep.

"Whatever is the matter?" Such sweetness, in his face, and real concern.

"I'm worried. About us."

Simon leaned over and took my hand.

"All couples have their ups and downs," he said with childlike simplicity.

"I sometimes feel my heart will break," I replied, unable to stop the tears. I didn't want Barnaby, not really; I had known this in some way all along. This was the man I wanted.

It was almost touching to see how awkward Simon seemed to be in the face of my distress, and how foreign to him the language of comforting. A little bewildered, he continued to pat my hand. How different, Barnaby's enfolding embrace.

"Of course I'll come to Ellis Park, darling," Simon said. I'd forgotten my request and now cringed at the thought of it. "If that's what you'd like."

* * *

It was disorienting, driving up to Ellis Park with Simon for the first time in more than a month.

Dinner was a torture. Barnaby was sitting at the far end of the long table. Try as I did to block out his presence, I felt the pull of him and sat in a terror of expectation that Simon would feel it too. He seemed unperturbed, however, calmly eating the salmon fillet I was unable to bring to my lips.

Simon excused himself after dinner.

"I'm going to work in Oscar's library," he said. "I'll see you later, back in the room."

"I might do some work myself, in the darkroom," I said nonchalantly.

"Of course. Work well," and he was off.

Not two minutes after he left, Barnaby was at my side.

"I see Simon has graced our presence again at last," he said. I was unable to read his tone; he was in full charade mode, which he'd perfected, these last weeks, for the benefit of everybody here.

"He leaves for Montreal on Monday," I explained, struggling to maintain the charade myself.

Barnaby lowered his voice: "I suppose you'll be joining him shortly in your rooms."

"Actually, no," I said, feeling reckless, looking Barnaby straight in the eyes. I squeezed his hand.

We took drinks with the others in the front parlor. I then said my goodnights and headed out, by way of the back entrance, to the glass house. Within ten minutes, Barnaby appeared.

"Marilyn, do you really think this is wise?"

"I told Simon I was going to work in the darkroom. He's in Oscar's library, already off in the land of imagination. There's nothing much that can distract him from that."

I was aware of my own madness, of the seesawing of my mood. Only a few days ago, sitting with Simon in the diner, I had felt aghast at the thought of my liaison with Barnaby. And yet, here I was again, drawn into the power of it. How wrong Barnaby had been that time when he said I was in the business of *teasing the truth out of things*. On the tatami mat now in the glass house with him, I was aware only of my dissimulation and deceit.

I looked up through the panes of the pagoda-shaped roof, up into the blurry dark of the night sky. Barnaby was stroking my neck, taking me in with eyes that could have belonged to anyone caught in the wet mist of loving a person he hardly knows, full of spirit and longing and fire. Barnaby rolled me onto my back then lay on his side, head propped on his hand, and looked at me. I closed my eyes. I could feel his gaze slowly crisscrossing the length of me, at the same time studied and free. Tiny beads of electricity roused where his eyes fell.

I reached out; my fingertips landed on Barnaby's chest. He was as still as I was. The rhythm of our breath slowed until it seemed to cease altogether, and it was not until the room had dissolved in the molten lead space between us that we drew together.

The night was finally lifting when I opened my eyes. Barnaby lay sleeping in my arms. I looked up at the limp bluish haze of the new day and listened to the early-morning sounds of the woods. I started at the sound of a snap—too loud to be a twig broken by a lizard or alighting owl, and too strong a silence following it. A blur at the corner of my vision, just above the screen, which rose to a height just shy, I'd guess, of six feet. I felt suddenly paralyzed, my eyes moved downward to the place where the blur had been. Under my left hand, Barnaby's shoulder was a smooth, warm stone.

There it was again, a white blur above a black shadow. I held my breath; the vision elongated and poured itself into the mold of a face. Two eyes pierced the thing and a pale slash hovered where a mouth would rightly go. I squinted my eyes and the dark form of a tree came into focus, but where the white blur had been was now just a last pocket of night-blood emptying into day.

When I arrived back in the yellow suite that morning close to dawn, Simon stirred. I told him I'd fallen asleep over my work in the darkroom. I climbed into the bed and spooning, we went to sleep.

Finally, close to noon, we awoke. Simon dressed and then sat in the chair by the window reading while I put on some light makeup.

"I was so stiff when I awoke in the darkroom early this morning that I went out for a walk," I said. "I wonder, did you step out too?"

"Why do you ask?" I detected a note of scorn in his voice.

"It's nothing, really," I said, fumbling at the back of my dress with the zipper. The heavy, airless feel of Simon waiting.

"Well, it's just that when I was walking in the woods, I thought I saw—a face." The zipper was stuck. I gave it a tug, which caught the fabric, making matters worse.

"You really think I'd follow you?" Simon asked, his voice glazed hard.

I stepped out of my dress and put my attention to releasing the zipper. I stared, for a moment, at the diamond design woven into the soft jersey cotton.

"Your life is your own," Simon added coolly. There was something savage in the way he said this, as if he were throwing me away. It was only then that I remembered the man on the beach.

"You don't suppose there's someone spying on us," I said. "I mean all of us. Here, at Ellis Park."

"Why would anybody be interested in trailing around after a bunch of privileged weekenders?"

"The man we saw on the beach. He looked at me. It was not the look of a stranger. He seemed to know me."

Simon picked up the book he'd been reading and flipped through to find his place.

"People walk on the beach, Marilyn. I wouldn't make too much of it."

Things became terribly muddled. I couldn't sleep; during the day, I felt dulled, exhausted, and at times confused.

When I was with Barnaby, I often imagined it was Simon who was so eagerly taking me in. I would store up the pleasure of it, and then look forward to the time when I would again see Simon. On one of those nights—they began to bleed into each other—for the first time, I experienced the reverse confusion, at a party in Oscar's grand room. I'd been dancing for hours, and I'd had my share of drinks. I found myself thinking it was Barnaby whose arm held me as I twirled to the sliding wet sound of the saxophone, the heat of the other dancers rising around us. The light in the room when I cracked open my eyes was a cold, faded orange. I almost cried out in surprise when I saw Simon's face above mine, and was even more startled to find his potent gaze filled with longing. There was a moment of terrible confusion, and I felt tears rising in my chest, a child's hopeless, furious tears.

I could no longer imagine my life without either of them; they had, alarmingly, become one. And then, an odd crashing fear that made absolutely no sense, and yet made all the sense in the world: that were I to break things off with Barnaby, I would also lose Simon. That our marriage could no longer bear the weight of—what? Of the depths of my own shameful, human need? The need to merge with another person in order that I might more fully own myself?

But then, that night, I closed my eyes again and forgot about Barnaby, forgot about Simon, forgot about the mess I was in. In the midst of the gentle cacophony, I thought about that dusk moment at Ellis Park, after the members of the quartet had packed away their instruments—the violin and viola in their velvet-lined cases, the clarinet and flute disassembled and wiped—and before the evening meal, when an agitated silence would fall on the house.

When I opened my eyes once more, we had slowed to the slowing music, we were hovering at the rim of the dance floor. On the far side of the room, through the parting crowd, I saw Oscar, standing in a rectangle of bright light. On the tables lining the walls, blossoms floated in glass bowls; the scent of jasmine and lilac drifted over and mingled with the hot dampness of the dancers. Above plates of salmon, and pastries filled with caviar, three towering ice swans melted into cold, crystal lakes.

The following afternoon, at lunch, Oscar invited me to go out riding. We rode for a time through the grounds and then headed into the woods. Where the trail ended, we tied our horses to a tree and took off by foot. We walked in silence, crunching over bark peelings and dried leaves, the summery air alive with birdsong.

"Oscar, I was wondering."

That frozen pause; I'd noticed it before—whenever Oscar was posed a direct question. Perhaps one of the reasons people seldom seemed, with Oscar, to inquire.

"Yes?"

"Barnaby has had so many adventures—you know how much he talks! But I have no idea what he did during the war. Do you?"

Oscar came to a halt: the practiced opacity, I could almost see it settle into his face. "Barnaby's a man who likes to speak for himself. But I don't need to tell you that."

His gaze lingered a little too long; I felt a slow blush rise in my cheeks. It was getting late, the sun had sunken behind the trees. Oscar leaned up against an oak tree and pulled a pipe from his pocket, along with a red leather pouch, then packed the bowl with tobacco. I'd asked about Barnaby, but now it occurred to me to ask about Oscar too—about his famously mysterious past. I opened my mouth to speak, but Oscar, as if intuiting an unwanted question, spoke first.

"You know," he said, puffing on his pipe, "in India, they have a saying. That when a man's head is cleaved with an axe, nothing is really changed. Matter has been rearranged, but not altered, in the scheme of things. A variant, I suppose, on the thermodynamic principle of entropy. Nothing in the universe is created, and nothing destroyed. It's all just rearranged."

There was a gentleness in his voice that seemed to have nothing to do with what he was saying. He looked up at where the setting sun had scattered coins of red and gold.

And then, Oscar cast me a secretive look, as if he had cleverly cheated someone and knew he would get away with it. It was an uncharacteristic expression that nevertheless seemed to capture some deep truth about him. In that instant, everything else I knew about him, which at other moments had the force and reach of his beloved oak trees, seemed suddenly less real: not faded, but the opposite—heightened, disconcertingly transparent, ghostly and illusory, like an overexposed photograph.

Why the alarming frisson of something sinister? I felt thrown: the questions—*And you, Oscar, where were you during the war? Did you fight?*—stuck in my throat. Unfathomably, another question lodged right behind it: *And on whose side?*

Oscar looked at me oddly, took two steps forward, a kind of fierce tenderness in his face. I stiffened, felt the desire to flee, but found I was unable to move. He stopped only inches from where I stood, raised his hand to my cheek. He leaned toward me, as if—as if to kiss me.

"Christine," he whispered, his eyelids fluttering strangely.

I jumped back. "Oscar!" I called out, feeling ridiculous. "It's Marilyn!"

He slowly lowered his hand, blinked once, twice, and

smiled. "But Marilyn, why on earth would you feel the need to tell me your name?"

I blinked myself. Had I imagined it? Was the uncommonly lovely sunset playing tricks on my senses? I let out a little laugh, hoping it would erase the evidence of panic I'd felt a moment earlier. Had Oscar slipped into a moment of transient insanity? Reaching up to touch my face, leaning toward me with eyes I did not know as he uttered the name of some other woman?

His normal, gracious expression returned, along with the distinctive mixture in his pale-blue eyes of careening sadness and a love fit to bursting: for his trees and gardens, for the stately house, wide and generous as a brood mare, for his guests, every one of them, no matter the folly (and there was a lot of folly). He sees it all, I thought, the world stripped to its barest realities. And yet believes in it just the same.

Oscar let out a good-natured laugh, looked at me in that knowing way he had, and waved his arm before him, as if to say the truth of it, whatever it was—the truth about Barnaby, about me, about himself, about everyone at Ellis Park—was nothing but a trifling problem we could leave for somebody else to solve. He crooked my arm in his, then pulled aside a low-hanging branch.

When he spoke again, his voice was buoyant: "Come on, I know we could both use a ride."

That night, the last before Simon's departure for Montreal, Simon and I stayed up until almost dawn, and then crept downstairs for a private toast. In the breakfast room, sitting together on the floral couch, I rested my head on his shoulder. The ceiling fan gently sliced at the air, making the heat flutter around us.

I felt Barnaby's presence before I saw him: looked up to find him in the doorway, a drink in his hand.

"Well hello," he said.

Involuntarily, I stiffened. I didn't know what to say, though I felt I should say something.

"Simon leaves tomorrow for Montreal," is what I said.

"I'd heard a rumor to that effect," Barnaby said. "Fabulous city. I've spent time there myself."

"A prior incarceration?" I inquired, attempting a smile. Barnaby looked down at us coolly from the doorway.

"Self-inflicted, actually," Barnaby answered. He half-raised his drink in Simon's direction. "Bon voyage."

Simon gave a slow dip of the head by way of reply. I fumbled for a cigarette. I could feel Barnaby's eyes on the crown of my head. And then: release—the warm air gone back to being stirred only by the fan. I leaned forward toward the flame Simon offered, glanced up to see that Barnaby was gone.

Simon waited for the cigarette to catch alight, a distant look in his eyes.

"You don't like him, do you," I said.

"Should I?"

"I don't suppose so."

"You like him, though, don't you, Marilyn," Simon said steadily. He shook out the match. I met his gaze, disarmed, as always, by its unwavering intensity.

"I'm not sure that I do," I replied.

Up the stairs, Simon's hand rested gently on my hip. In our room, the tender, slow caresses. He brushed the hair away from my face, in silence he removed my clothes—quietly, quickly; it felt as if they were simply falling away of their own accord. Still fully clothed himself, Simon took me wholly naked in his arms. With one hand, I unbuttoned his shirt; with the other I pulled it off, letting it slip to the floor.

"Simon?"

"Yes, little squirrel?"

"I'm going to miss you."

Nestled against his chest, sliding down, floating up, disappearing into that alive, burning place. I marveled for an instant at the startling possibilities of human travel: each of us pungently alone and yet quietly accompanied.

Oscar called me that week in the city.

"Why don't you spend the rest of the summer at Ellis Park? Now that Simon's away," he said. "There's no one much around during the week; you could work in peace."

Weekdays in the hot city were jangling my already frayed nerves. There seemed no reason to turn down Oscar's invitation. I loaded up the car and left the steaming grime of the city behind.

The next morning, the first of my full-time residency at Ellis Park, I awoke feeling unsettled. The mood hung around me all day and by the time evening came around, I didn't want to go down to the little shed and wait about in the darkness for Barnaby, or embark on the walk, by now so familiar that sometimes I took the lead. But we had planned to meet, so I went.

Curiously, Barnaby seemed unperturbed by my mood. As we walked, I could feel his lightheartedness, which made me more ashamed of the glumness that lodged rock hard in my chest.

In the glass house, he coaxed the life back into me, communing with my body as if he had a private, direct access that bypassed my conscious faculties. And yet, something in me was trained on the darkness outside.

Barnaby was in my arms, cooing endearments, running two fingers up my arm, over my shoulder, along the edge of my collarbone. I could not see his face but I knew he was smiling, I could feel the contentedness lift from him and mingle with the fraughtness of the room. For the hundredth time I scanned the windows, one pane at a time, teasing apart the layers of darkness outside: branches, bark, an endless variety of leaves.

* * *

The next time we made our way through the bushes and trees, the ground ferns flapping at our feet, I eased the thought of the face from my mind by counting our footsteps, listening to the alto chant of an owl, charting the subtle alterations in the air as we moved farther away from the sea.

Instead of our usual highballs, we made coffee, heating the water with a small electric element Barnaby had in his suite. Barnaby also brought some squares of dark chocolate, which he put on a little plate.

"I feel as if somebody's spying on us," I said.

Barnaby paused in his stirring of the coffee, a teasing look on his face. "An ill-wisher of some kind? Intent on exposing illicit doings?"

I shook my head. "It isn't that. I don't think it has anything to do with you and me. I know it's silly, but I have the feeling that something terrible is going on."

Barnaby placed his hand on mine. "What do you mean?"

I didn't know what I meant so I shook my head again. I studied our two hands resting together on the tatami mat. The feeling was of a piece with that unseen electrical flicker that had made me trip back into the apartment building to retrieve my portfolio that long-ago Friday morning at the beginning of the summer when Simon and I were packing up the car. An image flashed through my mind: a crumpled voodoo doll peering out from under coils of red cotton hair, its marble eyes growing feral.

I wondered what Oscar was up to, closeted away in his study, but I didn't want to intrude by asking. Working alone in the darkroom it was comforting, in any case, to look up from time to time, through the high window of the basement, to see the curtains of Oscar's study on the second floor glowing with light—to know that he, too, was awake, immersed in work of his own.

Deep into the night, I glanced up to find the opaque cur-
tained window rent by a bright splinter. Through the crack,
I glimpsed the wood paneling of the far wall. Oscar's fair,
neatly groomed head passed the opening, trailed by a plume
of pipe smoke. Again, the appearance of his head, another
waft of smoke. He was pacing, lost, no doubt, in his thoughts.
I turned back to my work.

When I looked up again some time later, I was surprised
to see the back of a smaller head covered with chestnut hair,
a man who appeared to be several inches shorter than Oscar.
He turned for a moment, revealing his profile. He lifted a thin
cigarello to his lips, drew on it sharply, then exhaled, twisting
his head toward the window so that I could see a slice of his
face full on.

Around the perimeter of the courtyard, Oscar had in-
stalled streetlights from England: old gas lamps, of the kind
still found on some London streets, which he'd had converted
to electricity. After the guests went to bed, all but one were
extinguished, and it was across the distance of the courtyard,
in the light of that one transplanted wrought-iron lamp, that
I intuited, rather than actually discerned, something disturbing about that unfamiliar half face, something inert and decided,
closed to discussion. An instant later, the man disappeared
from view. I studied the empty oblong of light. Then, Oscar's
face appeared. He peaked quickly through the opening before
pulling the curtains shut.

I put this occurrence out of my mind and was reminded
of it a few days later. Hours of scrabbling through notes for
my essay had left me feeling more at sea than when I'd begun.
I left the studio in a state of distress—not knowing how to
proceed or whether I could entirely trust my senses.

We were in the midst of a heat wave. It was Wednesday;
as far as I knew, Barnaby and I were the only guests at the
house. I moved slowly down the darkened hallway: around
me, sleeping servants, empty rooms. The hallway windows

must have been fastened because I remember that even in my light voile dress, I was sweltering. I leaned against the wall and fanned myself with the straw hat I was carrying; the hot fluttering of air around my face was pleasing.

I became suddenly aware of the sound of voices drifting toward me in fragments from the other end of the corridor. I continued down the hall. Yes, they were coming from Oscar's office. I stopped outside his door. Two voices—men— speaking in a foreign language, their voices so low I couldn't make out what language it was. Harsh though, and guttural. It was then that I remembered the man with the chestnut hair I'd sighted through the half-open curtain of Oscar's study. And only then that the memory of the man on the beach from earlier in the summer, that night of the terrible storm, flashed into my mind. There had been something imperious about him—I recalled how clearly I'd felt this—and now, hearing the throaty cadences coming from the other side of the door, I imagined it was the same man. Knowing how protective Oscar was of his evening hours, I couldn't fathom why he'd receive anyone at this time, or why the men would be speaking in whispers. I trained my ear on their voices, trying to penetrate the meaning of those opaque words. A burst of shame—what was I doing eavesdropping like this?—made me turn. I was still clutching my straw hat, which now felt as absurd to the moment as a freshly caught fish. A little louder, now, first one voice, then the other. *German.* The men were speaking German. I had not known that Oscar spoke German.

The sound of a door handle turning: the inner door of Oscar's study. I slipped off my shoes and hastened down the corridor. Whoever it was must have lingered a moment before opening the outer door as I had time to round the corner and start down the stairs without anybody appearing. The person who had left the room—the chestnut-haired man? Alone? Accompanied by Oscar?—must have used the back stairs and exited through the tradesman's entrance.

I took the long way back. And though I was very soon on the other side of the house, well out of earshot of the service entrance, I imagined the sound of riding boots clicking on shiny stones, and a whooshing as made by a cloak through the air when a rider swings onto his mount.

I went on a quick walk before dinner along a path I did not usually take, which wound behind the house and away from the Sound: through the kitchen gardens, past rows of curly headed lettuce, a bushy green quadrant of turnips and carrots, vines heavy with beefsteak tomatoes, and into a shady orchard of apple and pear trees in full summer leaf. Beneath the trees, the fallen fruit collected in mounds. I watched a sparrow choose a shrunken brown pear and set about his fastidious pecking.

I noticed somebody on the far side of the orchard, sitting under a tree on a rock. It was Oscar, immersed in a book. I was again struck by how young he appeared, a fact one seemed to put aside when engaged with him. His gave the impression of being seasoned, a man surely into his forties, though his boyish, unlined face suggested a man not yet thirty. I drew back behind a tree so I would not be seen, and peered around the trunk to observe him; I'd never before seen him alone in the open, away from the house. I felt a pang of guilt for spying on him but also felt unable to move. The person not a hundred feet away, intently studying the page, was strange in that baffling way that somebody you know well can defy your assumptions about them. From our first meeting on the second-floor landing of Ellis Park, I had known there was an elliptical quality to Oscar, but this was something else entirely.

How can I explain?

Long ago, I'd noted the unusual effect Oscar had on his surroundings, and the way this would waver and change. He did not so much fill a room as empty it of extraneousness. In his presence, people and objects acquired a salience, a relationship to one another, an order that seemed harmonious and precise and at the same time ultimately random. There was something translucent about his being, though not the least ill-defined—as if he were a glass sculpture through which one could see the world.

The effect was this: you were never quite sure whether Oscar was actually present at a gathering or not. You might turn to scan the room, expecting to see him leaning against the doorjamb, attentive and bemused, only to discover, having made a thorough search, that he was not to be found. Rattled, disappointed, you would feel as if someone you trusted had deliberately let you down. Then there was the opposite experience. Out with a group on a morning walk through the woods, knowing Oscar's habit was to eat breakfast alone in his rooms, I would turn my head and catch sight of him a little ways behind on the curved path, moving in and out among the trees.

Removed from the context of the group, Oscar was different again. The wide-ranging beam of his social attentiveness would narrow to become acute, and yet also gentle.

The only way I can think to convey Oscar's disconcertingly different auras is to compare them with the effect that differing light can have on the composition of a photograph. A landscape photographed on a sunny afternoon will of course differ from the same landscape photographed on a blustery evening (imagine spears of lightning or a darkening horizon), though the shape of the dead tree trunk against the shoulder of a mountain remains virtually the same in each exposure.

Until I stumbled upon Oscar sitting in the orchard engrossed in his book, I thought I'd had a pretty good grasp of his unusual, shifting nature. But there, in his mystifying solitude, I sensed a transformation of another order. Let me point you back to the example of the two photographs taken at different times of day. I draw your attention, now, to a third photograph. At first, you are puzzled; you have never seen a composition like this, though it is a strangeness you cannot identify. The same landscape scene, with a small house in the middle distance, a summer cottage perhaps, the retreat of someone who likes his peace.

The contours of the house are sharp and clear: they could not be better delineated. Every leaf on the trees surrounding the house and spreading unevenly toward the mountain is visible, even the veins standing out, which you know cannot be, given the scale of the picture. You scan the photograph for clues. What bubbles to consciousness is that in this picture, there is no sky. Moreover, you know, by intuition, that there is also an absence of air. And, while you know rationally that the photograph could not exist without it, you become convinced that what is most decisively missing here is light: no sun, no seepage of day through cloud, no candle or lantern or lamp, no flashbulb, not even the quivering, feather-tip flame of a match. It is impossible, but there it is: an earthly reality devoid of its most grounding ephemera—air and sky and light—a world buckled in on itself, though invisibly, life-defying as a vacuum.

Truly, what would this look like? What would you see?

"The East," Barnaby said.

I had come to Barnaby's rooms several times, now that Simon was away. I reached for a cigarette.

"All of it?" I held the flame to the tip. "Numerous countries, hundreds of islands, you loved them all?"

"No," Barnaby said. "But I did love Shanghai. Despite its cruelty. Or maybe because of it."

"Cruelty." I exhaled the smoke. "Do tell."

Barnaby took a cigarette from my silver case and struck a match. If it was possible for him to look even more comfortable than usual, it was when he was about to embark on a story about his travels. Was I imagining it, or did his happiness deepen the further away the country of his recounted adventure?

Now, he described a late-night rickshaw ride through streets that were alive with activity: spice merchants preparing their stands for the morning, an old woman sorting dried herbs, a butcher stringing ducks by their necks upon rows of metal hooks. Beyond the commercial district, prostitutes gathered in little groups, wearing tight-fitting dresses, slit from calf to thigh. He described how he reached an alley near the bay, where the air was filled with the stench of rotting junks. The only light on the street came from the doorway of a narrow building, and this was where the rickshaw man, his shirt soaked with sweat, let Barnaby off. Inside, Han Shu, the proprietor, took Barnaby to a large room lined with carved mahogany benches, where opium smoke hung in such thick clouds that the people, some seated, others lying stretched out, seemed to him to be very far away. He told me how Han Shu scanned the room, pointed to the corner, called out something in Chinese. A slender woman dressed in an evening dress emerged from the fog of blue smoke. Strawberry-blond hair framed her delicate features and she smiled, then handed Barnaby a pipe. She was an Englishwoman, and her name was Christine.

I flashed on that odd moment in the garden, when Oscar had looked at me as if I were someone else and called me Christine. Could it be a coincidence? The same name as the woman Barnaby professed to have known in Shanghai? Could Oscar and Barnaby possibly have known this same woman?

For a moment, Barnaby hesitated, casting at me a quizzical eye. "Funny," he said. "It hadn't occurred to me before."

"What hadn't occurred to you?"

"You remind me of her. And yet, the two of you couldn't be more different. Opposites, in fact."

"Barnaby, you're not making any sense."

"It's as if one of you is the negative, and the other the photographic print."

"Heavens—I'm not sure which I'd rather be. Mysterious

and transparent, or two-dimensional but well-defined."

Barnaby offered no rejoinder; he seemed lost in some complicated thought, as if puzzling something out.

"Barnaby," I prodded gently, my interest piqued. "You were telling me about Christine."

"Yes. Christine."

Whatever it was that had momentarily unsettled him seemed to vanish; Barnaby glided right back into his story. He talked for some time about her, and I found myself feeling more and more uncomfortable. Not jealousy—I still suffered those curdled depths when on occasion I would torture myself with thoughts of Simon and his first (his only?) great love. No, this was something else.

It was one thing to make a story of a panther, even of poor Charlie, who had himself made a narrative of his own life. But making a story out of Christine's life seemed another matter. I listened closely. There was a *beginning* and a *middle*, and now Barnaby was moving into the part that would be the *end*. It involved Christine's terrible decline—and then, something about her disappearing, but the details kept eluding me, slipping through my fingers like sand. As for Barnaby, I'd never seen him so engrossed.

The story ended as I knew it would: Christine desperate, Barnaby as savior.

"I looked everywhere for her. In all the seedier dens, where they offer a lower grade of smoke. The rooms were twice as crowded—almost all Chinese. Foreigners didn't go to those places much. I only had to mention that I was looking for an Englishwoman, and someone would remember her. But I kept missing her—once, by no more than an hour. Finally, she showed up on my doorstep. I scarcely recognized her. Opium can suck the life out of you, if you let it."

I rose, refilled Barnaby's glass, then emptied the crystal decanter into my own. "So it wasn't the whole of the Far East you loved," I said. "It was a woman. Christine."

"I'm not sure I'd put it that way." Barnaby's voice was serious, but I could see mischief in his eyes. We drew on our cigarettes, exhaled long trails of white smoke.

I walked to the window.

"I see," I said, drawing aside the blue drape and looking out at the black stretch of lawn. "So that's what you like to do. Save people."

Another broken night. Sleep, I knew, would not come now. I rose, glanced with a pang at Simon's empty side of the bed, and dressed. I'd been working too long on this project; it had been foolhardy to take on the essay for the catalog.

Frayed by tiredness, though my legs felt strong, I moved down the stairs noiselessly, two at a time. The basement studio was the last place I wanted to be. I headed toward the kitchen for a glass of milk.

I was sick of the work. I had begun to think of abandoning the project altogether. An image reared up in my mind: a woman photographer in a jeep, crammed in among a group of American GIs, bouncing along a narrow paved road. The driver turns onto a dirt path, the jeep careens. They all jam together; a soldier lets out a whoop. The woman holds her camera on her lap, tightening her grip each time the jeep hits a bump. The men are alive with chatter, excited to have a female companion. It is a fresh sunny day. The war is over, though an observer would sense, in the giddiness and the fragile edge to the banter, that this is not yet a reality the group can entirely believe. Of one thing, though, the men, to a person, feel certain: they are the liberators of Europe.

When they drive through the gates, the assemblage turns silent. They are out of the jeep now, scattered about the raked-dirt quadrangle. A white open sky emits an incantatory glow. The woman looks around her for some time. She sees everything, but what she photographs is the commandant's body. He lies in the center of the square, facedown in a three-day-old slick of blood crusted and cracked as dried mud. Two officers talk to each other in low voices. This she photographs as well. They are discussing the fact that the enlisted men don't want to remove the body: that they want it to remain where the recently freed prisoners left it. The officers are considering the practicalities: maggots, the threat of disease, the stench of rotting flesh.

I was not there, I did not see this. One of my exhibition collaborators described it to me. Neither of these photographs was among the ones she sent me; perhaps they were part of the group she destroyed. It made no difference. I saw them all, the pictures she gave me and those she just told me about. I don't know which imposed themselves more cruelly.

I am seeing it, I thought numbly. I did, in the end, stay away, but I may as well have been there all along. For a moment I hated every one of my collaborators, and I found myself gripped by the urge to set fire to their contact sheets locked in the metal drawer downstairs in the studio.

Alone in the kitchen, I glanced down to see an enormous water bug casually crossing the floor.

What do you do with a tainted eye?

In the blue suite, Barnaby asleep, I tiptoed from the bed to the sitting room. Still muffled by drowsiness, I positioned myself by the window and peered into the thickness of the woods beyond the lawn. I fancied I heard a clear ringing pierce the silence, as when a wet finger is slowly rubbed around the rim of a crystal goblet, only louder, more penetrating, and insistent. It seemed to be coming from where the moon clenched onto a knuckle of black sky, and I remember thinking that it must be the cold lamentation of moonlight, exiled to earth. On any other night, I might have taken this as an omen or sign, but that evening, everything was swaddled, allowing no movement, no meaning at all. Outside, the horizon was obscured by the jostling ovoid heads of trees. Nothing but flatness, and the ringing of the moon, dulled now to a cool and mineral whine.

The evening's work was done. I looked up to see that the yellow light in Oscar's study had been extinguished. I packed my contact sheets away in the drawer and headed back into the corridors of the sleeping house.

Outside, the air was cool. Halfway across the courtyard, hugging my cold arms, I realized I had left my sweater behind, draped over a chair. Tired, so very tired, I could think of little else besides the comfortable bed awaiting me in the yellow suite. But then, suddenly, I could not bear the idea of my sweater alone in that room, limp on the back of the chair. I sighed, turned back toward the east wing.

As soon as I entered the darkroom, I sensed that something was awry. I peeled the sweater from the back of the chair. A new wave of fatigue passed over me. I sank into the chair, rested my head for a moment on the counter. The cold metal surface felt soothing. My mind drifted: fragments, colors, snatches of sound, the shimmery descent into sleep.

A muffled crash awoke me. I sprang upright and scrambled toward the source of it, the cubicle on the other side of the room. I drew open the heavy black curtain. It was Oscar. Not the Oscar I knew, but someone else. His face looked somehow bruised—his eyes, usually the serenest blue, were those of a cornered beast: inward, dark, without language. His head turned slowly toward me and, though I could see he was trying to smile, could see, too, the jerky rise of his rigid shoulders in an attempt at a shrug, there was no hiding the inner collapse that had transformed my friend. I took in the rest: the brown leather portfolio in his hand, the vat of steaming chemicals in the trough. The portfolio was unzipped. It flapped emptily where Oscar was holding it above the vat.

"What happened?" I asked. "What's wrong?"

"I didn't know it was open," he said, looking dumbly at

the portfolio. "Stupid," he mumbled to himself. "The solvent wasn't ready, it was just acid. I filled it with acid and—" He looked down at the vat; I followed his gaze in time to see a tiny corner of paper dissolve to nothing.

"I was going to restore them," he said flatly, again not to me, his eyes fixed on the vat.

"Oh Oscar," I said, a bit too desperately, reaching for the pair of tongs on the bench and plunging them into the vat. He shook his head.

"It's too late," he said, his voice restored to his own. "They're gone."

I was back for a few days in Manhattan to scout through some files. I opened all the windows and watered my wilting houseplants, neglected by the neighbor who'd promised to tend them. I realized how overdue this visit was—how much I needed a break from Ellis Park.

I made some coffee, gathered my papers and books, and sat down at my desk. There was a lot to do: checking quotations and facts, hunting up numerous obscure details.

The river below was in the throes of its gentle commerce: egging two sailboats upstream, frilling prettily around a steamship, reflecting back bulging images of swooping gulls. Downriver, a barge: it must have been hauling a heavy cargo, I'd never seen a barge move quite so slowly. I stopped what I was doing to watch it, recalling a line from a poem: Walt Whitman musing on this same river, this same sky, thinking of someone not yet born—why not me?—addressing himself to this imagined somebody and saying that, once in a past that was his present, he too had felt what this future soul would surely feel, looking at river and sky.

I deduced from the streaks of soot on the deck that the cargo might be coal. A lone figure stood stern-side, looking up at the clouds. I watched, trying to calculate how much coal a barge like that could carry, how many men it took to load and unload it, when all of a sudden, the barge came to a stop. The man at the stern crouched, as if to retrieve something that had fallen. He righted himself and strolled toward the bow. From where I sat looking down from the eighth floor, he looked like a rickety puppet.

I watched him amble the length of the stalled boat. Holding my red editor's pencil in midair, peering down at the river, I had the sense that I was about to witness something dramatic. I felt a wave of regret for the little puppet man. Instinctively I reached for my camera, which was in the blue canvas duckbag on the shelf by my desk. But I withdrew my hand.

I had hesitated then too, that day in London, years ago, amidst the ruins, sighting the boy in the olive-green jacket in the viewfinder of my camera. "He made it down into the cellar through an open grate," the rescue worker was saying, his voice a dreadful distraction which threatened the harmony of the shot.

I had taken two steps away from the rescue worker, trying to brush him off, desperate to be alone with what I was seeing: the extraordinary power of the sky, with its unnatural metallic streaks—colors I might never again see, born as they surely were from the idiosyncratic mixture of gases rising from this particular site of devastation. I focused on the curve of the boy's shoulders, aware that the slight dip of his head was in perfect equipoise with the shape his foot made as it nudged the clump of charred timber. It ached, this composition; I could feel it as a human force. Here it was, my holy grail: meaning, unity, beauty, grief.

The rescue worker's voice broke through, shattering the harmony. "War," he said bitterly. "Don't you love it?"

For an instant, I took my eye away from the viewfinder. "Please," I responded a little desperately, struggling for some phrase that would keep him from saying another word.

My tone must have conveyed something, for he shrugged

and began to turn away, but then paused, and added in a low voice: "I understand he was the only survivor."

I slammed the camera back to my eye. The sky had changed: there was a bare remnant of that exquisite, awful, unearthly color that was as much shape as hue. The sky, those streaks, I could feel them dissolving in the full arrival of the day. *And the boy . . .* How could I not take the shot?

Now, outside my window, on the Hudson River far below me, I watched as the small fire erupted, watched as the puppet man flung himself about deck with what looked like a wet blanket and a bucket, struggling to get the little blaze under control. It was an old instinct which set my fingers to itching, that fierce longing to feel the weight of the camera in my hand.

Leave it be, said an inner voice. *Let the world get along without you.*

I turned back to my work.

Later that evening, I opened a can of soup, buttered some toast, and ate looking out the kitchen window at the round white moon, aware of a sense of calm at having the large spare rooms of the apartment to myself. I washed my bowl and plate and poured myself a bourbon. At the first sip, I was overcome by a crushing exhaustion. No more work this evening, I thought: a long hot bath and early to bed.

I was just stepping out of the tub, reaching for a towel, when the buzzer rang. Three long, hard rings: the doorman, Gerald, not a man who kept his emotions to himself, was clearly irritated. I reached over to the basin for my watch: eleven o'clock. I rubbed myself dry and wrapped a towel around my head.

"Someone to see you, madam," Gerald said over the intercom. "A *Mr. Harrington*." In his tone, severity and curiosity both.

"Thank you. You can send him up," I said.

Barnaby. Here at Riverside Drive. Not part of our unspoken agreement. I just had time to pull on my bathrobe before the doorbell rang.

I opened the door. There he was in a linen blazer, a single rose in one hand, straw hat and bottle of wine in the other.

"You're surprised to see me," he said, the half-smile now in his eyes, touching them with that hesitant, coaxing warmth that was in fact not hesitant at all. "You're angry."

He offered me the rose, which I unthinkingly raised to my nose. He must have taken this as a sign of invitation because a moment later he was behind me in the hallway, balancing his hat on the hat rack. He took my shoulder and turned me toward him.

"I wanted to see where my dove nests when she's in the city." He ducked his head so that he was peering both down and up at me at the same time, the little game of tender imploring fully at play in his face. In my absent haste on my way from the bathroom to the door, I must have picked up my drink; I noticed, suddenly, that I was holding it in my hand.

"Whatever you're drinking will be fine," Barnaby said, his finger was now on my chin.

I saw his eye wander up the hallway, sensed in him a flutter of excitement. *He must be very sure of me*, I thought.

"I don't think you should stay. I was just about to go to bed."

"Then I'll tuck you in." His finger traced slowly up from my chin, coming to rest behind my earlobe.

I could feel my irritation dissolving. But I also felt uncomfortable standing there in my bathrobe. I pointed toward the living room. "The bar's in there. I'll be right back."

I turned and walked through the dining room toward the bedrooms at the back of the apartment. Fleshy rounds of moonlight glowed on the varnished floorboards. The rooms had lost their calm.

In the bedroom, I unwound the towel from my hair, pulled on slacks and a light sweater.

When I returned to the living room, Barnaby was standing by the window with a glass in his hand, staring out at the flat expanse of river.

"Does it always perform so magnificently for you?" he said, his back toward me. "The river, the sky, the moon?" He swiveled around to face me across the width of the room. "But perhaps you take it for granted."

"We could go out for a walk," I said.

"I was going to tuck you in." Barnaby passed his gaze from my shirt to my slacks. "Although I see that you're dressed, now."

"I'll get my jacket," I said.

Back in the dining room, everything was disturbed, as if the building, after an unexpected blow, was struggling to regain its balance. In the bedroom, I sat for a moment on the green plaid chair by the window. I felt a terrible longing for Simon, pictured him in a small hotel in Montreal, sitting at the little desk found in such rooms, noting down images and thoughts for tomorrow's writing; pictured him setting down his fountain pen, stroking the back of his neck with forefinger and thumb the way he did when he was concentrating. I rose, took my purse and keys from the dresser, retrieved my cotton jacket from the closet, and clicked off the lamp.

Walking back through the dining room, I noticed a dim light issuing from the end of the passageway: Simon's study. Aware that I was almost tiptoeing, I headed down the hall, then stopped at the half-open door. I peered in to see Barnaby leaning over Simon's desk, half of him aglow in the light thrown up by the desk lamp, the other half obscured in the fuzzy blackness of the room—no moonlight on this side of the apartment, where the shades were drawn to keep the grimy airshaft from view. The sight of Barnaby's half-face was disturbing—not only because of the apparent loss of its complement, but because of the oddly prurient expression he wore. Barnaby glanced my way. He was holding up a handwritten manuscript page; delicately, he set it down.

"Let's go," I said. Barnaby pretended not to notice the curtness in my voice.

Downstairs, crossing the lobby, I noted the frank disapproval in Gerald's face.

Barnaby and I headed north on Riverside Drive, walking for several blocks in silence. He reached for my hand; reluctantly, I let him take it.

"Don't be cross," he said, giving my fingers a gentle squeeze.

I extricated my hand. "You had no business going into Simon's study."

"I just want to know about your life," he said. "Can you understand that?"

I stopped, Barnaby stopped. His face was shrouded by shadow. Above us, a canopy of leaves; beside us, the towering trees of Riverside Park, exhaling oxygen into the night air.

"Simon's study is not *my* life."

A veil softly falling, the smile that stole across Barnaby's face, taking full possession of his features.

"But Marilyn, it is," he said.

A woman in a white uniform and white lace-up shoes hurried anxiously toward us. A nurse, I supposed, coming off the late shift. I nodded to her as she passed. A convertible sped by roof down, a young rake in a checkered cravat at the wheel. Beside him, hair held down by a tightly tied scarf, a woman laughed into the onrush of air. I looked back at Barnaby, saw, for an instant, a vivid apparition—Barnaby swinging a child onto his shoulders, looking at me with those same knowing, relaxed eyes: sure of himself, sure of me, questioning nothing. It was a happy child, settled and loved.

"Honestly." I took a step toward him. "You really believe the rules don't apply to you, don't you."

He drew me toward him, looked at me happily and long.

"Darling," he whispered, "you really should try to be less serious."

* * *

Later, I lay on the bed looking out at the moon sinking by my window, unable to sleep, feeling trapped, somehow, between the layers of the river and the layers of the night. I kicked off the sheet and stepped from the bed. I dressed, threw a few things into my weekend valise, and took leave of the apartment.

When I stepped from the elevator into the foyer, Gerald rose from the night shift chair. "Do you have a car coming, madam, or shall I call you one?"

"I'm taking my own car," I said.

"But madam," he protested, looking pointedly at his watch.

"I'll be fine. It's parked around the corner." I pushed through the double glass doors.

The car was in fact a good many blocks away. Outside, not a soul about, but above me, in the high-rises I passed, signs of wakefulness: a random design of windows flashing light, like so many gap-toothed smiles. The streets seemed slippery with threat.

Once in the car, I headed along the quirky route Simon and I always took through Manhattan, aware of the differences wrought by the semidarkness. The shuttered buildings and halted commerce put me in mind of a great Egyptian tomb, constructed not for the living, but for some marvelous existence in the hereafter.

Across the bridge, the roads were quiet except for the occasional long-haul truck, piloted, inevitably, by a bleary-eyed driver sucking on a cigarette. I glanced up to see that the moon was sinking differently now, a round blade cutting through the black butter of night. I pressed down firmly on the gas pedal. The feel of moving through Queens: apartment buildings wearing the flimsy armor of their fire escapes, then tracts of newly minted houses, squat little things with awnings and porches and postage-stamp front lawns. And on, the roadway relaxing to twists and turns. Finally, the Long

Island townships, with the appearance of increasingly grand houses. Stretches of wooded land, a slight cooling of the air. The sky cleanly black above, the world ahead of me appearing as two hazy yellow tunnels molded into existence by the headlights of my car.

The familiar fork, an inverted arrow pointing away from Oscar's. I veered to the right and slowly released my foot from the accelerator, anticipating the bumpier surface of the road as it narrowed ahead. I misjudged the wide curve and swung up unevenly onto the grassy shoulder; my headlights glimpsed something shiny, also up on the grass, jutting out from beneath a large weeping willow. A fender: a shiny, jazzy fender. I slammed on the brakes, skidded into the center of the road. Leaving my car where it was, I stepped out onto the road. Little asphalt stones crunched underfoot as I made my way over to investigate.

Up on the grass, I pulled aside the curtain of leaves. It was a convertible, with the roof pulled closed, dark green and spanking new. Carefully parked under the feathery outlying overhang of leaves, clear of the heavier inner boughs that might have inflicted a scratch. I tried the driver's door, then walked around to the passenger side—both locked. A half-mile, by my guess, to the entrance of Ellis Park. I climbed back into my car, drew away slowly, and turned off the headlights. I sailed along, eyes trained on both sides of the road, each moment expecting to glimpse a moving form up ahead against the trees.

I reached Oscar's gates, left the car idling while I unlocked the bolt with the key he had given me, then turned onto the driveway, disembarking again to relock it. Two-thirds the way up the driveway, I pulled to the side and shut off the engine. I stepped onto the lawn and hastened up the incline, skirting the circular driveway and making my way to the back entrance.

It was rounding the house that I saw him emerging from

the rear. How odd, I thought; Oscar must have given him a copy of the key too. How else could he have gained access to the estate? The man paused, closed the top button of his sports jacket, and walked quickly across the patio. The back of the house was in darkness; the single converted London streetlamp, usually lit, tonight was blind. I knew, even from that distance, in the hazy darkness, that it was him, though we had never, in fact, met. When he had cleared the patio, I moved quickly along the grassy border. Alerted by the sound of movement, he turned. A moment of calculation in his face, then a practiced calm.

"It's you," I said.

"Good evening," he replied. A stray moonbeam stole across his face; I saw what a good looking man he was, though there was something disturbing about the mildness of his gaze, as if he were standing before something terrible and had chosen to look away. I saw, also, the color of his hair: a lovely shade of chestnut.

"You know me, don't you," I said.

He did not acknowledge that I'd spoken, though I noted a twitch of impatience around his mouth.

"What are you doing here?" I persisted. "What do you want?"

The man drew something from his pocket and handed it to me. It was a card, a business card with an elaborate seal, though in the near darkness I could not make out what it said.

"We may be contacting you. If, in the meantime, you feel you have any information that would be helpful, we'd appreciate hearing from you."

That mild gaze, I found it infuriating. I slipped the card into my pocket.

"I wouldn't count on it," I said.

He reached up to touch the brim of his hat in a polite doff, then turned and walked toward the lawn. I watched him cut across about midway down and pick up the driveway.

From there, I imagined him thinking that the sound of shoes crunching on gravel would not reach the ears of the sleeping servants up in the house. He kept the same brisk pace; there was tremendous assurance in his stride. I watched until he disappeared over the hump, then moved back to the house.

Inside, the hallway was sparsely lit by the wall sconces, which appeared to have been dimmed. No guests; I sensed the house was emptied out. I took the back stairs and headed toward Oscar's study. As I expected, there was a band of light beneath the door. From within, I could hear pacing, and shallow, erratic breathing. I raised my hand to knock when I was startled by a low voice.

"Madam, good evening." Wallace, materialized from nowhere, in full butler dress, bearing a silver tray which held a glass of water and a small bottle of pills. "A pleasure as always to see you, madam, but I confess we were not expecting you."

"Is Oscar all right?"

I saw a shadow of pain cross Wallace's face then dissolve into his usual expression of courteous distance. "Nothing that two aspirin and a good night's sleep won't take care of."

I hesitated. "Perhaps I should pop my head in to say hello."

"I don't think that's a very good idea. The master is feeling quite poorly."

I went back to my suite but felt too restless to stay there alone. I changed into comfortable slacks and blouse, then made my way down to the dayroom. Sitting in the darkness, I lifted the handset from the telephone and dialed the operator.

I thought the call would never go through. It was only an hour or two before dawn when the operator finally rang to say she had Simon, in Montreal, on the line.

That long-distance trip in the wire, my own heart missing a beat or two at the sound of his voice.

"Marilyn?" Just discernible, a note of concern.

"How are you treating Montreal?"

"A wary mutual respect, I'd say." That gentle catch in his voice—the sound, to me, of some hidden font of happiness in the cool reaches of Simon's soul.

"Marilyn, are you there?"

"Something's going on here. At Ellis Park."

"Whatever do you mean?" Simon replied, the catch in his voice gone.

"The man on the beach," I said. "I saw him leaving the house. From the servants' entrance. Simon, it was four o'clock in the morning." The telephone wire threw up a delay, which made for awkward hesitations. The conversation felt like a tennis game between mismatched partners.

"You know Oscar has all kinds of friends. Maybe he just wants to keep some things to himself."

I allowed a pause. I wanted something from him, though I didn't know what.

"Are you getting enough sleep?" he asked.

I let the next pause lengthen. "I wish you were here," I whispered.

"I'm sure there's nothing to worry about."

A crackle on the line, and the swelling feeling in the room of something sinister.

"Did you say something?" Simon's voice; it sounded like he was drifting away. "The line's cutting out."

"No, I didn't say anything." My own voice, loud in the silent dark.

"Well then—"

"I'll write soon," I said.

"Get some sleep . . ."

I placed the receiver back in its cradle, looked out into the blackness. The night had the feel of a photograph. I felt its hiddenness in my grasp: the throbbing stillness, the dense shroud of the living that hangs over everything in the deepness of night—birds with their heads tucked under wing, frogs statue-still on lily pads, horses upright and asleep in their stalls, even the cicada silent under its muffling. I wanted to hurl it back into the universe, this formless photograph. I had the urge to scream: *See? See what you have done?*

And then, right on cue, Barnaby appeared in the doorway.

"I thought I heard voices, but I see you're alone."

I did not turn around. I could not take my eyes off the window, the shiny dim surface, the heavy dark shapes in the blackness beyond.

"I thought you were in Manhattan," he said.

I heard him move toward the couch. The click of a switch, and then light, faintly rainbowed through the neat triangles and squares of Oscar's Tiffany lamp. I reached for a cigarette, realized there were tears dripping down my face and discreetly wiped them away.

"I can't say I was expecting you, either," I responded. The lamp's glare had reduced the window to a pale reflection of the room, featuring, off to one side, a ghostly likeness of Barnaby.

"I couldn't keep away," he said. He walked across to the alcove and poured himself a drink. "It seems as if I've been granted an early reprieve."

"Oh?"

"My sentence. It's been lifted. I've taken a new posting. It starts in two weeks."

"Let me guess. Someplace you've yet to conquer . . . Indonesia?"

"Not even close."

"Back to one of your old stomping grounds, then." I was trying, desperately, to sound nonchalant, though I was aware that my voice was shaky. I wanted a drink but didn't want to go to where Barnaby was standing to get one. Instead, I lit a cigarette.

"Guess again."

"Hmm . . . Closer to home . . . Costa Rica? Peru?"

"Try Washington." Barnaby said. "D.C."

"Washington," I repeated, exhaling a long, slow plume. "Rather less far-flung than I would have expected." And awfully close, I thought, to New York. To Riverside Drive. To me.

Barnaby walked over and crouched down by the couch, took my chin in his hand, his eyes tender and querying.

He said nothing. I said nothing.

"I have a new project brewing myself," I said, after a while. "I talked it over with my editor at *Life* when I was back in New York."

"Oh? Where to?"

I had not, in fact, discussed any such assignment with my editor; I have no idea how this lie sprang to my lips. I knew, however, upon hearing my own words, that I was tired, so very tired. Of my war project. Of longing for Simon. Of the brand of deception I had somehow, unwittingly, it now seemed to me, embarked upon in conducting this affair with Barnaby. Of being an intrigue for this man before me, a man I felt suddenly as if I did not know at all. Of the certainty in his face when he looked at me. Of the mess I was making of things.

I looked at Barnaby kneeling beside me: Barnaby, waiting for an answer.

"Rather more far-flung than I'd anticipated," I said.

It was Barnaby's turn to be surprised. He rose from his crouch, crossed the room to the bar, then turned and eyed me coolly.

"No guesses, I see," I said, trying to sound lighthearted.

"The suspense is killing me." A sneer larding his words. Yes, beneath the coolness, a flash of rage in those eyes. I felt the desire to be cruel. I could have stopped myself, but I didn't; I was curious to see how he would react.

"Then I'll tell you. Leningrad."

The yellow suite took on a forbidding emptiness, which made it even harder for me to sleep. And since chancing upon the

strange visitor, with his disturbingly mild gaze, I found myself seriously worried about Oscar. I couldn't imagine what
business this man had with Oscar or how it was that they
came to be speaking German. The more I puzzled over the few
facts I had at my disposal, the more stumped I felt.

So when, on the following Wednesday night, lying awake
in my room, I heard what sounded like a stealthy tread on the
stairs, I quickly dressed and stepped into the hall. Battered
by nights of insomnia, I felt uncomfortably jumpy and alert. I
made my way quietly to the other side of the house, expecting Wallace to spring out at any moment from nowhere in full
butler regalia, bearing some crucial item or other for his master. But no one appeared; I was alone, the only noise my soft
footfalls, muffled by Oscar's fine runners and hallway rugs.

I came to a halt outside his study. The crack under his door
glowed dully with light: the sound, from within, of purposefully lowered voices. The same lowered voices, again speaking German. But then, as if they had somehow been expecting
me, they switched to English. And as suddenly, one of the
voices became recognizable—it was Oscar's, surely and un-
mistakably, though the tremulousness I heard in it was new.

"How many are there now?" was what I think he said. I
pressed my ear against the door. It was unlikely that anyone
would be afoot at this hour and, in any case at that moment, I
cared less about being seen than I did about hearing what was
being said on the other side of the door.

"This brings the number of witnesses to four," the other
voice said.

There was a long silence. For an unnerving moment I
thought that perhaps the conversation was over, that the man
would open the door right onto my head.

But then, Oscar spoke: "I see."

Another pause.

"It is by no means certain how my office will proceed, but
I do recommend at this point that you engage legal counsel."

Neither of them spoke now, though I heard movement and faint rustling through the door. My instinct told me to take quick leave, which I did, and not a moment too soon. As I rounded the corner of the hallway toward the back stairway, I heard the sound of a door being gently opened and then gently closed.

Witnesses, I puzzled as I hastened back to the yellow suite. *Legal representation*. What in heaven's name could Oscar be accused of?

CHAPTER SIX

The days and nights were bleeding into each other. I had lost count of how many nights passed with no more than two or three hours of sleep. When I looked in the mirror, I startled at the sight of the black pools beneath my eyes and the angular cast of my features. Was it one night later, or two, that I was sitting in the darkroom—who knew the hour, it was certainly not before two a.m.—when I heard three quiet raps on the door. It was Oscar, his folded newspaper poking out of his jacket pocket. Cheeks drawn, jacket hanging slightly on his frame. But humor in his face.

"May I?" He gestured with his arm, indicating the darkened studio behind me, illuminated only by the lamp on the counter.

"I'm just fixing some coffee."

My little pot hissed over a Bunsen burner by the sink. When it was ready, I poured the coffee into glass beakers, added sugar, and handed one to Oscar. I returned to my work. We did not speak, but I sensed that he was even more distracted than he'd been of late. I looked up periodically from my work to find him staring absently above his newspaper at nothing in particular, his mouth pursed. How mournful he looked and, at the same time, emptied of feeling, like a marionette cast from the puppet theater. On one of those stolen glimpses he caught me watching him and attempted a wink, but it froze on his worried face into an awkward admission of distress.

I was distracted myself, that night, irritated by my work, too aware of the faults of the photographs, which lay in a stack beside my typewritten pages.

When I glanced up again, Oscar did not try to pull up the mask, made no attempt to still the trembling in his fingers that set the edges of his opened paper to rattling.

I removed my glasses, rubbed my eyes. "Oscar," I said quietly, "are you all right?"

He set down his paper, attempted a smile. "I've been a little under the weather," he said, taking out his handkerchief and touching it to his forehead.

"Oscar, what is it?" I could see the muscle working along his jaw.

He seemed about to say something, but instead drew the folded handkerchief across his mouth, as if to stop himself from speaking.

"Would you like to take a look at my photographs?" I asked unthinkingly, as if I were offering a harmless pleasure that might lift his mood. Immediately, I felt like an imbecile, speaking this way about my wretched material.

Oscar looked at me as if from across a great expanse. He put down his paper, peered at the stack of proof sheets I had slid toward him across the bench. Slowly, he examined the first. The second. The third.

The shadow of someone I had never met superimposed itself on Oscar's features, altering the set of the nose, loosening the lower lip, inking a disturbing chiaroscuro around the eyes. And something strange happened to his jaw—it was as if the bone has gone out of it, slid clear from the groove that held it in place.

Woodenly, as if of its own accord, Oscar's hand rose, removed the next proof sheet, lay it facedown on the bench. The hand dropped. He examined the sheet beneath. I had a sudden horrifying vision: I imagined I saw the flesh of Oscar's cheek hanging in a severed flap against his neck. I shook my head to clear the image. Oscar repeated the mechanical gesture, removing the next sheet. And the next. He continued this way for what seemed an excruciating length of time, until he'd worked through the entire stack. He pushed the pile a few inches away and stared toward the far wall. He seemed to be turning a problem over in his mind, trying to figure something out.

To my alarm, he started again at the beginning, but this time scanned each page very quickly. He was looking for something. It didn't take him long to find it: a contact sheet about midway through the stack. He angled it upward to catch the light from the lamp, examined it for several long minutes. It was a series of shots one of my fellow photographers had taken in rapid succession, the variations between them subtle: a shift of five or ten degrees, a step closer or further away, the almost imperceptible changes of light that occur with the passage of a few minutes. The scene, in each, was the same: a length of wire fencing strung along cracked posts, each of which bore a gas lamp, like a hat. In front of the fence, a thicket of barbed wire sprouted weedlike from the ground. At a bend in the fence stood a watchtower, its empty windows filled with the frosty whiteness of the sky. All along the fence, at roughly equal intervals, charred bodies lay in curious poses which in another context (children playing in a garden, clowns in the midst of a circus act) may well have looked comical: a man on his stomach, forearms crooked, legs flung high behind him; another corpse on its belly, head pressed to the ground as if listening for hoof-beats; and a smaller form, a child, head tossed upward, as if charmed by the call of a bird overhead. The images showed the northern fence of Erla, one of the first concentration camps to be liberated. In the center of the page, circled in red wax pencil, was the photograph I had chosen for the exhibition.

Finally, Oscar looked up at me with eyes I had never before seen. I had been about to say something, but those eyes erased the thought from my mind. I had the strange feeling that I had forgotten how to speak English: that all knowledge of my mother tongue had simply vanished. I felt as if I was drowning in those eyes; they, too, seemed to have forgotten something as absolutely fundamental. Oscar pushed back his stool and rose, took four or five steps and was upon me, bearing down on me with those empty, far-seeing eyes. He took my head in his hands, which felt oddly wooden; he bent down jerkily and kissed my forehead, while I stared helplessly at his chin. He turned, headed for the door, slowly rotated the handle, and was gone.

We set out at sunrise. As we drove through Oscar's Spanish gates, the sun blood-orange on the horizon, I felt a heady relief. Barnaby had suggested we spend a couple of days together away from Ellis Park in advance of his departure for Washington. With Simon away, it was easy enough to arrange.

I looked over at Barnaby, relaxed at the wheel, and felt a surge of uncomplicated joy, complete as religious faith, which made the world, including Barnaby, with his rugged face and strapping self-possession, bristle with benevolent intent. Everything my eyes fell upon seemed to have achieved an aesthetic harmony: the way the tree curved above the rust-colored barn; the composition of a mound of white stones beside a froth of late-blooming sweet william; the sudden ascent of a small flock of cardinals from an old stone bridge.

We arrived at the inn midmorning. We climbed the creaking stairs to the third floor, Barnaby carrying both bags in one hand, his other arm around my shoulder. Our room overlooked a summer garden in full bloom. I sat down on the enormous bed and fingered the wide cotton frills bordering the pillows. The open window did nothing to thin the viscous heat; it flowed in damply, spiked with hyacinth and honeysuckle and the reedy scent of sage.

Barnaby pulled the cord of tiny metal links hanging from the ceiling fan and it whirred into action, stirring the thick air and disturbing its fragrance. Little gusts slapped gently against my skin. Barnaby moved toward the bed and stood over me. He looked different. There was a stillness in his gaze I had not seen before, an intentness and focus. A dim memory from the distant past drifted into my awareness as we slowly fell among the pillows: a misty vague sensation of sunlight and height, of a room above a garden, a child's anticipation of something intensely pleasant; and then skimming down flights of stairs, the feel of my child's hair against my bare shoulders, the treasure in my pocket tinkling: three little spirals of barley sugar.

I opened my eyes. Embossed blue cornflowers stood out on the wallpaper, little bunches encircled by flat yellow ribbon. Another feeling, also dim, though threaded with certainty, wafted through the room as if borne by the fan: that I belonged here, and that Barnaby belonged here too.

It was late afternoon when we finally made our way to the lake. We didn't talk much; we walked holding hands. The sky above the horizon was streaked crimson and yellow, congealed brushstrokes of the leaden heat.

The lake was larger than I'd expected, with deep, clear water. A family of ducks paddling on the far side ignored us as we approached. We peeled off our clothes, stepped in, glided through the water. Afterward, we lay on the bleached grass of the bank looking up. Little pouches of cloud had gathered; the sky was glazing over with dusk. Barnaby leaned toward me, lowered the strap of my swimsuit, caressed my shoulder, smiled. Then the other strap. He looked oddly surprised as he passed the back of his hand across the length of my collarbone before leaning down to kiss me.

Leaving our swimsuits on the grass, we swam again. I clung loosely to Barnaby's shoulders; his long underwater strokes moved us silently forward.

The shower began as pointy little punctures on the surface of the lake and continued as a soft wash that soaked the clothes we'd left in a heap under a tree. We stayed at the lake well into the evening and walked back through the dark in our bathing suits, holding our wet garments. The darkness did not impede Barnaby's instinct for moving through terrain; he walked ahead and I wove in the clear space that seemed almost magically to open up behind him. The rain turned to a mist of fine droplets; from time to time, a head of leaves shook water down upon us.

Back at the inn, the dining room was closed. The innkeeper's shiny scrubbed face and the rollers in her hair indicated she was ready for bed, but she took pity on us, disappeared into the kitchen, and emerged with a tray, which held a cold joint of lamb, cheese, bread, and fruit.

The food tasted delicious; we were hungry and ate every morsel. Back up the stairs to our floral profusion of a room. Back onto the bed, the luxurious crisp feel of fresh linens.

Later, lying together, I propped my head on my hand and smiled into Barnaby's face.

"Have you decided yet how you're going to save me?" I asked playfully.

"Now, Marilyn. Saving. That's one thing you don't need." He tapped me affectionately on the rump.

"Well, then, what *do* you plan to do with me?"

Barnaby's eyes twinkled up at me; he surveyed me from head to toe, saying nothing.

"Whatever happened to Christine?" I asked.

A shadow passed across Barnaby's face and, in the instant before he broke out his easy grin, I saw callousness in his eyes.

"Why would you want to bring up ancient history?" he asked, stretching his limbs.

I watched a ripple of relaxation pass through his body, from the broad smooth feet, along his thighs, and outward to the tanned muscles of his chest. His eyes turned milky with affection; he reached across with one hand and tousled my hair. It was one of those disconcerting moments when everything suddenly seems off-kilter. I knew—everybody knew—this aspect of Barnaby so well, this comfort and strength and physical ease, the fluidity of action and the way he responded precisely, unthinkingly, to the rhythm of the person he was with. This was partly what made people love him as they did, beautifully and without hesitation.

But here was another side of it. I looked at him closely, wondering if I had imagined it, that fleeting flicker of—what? Was it contempt? The casualness, the unself-conscious stance seemed suddenly a perverse calculation, summoned to conceal. Watching Barnaby's eyes, which were hooded with confidence, I knew I'd not imagined it. A hair-thin blade of suspicion skimmed the innocence that generally colored our interactions, leaving in its place something raw and exposed.

"Really, Barnaby, I want to know," I said, trying not to let on what it was I had noticed. "About Christine."

"Fair is fair. You tell me about your Shanghai and I'll tell you about mine."

I felt caught off guard. I'd once mentioned I'd spent time in China with my parents when I was eleven years old. My father, a businessman, traveled for several months each year; every now and then, he took my mother and me with him. Now, images from that visit reared up. I tried to push the images away, but they would not yield. Lice; I could see the little black mites popping around the stringy-haired heads of children. Dark eyes, the chasm between us a mirage—nothing there, no pit, no divide, nothing but a few sorry feet of dirt. Me not much older than they were—and no camera, yet, with its paradoxical powers to protect me from, and yet also yield up the world: a widening of the chasm and at the same time a leap across the divide.

I could feel the trembling in my lower lip, tried to hide it, but too late. Barnaby gently touched his forefinger to my lip. He pulled himself up to sitting position.

"All right, then," he said. "Christine."

He looked away.

"Christine got herself into trouble. I don't know what you

know about the opium trade in Shanghai, but you don't mess with those guys. And you don't give them a hold over you."

Now, he was all business.

"Christine knew that as well as anybody. But I suppose she just—" He broke off, seemed to be holding his breath.

"Just what?"

"Lost interest."

"Lost interest? In what?"

"In life. In her life. I did everything I could for her. Finally, I sent her back to England."

"So that's what happened? She went back to England?"

"As far as I know. I put the ticket in her hand. She said she was going to go. There was nothing more I could do."

Lying next to Barnaby, I wondered why his words made me so uneasy.

"You never loved Christine, did you," I whispered. That hardness, again, in his eyes.

"I'm not sure that's really any of your business," he said quietly.

"I can't explain it, Barnaby, but I feel as if it is. I need to know—"

"What?"

"What you want."

Barnaby softened; I could feel it like a cooling of the air.

"It's hardly complicated, darling," he said. "I want *you*, that's all."

Why did I not believe him?

"But Barnaby, it *is* complicated. It's so complicated, I feel all tangled up in it."

Looking at him, I wondered how he imagined things proceeding. Did he picture us limping along in this fashion forever? Stolen hours, a weekend here and there, always the configuration of the tryst?

I spoke without thinking: "You've never asked me to leave Simon."

"No, apparently I haven't."

"And you have no intention of doing so."

Barnaby looked at me squarely. "No, I suppose I don't."

And then, it came clear. Barnaby said that he wanted me, but he didn't, not really. He wanted the idea of me, which meant keeping the living me at a remove. Simon was crucial in this equation—the fact that in the end, my husband was always there. I suspected there was some way in which Christine, too, had remained at arm's length for Barnaby, though I did not know the shape that had taken. Perhaps I'd been wrong to accuse him of never having loved her. In fact, he did seem intent upon loving. But to accept being loved back, wholly, and by an equal: perhaps that was not part of his nature.

"Marilyn." Now it was Barnaby who spoke softly.

"Yes?"

"You weren't serious about going to the Soviet Union, were you?"

"Why would you suppose I wasn't?"

"The way I see it," he said slowly, "New York is not so very far from Washington. Leningrad, on the other hand, is an altogether different story."

"It wouldn't be for long," I responded, having warmed to the idea of the place myself, even though it had only sprung to my lips when it did on a whim.

Barnaby seemed to take this as some sign that the little dispute, if that's what you could call it, was at an end. He rolled toward me, took me in his arms. I allowed the confusion to seep out of me, curled myself into him, allowed it all to drift out to sea.

At breakfast, I was quiet. I found I didn't have anything to say. Barnaby ate with gusto—eggs, bacon, toast. On the long walk to the lake, unpleasant dream-image scraps hung around me like cobwebs that clung more closely the more I tried to swipe them away. Hidden half-faces I didn't recognize, secretive whispers, a conspiratorial air. A mounting, unstoppable alarm.

After the cooling rains of the previous night, the heat returned full force and clamped against every square inch of my skin. As we walked, Barnaby talked happily of past travels. He wanted to show me the world. Africa, of course, and Melanesia. The mysteries of the Norwegian fjords. Bare-legged, I felt the reeds whipping my ankles, and the sting of prickly vines. We were taking a different route from the one we had taken the day before, though this did not seem like sufficient explanation for how different the landscape felt, how punishing the vegetation, and acrid the odors. An occasional crackling beneath my open sandals puzzled me. I slid to the ground and discovered the slippery remains of a beetle glued wetly to the sole of my shoe.

Barnaby laughed. "It's only a beetle," he said.

It was close to noon when we reached the lake. The air was thick, not a breath of wind; the water, still as glass, held plates of burning flame thrown down by the sun. We'd not thought to bring water or food. My throat ached with thirst.

Barnaby removed his shirt, pulled off his shorts, reached over and unbuttoned my sleeveless blouse. We walked down the little grassy slope to the water.

"I hate to disturb it," Barnaby said, dipping in his toe. Tiny ripples spread out. "Mmm," he murmured.

The water was warm as a bath. We separated, swam in opposite directions. Reaching the far bank, I took a deep breath and duck-dove down. I hovered alongside a deep ledge, looking in on watery blackness where I thought I could make out a tiny field of fronds, lazily waving, and the conical darting forms of hundreds of tadpoles. Barnaby's bicycling legs and arms splashed overhead. I rose upward and, the moment I broke through, felt the sun burning the crown of my head. Barnaby smiled. I expelled the air from my lungs in one long heave. The light was blinding after the darkness below. Before

I had time to gulp in some air, I felt the pressure of Barnaby's hands on my shoulders and the gentle plunge downward again, into the water. I could feel my own arms and legs thrashing about, suddenly clumsy from the need for air. A white hand reached through the bubbles and took hold of my arm. I pulled at the fingers to remove them but Barnaby, thinking it a game, tightened his grip. He must not have seen the panic growing in my face; when the bubbles cleared, he was still dreamily smiling, his tawny face creamy in white bands of light. He drew me toward him; a ballooning in my chest pressed at my ribs. I could see his half-closed eyes and his face, oddly swelling, leveling, then swelling again. The water slid noiselessly between us. My arms now seemed so heavy, I could feel them flapping against my legs. Warmth, like whiskey, poured through me, dissolving the ache in my chest.

I could feel my eyes rolling backward. I caught a glimpse of something floating by, something knotted and black, and was struck by the beauty of it.

A crack, loud in my ears. The pressure broke; a rush of water filled my lungs. And then, the crash into air, the heat, the heavy sweet air. I clawed at it, coughing, retching out water, and then an indescribable nothingness, soft and clear and vast.

I came to on the bank, Barnaby's worried face hovering above me, framed by the blue sky.

"What happened?" he asked. His voice was hoarse. Wanting to shut him out, I closed my eyes again and concentrated on the concentric circles of light behind my lids and the soothing sensation of air flowing along my windpipe and into my aching lungs.

I did not want to touch him, did not want him to touch me. Several times, with each new attempt, I plucked his hand from where he placed it—my arm, my waist, my throat—and set it on the sand. This clearly wounded Barnaby, but I found that I didn't care.

* * *

I don't as a rule believe in symbols. But, as we walked back to the inn, I noticed something unusual that I probably would have missed had I not, in my tiredness, paused on my haunches to rest. There, in the carpet of leaves and twigs, the wing of a bird pointed straight up as if it were a feathery seedling growing in the ground. I cleared the stones and leaves from around it, expecting to uncover the little body that went with the wing, hoping to find the creature still alive. But the wing sprouted stiffly from the ground.

Crouching by the buried bird's wing, I pried away the forest debris. Barnaby was ahead. I glanced up to see the receding soles of his feet. Then I noticed it, the crisscross weaving of reeds, a square the size of a handkerchief in the middle, a loose netting through which the little bird had plunged. It must have put up quite a struggle; the mesh was badly torn. Below, a small pit into which the head hung. I scrabbled some more in the surrounding area, flung aside fistfuls of dropped leaves and moss and dirt. Another miniature pit, about a foot to the left, a third, fourth, fifth, all in a diagonal leading away from the overgrown path and into the woods, a careful handiwork of traps. Nearby, a trill joined the growing dull drone of cicada. Something snapped clear, my thoughts eddied around a still point, an answer. I rose, looked around me, stepped firmly ahead. The forest seemed aware of its own perfection—seemed, almost, to sigh.

When I caught him up, Barnaby must have sensed I was rattled; he patted my arm and said, "You've had a bit of a scare. What you need is a meal and a good night's sleep." His sureness, shaken on the bank of the lake, was clearly restored.

We had dinner sent up to the room. Picking at my green beans, I struggled to tell Barnaby that our affair was at an end. Opened and closed my mouth several times, but could not find the words.

"What is it?" he said gently. "What's happened?"

"I found a bird," I stammered, feeling ridiculous. "A sparrow. Near the path. Dead in a trap."

"What are you talking about?"

I cast my mind back to the moment on the path, saw the little wing, relived the way the forest itself had suddenly seemed an explanation for everything hidden. I recalled, too, that feeling, dense and airy and uncatchable, that I had not stumbled across the sequence of odd little traps by chance.

"I hardly know you this way," Barnaby said softly, real distress in his voice.

I turned away from him and stared at the blue cornflowers on the wall. I felt flooded by everything troubling me; tears oozed from my eyes.

"What's wrong?" Barnaby said again.

How could I tell him? I now believed that Oscar was in real danger; but I couldn't possibly risk his well-being by discussing my concerns with Barnaby. And how could I tell Barnaby about the photographs? About how I had lost the ability to see, *really see*, through the viewfinder, how it no longer afforded me the protection it once had, so that now I had to face the world unprotected. Barnaby, swashbuckler that he was, or thought himself to be, would never understand this.

And what of Simon? How could I possibly tell Barnaby that I was only here, with him, because I'd been blindsided into loving my husband too much, that I feared being eaten alive by it, and by the awful knowledge that Simon suffered from a directly converse burden to my own—that of loving me too little.

"What's wrong?" Barnaby repeated, as if by saying the words again he might wrest from me an intelligible answer.

I held my head in my hands and wept. For Oscar, for Simon, who knew nothing of my betrayal: it was, after all, a betrayal, this affair, though I had never intended it to be. I wept for the boy in the olive-green jacket. And I wept for myself, choked with the bitter knowledge that the world had encroached on my camera, clouding my vision, it seemed, forever more.

"I'd like to go back. Tonight," I said quietly.

He was battling himself; I could see that his assurance was now shot to pieces.

"The story about the bird," he said. "It's a load of garbage and you know it." His tone had turned nasty.

Though I willed them not to, my eyes again filled with tears.

"Stop it," he said. "Don't pull that simpering act. It's not going to work. Not on me."

I bit the inside of my lip, hard.

"And you can forget about going back to Ellis Park tonight—it's too late. Besides," Barnaby continued, "we're not going anywhere until you tell me what's going on. Everything was fine. You had an accident at the lake. Okay, so maybe you're not the world's greatest swimmer. So what? You weren't alone. I was there. I got you out. Nothing broken. No permanent damage. It's plain childish, if you want to know what I think, turning this into a full-scale drama. Chrissakes, just drop it."

There was nothing more to say. I knew I could not tell him the whole truth; it hardly made sense to me and, in any case, he would not have understood. I could not tell him that our affair was over because of what I had seen in his face, the night before when I'd asked him about Christine; because of the way he'd said *my Shanghai*; because of what the water had done to his smiling face as I clutched for oxygen—those rubbery lips, swelling and askew, the eyelids two balloons over bulging eyes. Because of the terrible feeling that I was seeing him, the truth of him, for the first time.

Looking into his suddenly strange face, I made a quick calculation and decided that if I couldn't tell him the whole truth, I would at least tell him a part of it.

"It's because of Simon," I said. His face remained immobile. I turned away, saw in my mind's eye another face, Simon's: oddly serene, despite the frown marks in his brow. Open to truths, his truths as much as those of the world. And free of the need to possess. Not *my Spain, my Tunisia, my New York*, or *my* any of the numerous places he had lived in or visited. And certainly not *my Marilyn*.

I turned back to look at Barnaby.

"What about Simon?" he said. "Simon's been there all along."

There it was, incontrovertible: a faint shudder of fear, the search for safe ground.

I said nothing, and this seemed to steel him; I saw the confidence flowing back into his face. It was a strange thing to witness, like watching a felled creature spring back to life. He let out one of his easy laughs and, when he was finished, the tenderness had returned to his face.

"Sweetheart, is that it? Is that what's upsetting you?" Barnaby's voice was no longer angry. He walked over to where I was sitting cross-legged on the bed, pulled my head into his chest, stroked my hair. Again my eyes welled. Here I was, seeing everything. So why did his touch, the tender fingertip circles at the back of my neck where the hair grew in, feel so much like a lost home?

"Let's not fight, darling. Let's not spoil these last few hours together," he said.

"Oh Barnaby," I whispered, still weeping softly, misunderstanding what he had meant. "Let's not say goodbye angrily."

The words were hardly out when I heard the sound of breaking china, as the table Barnaby had upended crashed to the floor.

"I *will—not—be—left*," Barnaby said, his voice low, unfamiliar.

He stooped to pick up the car keys from where they had landed on the rug and walked out of the room, closing the door behind him carefully, precisely, without a sound.

* * *

After Barnaby had gone, I fell into a real sleep of the kind I'd not had in weeks. I slept for hours, blankly and well. By the time I awoke, the sun was high in the sky, blooming wild bright yellow into the room.

I extricated myself from tangled sheets and lay awhile, letting the thick, scented air bathe my bare limbs.

I dressed, descended, and ate a large lunch of brisket and salad, ignoring the innkeeper, who kept casting furtive glances at the unmanned place setting across from me.

When I'd finished my coffee, I asked the innkeeper to order me a taxi for later that evening to take me back to Ellis Park. I sat in the garden much of the afternoon, every now and then taking the short walk up the country lane to Main Street and back. When the light waned, I returned to the room, once again crushingly tired.

The floral-themed décor, which I'd found charming upon first stepping into this room, now seemed oppressive. I longed to return to the sanity and grandeur of Ellis Park.

I caught myself. *Sanity?* What was I thinking?

A picture leapt to mind: Barnaby, Oscar, the mysterious, nameless visitor, and me, all of us creeping about in the gloom of night, illicit meanderings in some vast below-ground cavern.

The visitor's business card; how could I have forgotten about it? The thought of it now propelled me to my feet. Had I brought that spring jacket with me? Yes! I'd been wearing it on the drive up. I opened the closet; there it was. I dipped my hand into the pocket.

I was puzzled by what I discovered, though somehow, at the same time, not really surprised.

Official lettering at the top, sitting above a distinctive, familiar seal: *Department of Justice.* Below this, in simple black typeface: *Office of Special Investigations.* And a name and title—*Jan van der Putten. Senior Investigative Officer.* A Dutchman?

Could this have something to do with those photographs

Oscar had attempted to develop, and lost? Clearly, his pictures of his family—the woman bore such a striking resemblance to him. Why was Oscar so terribly troubled? And how could any of this require Oscar to obtain legal counsel?

Impulsively, I picked up the receiver of the white telephone on the bedside table and dialed the number printed on the card. The phone rang emptily for what seemed a very long time. I was about to replace the receiver when I heard a gentle click, and then a voice.

"Mr. Van der Putten?"

"Speaking."

"Marilyn Whittacker."

A pause. "I hadn't hoped to hear from you so soon."

"Why are you stalking us at Ellis Park? What is it you want?"

"Stalking is a strong word."

"What would you call it?"

"I am an investigator, madam. I am investigating a case."

"War crimes. Isn't that what your office investigates?"

"That is correct."

"Why did you ask me to contact you?" I was aware of the hostile edge in my voice.

"It is notoriously difficult to build these types of cases; these people are masters of covering up their tracks. We rely on the minute slips. Typically, our most useful sources are those closest to the suspected perpetrator. Someone who is around the person day in, day out—as you are—who is likely to pick up some trifling, but telling clue. I had not planned to approach you quite yet. But then, when I ran into you on the lawn—well, I suppose I was just operating on a hunch. A hunch which, I daresay, if I might judge from the present call, was a good one."

A sudden recollection—not something I'd ever paid mind to before: the odd gesture Oscar exhibited, from time to time, of absently reaching up and rubbing a patch on his left upper arm, as if to ease a spasm or ache.

"Miss Whittacker?"

"I'm still here."

"Perhaps you will think about what I have said."

I found I was speechless.

"I'm glad you called. Please feel free to call me again. And if there's anything—"

Quietly, I replaced the receiver before he could finish his sentence.

A trembling took hold of me; it started in my fingers and coursed through my body—like a slap of fever.

That moment, on the walk, with Oscar: it came back to me like a punch to the jaw. The chill moment of frisson, the baffling desire to ask Oscar not only if and where he had fought in the war, but *on whose side*. It had seemed like an absurd thought at the time but now, in this moment, it seemed inevitable, even perfect: much like the feeling I would get when I sensed that a perfect photograph was about to erupt from the world and present itself to my eyes.

I lay down on the bed; a curdling confusion within turned to misery. I don't know how long I lay there. I shifted toward the window, watched as the sheer curtain billowed slightly and settled to stillness, watched as the rectangle of light moved through the room, then was snuffed to night.

I lay there in the heat, amidst all those ruffles; drifting into sleep, I found myself again back in London at the site of the bombed-out house. Time had stalled. I was looking up at the sky—seconds, fractions of seconds, I had no way of knowing. The colors in the sky were fading, the undoing of an image, like a developing picture in reverse—a return to the void. Inside, a terrible struggle: sensing, intuiting, somewhere deep within, that the only right thing would be to leave the boy to his grief, to simply turn away. But I did not want to let it go, I had to stop myself from crying out with the loss of it.

I took the shot.

My instinct had been on the money; the photograph of the

little boy before the rubble was extraordinary. It won several awards and widespread acclaim, became an icon of Wartime Britain. The shot that established my reputation, and also destroyed, for me, that intimate space of the viewfinder that had made my camera a refuge.

I was awoken by a loud rap on the door. I glanced at the clock on the bedside table: eleven p.m.

"Your cab, miss. It's waiting outside."

I hastily gathered my belongings and rushed downstairs, where I settled the bill and thanked the innkeeper. She appeared to have given my situation some thought and must have decided to pity me, for she reached over, patted my hand, and bestowed a reassuring look.

Thankfully, the driver was not the chatty type. We sped through the warm night in silence. I was aware of some feeling of resolve, though I had formulated no plan.

I had the driver drop me at the bottom of the driveway, by the Spanish gates, which at this hour cast fanciful deep shadows. I walked the driveway, aware, in a new way, of what Oscar had intended to achieve with the canopy of leaves overhead: an invitation not to pleasure, but to solace.

Entering the house through the back door, I made my way directly to the blue suite, Barnaby's rooms, knocked twice, waited, entered. As I expected, the rooms were empty. I opened the closet, pulled at several drawers: all empty. Barnaby had taken full leave of the place.

I felt eerily ghostlike as I headed toward the yellow suite on the other side of the house. Once there, I deposited my weekend bag, splashed cold water on my face, pulled a comb through my hair, and brushed my teeth.

Back in the hallway, I felt sure-footed again; whatever its complications, I realized that I had made Ellis Park mine. Outside Oscar's study, I hesitated. I had no idea what I was going to say. I knocked, turned the handle, first of the outer door, then of the inner, and stepped into the room.

Oscar started, his face exhausted. Seeing it was me seemed to have little effect; he continued to look as if he were in some kind of shock.

"Oscar, it's only me," I said unnecessarily.

His hand rested on his pipe. I sat in the chair facing his desk. He scrutinized my face, as if trying to decipher something.

"I'd like to help," I said.

He was silent.

"Marilyn, there are some things there's no helping," he said finally.

"What is it? What's happened? Is this about those people in the photographs, the ones that fell into the vat? They're your family, aren't they, Oscar? Your mother, your father, your sister."

His face darkened. I knew I was intruding, but I could not stop myself.

"Where are they? What happened to them?"

"I don't know, Marilyn. That's the thing. I'm trying to find out." Oscar gestured to the papers arranged in neat piles on the desk.

"The man who's been following us all around, does he have anything to do with this?"

Now Oscar looked like the wind had gone out of him, as though he'd been kicked in the gut. "What man?" He seemed unconvinced by his own feigning.

"Your late-night visitor."

Oscar reached into the drawer of his desk and drew out his tobacco pouch. "Have you spoken to him?" he asked calmly.

"No. Well, yes. Not really."

Oscar looked at me inquiringly and waited.

"Just once. About two weeks ago. I saw him sneaking out the back entrance. I asked him what he wanted. He looked at me rather arrogantly, I thought. He didn't answer my question, needless to say." The rest I left out—the business card he'd given me, and later, the dreadful telephone call.

Oscar carefully filled his pipe. I could see he was waiting for me to say more.

"I came by your office one night. To talk. Oscar, I heard you speaking German. At least I think it was you. It was hard to tell."

I saw it now, for the first time. Something beneath Oscar's extraordinary control. Sensed that he was embroiled in an ongoing struggle to appear calm, against great odds—battling always, and with great effort, a mighty, invisible storm.

"What is it he wants?"

And then Oscar's control slipped: only for an instant, but I saw again that rawness I'd glimpsed in the studio the night I'd showed him my desperate pictures of Erla; for a moment I felt I was looking at someone I'd never met—not Oscar at all, but a stranger, inhabiting his flesh.

I looked away. When I cast my glance back, Oscar was restored. He picked up a match, touched the flame to the bowl of his pipe. As he puffed to get it going, he seemed to be measuring his words.

"Things are seldom as they seem. I know you know this; I've seen it in your photographs."

Oscar could not have known the impact of his words. The image reared up, the boy in the green jacket, little poisonous flecks of soot, almost invisible, dancing about him in the air. I spoke without thinking.

"Sometimes things *are* what they seem. Isn't that what you intended to create here, at Ellis Park? Nothing but pleasure and calm and grace?" I hardly knew what I was saying. "Only superficial people don't judge by appearances—isn't that so?" I continued, a tremor in my voice, throwing back at him a line from Oscar Wilde that he liked to quote.

I'd spoken about Ellis Park but, in fact, I was thinking of what I had done—saw, in that moment, the true nature of my own actions, though I suppose in some sense, I'd known it all along. This was my crime: showing Oscar the photographs that evening in the darkroom, the photographs of Erla. Showing the world the orphaned boy, there, before the rubble of his house. Ferreting it out, exposing.

And now, here I was. No camera, it is true, but equally presumptuous. In a room bursting with secrets and pain.

"I'm sorry," I muttered, feeling the spill from my eyes. "Really, I am."

I rose, walked around the desk. Oscar rose too. Unthinkingly, we embraced: a long, slow embrace, Oscar still, utterly still.

I knew, in that moment, that whatever the disconcerting man from the Office of Special Investigations might believe, Oscar could not possibly have committed the kind of crime to which he'd alluded. It was simply unimaginable.

I drew away, averting my eyes, understanding only now, and too late, that it was not always my business to see.

"He's mistaken." Oscar said this in an unfamiliar voice; I fancied I detected the trace of a German accent. "Whatever he told you—"

"Yes?"

Oscar had frozen; he was looking at me from some dark place. I'd been to dark places myself, but this was something else entirely. I took a step toward him; he held up his hand, keeping me at bay. Still, he said nothing. I stood unmoving; the heavy silence hung between us.

"I'm tired." Oscar seemed to be speaking to himself. "Terribly, terribly tired."

I remember every second of that meeting. It was the last time I lay eyes on Oscar.

PART III

Oscar

The North Shore of Long Island. Summer, 1951.

CHAPTER SEVEN

Another witness apparently has surfaced. This brings the number to four. From what I can piece together, my visitor's organization generally does not proceed unless a larger number can be produced. They have their reasons to be wary, I suppose, beyond an interest in justice: legal suits, libel claims, and the like. Who the witnesses are, how they came to light: on these issues, my visitor has remained silent. Not surprising, given the nature of the investigation and the fact that he is, for the most part, a man of few words.

The one exception to his general taciturnity was on his first visit, when he talked at length about his organization, giving a detailed account of the dossier they had amassed pertaining, as he put it, to my "case." When he came to the end of his monologue, I was speechless, so great was my astonishment. I detected a measure of embarrassment on his part at my reaction. I was standing by the window and it was only then, the two of us silently facing each other, I noticed the curtain behind me was not properly drawn. I quickly rose. On my approach, my visitor sidestepped me in the direction of the door, his green eyes cool. He flinched as I brushed past him. Before pulling the curtains to, I noted with some relief that the courtyard below and the wing opposite were in complete darkness.

In subsequent meetings, my visitor has restricted himself to the fewest words necessary to convey the latest information. Once, he had nothing to communicate. When I asked him that evening about the purpose of his visit, seeing he had nothing to report, he replied that these *briefings*—that was the word he used—had been scheduled at prearranged intervals, that they did not depend on new developments.

I am having trouble staring down the multiple horrors before me.

I cannot bear to learn about my accusers or their circumstances. One thing I do know is their method of identifying me.

Posing for that picture was a grim business. That first evening, my visitor was carrying a leather satchel, which he set down on the end table by the door. After his little speech, he removed from the satchel the most compact camera I have ever seen, and a tiny flash to go with it.

"Over there," he said, indicating an unadorned section of the wood paneling where I understood he wished me to stand.

I walked to the spot, instinctively straightening my cravat, feeling like a fool for having done so.

"It would probably be better to remove that," he'd said, keeping his eyes on me while he fiddled with something on the camera.

I untied my cravat and, not knowing what else to do with it, stuffed it into the pocket of my jacket. I looked straight into the camera. The miniature lens glinted at me before disappearing, along with everything else, in the tiny but potent light of the flash.

It's a wonder with all his comings and goings that no one has spotted my troublesome visitor. But then, he comes only very late at night and is, to his credit, a model of discretion.

I can move quite freely around the town but I've been told not to leave the county. It did not occur to me that they would doubt my honor on this point until I noticed, three days ago, on my way to the bank, that a shiny blue car seemed unusually evident wherever I went. Once I made a point of looking out for it I found that the car, driven by a pleasant-looking middle-aged man, was trailing me in the most obvious manner as I went about my business. I have no intention of removing myself, although I suppose they can't be blamed for thinking that I might.

I must try to remain as unemotional as possible. I need to conserve my energy for the critical task at hand—of conducting my search. Strangely, this unexpected and alarming development has renewed my vigor; whatever happens, I must do my utmost to track down my mother and my sister. I have uncovered several new leads and am pursuing them with all the hope of the early days, which I thought was lost to me forever. The rest of my life—the house, that is—continues to run smoothly.

Now that I am reembarked on my search for Mama and Else, the memories are coming back unbidden. Almost six years of freedom, of having truly *fled*: undone. I find myself back in my childhood home, the redbrick house on Kirchstrasse. Back with my sister and mother, reliving the details, scouring each moment for clues as to how I might have—should have—acted differently. Seeing only, and everywhere, missteps.

After the world performed that peculiar somersault that changed everything forever, I had wanted to ask my mother if Papa had known. I wanted to know if Papa had been as surprised as I was when the soldiers had come to our own door. For months we'd heard of the nighttime arrests—and, some weeks earlier, I'd heard my mother and father arguing about whether to hide our elderly neighbors, the Bergmans, in our attic.

"Absolutely not," Papa had insisted, his handsome face marred by the thick blue vein that appeared in his forehead when his ire was aroused. "We have the children to think of."

Mama's response had puzzled me. "But it *is* the children I'm thinking of," she said sadly, letting the lace curtain fall back across the window.

Two weeks later, the Bergmans were taken away, with the usual theatrics. Clear across the street we heard the banging on the door, and then the sound of crashing and thudding from within—furniture being toppled, china and crystal smashed. The old woman must have been prepared: I knew that they did not allow people to collect belongings, and yet when she was led away, she was wearing her good felt hat. I pictured her, Mrs. Bergman, whom I'd known since my earliest days, sitting night after night in her parlor, the hat pinned into place on her head. I wondered what it could have meant to her, anticipating that when they led her away, she'd be wearing her good felt hat.

They did not smash our door in, though, and they did not take us all away. Just Papa—*For questioning,* we were told. *Your wife is suspected of being a Jew. It's a crime to be married to a Jew. We need to establish the facts.*

I had long closed my eyes and ears to the awful realities of the new order—including the arcana of details surrounding the laws of racial purity—realities that had not, until now, pertained to me or my family. When they came for Papa, a vague and pertinent recollection seeped back. That while all Jews were considered racially impure, slated for eventual "resettlement" or "special work assignments," to be married to a Jew was a crime, a treasonous act worthy of immediate action. This was partly a matter of public pageantry; such *criminals* were paraded through the streets wearing signs declaring their treachery. It dawned on me with horror that Papa would be put to such use. And, once *the facts were established,* we—my mother, Else, and I—would be put on the list for a late-night seizure.

My father had not moved with the stunned stillness of the elderly neighbors but had gone in a panic, the blue vein writhing on his forehead. Papa gave us each a hasty kiss as the flax-haired soldier stood silently tending to his military posture. Some minutes later, I watched through the window as Papa descended the stairs. He cast a quick backward glance and I saw a terrible knowledge slammed into those gentle eyes, and something else I could scarcely believe: the strong, square jaw of my father, quivering.

"Your father will be back," Mama had said evenly, walking to the piano and raising the cover. "He's only been taken for questioning. Their claim is absurd; they'll find no records to back it up. They'll admit their error and things will go back to the way there were." She pressed a few chords into the keys, slowly, as if the care she took with the notes would ensure Papa's safety. Else settled next to Mama on the brocade piano stool. Leaning over the belly of the instrument, I watched my mother's wrists float above the keys.

It was my idea to move to the attic.

"I suppose it can't hurt," Mama had said. "As a precaution, until your father returns."

We dragged the cot from my room up the stairs. I see Mama in her tan wool dress, which kept catching in the springs of the metal frame. By the time we reached the attic, the front of the skirt was speckled with little brown holes. I managed the small table and chairs on my own; Else and Mama followed with armfuls of clothes. We brought up supplies in the wooden buckets Hilde used when she scrubbed the floors: bread, dried meats, sausage, jars of vegetables and preserves, three enormous cabbages with loose ruffled skin. I remember turning to see Else, a smaller dark-haired version of Mama, straining with the heavy buckets. In the dusky light of a single candle, I could see the grimness in Mama's face. Pointless, after all, I remember thinking, to move to the attic. No matter how we barricaded it, the door to the attic would yield to the soldiers' axes like butter.

No records to back it up. I chewed over Mama's words and found in them this meaning: that though not provable, the claim itself was true. But that evening, my mother's face was closed to questions, so I resolved to wait out her mood and broach the matter in a day or two.

Later, Else and Mama knelt by the bed, then looked toward me expectantly, though I did not join them; it had been years since I'd prayed. That smooth Latin chant, a layer of syrup to coat the dread. Mama made the sign of the cross over Else, then rose and did the same to me, her fingers curved like a dancer's, pausing at my forehead, dipping to my chest, passing slowly across my shoulders. Her lips worked silently. I knew she was whispering to Jesus to protect her *kinde*.

The needle flew in the wavery near-dark. A single taper, placed in the corner of the attic farthest from the window, was our only illumination. I'd never before seen my mother sew yet her movements were expert and unthinking. Where Mama was concerned, I was used to such little mysteries. Once—I couldn't have been older than five—I was helping Mama in the rose garden. She'd turned and looked into my face, a sudden light transforming her features. The heaviness of the shears in my little boy's hands; I'd managed to keep them aloft, just the right distance from the coiled bud.

"I tended a garden like this when I was a little girl, just about your age." The way she addressed me when we were alone: as if the rest of the world had ceased to exist.

"The nuns planted it, just for me," she continued, drawing so close I could feel the whisper of her breath on my cheeks. I exerted all of my strength to keep the shears up high against the stem, as if letting them fall would shred the splendid cocoon that had sprung up invisibly around us.

"Before the convent," I whispered. "Where did you live before you lived with the nuns?"

"In a palace on a diamond mountain, where I took baths in tubfuls of rose petals." She kissed my nose. The shears dropped from my hands, landing with a thud in the dirt. Mama turned back to her work, the brightness fading from her smooth oval face.

She'd probably learned to sew in the convent; there, in

the attic, I watched as Mama's needle looped through the air. I glanced over to Else. It was then, when I saw my sister's straight shoulders and closed, numb face, that I knew she would not be coming with me.

"Here," Else said, handing me a small scrap of paper. "My friend Klara, do you remember her? She has an uncle in England; his daughter and I wrote to each other for a while—*pen pals*, that's what she called it. I kept her address. Take it."

The words were barely visible in the weak light. *47 Park Street, Mayfair. London.* I folded it three times into a tiny square and handed it to my mother.

The work done, Mama passed me the jacket. I examined the series of little pockets secreted in the lining at waist level, admiring the tiny, even stitches. I passed the jacket back to Mama, who slipped the gold coins, one by one, into the new pockets, tucked the tiny folded square of paper in with one of them, then set about stitching them shut.

I did not sleep. I sensed the arrival of morning, even before lifting a corner of the oily cloth covering the small window of the attic. Redbrick houses, side by side; a rusted bicycle leaning against a wall. Winter light slanted coldly across the gray length of the street, etching the shapes of naked branches onto rumpled patches of brown grass. I let the cloth fall, walked to where the wooden trunk, fastened with a brass latch in the shape of a lion's head, sat under the eaves. I pulled up the protruding tongue of the lion and the trunk sprang open, releasing a musky, yellowish breath of cedar. Folded on top was the heavy navy jacket; beneath that, a blue woolen cardigan and navy flannel trousers. I removed each piece and put them on over the clothes I was already wearing. I glanced over to where my mother and sister lay sleeping on the mattress. I stood there, unmoving, for quite some time.

So many conversations about leaving. Always the same, my mother's tightly drawn mouth, her unshakable resolve. "I am not leaving without your father. He'll expect me to be here when he comes back." And Else's girlish optimism: "It's all a dreadful mistake. We're Catholics, after all. Mama, isn't that so?"

I knew what they would say: "Go," the two voices one. "We'll see you when it's over."

When I had finally summoned the courage to ask Mama about her background, she answered cryptically, though her meaning, in the end, had been plain.

"I have no memory of any of the nuns ever telling me this story," she'd said. "Although they must have, perhaps when I was a very little child. The image has been plaguing me since they took your father away. I always thought it was simply a very odd dream. It never occurred to me there was any truth in it."

I walked over to where Mama and Else lay sleeping. I leaned over my sister: the warm imprint of her cheek on my lips. Then I placed my own cheek against the face of my sleeping mother.

The hallway, cold and wide after the confinement of the attic, was softly aglow with early-morning light. I stayed close to the wall as I took the stairs, ducking beneath the window at each of the three landings.

I descended the last flight to the maid's quarters and turned the glass door handle with care. Hilde's room was as she had left it—the crocheted bedspread drawn tightly across the bed, a half-drunk glass of water on the windowsill. Four stockings dangled from the mantle, each describing the shape of Hilde's short thighs and muscular calves. An open book lay spine down on the table by the window, splattered with faded rose petals, and beside it, in a glass vase filled with murky green water, a half-dozen stems stood with drooping puckered heads. Hilde's familiar odor lingered in the air, a curious mixture of molasses and slightly rancid milk.

Through Hilde's room and into the adjoining workroom, used for storing wood, which opened onto the garden. Out and across the little vegetable garden Hilde had tilled for so many years, now dormant under a cover of sackcloth.

The gray stones of the alley collected my footsteps into echoes, which sounded dangerously loud. The leaves, the sky, the occasional crop-haired bullfinch—all were startlingly vivid, unnervingly still, as if everything around me was readying to pounce. I felt something brush up against my leg and started to run. I swiveled my head back to see a small white dog with a wounded expression on its face. I slowed back down, attempted a casual gait.

Walking. A welter of streets. I was aware of an alarming, invisible shift that had taken place in the world. I'd had no reason, before this moment, to question my place in the order of things as I walked down the street. But now, the world vibrated with awareness, bristled with the threat of being seen.

I found myself taking the familiar route to my school—I would have graduated with honors in the spring, only days shy of my eighteenth birthday, and therefore of the draft. I came to a halt before the building. Flashes of my life there: crouched on the tarmac of the schoolyard, shooting marbles, lining up when the bell rang to file into class. Always a crowd of boys in boisterous motion. It was here that the world of art and artifacts had been opened up for me, through the person of Professor Eisensdtadt, a junior curator from the Zwinger who taught several afternoons at the school. The darkened classroom, the procession of illuminated slides beamed onto the wall, the feel of slipping into a new dimension. Sometimes, in that brief moment before the lights flickered back on, I'd feel almost drunk, my imagination reeling with these images in their slow-motion brilliance.

More recent events at the school were bleached out and unreal, like overexposed photographs. There were the gradual disappearances—senior boys pulled out for the draft, the day they came of age—and the other empty chairs about which no one spoke, the age of the boys in those cases irrelevant. I had now joined them myself: one of the vanished. Were my friends alarmed? Agitating to find me? Or doing what we'd all done before: simply taking this latest disappearance in stride?

The building was locked; no one was yet about. I looked up at the curved inscription on top of the tall iron gates. Light pulsed behind the steel-gray fabric of the sky, turning it to a sheer funereal veil. Standing there before the school, I counted my own breaths, one through ten then back again. A flutter, inside, of recklessness. I turned in the direction of the city center. I wanted to put to the test that new feeling: to see whether there really were eyes everywhere—in the coats of the birds, in the street signs and buildings and lampposts.

By the time I reached the center, the streets were coming to life. Older men in heavy overcoats carried briefcases, purpose in their stride. Women hurried to their work; others walked, small children in tow. Everywhere, the brown uniforms. They'd been around, it seemed, forever—since I was a boy of eleven. Now I felt I was really seeing them for the first time.

I walked purposefully, flexing my shoulders and the muscles of my back to ease out any possible sign of fear.

Up this street, down that, drawing in the bracing air: Heidelberg, my city, even as I fled it, tracing itself into the soles of my feet.

Before the department store, a small line of mostly younger women waited while a guard struggled with an unwieldy set of keys. It was risky, even crazy, but I was gripped by a desire to see if I could disguise the new knowledge I had about myself. When the large entrance doors finally opened, I followed the group of women into the foyer, with its minimal attempts at Christmas cheer—a bedraggled artificial Christmas tree, no more than three feet tall and missing handfuls of branches, and drapings here and there of tatty red tinsel and worn green felt.

I wandered around the ground floor; the oddment of

salespeople and poorly stocked shelves contrived an atmo-
sphere of grim deficiency. I stopped to examine a display of
ties, frosted with fine dust. The unnerving sense, again, of
watching eyes. I mounted the stairs, aware of the feel of my
hand sliding slowly up the polished banister. Above and below me, on the two levels joined by the stairs, the number of
shoppers seemed to be increasing. I was sweating beneath the
multiple layers of clothing I was wearing. I reached the top of
the staircase and there he was, a middle-aged man, paunchy,
with a babyish round jaw, wearing a uniform. A presumptuous look on his face, eyes that had come to some conclusion.

Relax, relax, I said to myself over and over, desperately trying to appear indifferent.

"Over here, boy," the guard said as I stepped onto the
landing.

"Good day to you, sir," I replied, intending to keep moving. I was stopped by the dangerous gleam in the man's eye.

"Doing your Christmas shopping?" The guard's voice was
thick with derision.

"A vase for my mother, sir." I looked him full in the face.

"I don't see why your *mother*," he emphasized this word,
"would want to soil perfectly beautiful flowers with her filthy
Jew hands."

I looked at the man a long moment. The man stared back,
seemed to be waiting.

"What do you want?" I asked, and the guard jerked his
head in the direction of a booth on the other side of the
mezzanine.

"Gestapo. Temporary office," he said. "Let's take a walk
over there, shall we?" Just hardness, now, in his face.

"If it's money . . ." my voice was steady.

Without hesitation: "What do you have?"

I named an amount of gold. Several emotions cycled trans-
parently across the guard's face: greed, anxiety, and, oddly,
temperance.

"Wouldn't want to clean you out, son," he said, his tone now strangely avuncular. I unbuttoned my coat, reached in at the waist, pulled at Mama's stitches, closed my hand around one of the gold coins she'd sewn in. I stretched my arm out, as if to shake hands. Our palms met.

"Holiday season, after all," the guard said. I lowered my empty hand, nodded.

"*Guten tag,*" I said.

"*Ja,* and to you," the guard replied with a trace of courtesy. I moved on, aware of a repugnant surge of gratitude toward the round-faced guard.

Out again on the street. I emptied my mind in order that my face might show nothing. My feet moved of their own accord.

Her filthy Jew hands. What had tipped off the guard? The extra layers of clothing? A furtive look in my face?

I rounded a corner and saw the sloping shapes of very old tombstones. Before me, in the small square, a circle of birds dipped and shook themselves in the froth of the fountain. The patina-green dome and steeple of the church rose prettily above the plain boxy roof of the vestry. Pausing beside the old graveyard, I peered at the largest of the markers, as I had done a hundred times since I was a boy, in an absent attempt to make out the faded lettering. Two letters only were decipherable, a D and an S, the others reduced to a bare indent or curve or else altogether dissolved into the stone.

I walked up the stairs to the church and rapped three times. The door was opened by the priest, whose face, with its bland watery eyes and loose, double chin, was as known to me as the faces of my own parents. Sunday after Sunday, year after year, I'd sat on the smooth oak of the pew, taking in the week's homily, glancing sidelong at the unmoving, absorbed forms of Mama and Papa, sometimes holding Else's hand to keep her from fidgeting. The weathered, resigned face of the Pater presiding over us all, his kind, distracted eyes sweeping the congregation in a gesture of ingathering.

Now, standing in the doorway, the old Pater's eyes flick-ered with surprise.

Inside, the familiar cold stone stillness of the air. I fol-lowed, the echo of several hundred years rising upward from my feet, up into the steeple's point. The priest took me to the room behind the chapel, where the choirboys dressed for mass. Sitting across from him, on a low stool, I told him what had happened.

When I came to the part about my mother's suspected Jewishness, I found myself hesitating. I felt absurd having to utter the words. The priest sat very still in his brown leather chair, his back to the heavy red drapes drawn across the win-dow, his only movement an occasional nod of the head.

When I finished speaking, he leaned forward and gripped the arms of his chair with thick-knuckled fingers.

"There's a milk cart that makes deliveries in the hills," he said. "Twice a week. It leaves tomorrow morning. Six o'clock. We've sent Jewish boys out that way before. As far as I know, the escapes have been successful." Barely noticeable, the slight indrawing of the Pater's breath at the word *Jewish*.

"Alfred is the owner of the cart. He'll tell you what to do once he drops you off. He has made a study of it. You will make your way by foot—far and away the safest bet—and eventu-ally cross over to Marseilles. There, you will find a barge that sails for England." Another pause. "Do you have money?"

I nodded, absently fingering one of the gold pieces my mother had sewn into the lining at the waist of my jacket.

"You'll need it for the boat. A piece or two of gold will suffice. Now, about tonight. It's not very comfortable, I'm afraid, but there's a closet under the stairs behind the sanctu-ary where I keep my vestment garments. It would be best if you stayed there."

It was stuffy that night, in among the priest's garments, the long stifling hours measured out in lungfuls of mothballs and starch and stale body odor. The idea formed, and then

I could not let it go, that I would make a detour in the early morning, en route to the market, to take one last, brief look at the river—my beloved Donau.

I slept very little, dozing off at intervals, for what seemed like only minutes. The airless closet had a skylight; I watched the night sky lighten to a misty, early dawn, then quietly took my leave through the silent cold church, moving one last time past the ancient wood door, tall as three men, the old metal hinges creaking quietly as I carefully pulled the door shut.

The backstreets were empty. I walked quickly—I could feel the exertion in my ankles, calves, thighs; the pavement rushed beneath my feet. And I felt I was moving in terrible slow motion. All around me, darkness diffused to grainy, hazed light. I broke out from the side streets to see the glimmer, ahead, of the river. Down by the water, where the brown grass thinned to a crust of dried clay, I crouched for a moment and closed my eyes, sensing the dark ache of the river's passage through the hardening winter earth.

Looking at the rumpled green surface of the water, I puzzled over why, the night before, of all the benedictions I could have chosen, it was the Absolution I had asked the priest to recite.

Back on the side streets, hugging the shadows, I studied the universe of cracks at my feet as one might the constellations. Turning into the square, I saw that the market, like everything else, had narrowed to its own bare outline. Four or five ragamuffin stalls, each frayed awning flapping above a meager offering: several rounds of dark bread, charred at the edges; a trayful of gloomy-eyed fish; spotted apples in a barrel. The bread seller, no audience yet, barked to nobody, with the vaguely insulting gusto of the professional hawker. By the gate, a stooped man entreated an old mare laden with wares to get moving, but the beast only stared into the distance.

Alfred, the milk carrier, was exactly where the priest said he would be, in the far corner of the square, under the branches of a mulberry tree, busying himself with the hoof of his dray. He looked up at the sound of footsteps, lowered the animal's leg. With no word and barely a glance, he opened the door in the house behind him and absently stood aside.

I found myself alone in a small hallway smelling of cat urine. Through the door behind me I could hear rhythmic, clanking thumps—the sound of the man loading the milk urns into the wagon. The door cracked open, I glimpsed the man's eyes, bright and eager as a boy's. He slipped in, then thrust me down the stairs.

Below, in the cellar, the man pointed to a grate high in the wall. "Five minutes. I'll be there with the cart," he said, and he was gone.

How to judge five minutes? Through the muddy darkness, across the cellar. The handle of the grate was stiff with rust. I tugged and it gave. I heaved myself into the opening, aware of the smell of fresh horse dung.

Two arms seized my shoulders; I was pulled out through the window and shoved into the back of a closed wagon. The clanking sound from earlier continued, amplified. Milk urns were being loaded into the wagon all around me, and then on top of wooden planks inches from my head.

The horses let out several loud snorts as they heaved the cart into motion. A tune reached my ears, the same peasant ditty my nurse had sung to me as a child, whistled through the milkman's teeth. I focused on my breathing and tried to lose myself in the jolting of the cart.

The steady loping movement. Vague, unsettling moments of sleep. The slow assault, in my gut, of hunger. Staring into the closed darkness.

The hours congealed; time became the long, cold, intensely uncomfortable jolting of the milk wagon, my ears deafened by the clanking, my spine and bent knees reduced to an intensity of numbness that sparked, every now and then, into pain.

Many hours into my journey, I fell into a dead sleep. I awoke with a feeling of dread. Nothing but the cursed clanking all about me, the world a cacophony of metal making busy contact with metal.

An ear-splitting explosion. Soldiers' boots. Voices, shouting in German. "Pig! Jew lover!" The wagon reeled, then crashed onto its side. A foaming white torrent poured through a vent in the crate; the cool rain washed over me, soaking my hair, trickling into the crevices of my clothes.

"Find the Jew! He's hiding a Jew!"

And now Alfred's voice, anxious and solicitous. I opened my lips; sweet cream seeped across my tongue. I held it in my mouth before swallowing.

The approach of more heavy boots. The door of the cart, partly in splinters, pried from its hinge. Urns heaved from the toppled cargo. Gunfire, more shouting. The roof of the wagon flew skyward, the urns opened, metal flowers in fitful bloom, sending pure white geysers into the night air. A crater appeared in the floor of the wagon; I tumbled through, thudding to a stop with my face against the wet ground.

Crawling, clinging to a ridge of dirt, I waited for the next, fatal explosion. But there was only an eerie creaking: the damaged axis of the earth, trying to right itself?

Inching along the ground for an eternity. The smell of mud turned slightly foul. I tumbled into a shallow ditch. With my hands, I began digging. The soil was soft and gave easily. I packed the mud high on the sides to form a lip, and waited. Images from the weeks in the attic with my sister and mother flooded my mind: snatches of our intermittent conversations. Odd new glimpses of each other, in that shuttered world, that existence shorn of daylight and daytime realities. The dream Mama told me about, a strange dream that had visited her throughout her childhood. I heard her voice again:

I have no memory of any of the nuns ever telling me this, but af-

ter they took your father away, the image of it kept coming to my mind.

A wide lawn late at night, I'm standing alone. It is very cold; I'm inadequately dressed. Looking at a large house on a hill. Below me, beautiful countryside I do not recognize: fields and orchards. A forest in the distance. I'm shivering in my short-sleeved blouse. Two people come out from a clump of bushes: large, draped figures, moving quickly. Each holds a hand to her head to keep her winged headgear from flying away in the wind. They are nuns, older members of the convent, the only home I ever knew.

They hurry up the incline; one disappears behind the house while the other stands watch. The first reappears, carrying an enormous ladder. Together, they maneuver the ladder into position against a window of the third floor, and then the first woman climbs while the second steadies the ladder from below. She opens the window and squeezes through. Minutes pass.

Finally, the plump nun reappears at the window and makes her way down, supporting herself with one arm. In her other arm, she carries a bundle. Leaving the ladder where it is, the two women move quickly across the open lawn. The bundle is moving, wailing. In the dream, I know two facts: that it is a Jewish household the nuns have robbed, and that the baby one of them holds in her arms is me.

I remember something else: hearsay, rumors. About rogue nuns who stole Jewish babies from their beds. They thought they were saving souls.

Lying in the ditch, Mama's dream image was as vivid as if I'd had the dream myself.

After they took your father away.

It was cold in the ditch, but there was give to the dirt; it was a comfortable place to rest. Night fell fitfully. And then, darkness all around, pressing down from the sky and up through the damp soil. I ground my face into the mud: the feel of crushed worms against my cheek; I can feel it still. And smell the milk, which had turned, a sour stench lifting from my trousers, clammy against my skin.

After I began my apprenticeship with Mr. Harcourt at the London brokerage house of Harcourt and Goode, I realized I could tell the future. It was a kind of double exposure—the events recorded in the newspaper superimposed on the numbers flying off the ticker tape. Together, they formed a crystal ball; I had only to glance at it and it was as if I knew which stocks would rise: which business initiative was certain to thrive in that climate of war.

It started as a game. I felt a certain glee, watching the little rubble of gold coins my mother had sewn into the waist of my jacket grow into the town house I bought in Kensington, not three years after being taken to the Internment Center on the outskirts of London. Magic, sorcery, call it what you will; the pleasure was in the trickery, in the feeling that I was making restitution, irrational as that seems to me now.

I sold paintings too. Was that also a game?

Mail from Germany is taking an inordinate amount of time to reach us. *Normalizing relations*—that's the term that's used. But an astounding amount of disorganization remains; even six years later, the newspapers give no indication of the extent of bureaucratic disarray that is still to be found there. I have exhausted all the relevant bureaus dealing with displaced persons and have decided that I must now widen the search to include those horror pits I can scarcely bring myself to think about. I find myself fighting the deed, so afraid am I of what I might discover. But I will grit my teeth and barrel through. Tonight, I will stay up until dawn, if necessary, writing to the relevant authorities that have been set up to deal with inquiries for each of the *camps*. How elastic language is—this word, once innocent enough, now yielding to its heinous new meaning.

Here am I, my identity confused with that of an SS officer, second-in-command of one of the smaller camps, at the same time as I am forced, in my search for my mother and sister, to consider that such a place was their fate.

And me, a Jew, accused of such things.

I tell myself that I owe the fortune I amassed to that odd precognition I had—the ability to map developments in the theater of war onto the happenings of the stock market. (Although why should this have assuaged any hidden sense of guilt? After all, is there not something unsavory about putting to use a talent for bleeding the jugular of the war organism?)

In any case, there were also monies made elsewhere.

I have never tallied the amount I made selling paintings. Now, despite my efforts to silence the inner voice, the numbers ricochet in my mind, sums in pounds sterling, as if they are insisting on being counted. Large sums, defying me to ignore them. Sums I ploughed back into my workaday financial schemes, which then multiplied beyond any expectation I might have had.

Memories of that sorry undertaking of my life visit too, unbidden. This happens often when I am sitting with Marilyn, late at night in the stainless steel surrounds of the darkroom I constructed on a whim when I first took possession of Ellis Park.

I find myself reliving negotiations, deals, the handing over of the booty. Last night, for example, to take just one of the many moments I would rather forget, I was sitting in the basement with Marilyn, trying to read the newspaper, and one face kept insinuating itself into my mind's eye. I tried to push the image away, to no avail. This inner tousle ended as it always does: with the meeting of long ago playing over in my mind from start to finish, like a newsreel.

The gentleman, whom I shall not name, was titled. By that time, I had become accustomed to the homes of the aristocracy, partly because of having lived those two years with the Harcourts, and partly through escapades of my own. So I was not particularly overwhelmed by the splendor of his home, though I did register the massive entrance hall, the sweep of the curved stairway, the sequins of refracted light sloughing from the cut-glass surfaces of the chandelier.

The butler showed me into a private rear parlor. Though we had corresponded, the gentleman and I had not actually met. I was thrown off by his appearance—not the silk smoking jacket or his refined features, but the unexpected and baffling expression he wore: a mixture, it seems now, looking back, of high sensibility and prurient greed.

"I see you have brought it with you," he said, even before rising or offering his hand. And when he did come toward me with an outstretched arm, it was not to perform the appropriate social gesture but to relieve me of the package I was holding, which was wrapped tightly in brown paper and tied with twine.

"Do forgive me," he added, a head nod to his discourtesy. "I'm just so anxious, finally, to see it."

He went at the twine with some dexterity and in less than two minutes was gazing at the rich reds and gold of the Cranach, a panel from one of the lesser, yet still startlingly beautiful altar pieces. I stood in the shadows, beyond the lamplight, watching his face, a face soft with privilege and lit from within by inspiration. The dead artist had crossed the Channel, the centuries, the Life-Death boundary, to chase out the lassitude and frivolity of this parlor with a breath of truth.

"I trust you've made the necessary arrangements," he said, searching the details of the canvas.

"Everything's taken care of," I replied, feeling suddenly defenseless, as if the brown package I'd been clutching had been a shield.

"You'll find the funds in place as we discussed," he explained. "It will take no longer than two or three days."

This was typically the moment of awkwardness, and I found myself thinking that a more precise etiquette for such situations would certainly be helpful. I imagined, for an instant, writing a manual myself: *Manners for the Black Marketeer*. I bowed slightly before making a discreet exit.

This evening, my visitor was carrying a portfolio under his arm. The usual courteous greeting, and then instead of positioning himself by the window (I now make sure the curtains are properly drawn), he sat in the hard-backed chair by the door, placing the portfolio on the side table next to him.

"I will repeat my earlier recommendation," he began. "For your protection we strongly advise that you engage legal counsel. This is not to say that proceedings against you are imminent. They are, however, a possibility. I have here copies of the relevant documents."

Stepping around my desk, I glanced at the portfolio, which was made of heavy black card and embossed in gold with the seal of his office.

"Witness depositions." He fixed me with his green eyes. "Memos. A portion of our correspondence about your case with the Department of Immigration and Naturalization."

I could feel it tonight quite distinctly—that he was watching me. And waiting, I'm not entirely sure for what. For some sign, perhaps, some indication that would help him move this business along? Was he wondering if I perhaps planned to do myself harm? I can't help imagining there's more to it. He's a difficult man to read. Something about the way he looked at me tonight makes me think he has a personal stake in this: that he's looking to me, or rather to my *case*, as he calls it, for clues that might settle some important dilemma of his own.

He's an interesting young man; one senses in him a pure-ness of spirit, but also an element of mystery. One of those people who seems to have no dark secrets and at the same time everything to hide.

It's been awhile since he left—maybe an hour. The black folder is sitting where he left it on the side table. From here, the seal looks like an upside-down smile, and the lettering on the inside of it like polished little teeth.

I've fallen behind in the matter of my search. There is so much to do. How could I have energy or time to take steps in the direction of my *own* protection or defense? The search for my mother and sister seems so much more urgent, so much more the driving reason for my life.

Half of this week's mail is still lying unopened on my desk. I will stay up as long as I need to catch up on the correspondence. I find myself once again, as in the early days, holding on to the possibility of finding them.

Between calls from my visitor, my efforts to keep *this business* out of my mind are, for the most, successful. Every now and then, however, I catch myself in the midst of a disturbing daydream. Someone I've never seen is holding a photograph with trembling hands. Sometimes it is a man, sometimes a woman, and the age of the person varies from very young to quite old. Once, the figure I pictured was not much more than a child, a girl with long brown hair and a self-possessed air. In this reverie I watch, alarmed, but also horribly fascinated, as a hundred recollections and feelings flitter across the face: slight shadings of a taut skin when the face is a young one, a deepening and rearranging of creased furrows when it is old. In this daydream, no words are spoken. There is only the awful pulse of recognition as he or she examines the photograph, the play across the face of the kind of memory that excites all the senses, that is relived the instant it is aroused. The individual then looks up, gives a quick nod, and hands back the picture, holding the corner pinched between forefinger and thumb, as if to avoid being contaminated. It is usually at that point that I catch myself and try to dissolve the image, though it is already too late.

At these moments, I have the urge to leap to some kind of action—to call for the car and rush into town and somehow try to set things right. To search out those nameless souls and change their lives, bringing to bear whatever resources I now have at my disposal: to undo their experiences, that they might never have set foot in that place where these witnesses now say I committed the crimes of which I stand accused.

Memory can be tamed, I want to say. *Let me show you how.* I look over at the portfolio with its insinuating upside-down smile. The actual accusers—not the changing, nameless faces that have been haunting me of late—are listed there. Their names are perhaps neatly written in my visitor's professional hand— no surnames, no addresses, I should think; the agency would be cognizant that these people would surely fear me still, or, should I say, fear the person they believe me to be.

And here, of course, I must stare another irony in the face: that having spent a good many years pretending to be someone I'm not, I am now taken for another *someone* far removed from any impersonation I have in fact committed.

I see I have used the word *committed.*

And aptly—for how could I not be aware that, along with everything else, I have also betrayed the past?

In the nightmarish daydream, after the accusing faces flash before my mind's eye, the thought of myself frantically tracking down these people inevitably brings me to my senses in such a way that makes me want to laugh out loud. Were any of them ever to see me in the flesh they would recoil in horror, for they are my accusers, and the face in the picture they cannot bear to touch is my own, staring bleakly, unblinking, into the closing black shutter of my visitor's sophisticated miniature lens.

And in any case, there is no setting this right. I know that in my bones.

CHAPTER EIGHT

We never did talk about Christine, Barnaby and I, except for briefly, the day we first met.

Christine bequeathed Barnaby to me (or perhaps me to him), informing him of how he might track me down. I do not believe she did this lightly; Christine was not a person who did things lightly. *I think you and Oscar could be friends*: according to Barnaby, those were the words she'd used.

I knew, when I first saw Christine in that bleak little classroom at the Language School in London's East End, that she would change my life. I'd been at the Internment Center five months, and though I'd made good progress, building on the solid English-language instruction I'd received at school, my accent was appalling. Christine was known for working miracles with pronunciation, so I was delighted to learn that for my third session—the last we were entitled to as alien, "interned" refugees—I'd been assigned to her class.

I believe Christine felt it that first day too, though she maintained a professional posture.

On the last day of the six-week session, as we all filed out of the small bare room, that was painted the sickly wartime green of all government agencies, Christine asked me to remain behind. It was then that she offered me private lessons, insisting on waiving the fee. Desperate to eliminate the guttural German burrs from my speech—and eager, too, for an opportunity to be alone in Christine's company—I swallowed my pride and accepted her offer, assuring her I would reimburse every farthing, once I'd secured employment.

Sitting with her that first evening, the two of us alone

in the sterile classroom, it was as if someone had flipped a switch, effacing the appalling numbness that had engulfed me since leaving the redbrick house on Kirchstrasse. It was cold in that room: the bare walls and tile floor set up a disconcerting echo that reduced us both to whispers. Looking into Christine's vivid green eyes, aware of her subtly mobile features, which remarkably displayed both world-weariness and great cheer, I felt warmed back into the fullness of life.

By the end of the lesson, something had changed between us: no longer the *teacher* with one of her refugee students, but two people, leaning urgently toward each other.

Soon, I was spending long evenings with Christine at her lodgings in Bethnal Green. We continued to meet twice weekly at the school, teacher and student, the two involvements remaining distinct and yet drawing us closer together.

Later, on the heels of my early success at Harcourt and Goode, when I was ensconced at my Kensington town house, we kept to my rooms there, enjoying the spacious elegance and grateful for being completely in our own space.

I recall an odd thought. Christine and I were celebrating my birthday—perhaps two years after we met; Christine had fashioned an apple pie from coarse ration flour, lard, and a single spotted piece of fruit, and we were savoring a bottle of wine I'd managed to get my hands on. I remember thinking, looking into Christine's clear eyes, startled by a happiness I thought I'd never again feel, that we were twins, both ageless and aged, outside of time, outside of place.

Here I am now, sitting in the soft round of light cast by the desk lamp in my study at Ellis Park, the rest of the room sunk in comforting shadow, quickening to the feeling of being united with Christine. For six long years I have cast her from my mind, along with everything else; I had supposed her lost forever. And now I am almost giddy with the sense of her. I have only to close my eyes and she springs to life: here, really here—and also there, really there, *back then*. The past no longer the past. I see her crossing the room to where I await her by our usual table at the club. Other eyes, too, follow her progress; she is a figure one wants to watch—the strawberry-blond hair pressed close to her small head in glossy ripples, the clear complexion, the nonchalant and absolute self-possession of a woman who has all her life known the power of her own beauty. As she comes closer, I see the unsettled intelligence of her face—eyes in search of something, an un-yielding impatience about the mouth. And when our eyes meet, the dazzle of her generous, uninhibited smile.

I never tired of watching Christine move. I never tired of listening to her expound on this or that enthusiasm. I never tired of touching her, of breathing her in.

I recall another moment at the club, something that puzzled me at the time but which I'd put from my mind until now. We were at the award ceremony, the night I was honored by Harcourt and Goode for the work I had done. All evening, I'd been aware of something slightly altered in the way Christine looked at me. I'd assumed it was simply the newness, for her, of the situation—seeing me, well, at the center of things. Toward the end of the evening (which had, to my embarrassment, been rather too glittering, given the circumstances; we were still a nation at war, though the end was in sight) I was surrounded by a little group of well wishers when I found Christine suddenly at my side, that odd, appraising look on her face. I was doing my best to utter the expected gracious remark to yet another compliment when Christine stood up on tiptoe—not easy, I imagine, in the high-heeled silk evening shoes she was wearing—and whispered in my ear: *Who are you, Robert?* (My old name. My real name. I was not yet Oscar.) *Really, I'd like to know.* I was more than a little thrown by the question and responded, I'm afraid, by simply pretending I'd not heard what she'd said.

Upon meeting Barnaby, I saw in his eyes that he, too, had loved Christine. Strikingly, this inspired in me little jealousy.

Though Barnaby has tremendous erotic magnetism, I imagined that Christine, with her near incapacity for returning love—I count myself as the only exception—would have had for Barnaby no more than light affection. He was simply too, well, conventional; and likely to have come in too close (I picture troops astride steeds, crashing across the drawbridge), not knowing how to keep the right distance. Another might suppose me self-deluded here, but I really knew Christine (I fancy I know her still) and feel certain that whatever the liaison with Barnaby, our own intimacy—exclusive, irrevocable—remained unrivaled. So rather than being the cause of any friction between Barnaby and me, our shared knowledge of Christine actually bound us from the start.

As far as covering my tracks was concerned, it was my only lapse—dropping that postcard to Christine, newly arrived in Shanghai, into the mail. I sent it to the American Express office in the Foreign Quarter. Christine used the service in London; I assumed she'd do the same in Shanghai. In any case, the expatriate community was legendarily insular; I had no doubt card would end up in her hands.

What sort of disappearing act is it, you might ask, if you let people know your new alias as well as your whereabouts? Well, it wasn't people, it was Christine, and what I wrote on the postcard was my new name and the name of my solicitor in New York, nothing more. She knew my handwriting—she had, after all, been my teacher—so I was certain she would realize it was me.

I'd had a premonition that one day she might need my help. Though I admit it cut more deeply than that: a feeling that I couldn't go on, couldn't seize my new identity, with Christine completely in the dark. It was easy to slough off the rest; I could quite happily never set foot on European soil again. But leaving behind Christine, truly disappearing from her consciousness: that was not something I could bear.

* * *

Had I not so assiduously covered my tracks (my reasons for doing so were, of course, entirely unconnected with the matter at hand), I would not now be under this suspicion. There are certain things, though, that one cannot foretell.

"Two more witnesses," my visitor said last evening. "I suspect the case will now proceed." I detected a trace of sympathy in his voice.

I knew the paintings were stolen; I do not deny that. I had, however, incorrectly assumed a different act of theft from the one that in fact had taken place.

You will think I am making excuses, and perhaps I am. But I believed my source, especially concerning the Cranachs. They looked like they belonged in a museum, and the story about their theft—rescue, really, during various bombardments, including, toward the end, the destruction of Dresden—convinced me thoroughly. Yes, a more honorable man might have questioned the veracity of my source's claims. But the fact is, I didn't; and the fact is, I passed the paintings along. To dozens of aristocrats, of whom the culturally inflamed gentleman I spoke of earlier was but one.

The painting is homeless, I reasoned; it needs a home. I was simply uniting a wayward work of art with a soul in search of edification—I prided myself in supplying only those I deemed deserving, having developed a set of criteria to determine who was and who wasn't. *Sold*: to the screened and willing adopter, who expressed his gratitude in a gaze of disbelieving joy directed at his new foundling, and in a significant sum of pounds sterling, wired to one of my off-shore accounts.

The story my source told me had gripped me from the start. Paintings whisked out by some rebel underground from the basement of various German museums in the midst of unearthly poundings—I envisioned a building shuddering and, within the sound of shrieking alarms, the ghastly silence of the newly dead. Who would not cleave to the idea of rescuing from Germany the art it no longer deserved?

My original intention was naïve. That I would donate the paintings to the British Museum. My source pointed out that their origins—the alleged museums (which turned out to be a lie)—would soon be determined. That the war would end and then, some years hence, an impossible snarl of international controversy would ensue. Who knew where such a turn of events might lead.

No, my source said. There are buyers here, in England. Let some Englishmen take possession, my source said. He knew how the aristocracy functioned: a painting would stay in the family two, maybe three generations. Ultimately, it would find its way to the public weal—too long after the fact for anyone to bother about its provenance.

Needless to say, he did not in the same breath mention the rolls of banknotes that would change hands, half going his way, the other half going mine. Though he did add knowingly, "I'm sure you have pet causes, a man like yourself."

There really is no connection between the crimes I am accused of and those I have committed, if you can call my go-between activities crimes.

Or is there?

Yes, the paintings.

But there were also other crimes.

I knew Marilyn was working on an exhibition. I suspected it might have to do with the war. I'd presumed the focus was on England, as I knew she'd spent time photographing there. How could I have known she had a friend whose photographs are to be shown alongside her own? A friend who had gone in with the Liberators. Who had been among the first Americans to see, to really see, just what they (*they*? I must say *they*? Am I not a German?) had done.

How could I have known that the large stack of photographs Marilyn slid across the stainless steel bench in my darkroom, a room I'd never taken the time to use myself, would contain those hellish scenes? Scenes depicting the camps, mere days or weeks after their liberation—places I am now forced to consider in my search for my sister and mother. Erla. Dachau. Bergen-Belsen. Buchenwald. Visited and documented by Marilyn's photographer colleague, who carefully marked the names, in red, in a bottom corner of each proof sheet.

My right hand flies to the spot on my left upper arm; I stroke it, though I know this will not ease the poisonous ache.

The wooden door, I see it now, the patchwork of faded color: generations of old paint long since flaked away. A tint of blue, the merest hue of rose, a cross-hatch band that perhaps once was green, now muted to grayish-white. In among the hints of color, I see the battered grain—feel, as if I might reach up and strip away long splinters by the fistful.

The sound of Klauss's phlegmy cough—hacking, insistent. His boot on the door, caving it in.

I will not recover from having seen Marilyn's photographic images.

My visitor has not gone unnoticed, after all.

Marilyn seemed quite distressed this evening, here, in my office. I don't know what she was trying to accomplish. I felt at a loss—betrayed, in that moment, by my years of strategizing, of carefully constructing every action and response, left not knowing how to respond. Of course, she has no idea what is really going on. How could she? Perhaps she is trying to help. But it seemed impossible, like trying to unweave a spider's gossamer creation. Where would one begin? And what would be the point?

I do not believe she was telling the truth; I am sure my visitor must have said something damning about me. How else to explain, at the end, the look in Marilyn's face of fright?

What other reason could she have to fear *me*? I dread to think of what he might have said. And dread the thought that Marilyn would believe his words to be true.

When the envelope arrived today in the mail, there was something unreal about it—I'd waited so long for news about them. I knew that the odds of the news being good were extremely remote, virtually nonexistent, in fact. But the human heart is blind to probability—a shred of hope is the same as a great mountain of it.

I left the envelope on my desk and paced back and forth before it, holding onto this last moment of—what? Of not knowing the truth, whatever it might be? Terror, exhilaration—both coursed through my veins. And a sudden awareness, that whatever the outcome, I would be brought closer to them—to my mother, to Else. The perhaps of: oh, wonder of wonders! To know I might see them again! Or the other, unthinkable perhaps: to be brought to the fullness of grief, the great pool of sadness itself a dark rejoining.

Aware that until I opened the envelope, neither possibility had any claim to certainty.

I do not know how long it lay there, the letter, unopened.

I could not get the photographs out of my mind's eye, the vision of Marilyn's proof sheets. The diffuse gray sky in one grainy shot of wire fencing, a guard tower. The cloudy light that fell upon the photographic paper to make the image—could it have been the same light that fell upon my mother and sister in their final days? Hours? Moments? Or was this the light only of other people's ends?

I must have opened the envelope, though I have no recollection of doing so, because here it is, on my desk, the top neatly sliced by my silver letter opener.

I see them, taking off their clothes with everyone else, walking naked into the chamber where they would breathe in deeply and die.

The blow is worse than I could have imagined.

Was it the last thing they saw? A brown uniform? The arm-band: red and black, black and red?

And the woman, rocking by the hearth. Looking out from dark eyes that seemed not to see and yet saw nonetheless—their movements proved this well enough. Klauss's brown uniform—or perhaps my own?—was the last impression her eyes would claim.

After the explosion that destroyed the milk cart, I stayed in that cold ditch all night. If I slept, it was the sleep of purgatory.

Cold morning light slapped me to consciousness and I crawled from the ditch. Such a heavy silence. Before I saw the grisly scene I remember thinking: *This is the silence of the grave.*

How could I have not known that Alfred was dead? My mind was not working; it had slipped from its moorings.

Alfred's body lay by what remained of the cart in an oddly strewn posture—a rag doll flung down by a distracted child: elbows, ankles, wrists, and knees working against the usual mechanical positions of joints. The fatal wound was to his gut; his entrails hung casually from a gaping slash, like a bunch of bruised wine-dark grapes. No more than a pace away lay another dead man, his body by comparison orderly and neat, the limbs arrayed cleanly like those of someone in sleep. Brown uniform, black and red armband. As luck would have it, Alfred must have dispatched the soldier with a single, close-range shot to the face, which no longer resembled a face: just shattered bone and black-red blood and a halo of splat-tered brain. I saw the gun still clutched in Alfred's hand, the fingers curled—already turned to granite—around the handle and through the mechanism of the trigger. I tried to figure the logic of the scene: Nazi soldiers, tipped off that this milk-man is harboring a Jew. They attack. One of them lunges at Alfred with a knife; Alfred manages, perhaps while falling, to execute a perfect close shot to the enemy's head. The others, not finding their Jew, head off in different directions to track him (me?) down. Perhaps they would return later for their fallen comrade.

I quickly removed my navy jacket, and then the outer of my two sets of clothing—the woolen cardigan and flannel pants—leaving them crumpled on the ground, then put my jacket, with the secret pockets my mother had sewn, back on. I approached the dead soldier and found myself removing his jacket, aware of the sticky red rim on the inside of the collar. The blood must have flooded down his neck, as the inside of the jacket was drenched to the waist. From the outside, the dark blood was visible at the collar's edge; the front of the jacket had spatterings, as did the pants. But this was war: blood was a normal enough stain. I removed the pants too, my hands working free of thought. The dead soldier was larger than me, though not by much. I avoided looking at him; I continued my actions by feel. And then, I walked away—from the soldier, and, with a tremendous pang of grief, from Alfred. He had saved my life twice: once while alive and again in his dying moment, when his finger squeezed the trigger of his gun, giving me a relatively clean brown uniform in which to take cover.

I continued to sleep in ditches by day, rising to walk endless cold hours through the night. Though the uniform made me less visible, I still felt I was a target.

Snatched from sleep—a rough shaking at the shoulder—a moment of panic as I saw that the man shaking me was wearing a brown uniform. A flash, and then I recalled that I was wearing a brown uniform too.

Why, then, the suspicion in his face? It was a square, blunted face, with eyes that were resentful and dull with ignorance. His name was Klauss, and we trudged alongside one another—I don't know for how many miles. He was not given to much talk, which I welcomed. Now and then, I felt the sting of a sidelong glance filled with that same suspiciousness of his first regard.

Why he stopped at the moment he did, I do not know. He grabbed my shoulder with such force I felt a pain shoot down my arm.

"Drop them," he said curtly.

"I beg your pardon?" I had no idea what he was talking about.

"Your pants. Drop them."

I did what I was bidden, turning my face away while Klauss inspected my naked penis, which shrank toward my body at the cold breath of the wind.

He seemed disappointed at the sight of my intact foreskin. He issued his hacking cough and wiped his dripping nose on his sleeve.

"We'll find a use for that," he said crudely, indicating my private parts with a jerk of his head. He resumed the march, leaving me to fumble at two sets of flies—I'd been careful, in pulling the two trousers down in one swift movement, to make it seem I was wearing only the one pair. I saw that light was beginning to wash over the heavy black sky.

The previous night, which was our first together, I'd intended to steal away, make my escape from Klauss, the minute he fell asleep. I'd willed myself to stay awake but had failed, finding myself awoken again some hours later by his rough shaking. Now, I vowed to myself anew that when we next stopped to sleep, I would dig my nails into my legs, bite the inside of my lip, anything to keep exhaustion at bay so that I might free myself of Klauss's unpleasant and dangerous company.

It was not, however, to be. Not until too late—until there would never, for the rest of my days, be any possibility of escaping Klauss.

I am, after all, to be arraigned. Remarkable, the way the manner of my late-night visitor, through everything, has remained professional; he treats me with no sign whatsoever of condemnation. After conveying the news, he took his leave for what we both knew would be the last time. After he was gone, I removed all the materials from my file drawers: ledgers and notebooks and numerous files of returned mail. I had not seen it all gathered together before and was surprised by the sheer volume. Useless, dead documents. The search over.

I hear the voice of my friend, Oskar. The *real* Oskar. My fellow refugee from the Internment Center next to whom I'd slept in the dormitory. Oskar, who had dressed the wound on my forearm—the blackened gash that might have become gangrenous but did not. I had willed the wound to go bad, fixated on this, as if losing my arm might relieve me also of the burden of my actions (and inactions); as if losing some of my capacity to reach out might serve as punishment, and permit me to go on as a free man.

But against all the odds, the arm healed. Oskar took this as a point of pride. "I should have been a nurse." He said this drily. I'd turned away to hide my distress. And disgust at my own failure of courage: that in plunging the wet red tip of the knife into my arm when I did, that long-ago cold and distraught day, I'd not done myself a greater injury.

And how did I repay him? This friend who helped deprive me of the punishment I deserved?

I took his name. I should say stole, for it was not a name he freely gave or to which I had any right. I hear him now: *Over? How could the past ever be over?*

I know it now: the dead do not die.

I shed the uniform as quickly, as effortlessly, as I have shed outer garb before and since. For this, I believe I have a singular talent. Two counts of good fortune: that it was terribly cold, and that the uniform was too large. Which made the wearing of my other clothes both possible and an advantage. Later, when I was finally able to break away, I could peel off the uniform and stash it in some bushes, and find I was still fully clothed.

It took me awhile to adjust to the loss of the layer—the cloth had been heavy and had served well against the wind.

Afterward I felt foolish recalling how, unthinkingly, I had folded the jacket and pants before shoving them into the hedge, which had materialized the instant I had need of it.

But I am leaving out one other detail. Before folding the jacket, I ripped the black and red armband from the sleeve, folded it into a tiny square, and stuffed it into one of the little pockets my mother had sewn inside the waist of my navy jacket.

The rest had gone without a hitch.

I'd become a true night creature. I had the map Alfred had given me, though no need to consult it, as it was long since committed to memory. When I reached Marseilles, I found my way easily to the dock. The barge was where Alfred said it would be: not a day or a week earlier, or a day or a week later, but right when I needed the boat to be there. I gave no thought to the serendipity of this; I was beyond such musings and besides, there had already been too many dark turnings of Fate for me to have any real regard for her occasional glitterings of gold (fool's gold, only, after all).

On the practical side of things, I was, however, in possession of real coin; when I approached the helmsman of the barge, who eyed me coldly, the two gold coins I offered glinted in the oily moonlight. The helmsman examined them briefly, nodded his yellowish face, and blinked slowly once, twice, a hooded reptilian gesture that drew attention to his alert eyes. Raising his soiled shirt, he slipped the heavy coins into a pouch strapped to his waist. I approached the trapdoor in the middle of the deck, kept slightly ajar by a stump of wood, and caught a glimpse of what awaited me in the hold: a wedge of pure darkness.

It was a relief to be below deck, away from the wind, which had made light work of my clothing. I inched along the wall until I could feel the contours of the fourth bin, a rough hardwood box long enough for a man to lie stretched out and tall enough to crouch. Holding up the lid of the crate, I climbed in. Numerous holes the size of large coins had been bored into the side; I hunkered down in the boxed-in darkness.

Sounds filtered in from the upper deck: voices speaking French, comings and goings, objects dragged from here to there. Then the stir of engines, distant and near as one's own internal organs, and soon I felt the grinding pull away from the dock. I breathed in the soot that coated the inside of the coal bin and trained my ears on the darkness. The arcing motions of the barge steadied to a slow gliding. The sounds from above deck waned.

But then, the beat of a single set of footsteps. Moving down the iron ladder, across the old boards of the below-deck, toward my bin and right up to the side of it. The lid to my crate was raised, and in the pulpy light of a small kerosene lamp, I saw the helmsman's bulbous forehead and thin cheeks. He dropped in a heavy loaf, which bounced off my shoulder and thudded to the wooden floor of the box. The helmsman reached up and handed me a tinful of watery soup: various lumps and agglutinations floating in a thin, brown liquid. The lid above me was replaced. Again, the footsteps, this time leading away.

Sitting cross-legged, I broke off a piece of bread and chewed. I remember the gritty taste of the dark rye; I washed it down with a mouthful of liquid, which was faintly flavored with garlic. My meal over, I repositioned myself from the crouch to the lying-down-on-my-side position and stayed that way for some time, listening to my own breath—time and space reduced to numbness and bottomless, damp cold. After the nightmare weeks of endless marching, the constant threat of being seen, the coal bin encased me like a sanctuary. I gave myself over to a dreamless sleep.

✳ ✳ ✳

I took two names—a first and a last, but only Oscar feels stolen. The name Harcourt, that of my mentor and now mine these last six years, was freely given, and also, somehow, my right.

A monochrome day, the London sky even flatter than usual, the light wan and diffuse. I remember my ill-fitting hand-me-down shoes rubbing against my feet as I hurried along the thoroughfare. My suit, also given to me upon my arrival at the Internment Center, was a size too small; the knees rode high and there was a crease at the ankle where the fabric had been let down. (My own clothes, irremediably infested, had been immediately burned.) The ache in my bones, from two months of night trekking, the days spent sleeping in ditches.

Every so often, a house reminded me of home; I pushed this from my mind. London, I kept saying to myself—and in English (*practice, practice*)—London on its own terms.

The streets got wider, the houses more grand. Here and there a rupture in the neat array: a house or two in ruins. A skeletal stairway or slab of wall presiding over mounds of brick and the entrails of a family's life—broken crockery, pieces of metal twisted to beautiful shapes, partly burned items of furniture. I paused to examine one such ruin—a slim pillar of wall, the ghost of each story evident in panels of discolored wallpaper: rose chintz at the bottom, green velvet above, then embossed blue, and finally, at the top, capped in a remnant of red roof tile, the serviceable gray of what had probably been the attic. A fragment of floorboard jutted between the upper two patches of wallpaper; absurdly, a china teapot balanced on this tiny ledge.

And then, it was upon me. *47 Park Street*. Miraculously intact. An impressive entryway, flanked by four columns, was set back a little from the street. A brass knocker in the shape of a leopard was affixed to the carved door. I shivered in my thin suit. A faint cry, no more than a whimper, echoed in my mind: for an instant, the feel of my sister Else's cheek on my lips. I reached for the leopard and gave two firm raps.

The maid looked at me oddly when she opened the door, and quickly ushered me into an opulent foyer, unmarked by wartime scarcity. I waited until the maid returned, followed by a handsome middle-aged woman dressed in a gray velvet dress, her brown hair swept up off her face.

"Mrs. Harcourt," the maid announced.

There was a strange look in the woman's face.

I tried to quell the panic that had arisen on hearing her name—not the name I was anticipating, not the last name of the uncle of Else's school friend.

"It is a Mr. Pettigrew I am looking for. Edgar Pettigrew," I stammered.

"I'm so sorry," Mrs. Harcourt said, the peculiar look still on her face. "He lived at number 13. Our neighbor. But he passed away in the spring. I understand his widow has retired to their Yorkshire estate. Their house has been closed for months."

Harcourt. The wrong address. Not the uncle of Else's old schoolmate: that would have been number 43 Park Street. Mr. Pettigrew gone these six months, the widow in seclusion up north.

And me standing there speechless, the worn scrap of paper dangling from my hand.

"I'm so sorry," Mrs. Harcourt repeated. Yet she seemed strangely exalted. "Come. We'd be more comfortable in the parlor."

She turned toward the hallway. Hatless, I followed, taking in the faces of Harcourt ancestry floating on the wall in hunting gear, morning suits, frothy gowns. Sharp faces, angular and fine-boned, the same blue eyes in different configurations, wider or rounder, with more humor or less, or a hint of timidity; and in more than one portrait, a potent gleam of intelligence. All of them gazing out from the past, neither curious nor accusing. A sense that these painted forms were awaiting something—the breaking of a spell?—so that they might resume what they were doing, get on with things. I paused before a life-sized portrait of a man, youthful but prematurely gray, dressed in military attire from a long-past era, astride a palomino. Something in his hand—a parchment covered in writing; in the background, a battlefield, still smoking from the fire of cannons. There was a sober expression on his face: not victory, not defeat, but something uncannily modern.

Mrs. Harcourt pushed open curved mahogany doors to reveal an elegant parlor: plush chairs, velvet walls, heavy curtains in different shades of hunter-green, and here and there a shiny, well-cared-for wooden piece—a rolltop desk, a sideboard inlaid with mother-of-pearl, a small oval table with clawed metal feet. My eyes flew to the framed photographs arranged on the marble mantelpiece, and to one in particular: a portrait of a youth in uniform, touched up with watercolors. The youth had pale eyes, the same hue of the ancestors hanging on the hall.

"Andrew Harcourt. My son," she said simply. "He was killed early on, shot down over France." She fell silent.

We stood there together in that opulent room, strangers from such separate worlds, worlds which had no business colliding as they had astoundingly, absurdly, against all the odds done. Joined now, without any sense or reason, by an impossible *coincidence*—though of course this word, now that I think it, rings hollow and nonsensical. And yet, I can find no other.

"It's remarkable, isn't it," Mrs. Harcourt breathed after a while. I looked again at the photograph. I knew I should be amazed: to be here at the wrong address, as it turned out, peering into the face of a felled English soldier who, on the basis of physical likeness, might well have been my brother, almost a twin. And yet, I found myself looking into those

touched-up eyes—fierce beneath their surface gentleness—
with an uncanny sense of inevitability. The wrong house, the
Harcourts' son no longer alive; all these years, a boy growing up in London, bearing such a close resemblance to me.
And why not? My own mother not who she was, me not who
I'd thought myself to be, all of it pieces of colored glass that
tumbled and shifted into vivid, random arrangement.

Mrs. Harcourt was staring at me with a disturbing mixture of disbelief and joy. I stood, in my worn suit, which had
most likely once belonged to another young man killed in bat-
tle, shredding the scrap of paper with Else's faded schoolgirl
script.

A smell of baking bread wafted into the room. Faint
with hunger, I stared down at the lacy pattern of light sifted
through leafy trees and falling through glass onto the floor.
My face felt wet and I wondered how I could be sweating
profusely when it was so cold outside.

Mrs. Harcourt came toward me, holding something out:
a white handkerchief. I took it; it was made of the softest
silk. I wiped my nose, wiped my dripping eyes, felt something
slightly itchy on my skin. I unfolded the handkerchief to see
the spidery lines of embroidered initials, *A.B.H.* I wondered
what the *B* stood for. I moved to hand the handkerchief back.

"Keep it. Please," Mrs. Harcourt said.

I have it still, that handkerchief. On occasion, I place it in
the breast pocket of my jacket.

Mrs. Harcourt invited me to move in with them that very
day. Just the two of them, she said, she and her husband,
rattling around in their large house. She seemed to take it as
a favor when, without really thinking the matter over, I accepted her invitation.

"So"—a whisper, through the film of sleep—"I understand
you're leaving. I wanted to wish you luck."

I opened my eyes to see my fellow refugee, Oskar, sitting

in the gloomy light of a yellow taper. Before he'd been made to wear the yellow star, Oskar had been a concert pianist. Around us, in cots along the length of both walls, the other residents of the Internment Center slept their unsteady sleep.

We'd been fast friends since the day I arrived at the Center, almost a year earlier. We'd worked together on a crew clearing rubble after air raids and attended the same language school, though we'd already begun to take different directions—me attending a night course at the business school, Oskar training as an assistant teacher at a primary school in Hendon.

There were unspoken rules at the Center. First and foremost: the residents spoke only English—to the staff, to each other, in the outside world.

"I can hardly believe you're getting out," my friend had continued.

Oskar's fingers rapped a complex rhythm onto the narrow bed, off beyond the reach of the candlelight.

"Who are they, these people with the big house, who hand out jobs?"

I told him about the Harcourts and their unexpected offer of help.

"When do you leave?" he asked, averting his eyes.

"Tomorrow."

His fingers were still lightly drumming. I was aware of our silenced mother tongue, hanging between us like a lament.

"This is it, then," he said, his voice suddenly distant. "You're pointed in the right direction. The future. That's what we're all of us here supposed to be thinking about."

He waved his arm to indicate the room, the steady sounds of sleep issuing from the dozen other beds floating in the tarpaper darkness.

"I have a favor to ask," he said, lifting a silver object from his lap.

I saw in the flickering candlelight that it was shaped like a small flute, and intricately engraved. Some religious article,

I supposed, though I'd never seen anything like it.

"You don't know what this is, do you?" he asked, a slightly odd look on his face.

I gave an almost imperceptible shake of my head. I knew that, through this little gesture, I was revealing more about myself than the etiquette at the Internment Center generally allowed—the second and most important unspoken rule: no stirring the ashes of the past.

We were all Jews, or appeared to be—whether from enemy or collaborator states: Germany, Italy, France. It was generally understood that our internment was a formality; the residents saw themselves as refugees and were treated that way by the staff.

But I knew that I stood out among my fellow internees. There was the matter of my looks but also, I sensed, something about my deeper being that aroused discreet curiosity. Here, now, was another of those little queries I'd become accustomed to. Not knowing what else to do, I allowed the ripple of revelation—that I had no knowledge of Jewish rituals or customs.

"It's called a *yad*," Oskar continued. "It's used as part of the ceremony for bringing the Sabbath to a close. My grandmother used to carry this around with her—she wore an old blue cardigan, I would see the tip of it poking out of the pocket. She'd brought it to Germany with her when she fled Poland—the pogroms—forty years ago. I think she believed it protected her."

I remember the way my friend stared at the pointed silver object, as if imploring it to yield some answer.

"I grabbed it—I don't know why—when I left. Perhaps I shouldn't have. I don't know how I managed to hang onto it . . ." His voice was barely audible. The candle was almost burned to nothing. "When I used to play the piano on Shabbat, my grandmother would pace back and forth by the door of the music room, muttering to herself in Yiddish. *You've for-*

gotten who you are! she would say. *What does any of it matter if you've forgotten who you are?"*

Oskar crossed one knee over the other and studied his foot, his face clenched in private thought.

"She was always so afraid. I hate to say it, but it disgusted me."

Now he leaned so close that shivering under the thin blanket I could see tiny beads of sweat high on his forehead where his thick hair sprouted.

"You don't know about that kind of fear, do you?" he asked, an urgent glow in his eyes.

"I'm not sure I know what you mean," I replied.

My friend's shoulders sagged; his eyes went dull. "Forgive me," he murmured.

I remained very still, I remember staring down at the worn border of the sheet peeking out from under the blanket. My friend cast his eyes hesitantly around, as if discovering for the first time his whereabouts. The tuneless music that had poured from Oskar's fingers had stopped; his strong hands lay crumpled on his thighs.

"When I heard you were leaving, it made sense. I can't explain it, but I realized that all this time, I'd been imagining that you were going to lead the way out. Not just for me, but for all of us."

Imperceptibly, the deep breathing around us altered. It was as if the collective dreaming of the sleeping residents had simultaneously ceased, leaving the room adrift in the shallow pause between sleep and wakefulness.

"Take this," Oskar said, pressing the pointed silver rod into my hands. "I'm not asking you to remember anything about it. Not my grandmother, not me: not her fleeing from Poland to Germany or me fleeing Germany for here."

"What *do* you want," I asked softly. "What is it you want me to do?"

"They're not your memories. I know it's crazy, superstitious, I don't know what. Just take it. I believe it will bring you luck."

Mr. Harcourt, being the man of influence he was, was able to provide the necessary assurances and guarantees to gain my release from the Internment Center. And in offering to take me into his venerable financial institution, Harcourt and Goode, it was clear there was more to it than a passing altruistic whim. Clearly, for the Harcourts, I was stepping into the shoes of their dead son, whom I so uncannily, impossibly resembled.

You might think that my precipitous success in the company was spurred by a desire to repay my hosts and mentors for their extreme generosity and faith. I wish I could claim this as a motive. The truth is, I was driven by what felt like a demon: ugly and vengeful, greedy and frothing with lust. A demon with appetites I did not understand or care to understand. The effects of my success, however, gratified my new "family" as if my efforts were aimed solely at this end. This pleased me, as they were kind souls and deserved some rewards for the belief they had placed in me.

Two months before sailing for New York, I paid a visit to the city Deed Poll office to change my name. When the clerk remarked, "Oh, a refugee—refugees often request a name change," he seemed to pointedly, rudely eye the expensive cloth of my suit. When I spoke, the name Harcourt fell from my lips: as if it were meant to be, as if it were already fully mine.

But when I leaned over to sign my new name, it came as some surprise to find myself prefacing *Harcourt*, the name of my patron, which had rung out over the generations in the House of Lords, with *Oscar*, the anglicized spelling of my friend's German name, not particularly Jewish in character, and yet steeped in the Jewishness of his family history. In snatching my old friend's name, I gave birth to a peculiar hybrid that the real Oskar would surely have cringed to hear. Without his knowledge, without his permission. And a deeper shame, still: that I'd made a point of not keeping in touch. That I'd taken the *yad* he'd asked me to keep, pillaged the luck that had come with it—yes, *the paintings* again, they tighten around my neck like a noose—and then sloughed Oskar off as quickly, as silently, as I had all the rest.

The search was over. I could scarcely hang on to this fact. It slipped through my fingers like sand. I stared at the papers littering my desk, rested my head on my arms for a moment in the hope of clearing my head.

I must have dozed off. Wallace's firm rap on the door roused me. I will not quickly forget the ashen look of resolve with which he greeted me. In the years I have known him, I do not believe Wallace has ever before issued me a direct instruction: advice, certainly, a casual suggestion phrased with his customary tact in the form of a tentative if pointed question, but never more than that. So, when he announced that he had taken the liberty of packing my bags, and had brought the car around to the back of the house where it now sat idling, I searched his face, finding nothing there that might lead me to question his judgment, then quickly set about gathering the papers and files from my desk.

"Will you really be needing those, sir?" Wallace asked.

I nodded, packed what I could of them into my briefcase, passing over the black binder with the gold grinning teeth that still lay unopened on the end table, and followed Wallace through the door, taking care not to glance back at the room where so much and so little had taken place.

Wallace appears to know what he's doing. He's taken care of everything to the last detail. He must have been planning this for some time. Outside, it is pitch dark; the car seems to be moving in complete silence.

✳ ✳ ✳

I have been writing in this notebook now for some weeks—since the unwanted visitor first appeared at my house. I grabbed it, along with the papers on my desk, when Wallace appeared at my door to tell me that the car was waiting and that we had no choice but to steal away, as we did, like criminals. These last entries, I have penned as we speed along through the night.

I know where Wallace is taking me; I'm not sure I'm up for the journey. But what choice do I have?

Wallace is convinced that his scheme will take care of matters once and for all. I'm not so certain. To go along with it would be to repeat myself in a way that has shown itself to be a failure of the greatest magnitude.

And what would it mean to enact another erasure? To erase all I have been, all I have done, here, in Long Island, at my estate?

What does it mean to cover tracks that were themselves a cover?

It is now very dark outside. Earlier, the moon was fairly bright, but now it seems to have disappeared, and I can scarcely see the paper I am scribbling on; what I am writing is no doubt illegible. I do not mind this—there is no purpose to this scrawl beyond the slight relieving of pressure in my chest, and the distraction from all I have left undone.

I can hear my trunk rattling in the capacious boot of the car. It surprises me that Wallace failed to secure it. But then, we left in some haste. The very trunk, it occurs to me, that I so carefully packed in preparation for the journey that brought me here, to America. (I have so few objects from that time; I could probably count them on one hand.)

I put my pen down on the seat of my car. The darkness outside is whirring. I open the window, close my eyes, give myself for a moment to the cool moving air of the night. I rewind the window and sink back into the soft leather. From where I sit in the backseat, diagonally behind Wallace, who is steering us along at skillful speed, I can see the determined set of his profile. He has been a fine and trustworthy friend. It is a mercy to be in his hands.

CHAPTER NINE

Oscar

Atlantic Crossing. September, 1951.

I don't see how the plan can work. Wallace, however, is resolute: convinced that his Man Overboard scheme—those are the very words he used—will take care of matters once and for all.

My attorney, a trusted friend before I ever requested his legal services, is in on the plan; Wallace saw no way around it. He called him just before we left Ellis Park, waking him, no doubt, as the hour was late. It was my lawyer who suggested a five-year clause; that we allow some time to pass before the will is activated. Give the "heat" of the accusation a chance to dissipate. I realize we are putting him in a highly compromising situation, in effect making him complicit in my escape. This troubles me a good deal, though it is too late to undo it.

I wonder how my friends will react to my simply disappearing. I can only imagine what Marilyn and Simon, along with Barnaby, might feel five years hence, when they discover that I have bequeathed the house to them.

The scheme has become complicated, which Wallace reminds me is a critical element to its success. He has made a close study of the entire staff of the ship, a cargo vessel that accommodates a dozen or so guests, having been fitted out with a corridor of cabins, a modest dining room, and a good-sized lounge where the passengers gather in the evening. Wallace has settled on a member of the cleaning staff, a Polish boy of eighteen or nineteen who cleans the living quarters and is confined entirely to the below-deck. Because he cleans when the cabins are empty, he is more or less invisible. Wallace appears to have befriended him—and assures me we can trust him to "within an inch of your life" (he winced when he said this; we both let it go unremarked). Money has, of course, changed hands—a good deal of it—but I suspect Wallace is depending more on some other kind of incentive: a promise, perhaps, that drags in the boy's nearest and dearest, some classic detective-story move so that a betrayal of me would bring harm, or else loss of significant advantage, to some person or cause close to the boy's heart.

Wallace has given me to understand that the Polish youth is timid to the point of fear, which of course aids our plan; his contact is apparently limited to his supervisor, a beefy woman of advanced years, whose complicity Wallace also has secured.

I should follow Wallace's instruction—to leave the plan and its execution in his hands, focus on the part I am to play and not worry about the details.

The scenario he has concocted is an elaborate piece of theater, to take place one full day before we pull into the Port of Southampton. The timing is important: the goal, to minimize the necessary duration of the charade while ensuring that the full force of land resources is not immediately brought to bear. The boy will go into hiding at exactly the moment of the unfortunate accident, whereby the reclusive passenger, who has spoken to no one the entire voyage, is lost to the sea. I am to resume the youth's place, carrying out his molelike duties for the course of one day.

Again, I find myself indebted to Wallace, for whom my admiration continues to grow. In executing his plan, he has demonstrated both an eye for the critical detail, and some mastery of the art of diversion.

I spend the whole of each evening on deck; it is the one place I can count on being alone.

The gods appear to be on our side.

Beyond furnishing us with a highly suitable stand-in whose place I will take, better in all ways than we could have dreamed up ourselves, we have also been graced with unusually bad weather. The captain claims, according to Wallace, that in twenty-nine years of seafaring, he's not seen the ocean more turbulent. Those passengers not felled by seasickness— and most have been—are unwilling to brave the challenging condition of the deck: great slaps of icy sea water, violent gusts that feel, in the moment, sufficiently powerful to capsize even a vessel as large as this, though I imagine that it feels more dangerous than it is.

The fact that I spend so much of my time on deck, and in such dreadful weather, will make my alibi—if one can call the staging of one's own death an alibi—all the more convincing.

Up here, in the open, the elements in full force, I find the past flinging up in fragments, as if from the raging sea. There have been so many layers of forgetting, of attempts to keep memory at bay, that I find myself confused, at times, by the snatches of different epochs, snatches of different selves.

The first attempt to eradicate: it was set in motion, I now see looking back, the very moment I stepped out of the red-brick house on Kirchstrasse to embark on my initial escape.

I did not flee to save only myself.

I fled because I could not bear to do nothing.

I fled in the name of my family, so that one of us might find a safe ground from which to stage a rescue of the rest.

I see now that I had even then, without fully acknowledging it to myself, given up hope regarding my father. The Gestapo, I am certain, made an example of him soon after his arrest—probably while Mother and Else and I were still hiding in the attic, with our wooden buckets of vegetables and dried meat.

From the moment I made it to safe soil—that's how it felt when I docked at Dover—I wanted only to find them. To find my mother and sister and put things right. Though I closed my mind to Germany, I erected in my mind a kind of altar of intention: I spent hours upon hours strategizing how I would go about finding them long before I could actually do much about it. I dreamt about them, saw myself back in the house of my childhood, a pleasant twenty-minute walk from the Court House. I dreamt I was chasing Else up and down the stairs. I would hear her laughter, watch my mother as she leaned to snip the spray of sterling roses she would carry indoors and set in a crystal vase on the sideboard.

Then, last night, up on deck, I remembered this.

I was a teenager; we were visiting my father's sister in Frankfurt. Already, there were disturbances, but nothing, yet, like that night.

Respectable people stayed indoors. It was my mother who wanted to go out. I hadn't seen her like that before, her whole body wracked with distress.

We walked the streets, the four of us: Mother, Father, Aunt, myself. (Else had stayed behind, in Heidelberg, with the family of a friend.) We picked our way through the fresh rubble—broken glass, mostly, but also upended pieces of furniture and store goods. I remember a collection of ladies hats, trampled, for the most part, also a basket of fresh apples, unharmed and rosy cheeked. For all the disarray, it was eerily silent; the crowds had cycloned onward toward the city center. We followed the path of destruction. Here and there, we stepped over sticky patches of what must have been blood.

The eye of the storm, when we reached it, was not silent. Huge panes of glass being hit by brick and rock make terrifying music, beautiful in its way. And light, great streaks of light: torches and headlights and who knows what else. The action slowed to unreal motion, a crackling, flickering film reel: people dragged into the street, men and women both—now a shoe brought down as a weapon, now a chair leg, a crow bar, a hammer—their children made to watch. My mother's hand gripped my arm and dragged me back along the route we had come, sidestepping the dangerous shards. I scrambled beside her, happened to turn my head to see a dress-store mannequin thrust through a broken opening. Her glazed eyes gave an unseemly glare.

Kristallnacht, they later called it, a word that could conjure the image of beautiful Austrian crystals tumbling from the night sky.

I was a teenager. This terrible theater was not about us, it was happening to the cruelly victimized *them*.

After the Allies finally realized what it was going to take, and America set about the business of bringing the whole thing to an end, I managed for a short while—in the interest of holding on to my sanity—to keep an almost unfeeling distance from it all. Of course, my family was never for a moment out of my mind. I'd been in England for almost four years and had taken to my role as an immigrant with a vengeance; I was able, therefore, to busy myself in the myriad tasks of my new life, endeavoring to put Germany and all its goings-on out of my mind.

But when I saw the photographs of the massive Dresden offensive of February 13, I could not avert my eyes from the devastation. (I was sitting in the club with Christine, as it happens.) It was clear from the pictures that the aim of the Dresden bombing was to pluck Germany's prize jewel and trample it underfoot. Seeing those images was for me a confusing business: the Zwinger, its golden dome in tatters; the mighty Frauenkirche reduced to three giant disembodied pillars; the Semperoper flattened to rubble; the entire city a disgrace of severances heaped around its own squat remains.

The truth is, I don't really know who the enemy is. I do not recognize the blood that runs through my veins.

I am reminded of Gandhi's quip when asked what he thought of English civilization: "I think it would be a very good idea." But Germany is more deserving of such judgment; there was always so much savagery there, beneath the cultivation. If I had any mirth left in me, I would laugh at the arrogance of anyone believing that Germany's cultural ascendancy could be crippled through leveling Dresden, its most beautiful city, a city crammed with music and art. I see those swaggering GIs, conquering and proud. But they were only sweeping up the scraps. Germany can take the credit for its own demise.

And yet, examining those pictures of destruction, something caught in my throat: the memory of the redbrick house of my childhood on the mottled sunny street. Heidelberg sustained significant damage, I know that. The house, therefore, may well have been destroyed. But that was something I could not imagine, no matter how hard I tried to visualize it. I could only see the house as it had been—the white lace curtains, the petunias in the window boxes. All the other ruins I could visualize—the remains of other families' lives: charred mementos and the undone pages of books, shoes scattered among split beams and stones, broken china and rotting foodstuffs. But not the redbrick house. How could it not have been spared?

I feel oddly grateful for the opportunity that Wallace's Man Overboard scheme affords: of tasting my own death, so that I might begin to live more sweetly. I find myself feeling mournful about every sensation, each perception, and even the most quotidian action. A mouthful of soup tastes exquisite; washing my face in the morning is exhilarating; even talking to Wallace about nothing in particular (now that the plan is in place, we studiously avoid that subject) seems to embody the fineness of human intercourse.

I am also aware of how different the business of erasing

myself is, this time around. When I struck the name Robert from my life, there was a violence to it; something heartless about the way I systematically dismantled everything about my person—all that I had been and all that I was but had not known about. (I speak, here, of my *Jewishness*; even now, the sound of this word has, for me, a hollow and unreal feel.)

This time, the identity I am undoing—that of Oscar—was a lie from the start. A lie of convenience—and also of longing. Which brings me to an interesting question, one which has of late quite gripped my imagination, though for all the mental attention I have given it—pacing the heaving deck, swallowing gusts of wind and breathing in the stinging salt spray— has yielded no inkling of an answer: Does the erasure of deceit result in the revelation of truth? Or is there, behind the crafty Oscar edifice-façade I erected, only a bare windy plain, populated by nothing more honorable than lowly tumbleweed moving pointlessly through timeless time and no-place space?

I find myself thinking constantly of Christine. I am beset by a new and most unrealistic sentiment; that this ship I am on is delivering me not just *out of harm's way* but *home, to Christine*. Of course, this is an entirely absurd fiction: I have no idea where Christine is, what her life has become, whether she would have any interest whatsoever in seeing me. But the fact is that here, in the confines of my solitude, wrenched from the life I have led these past six years—from the person into whom I had fully evolved—I have only to conjure Christine's lively, impatient features and I find myself feeling truly alive again.

So many evenings in Christine's cozy rooms in Bethnal Green—and then later, in my own rather grand rooms in Kensington. I'd shut it all out, not knowing that Memory has her secret hoarding tricks; standing up there, on deck, deafened by the sky's wet tantrum, moments—long stretches of time—pour themselves out into my consciousness, vivid in the reliving.

I see the moon in full throat through the small high window of Christine's bedroom, the window so aglow one could read by its light. I feel us lowering to the bed, Christine, wordless, moving slowly into my embrace. She is wearing her beige silk blouse; I feel the silk in my fingers, smoothing it with the palm of my hand, the button a shell slipping through colorless sea, another shell, a third. Her warm breasts beneath the flats of my fingertips, the fluid sweep of her beneath my hands. On her white skin, the moon's light seems wet; in her fair hair, it is muffled to smoke. The wailing begins: the air-raid siren. And then, some distance away, the first strikes. The delicate shuddering of the earth. Christine moves in my arms; the break in her voice, when it comes, is the sound of a rising wave curling up and over itself—a salt spray, a powerful sliding. Christine is touching my face. I close my eyes, shut her out so I might take her in, sink myself into her so that I might rise to the surface and float.

Now, we are floating together. The tiniest movement, then Christine's liquid response; I am holding her there, I do not want to release her and she, her arms tight on my back, does not want to let go.

The world, what there is of it, shuts down. And now, nothing but the free fall, a movement through silence and darkness: impersonal and yet intimate, with nothing and everything to do with us, like the music that hangs in the space above the orchestra, having issued from instruments but become pure sound in air, attached to no person or thing. We hang that way in the air, merged, as the sounds of the strings merge with the winds, but also wholly separate, as the wood of the violin never makes contact with the metal of the flute.

I open my eyes to see that Christine has closed hers. Beneath the fringe of her lashes, a whisper-soft shadow on white.

She left. Christine went to Shanghai.

She'd talked about it once or twice but never in a way I took seriously. Christine was given to passionate enthusiasms, many of which led to nothing beyond the moment of their expression. I suppose I placed her musings about visiting the Far East in this category.

I'd have stopped her if I could have. Stay, Christine, I would have said. I, too, know the call of pleasure; but let me show you a different way.

She'd only have looked down her elegant nose and laughed. Not scornfully, but as if to say, I know your trepidations, I know the kind of safety you seek: the bricks, the mortar, the history. The illusion of permanence, of culture, of belonging, of inalienable dignity and rights. *I'm done with such playgrounds.* I see her sitting back in her chair, sipping a martini, the agitation around her mouth at odds with the deep seductive sparkle in her eyes.

But the fact is, I was not given the chance to stop her, not given the chance to ask her to stay.

I don't know why I became possessed by the idea of telling Christine everything. But once it took hold of me, it wouldn't let me go.

I confess that at times I entertained the fantasy of a clean new life—of Christine and me married, perhaps even a child or two—moving forward into clarity and happiness and light. But then a terrible gloom would settle over everything, snatching the fantasy away, leaving me deriding myself for such baldly foolish hopes.

Somehow I convinced myself that if Christine knew the truth—the truth about me—together we could bury it, snuffing out the shadow of undoing once and for all.

We stopped at my house on our way to a dinner party, having met at the club at the end of my workday. Christine had changed before meeting me; she was resplendent in yellow chiffon, a cluster of crystals glittering at her throat. We paused for a drink in my study before I was to repair to my dressing room. I remember pouring Scotch whiskey from my crystal decanter, the shimmer of amber liquid as it splashed onto ice in the cut-glass tumbler. I loosened my cravat, brought the glass over to Christine, who was seated on the divan beside my rolltop desk.

On occasion, a stillness would settle over Christine, quieting the current of agitation that otherwise seemed constantly at play in her being. As I handed her the drink, I could see the steady calm in her eyes, feel the fullness of her vitality—and then the distinct sense that she was offering all of herself, all of her being, to me.

"Darling," I said quietly (I can hear my own voice, all these years have passed and yet still I am there, uttering those words). I peered deep into those terribly alive eyes, eyes that were taking me in, and I knew it was time to put words to the *all of me* that was holding me hostage. I believed she was offering—willing—hoping—to see.

"Darling," I repeated—it was there, in my throat, preparing to tip from my very core.

But then I saw it: the flutter of anxiety, the unsettling ripple in her eyes.

"Sshh," Christine said, her face now unreadable. The tip of her finger floated to my lips.

"Not now, darling," she said, silencing me (silencing me, though she was not to know this then, and neither was I, forever). "Not when it's all—so—perfect."

A rattle of confusion. I did not know what Christine meant, exactly, but I sensed she'd intuited the contours of the confession I was about to make, and that instinctively, she was warding it off, pushing it—pushing me—away.

Her finger still on my lips—and me, trying desperately to mask my bewilderment—she said: "Why don't you go and dress? There'll be time later to talk."

I rose, paused to take a sip from my glass, which I'd left on the side table. Before leaving the room, I turned to see Christine, her equanimity restored, lovely in yellow against the brooding deep red of the divan. The curve of her bare shoulder beneath the sheer sheath of her stole, the play around her lips of the sweetest, most loving smile she'd ever given me. And something secretive, even shy, in her face, as if she were planning some little declaration of her own. My disappointment and shame of a moment before vanished, replaced by a renewed and even more vigorous hope. I'd misread her, I thought; yes, we'd talk later. Later, I would have my chance.

But we wouldn't talk later, for that glimpse of Christine, a vision in yellow on the divan, was the last time I ever saw her.

When I returned, some thirty minutes later, the air in the room was a frenzy of alarm. Her drink was where she'd left it, stained pink at the rim, but Christine and her things—her chiffon stole and heavy wool cape and silver evening bag—were gone.

It made no sense to me. I waited for her all that evening and again the next day at the club. Shameless, desperate, I went to her rooms to find she'd packed her belongings and left, instructing her landlady to inform me there was no forwarding address. (Later, on the eve of my own departure, when I'd gone one last time to Christine's lodgings, the landlady let slip that she had sailed to Shanghai.)

Gone, too, from the Language Center.

Gone. Gone from me, gone from my life.

It was then that my own leave-taking plan sprung to mind. A leave-taking that now, I see, was inevitable.

You see, there was the matter of the paintings. The war enacted its own abrupt end and I found myself in the position of needing to bring about my own erasure. I had a new passport, a new name. I was in a position to construct a new life.

At times, over the years, when the bewilderment of Christine's disappearance has felt too hard to bear, I have reassured myself with this thought: that whatever happened that long-ago evening, the evening that Christine, gently touching the tip of her forefinger to my lips, silenced my confession—I was going to say banished me—we were perhaps in any case moving in opposite directions. Had that evening not happened, perhaps she'd have gone anyway. (Don't we always find reasons to do what we are fated to do?) The heart of things, she'd said. That was where she wanted to go, Shanghai as good a version of it as any. And I, I was headed to the periphery, embarked on a retreat from exotic human truths. Gardens, boathouses, and frivolity; these were the coordinates of the world I would construct.

The paintings I sold had not, in fact, been rescued. Not rescued from the Zwinger or any other museum felled by the weight of the Fatherland's homicidal-suicidal rage.

The paintings had had owners: had hung on the walls of people's homes, witness to the lives unfolding before them.

I know no names, I know only a smattering of detail about circumstances.

I tell myself the paintings would otherwise have been plundered or destroyed.

I tell myself the money I made as middleman would have done those people little good. From what I understand, there was no practice of bartering or bribes, once you were crammed into a cattle car. (I don't know how the paintings came into the hands of my source: one more question I never asked.)

Though I say this, I know, of course, that it was two gold coins, glinting in the moonlight—two gold coins my mother had sewn into the waist of my jacket, two gold coins that I handed to the helmsman with the hooded eyes—that took me away, brought me toward, and planted me in the city of multiplying money, then across the Atlantic to the peninsula of Long Island, a crooked finger pointing back at the place from which they, the owners of the paintings, did not escape. Five ounces, maybe six, of gold: that was the price I paid for my life.

Another tortuous turn of the screw sometimes rescues me, for the briefest moment, from guilt (this is worth more to me than anyone can know, though I am ashamed to admit this even to myself). For surely I am not after all a Jew, not really. Maybe this is the reason I was able to flee, this the fact that saved my life. Not the gold coins, but the simple fact that I was not, in my being, what had come to define a person as a criminal and bring about a death sentence.

And though I occasioned suspicion twice on my journey, many more critical strangers helped me along the way (and Alfred, at the cost of his life). Did they do so because they sensed that my escape was not doomed from the start, but a real possibility? My looks were obviously part of this equation: my features, my coloring. But most important was what I emanated from the core of my being: I did not think of myself as a Jew.

If it was not money that saved me, then surely money—or valuable paintings, as good as money—could not have saved them.

I still cannot put the accusation out of my mind. Wallace tells me I am safe, though it is clear that any such declaration is premature. In any case, it is not fear for myself that plagues me so much as the reality of what happened: the crimes that were in fact committed. Not, of course, by me—I must say again that I am innocent of such crimes.

I hesitated. What was I to do? Is that a choice to put to a man?

In any case, though, what does it matter who committed the crimes? It was someone. There were many, too many, someones.

Mama. Else.

Else. Mama.

I do confess that I sold paintings.

I do confess that I took Oskar's name and discarded my own (it's been six long years, already; if someone called out *Robert*, I do believe I would not even flinch). I had thought it an act of restitution: there, in the New World, the world of remakings, of new beginnings, of happy endings. I would take Oskar's name and plant it in the fresh, clean-smelling earth.

What did I expect would grow from it? A tree of innocence?

And Christine. Did I siphon from her too? Or was it she who took from me?

There is something more.

I wore the uniform. I feel the swastika still, burning into the skin of my arm. But I wore it as an act of self-preservation. What crime is there in self-preservation? (*Hypocrite, hypocrite.*)

Last night, up on deck, the vehemence of the storm effacing all else, I looked death in the face.

It was not the first time on this voyage that my mind flew to that other sea voyage I undertook all those years ago across the English Channel, from Marseilles to Dover.

There I was, anchoring my body by sheer will, down through the failing muscles of my legs, on to the water-drenched boards, the harrowing waves that joined with solid wind gusts so that the force of one became indistinguishable from the other. I clung to the railing, allowing the storm to have its way, giving over, in a sense, to its power.

It was when I stopped fighting it that my mind cleared. The storm suddenly seemed human, alive not only with threat, but with hope. I had been tagged for death so many times since my father was taken away—perhaps most of all by my own nullifying self, burying, always burying. And now, finally, here I was standing above this great agitating sea; it was telling me, as I thrust my face into its gusts, saying, again and again: *Now*, Robert, Oscar, Alfred—my new choice of name—whatever it is you call yourself, whoever it is you are. This is the destiny you have set for yourself, the truth of your being. Now is the time to seize it.

I could not have saved her, I know this. And yet—I hesitated. And what of my sister, my mother? What if I'd stayed?

If only to provide some comfort, if only to breathe in deeply, alongside them, in that bare concrete chamber. I could have held them; the three of us, together, we could have held each other.

It has been many years; I have told myself a great many things.

But this: I wanted to live.

I had it, the sea, in my arms, on my face; my clothes were heavy with its cold, wet promise. I had only to answer the call.

The fact is, I was going to jump. The fact is, I felt a moment of rushing grief that was the sweetest release I've ever known. I turned—one final glance on to Life—to find Wallace standing behind me. Wallace, dignified, calm, as if he were simply summoning me to dinner. He was, as always, the picture of professional command, though he was as drenched as I was. When he opened his mouth, it was to shout, in order to be heard above the storm, though of course, being Wallace, the utterance had the effect of a softly spoken suggestion.

"Below deck would be wise, sir," is what I think he said, and he placed a hand on my arm—actually, it would be more accurate to say that he took firm hold of my whole drenched, ecstatic, desperate self and pulled me away from the railing, wrenched me from the leap I felt certain, in that moment, was the most important, self-defining moment of this life-death I have been entrusted with in the short time that any of us have. He clutched my arms, an embrace, of sorts, and led me away. Away from the sea and the storm and toward the metal rungs of the ladder leading down to the warmth of the below-deck.

It is here, now, that I sit, having slept long and dreamlessly, and dined on the simple meal of cold pickled beef and boiled potatoes that Wallace brought me from the dining room. It is here, now, that I sit, awaiting the ruse that will, if all proceeds without incident, land me in a new life—which is to say, a new fiction, one which I am counting on to be my last. A fiction—and I say this with full awareness of the minimal credibility it would hold for anybody knowing the full sweep of my life, of the choices I have made (no such person exists, as it happens, which is both a relief and perhaps my greatest sorrow)—a fiction that I intend to imbue with Truth.

CHAPTER TEN

Marilyn

The North Shore of Long Island. Winter, 1956.

I had never seen the lawn turned brown, having been to Ellis Park only in summer months. Looking out the morning room window, it seemed so altered, with the little crust of snow melting around its perimeter, all that remained of the light nighttime fall.

The room was bare but for three chairs and a desk with a red leather top. Glancing back down the corridor I glimpsed, through large open doorways, several white-sheathed edges, the corners of furniture I remembered so well, covered now in sheets. I turned back to the window, watched as my breath formed a circle of fog on the glass. I heard footsteps behind me, on the polished wood floor of the hall. I knew them at once. They continued into the room.

"It seems we're the only ones," he said. "Not counting the attorney."

I turned. There he was in the doorway, leaning on the jamb.

"Hello, Barnaby."

"Hello, Marilyn."

Five years had passed, but now they fell away, along with that final weekend at the lake—dragging out to sea, leaving only the yellow suite, the green room, the blue suite, leaving, most of all, the glass house. For an instant, I could see the fingers of moonlight dancing across Barnaby's olive-skinned back and limbs, stippling his rugged face.

Now, he was smiling an unfamiliar smile. It startled me. No pretense, no swagger, no plan. I saw that he had changed. I wondered if he saw change, too, in me.

"I don't believe it for a minute," I whispered. "That Oscar's dead. Do you?"

Barnaby shook his head.

"Do you have any idea what he's up to?" I asked.

"I suspect there's not a soul on earth who knows what Oscar is up to," Barnaby said.

Looking at his broad, welcoming face, I had the feeling that I knew Barnaby better than he knew himself. In that moment, I was grateful that Simon was away on a book tour and not here. It seemed right—Simon had never belonged here, not the way Barnaby and I had. I was grateful to be reencountering Barnaby now, these five years later, in private.

He walked slowly toward me. Peering into his eyes as he approached, I could feel his lips before he even leaned down and, when they were on mine, I almost gasped with that old feeling of home. Ellis Park, this room, that summer, somehow my life, such as it was—and Simon too—arranged in equipoise: all of it on an axis, the world set to right.

But we drew quickly apart.

"It was always only this, wasn't it, Barnaby?" I said, not knowing exactly what I meant. Barnaby, sweet smile at play in his eyes, soberness in the rest of his face, seemed to understand. With the tip of his finger, he made a line from my cheekbone to my chin.

I glanced again around the room. Every detail so precise and so familiar—the molding around the window, the curve of the drape, the pale aquamarine of the wall. And yet, the details of that summer strangely eluded me, leaving only mood: the nuances of weather, the undulations of feeling that pass between people. But then, who is to say that memory is not as much the texture of events as the hard nubby this-happened-that-happened facts, lined up in stark little rows? That the whole of it cannot be found in the boiled gray shade of a day, the tremulousness of raised spirits, the mossy green odor of deceit.

Standing there, I realized I would never really put that summer—or Barnaby—behind me; that when something changes you, it becomes part of you, and you can't leave your self, even a little bit of it, behind.

At the sound of footsteps in the hallway, we both turned to see the attorney, sturdy in an expensive blue suit, stride into the room.

"Mr. Harrington, Mrs. Wright." He offered his hand, which we each shook in turn. "Thank you for coming. Let me again say how sorry I am about Mr. Harcourt. It must have been very difficult, these past few years, not knowing for certain what happened to him. Perhaps now, it will be easier to put the matter to rest."

It was clear to me from the way the lawyer was speaking that he didn't believe in Oscar's death any more than Barnaby or I did. For a moment, none of us spoke, as if we each needed a chance to decide how to proceed with this awkward yet necessary charade. I wondered, had Oscar communicated with Barnaby too, the way he had cryptically, through that single postcard, communicated with me? But this was not something I could ask Barnaby. To do so would risk betraying Oscar's unspoken confidence in me. Perhaps Barnaby was wondering the very same thing.

It was the lawyer, finally, who broke the silence. "Perhaps we ought to get started. Let me first say, I'm sorry Mr. Wright could not make the meeting today. I trust you will relay all the details. In the will, your two names appear together: always Mr. and Mrs. Simon Wright—though I know, Ms. Whittacker, that professionally, you go by your maiden name."

We sat down: Barnaby and I in the two armless chairs with tapestry seats. The attorney sat facing us in the leather wingback. He shuffled quickly through the pages of a lengthy document, and arrived at the place he was seeking. He read aloud several legally technical sentences, which stated that Oscar had bequeathed the three of us the house. I looked over to Barnaby; he wore a clouded, perplexed expression. Joint ownership, the lawyer was saying, Simon and me one party, Barnaby the other. With right of survivorship.

When Oscar had disappeared, one week after I returned from my disastrous weekend with Barnaby at the lake, everyone but me went into a state of shock. Numerous theories were put forth, one more fanciful than the next. I paid little heed to any of them. One point, though, was clear: the Ellis Park world we had known was over. In took only two days for the place to clear out.

I knew that Oscar's leave-taking had something to do with the German-speaking visitor, with the mysterious, and surely dire, accusation, and with the finding of witnesses I'd heard mentioned while eavesdropping late that night by Oscar's study door. The phone call with the investigator—how odd, his name slips my mind—only convinced me that Oscar was the victim of some terrible mistake; the idea of his being the perpetrator of a war crime came to seem more unlikely as the years passed.

For a time, I tried to put content to the contours of what I knew. But none of what I came up with made any sense, so finally, after months of anguish, I tried to put the matter to rest. I took comfort in knowing that Wallace was gone too, which suggested not only that Oscar was in his responsible care, but that they were operating with some kind of plan. In any case, the investigation, whatever its details, must have failed, else we'd have heard about the matter in the press.

Even had I not received that postcard almost a year ago, postmarked *London*, I'd have known Oscar was alive and well, simply from the filaments that bound us, delicate and steel-strong as spider silk. The card bore the typed name and address of a solicitor in London, along with an ink drawing of an Indian man in a loincloth, his head cleaved in two. Clearly, to my mind, a reference to a conversation we'd had that summer while out, if I recall correctly, for a ride. This was how I understood the message of Oscar's drawing: *All is as it was, nothing is changed.*

Now, the attorney scanned silently down, flipped to the next page, and scanned that one too.

"There are some details concerning the contents of the house. A few pieces of furniture and the odd painting are left in bequest to some other party. The majority of the contents, however, are to remain."

He handed us copies of the relevant pages.

"As you will see, it was the wish of my client that the bequest be made in the winter of the present year, and that it be announced here. Our dealings from here on may be conducted at my offices."

He handed us each a business card.

"Call me when you've had a chance to read everything through." He gathered his papers and stood. "And feel free to linger—it's yours, now, after all."

He extended his hand and offered a quick professional smile.

"I've instructed the groundskeeper to give you keys. You know where to find him, I trust."

We did not linger, however, but rose soon after the attorney had taken his leave. We walked together into the hallway, past the familiar rooms with their unfamiliar shroudings and dustcovers, empty vases, and unlit lamps. I was struck by how clean everything looked—not a dust ball or felled insect in sight. I pictured the staff going about their business with lonely, closed faces.

I still sometimes think about the mysterious events that

led up to Oscar's disappearance, and about the late-night visitor, with his peculiarly sinister mildness, though I no longer try to solve the puzzle. I see Oscar as I last saw him, sitting at his desk, in the greenish light of his lamp, and recall how small he had seemed beside the outsized tapestry of the fox hunt, and yet also somehow grand. Much like any individual human reality, I suppose: potent and inconsequential both. As I left the room that night, I'd taken one last glance at Oscar sitting there; I still wonder if I saw him mouth the words, *Thank you*, or whether this was something I imagined.

Though it was the last time I saw him, Oscar is with me still, as are the collection of days from that heated summer, which I imagine will always emit for me a disconcerting light: both too shadowy and too bright, disarming the capacity for focus, disabling the mechanism of the shutter.

I still get requests to go out on assignment. Now, when I politely decline, I no longer feel frantic with grief. It is true, I suppose, that a piece of me has—I was going to say *died*, but I think *been put to rest* is a better choice of words. I find I am surprisingly content in my role as mentor to my students. I value the privilege of helping them uncover the shape that their own struggle will take, and then nudging them into the work of it.

It was in Oscar's study, I think, that Barnaby had said, of my work as a photographer: "Isn't that the business you're in? Teasing the truth out of things?" My camera, my eye, to his way of thinking, was trained on the world with the purpose of showing up Truth.

Thinking about Oscar sitting there in his study, remembering the look of intolerable pain on his face, which he seemed unable to mask, I take consolation in a new thought. That sometimes the closest one can get to the truth is to look away.

Barnaby and I stepped onto the wide front steps and looked out over the circular driveway to the brown, wintry lawn. I turned, force of habit, to catch sight of the sea, from here no more than a dull metal band joined to a heavy expanse of white-blue sky. A faint echo sounded from the woods: a few birds deep in the trees, taking shelter from the cold.

"Can I give you a ride somewhere?" Barnaby asked. There was that dip in the eyes: both of us aware of other questions, other offerings, and everything else besides. The cold air smacked up against me.

"Barnaby, obviously I haven't discussed this with Simon, but on matters like these, I know how he'd think. I'm sure he'd agree to us signing our share over to you."

"I was going to say the same thing," Barnaby responded in a husky-soft voice. He reached for my hand, then, lifted it to his lips, his eyes holding steadily on mine, head lowered in that way he had so that in looking at you, he was looking up and over, as though peering out from some enclosure—not confined, but pleasantly ensconced and inviting you in. And me, my resolve dissolving, wanting to go wherever it was he intended to take me. But knowing that I wouldn't, that I'd found my place, at last, with Simon; that the two of us had, in our odd and unencumbered way, divested of claims to owner-ship, made for ourselves a home.

I nodded to my car, parked at the other end of the drive-way, where the loose gravel met the first tufts of lawn.

"I brought my own car," I said. Barnaby's lips lingered on my hand. I could feel the smile on them as I looked deep into the lithe gleaming smile in his eyes.

We must have stood that way for some time, as I became aware that through the leather of my boots my toes were feel-ing quite frozen. I was thinking how strange it was, and yet how right—and, of course, this had been true all along—that at this moment, I felt Simon's presence so strongly. A peculiar triumvirate, to be sure.

Barnaby leaned toward me, I leaned toward him, we leaned toward each other.

CHAPTER ELEVEN

Oscar

I was surprised to learn that Christine had returned to England; it appears she has been back for some years. How could one not have been struck by the intense loathing she'd felt for this place when I knew her, so many years back? That great ache to be elsewhere; it followed her around like a fog.

There's symmetry here, as there has been so often in my life (in everybody's life?)—the postcard I sent Christine years back, when she was still in China, giving a clue to my whereabouts in the United States, and the postcard Christine recently sent to the address I'd given her then—my lawyer in Long Island, forwarded now by him (bless his loyalty, and the inviolability of his discretion)—imparting the same kind of clue.

I do not know the circumstances of her return, but something in the tone of her quick note—five sentences, that's all it was—informed me that her sojourn in the East had not proved to be the escape for which she'd hoped. I suspect Christine's mission was doomed from the start: that what she was fleeing is not something one can, in fact, leave behind.

There was hostility in that note—lightly disguised, but clearly there. She blames me for what happened between us; I feel this, though I could not identify what she sees as my crime. Needless to say, I have spent a good deal of time mulling the matter over. After considering and reconsidering a number of the most likely permutations, I remain loyal to this view: that, upon intuiting the imminent confession of my crimes, Christine fled. Which is to say, she was not up to the truth: Christine chose to stake her claim to life in artifice and illusion.

I say this with compassion; I am in no position to judge. In any case, I do not believe Christine's choice had anything to do with being shallow. I am certain it was simply a question of survival.

Perhaps it would surprise her to hear me talking this way. The fact is, I knew Christine better than she thought I did.

I have set up a home—nothing with the grandness and sociability of Ellis Park; it's just the two of us now, Wallace and me, in a handful of pleasant, furnished rooms overlooking the heath. I rigorously avoid all districts to which I formerly had ties. I have, through this necessity, found that London is indeed the sprawling metropolis it is famed to be: a haven of anonymity for whoever chooses it to be so.

I do my utmost not to think of the past and often enough I succeed. I can go from day to day in a kind of self-imposed temporal confinement, willing my mind to occupy itself only with the next twenty-four hours. It is a strange limbo, this living without a past; when I see amputees—and they abound, of course, because of the war—they feel to me like *landsmen*: others, like me, who go on with a damaged part of themselves cut away.

It didn't take me long to track Christine down. It was a further surprise to find she is trying to establish a girl's school: in a sense, right back where she started. I understand that she has a partner in the endeavor—a young Chinese woman she brought back with her from Shanghai.

But how was it for her? Did she feel, in coming back to England, that she was coming home?

Only once—it was last week, as it happens—did I risk venturing into dangerous territory in passing by the library. I stopped, for a time, and looked up at its imposing façade. The home of my long-ago researches—where I sat researching the paintings that would pass through my hands.

I knew, incidentally, that Christine had followed me on several occasions, including one time when I came here. What I still do not know is what she was seeking in tracking my movements.

I do not believe, though, that Christine ever trailed me on an appointment with a customer (I speak of the paintings); I was especially careful about this.

Standing outside the library, a fragment of the past erupted, as if coughed up by the great building itself: that strange night I spent here, locked within the institution's daunting emptiness.

I'd been sitting in the stacks, examining the large volumes with their beautiful reproductions. When I heard the *tap-phh, tap-pph* of the guard's step, I found myself scooping up my belongings and ducking behind a wall of books. I don't know what made me do it—the odd whim simply reached out and grabbed me.

I hid in a cleaning supply closet that appeared just when I needed it, managing to tolerate the burning admixture of ammonium and lye for as long as I could. When I pushed open the door and, faint from the chemical fumes, almost fell from the closet, I could feel from the heavy emptiness that the guard had gone and that I was alone.

The library lights flashed off. The blackout cloth on the windows had been scrupulously fitted, and in that corner of the massive room all signs of the waning day were banished. I stood alone in the blackness. The air was heavy with dust.

I'd been careful about my study sessions here: kept them

to a minimum to avoid drawing attention to myself or to the subject of my researches. The few hours I spent here, though, I'd enjoyed a sense of calm and peace long denied me. Blocking all else from my mind, I'd given myself over to the blinding majesty of the Art.

Alone, free to wander unnoticed, the place deserted and locked for the night, I found it was not the paintings I wanted, but something else. I walked behind the librarian's desk and struck a match. The matchstick-length life of the flame was just enough for me to identify the whereabouts, from the map pinned to a notice board, of the modern German literature collection. Two flights up, three rooms across: sufficiently simple for me to negotiate in the near darkness.

As I was taking the stairs, I heard the distant cat wail—the familiar beginning of the air-raid siren's arc—muffled by the wall of books between where I was standing and the windows. I walked the length of the stack, feeling along with my hands, winding my way in solid darkness around rows of books, the siren outside rising to a screech.

I reached the window, peeled back a corner of the tarpaper just as the first missile found its target. But I saw nothing; only heard a padded thud, like a rock falling into snow. Then, the tremor rippling through air and steel and brick.

I crouched at the window, lifted the paper several inches, and beheld the spectacle—shooting stars in graceful arc, giant thrumming projectiles coursing blackly across the skies.

It didn't last long. The horizon was bright with flames. Medical workers, salvage teams—I pictured everybody preparing to emerge from cellars like so many ground-dwelling night creatures. But for now, only the eerie fire-scape, elongated buds of oranges and yellows leaping and cowering, and everywhere wavering columns of grayish-blue smoke.

It was a strange and beautiful nexus—past, present, future, folding and unfolding into one another: history in the throes of being destroyed, the sudden appearance of empty space which would one day hold new constructions, all of it a smoldering of the present.

I let the tar cloth fall, stretched up from crouching position, my knees creaking painfully. There was no obvious source of light now, only slivers, here and there, filtering in through a glass door panel, a vent in the floor, a hidden skylight up near the rafters. But I had no trouble finding my way; I was suddenly once again a night creature myself. Not from the ground but of the air—an owl, perhaps, or a bat.

I passed by row upon row of books: the delicious proximity of abundance. Not for the taking, but for the destroying. Here I am, I remember thinking, among the flawless works of genius that had haunted my youth and haunted me still: leather-bound volumes of Novalis and Goethe, Schiller and Schopenhauer and Nietzsche. An intense longing: to do damage, real damage, to the weight of work around me, to the productions of a culture that had made me who I am and then turned murderous. A terrible image filled my senses: blood, everywhere blood, the blood of my family—*her blood too, the woman, rocking by the stone-cold hearth*—there, in the library, dripping down the dusty pages, dripping down, onto the great slabs of stone at my feet. An urge to set fire to it all—to cleanse it all away in a roaring blaze. The power of ritual destruction, the desire to enter the darkening calm, the holy hush of ancient sacrifice.

Around me, the smell of vaulted stone, the infusion, in air, of millions of pages in thousands of spines.

I plucked down a volume, gingerly at first, and then more clumsily, loading my arms. Carrying a small tower of books, I walked to the nearest study table and set them down.

I could not burn them but I determined that I might in some way perform an exorcism. Staring at the stack of books I felt, wildly, as if something ceremonial should be said. The only Jewish prayer I knew, taught to me by my friend Oskar (I say this again because I must: the real Oscar) when we were together at the Internment Center. *Shema Yisroel Adonoi Elehaynu Adonoi Echod. Baruch Shem K'vod Malchuso L'Olam Va'ed. Ve-Ahafta es Adonoi Elohecha—*

I stopped. What business had I with prayers? I remember thinking. And what business had they with me?

I looked at the books: dumb objects, already the life of them—once so aflame within me—extinguished, reduced to ash. I swept the books from the table; they crashed to the floor, filling the space with a single bright echo, godly and inanimate as a thunderclap.

That night, I slept where I sat, head on my arm, at the study table. Instinct woke me, snapping open my eyes. Not two minutes later, I heard the distant tapping of the morning guard's shoes on the stone stairs. I cut across to the other side of the vast room and made my way down the back staircase.

Mercifully, the back exit could be opened from the inside and was unmanned. I pushed open the door and stepped quickly out into the gray London morning.

What stopped me, that evening, from confessing everything to Christine? Surely, I might have removed her silencing finger and spoken the truth? Why did I choose, in the end, to keep it all in the dark? Was this my undoing?

I remember the line from Nietzsche that was popular among my classmates: that without illusions, man would die. But this is too generous; I am aware that it is a mere half-truth, and self-serving, as half-truths tend to be.

Though perhaps I am romanticizing matters. Perhaps we are all just—well—what we are.

Foolish theorizing, this. The simple fact is I want to see her. I want to see Christine.

Rather than unnerve her by simply appearing on her doorstep, now that I have tracked her down, I am planning first to send her a letter.

I've had a devil of a time drafting the thing; my wastebasket is heaped with failed attempts. I will turn to it again this evening. It seems silly, after all this time, to invest the wording of the letter with such importance.

Five years into it, and the idea of my new alias still jars. This time, however, I was faced with no choice: circumstance forced my hand. Though I took on Alfred's name to honor him, I cringe at the thought that it is, in the end, a taint, for his memory to be linked in any way with my existence. It is too late, though; as much as any name can be for me, his name now is mine. I hope Christine will not think it forced.

I hope Christine will want to see me.

I don't know what I was expecting. I can say that I was not expecting what I found.

The building in which Christine is hoping to establish her school is a simple affair. Having secured government funding for the project, she has rented a structure that more than a century ago lodged a poorhouse, long since stripped down inside to the bare walls. Small clean rooms have replaced the cavernous pit it once was; there is no embellishment, just plaster walls and low ceilings, the plainness broken by cheerful green gingham curtains that adorn the windows throughout.

When, after standing before the building some ten minutes, I finally mustered the courage to ring the bell, I was surprised by the serious face of the young Chinese woman who opened the door. She looked no more than seventeen or eighteen (later, Christine told me she is well into her twenties), and had about her an air of such clarity—a sense of being wide open to the forces of the world while also knowing deeply who she is and what she wants. Unusual, in a person of her youth.

I suppose I should not be surprised that this young woman—she introduced herself as Ma Ling—reminds me of Christine. Not the Christine I saw yesterday, but the Christine I knew some twelve years ago here, in London, before either of us set out on our respective escapes.

Ma Ling led me to the rear of the building to where I would find Christine—Christine, whom I'd not seen in so many years, whose beauty and troubled largesse and unwavering focus on *the search* were inscribed into my being; Christine, for whom I'd never stopped longing. Before opening the door, Ma Ling looked at me so openly that I was taken aback. It was a look that both took my measure and assuaged the deep anxiety I was feeling, a look that was at once deeply attentive and a clear-eyed challenge. Peerless Christine, I thought—elegant, alluring, anguished Christine, steeped in the pleasures of masquerade and at the same time defiantly authentic; perhaps in Ma Ling she had met her match.

Ma Ling opened the door, and there she was, Christine, seated in a wooden chair in the cold glare of a fluorescent light. Anger, grief, resignation: I saw them all in her face.

"I never thought I'd see you again," she whispered.

I entered, closed the door, leaving Ma Ling in the hallway outside. I heard the sound of her footsteps heading away.

Christine was aged—I'd somehow not expected this—and seemed smaller, giving the impression that she'd lost several inches in height. In place of the brilliant smile was a muted warmth that gave a soft glow to her now more angular features. Her hair, having lost its strawberry sheen, was a common shade of blond, cut stylishly short. It suited her, as did the simple tailoring of her beige wool suit, which showed her narrower though still lovely figure. She was altered, yes, there was no denying it, though her beauty, for me, was in no way diminished. I was aware of something I'd not experienced in a very long time: a flutter, within, of joy.

"Christine." It cost me some effort to utter her name aloud; I'd not done so in many years. She did not rise; I sat opposite her on a compact divan.

"I surprised myself," she said.

"Oh?"

"I felt so very happy when I received your letter."

"Should you not have been?" Christine looked at me squarely. "You must know why I left. After all these years, surely you worked it out."

I shrugged. It was a gesture entirely inappropriate to the situation, but I found it was the only one I had.

Christine leaned forward. Suffering and hatred—I saw them, visible forcefields in the back of her eyes.

But then, a growing look of astonishment in her face.

"You don't know, do you," she uttered, her voice an echo of disbelief. A long pause. Too long, uncomfortable. When finally she spoke, her voice was a whisper. "I discovered the truth. About your *past*." She breathed this last word with discernible distaste.

"My past," I repeated idiotically.

The fact is, I was confused. I didn't know which past Christine meant.

"I'm sorry, Christine. I don't understand."

She strode to the window, the old agitation evident in her taut movements. She stood there for a moment, her back toward me, peering out.

"It's strange not to be able to use your name when addressing you. I want to say Robert, but then I know you stopped calling yourself that long ago. And now—" She turned to face me. Her cheeks were streaked with tears. "You took it all away. All of it. Smashed it to bits. Don't you see?"

"What are you talking about, Christine? I have no idea—"

"No idea? Of how you took my one chance for happiness and killed it?" There it was again, hatred, through the tears, only this time it was very clearly directed toward me. "Just one more death to you, no doubt. In a string of how many?"

Just the wrong thing, a terrible thing; for some unfathomable reason, I did it again—that peculiar, helpless shrug.

"Such things cannot be shrugged away," she said in a strangled voice.

It was all pointless. I knew this in that moment. My coming here. My hopes that—what? That Christine and I could make some sort of life together? Salvage something from all this wreckage?

The truth is there *had* been a string of deaths. Though how could Christine have known about any of it?

"What did you discover, Christine?" I said quietly.

"That night—you went to your dressing room to change."

"Yes." Of course I knew exactly what she was talking about; I'd been over the moment so many times in my own mind. Clearly, she had relived it too.

"You didn't lock your desk." Christine's tears were coming faster. I'd never before seen her cry. I felt a pang of tender concern. "You always locked your rolltop desk, but that night—we had kissed, you seemed distracted, as though you had something to tell me. You fled the room, forgetting to lock your desk."

It was coming at me, some inchoate realization, though Christine's meaning was not yet clear.

"As it happens, I was planning to tell you something myself that day, words I had never uttered to anyone in my life. It was too difficult for me, so I decided to write you a note and leave it for you in your desk where you would find it later, when you were alone."

My desk, I scrabbled in my mind for *the thing.*

Yes, I now saw what she knew—or thought she knew.

The past, yes. The past.

Another mistaken identity.

Christine had fled the wrong man. My own story: a fleeing of her flight.

Though I suppose there was more to it.

There's always more to it, isn't there?

"You followed me, sometimes, didn't you," I said, curiously calm now, waiting for this scene to play itself out.

Christine nodded. "I never found out what you were up to, but once I found the armband, the details no longer mattered."

Silence. A minute. Maybe two.

"All these years, I was waiting for news that you'd been captured. Turned over. I expected to see it in the papers."

"Why did you send me that postcard?" I asked.

"I don't know," she whispered, misery in her voice. "I suppose I just couldn't bear it."

"What, Christine? What couldn't you bear?"

"Believing it was true. Losing you so completely."

I saw no reason to tell her the whole truth—that truth I'd been readying to tell her many years ago, on that evening I apparently neglected to lock my rolltop desk. It was too late now, for that. It was not that the passage of time had made my crime worse. But it had made my crime clear, at least to me. Perhaps back then I thought that love could change things. That a sharing of hearts could relieve the burden—perhaps commute the charge to a lesser offense.

I know now that nothing can change what is done.

I know now that the past is never over.

Again I am treading the path to the door. Again I hear the crunch of loose stones beneath my boots. Again I am staring at that battered door—the patches of faded color, the rough weathered surface of it. I am used to the sight, now, used to the sounds; they will be with me always.

This time, though, in my mind's eye, I allow the door to open.

Klauss's hacking cough; all this time, I've been hearing it as we trod the pathway. No, it did not come before the creaking open of the door, but after. After we had both taken in the hellish scene, which would become even more hellish, and soon.

Old blood on the table, the floor, the walls, splattered up and around; the woman's family members, whoever they were, whatever configuration of genders and generations, must have put up a struggle. Rotting foodstuffs too, on the table, by the sink, the overall stench of the place was putrid.

Sounds, coming from the far side of the room—soldiers, two of them, in uniforms like the one I'm wearing, sitting on a wooden palette. One is hunched over; he heaves, spews forth a dark stream. The other swigs from a bottle; he holds a gun, which points slackly toward the hearth. Momentarily, he swings the gun our way. Our uniforms, brown like his own: he laughs drunkenly, swings the gun back toward the hearth, where a woman sits rocking. "We were wondering what to do with her. We've had our fill." The other, finished with his vomiting, lies back on the rough bed. He waves his arm.

"She's yours," he says wearily, hand on his own gun.

I look over toward the hearth. I can see that the woman has some kind of injury on her forehead. Perhaps she was banging her head, as she rocked, into the brick of the fireplace; the broad lesion looks like it could have been sustained this way.

"Robert, what is it?"

My name, the name given to me by my father and mother. I'd not heard it now in so many years, it came as a shock.

"Christine," I said, "I did not choose to wear the uniform. I stripped it from a dead Nazi soldier. It's what allowed me to escape."

"What?" Disbelief in her voice.

"Christine, I'm a Jew. My mother and sister were murdered at Bergen-Belsen."

She swayed a little and I thought that she might faint. Then, she looked at me with a kind of horror. There was no reason that she should believe me, and yet I'd assumed, simply, that she would. The stunned look melted, and then—for a moment I saw the old Christine, there, on the couch. Her eyes, her face, all of her—looking at me in that old way, giving herself, taking me in. I heard a sob and realized it was coming from me. Then Christine was at my side, kneeling on the floor, pressing her lips to my hand. No tears from her, though I could feel that my own cheeks were wet.

"Why didn't you tell me? And what possessed you to save the armband?"

Klauss's hacking cough. He walks over to the woman—slowly, wiping his nose on his sleeve. He rips open the woman's dress and laughs.

"Look, Robert. Beautiful, no?"

He seizes her breasts and twists them, hard. He moves roughly, with deftness; only for me, his actions are in eternal slow motion. I see the gun at his side, in his halter. He needs no further show of force but nonetheless pulls his knife from its sheath and shows the woman its gleaming surface.

"For you, my darling," *Klauss says. I see him pulling from his trousers his erect member, pushing the woman against the brick, and falling on her; hear the laugh transposing to a grunt of animal greed.*

Three guns in the room, none of them mine.

I cannot take my eyes from the hearth; she is still, beneath him; I hear the echo of the crack made by the back of her head against the stone.

Slowly, her head turns; the beam of her eye meets my own, the other is in shadow. An eye that is living, yet no longer has life.

The gun in the hand of the drunken soldier; I might leap at him, wrench it away. Turn it first on the other soldier, then on Klauss.

I've never fired a gun in my life; I don't know how.

It's over so fast: Klauss is buttoning his fly, again drags his sleeve across his nose, walks from the woman's splayed form to the seated soldier who, grinning, hands him the bottle.

"She's yours," *Klauss says, then takes a swig.*

All eyes on me; I am frozen.

"Not good enough for you?" *Klauss thrusts toward me; shoves me roughly in the direction of the hearth.* "You want a virgin?" *Rage in his eyes, red-hot, deadly.* "She's good enough for us," *he hisses, pushing again.*

My body lurches forward with each shove, and then stops. I scan my eyes back and forth, from the woman to the soldiers. The three men are waiting, they're enjoying the show. Both of them now holding their weapons.

I'll grab both guns, I think, one in each hand. One of them is looking at me; I must wait for my moment.

Klauss is there, back at the hearth; he must have bounded. He has the woman, he is cradling her in his lap, pulling her head back by her hair, to show me her neck.

"Well then, we're all done with her."

But then I realize: it is already too late. He has already drawn the blade of his knife neatly, cleanly, across the white of her throat, which yawns open for a moment before the black-red gush. He flings the knife toward me—it lands a few feet away.

I leap back, leap away from the spurting blood.

Coughing, drunken shouts, the woman is dragged across the room, through the doors. Table knocked over, chair kicked aside. The other two supporting each other—high spirited—follow Klauss outside.

The rough, desperate room rings with emptiness. I lunge across the spreading slick, by the upturned table with its stiff legs thrust awkwardly sideways like a slaughtered beast. I cast my eye out the window: a sky with no moon, not even a sliver. I scan the black surface of the sky for some pinprick of light. Nothing—no star to hang a prayer on, no possibility of other worlds.

I am in this room, I look back at the spreading pool; it glints, fanning to a strange, amoeboid shape. The glint—no light in the heavens but here, this: a pinpoint signal from hell.

I skid, grab at the knife. Plunge it into my own arm—deep, deeper, until the wet, now twice-bloodied tip finds bone. Draw it across, yank it out, flinging the knife onto the hearth and flee, dripping hot, wet blood as I run.

And now, Christine—oh, so many years have passed—Christine, in my arms. And me holding her, breathing her in.

There was so much of the past there, in that odd room, where yesterday I met with her—my body ached with it: the phantom-limb pain of the amputee. Sitting there with her, I had the distinct feeling that there was nowhere further to go, that we had arrived, the two of us, at the end of the line.

For some time, neither of us spoke.

I was aware of how little we knew of the facts, of how these past years had played out for each of us, though it was entirely clear, I believe to Christine as much as to me, that there had, for each of us, been trouble.

"Have you been in touch with Barnaby?" I asked.

Christine peered at me soberly. "So he did contact you, then. Where you were living. In Long Island."

"I'd say so. We were inseparable for a good many years."

"No, I've not had word from him for some time." She paused. "Though I've been meaning to contact him. To try to find some way to thank him."

I knew there was weight behind her words; I waited for Christine to make her meaning clear.

"I don't mean to sound melodramatic, but I wouldn't be here if it weren't for Barnaby. I was ill, very ill; Barnaby nursed me back to health. Day and night, really, for more than a month. He took care of Ma Ling too. She was also unwell, though not on death's door, as I was."

"He's a dark horse, Barnaby—and not of the usual stripe," I said. "I always knew that behind all that bluster was a sense of what really matters."

Christine rose, walked over to the window, pulled aside the gingham curtain, peered outside. Though I could not see it, I imagined a view across an alley where rubbish bins are kept, onto the back of a commercial building, with a smoke-darkened façade and, on its rooftop, an unruly assortment of clay chimney pots.

Then she spoke: "There's something I've wanted to tell you, these past years. Funny, isn't it, what ends up preying on one's mind. When I knew you . . ." She hesitated. "When I knew you, I was in the habit of, well, fabricating things. I'm not actually a deceitful person; I don't understand it fully myself. I just made things up—to suit the moment. I suppose we all make up our lives as we go along—I thought it didn't make much difference. It's all just a kind of storytelling.

"It was only later that I realized the stories I told you were different." Here, she turned and gave a sad little smile. "You see, in this case, the fabrications were on your behalf." She let out a clipped sound that was half regretful laugh, half sigh.

"You can also see that I've given this matter a good deal of thought. It seems to me that it's one thing to make oneself up for one's own purposes, and quite another to play god for someone else. It was not for me to decide whether or not you could tolerate the truth of who I am."

Christine's words came at me like a blizzard which freezes and burns at the same time. Had she not been the one to silence me, now many years ago, at the very instant I was preparing to tell her everything of who I was? All the desperate, damning truths of my own sorry existence? I had not known that she had been silencing, also, herself.

"What I wanted to tell you is this. My own mother died a long time ago." Christine was still looking out the window. "Of alcohol poisoning. In the little flat in Manchester where I grew up. Everything I told you about my mother, about my perfect family life: none of it was true. I never had a father, not one that I knew. I made it all up. I thought that's what you wanted to hear, and I didn't have the heart to tell you the truth—"

"The white dress with the eyelet collar . . . ?" I said, trying to keep the desperation out of my voice.

"There was no white cotton dress."

"Then, what?"

Christine had left the curtain open; from where I sat I could see a gray wash of sky and the single branch of a tree creaking in the breeze. She seemed to be thinking something over. Her office was so plain—the walls bare but for a single watercolor of a nondescript English beach—and yet the room was alive with feeling. When she turned, I saw that she was assessing me.

"Well, there was heavy blue silk, and taffeta. And sometimes nylon stockings." She spoke carefully, her eyes unreadable. "And my mother's friends. Gentlemen friends."

Christine must have seen something in my face, though I believe she misinterpreted what she saw, as she said: "Don't feel badly for me. I've gone where I've wanted to go."

I was not sure what she meant, but in her eyes there was a trace of the old passion—though less personal, somehow, and stripped of anguish.

"We'll build a different kind of life for girls here," she continued. "There are a lot of orphans in England who lost their parents in the war. We're going to have a strong academic curriculum; we will be serious about preparing them for rewarding work. But, most of all, we hope to teach them to shape their own lives. Not to be at the mercy of their circumstances."

Christine searched my face, uttered a self-mocking laugh. "I know, it all sounds terribly earnest. I'm afraid I've come to see life as rather an earnest business."

How small she looked, and yet also less vulnerable than she had been, those many years ago.

"I've rather come around to that opinion myself," I said, wanting to say more, not knowing where to begin, yet feeling, in that functional room, the office that Christine and Ma Ling shared, that perhaps we might begin anew.

"I'm sorry," I said finally.

"Sorry?"

"About your mother. Her life. Her death."

We both knew there was a lot more to be sorry about; but then again, perhaps we were talking also about everything else besides.

"Don't be," Christine responded, a shade of her former brightness touching her slightly wan features. "She lived her life as best she could. What more can any of us do?"

* * *

I do not know where things will go from here. I do not know what tomorrow will hold.

I wonder how Barnaby, Marilyn, and Simon felt about my handing the house over to them. I assume they do not believe the fiction of my death and that I therefore did not burden them with grief. Yes, I sent another postcard, this one to Marilyn. I know her well enough to be sure she understood it was from me.

I imagine Marilyn has no idea, however, just how painful, and also important, her famous photograph was to me, the picture of the little boy in the green jacket, standing in front of a pile of rubble that had, only the night before, been his home.

When I saw it on the cover of *Life* magazine, I felt a terrible bolt of recognition that was disorienting and also—this may sound strange—reassuring. I had long harbored the belief that through sheer will I could create a sustaining world, rich with nature and history and alive with pleasure. This was what I had been hoping to achieve with Ellis Park. Marilyn's picture brought me face-to-face with myself in a way that nothing else had done (this may sound unconvincing, given what my life has been, but the psyche has its ways of protecting): face-to-face with the sheer force of desolation. Studying that picture, something died within me: the belief that it was possible to rebuild.

It was only much later—back in London, here in this room—that I realized Marilyn's photograph of the little boy bore a relationship to hope. Seeing that boy, intuiting the windy bare habitat of his soul, I knew that, though I could no longer be a citizen of the arboreal world of the hopeful and unbereaved, I was neither mere tumbleweed—was not, in fact, doomed to eternal homelessness.

The details, the details aside: the sum of my life is a certain vision, and I have come, finally, to believe that if one has a mind of winter, the January sun, though cold, sheds light of a startling clarity: that what I behold is every bit as much a part of the world and, in the end, some sort of legitimate place within it.

The charitable trust has been set up in Wallace's name, for obvious reasons. I run the organization, though Wallace does lend a hand. While the focus of the fund's work is on providing aid to camp survivors, we have also begun to furnish monies to victims of bombings here, in London. I have in mind the idea of tracking down the boy in the green jacket—he'd be fifteen or sixteen by now—and others who were orphaned, as he was, in a blitz. I would also like to provide anonymous funding to Christine's school.

These rooms are well appointed; I have never seen lodgings designed with such taste. Several of the objects within them are beautiful and also unusual. One, in particular, captures my imagination. It is a Chinese urn—not an antique but a fine reproduction. It sits on the white marble mantelpiece and I find myself often drawn to contemplate it; standing before the fireplace, I regard the bucolic scene etched into the finely cracked glaze: a vertical array of hills, delicate trees in full leaf, several with papery blue flowers. A lone farmer bears two buckets of water on a yoke across his shoulders and amid wafting banks of cloud, tiny birds dot the sky.

It is a funeral urn. Perhaps it holds the remains of some long-departed stranger, though I've not had the courage to remove the lid to find out if this is the case. At times, gazing at the lovely, distant, peaceful scene—another world entirely, a forgotten era—I feel that I am somehow like that funereal porcelain, a vessel for the ashes of the dead.